I0575014

HER COWBOY BILLIONAIRE BEST FRIEND'S BROTHER

CHRISTMAS AT WHISKEY MOUNTAIN LODGE, A HAMMOND BROTHERS NOVEL, BOOK 3

LIZ ISAACSON

Copyright © 2020 by Elana Johnson, writing as Liz Isaacson

All rights reserved.

No part of this book may be reproduced in any form or by any electronic or mechanical means, including information storage and retrieval systems, without written permission from the author, except for the use of brief quotations in a book review.

ISBN-13: 978-1-63876-168-6

CHAPTER 1

G ray Hammond checked his teeth one more time in the rear-view mirror, though he hadn't had anything in them when he'd left Wes's house. Gray never went anywhere without all the proper pieces in exactly the right place—at least he hadn't for the past twenty years.

Now that he was done at HMC, he had no idea what his days would hold. Probably a lot of time spent in pants with an elastic waistband and hours on the farm his parents refused to sell. A frown marched through his eyebrows at the thought of them on that piece of land, with all those animals, none of which they could take care of. His father tried, but he was almost eighty years old, and Gray had started talking to Ames about staging an intervention.

If there was a brother who would take such a thing seriously, it was Ames. The man took *everything* seriously, and most of the time, that grated on Gray's nerves. And *he* was the lawyer in the family. He, by profession, took things seriously.

But an intervention with Ames involved would have steps and rules, and Gray had told him his concerns for a reason. Their parents simply couldn't stay on the farm much longer.

Ames and Cy had gathered to the farm in Ivory Peaks for the holidays, just to give Gray and Hunter a break. Gray felt like he needed a vacation from his life, and he was having a hard time not to take one. The only thing anchoring him in one place at the moment was Hunter. Hunter's school.

He couldn't just pack a bag and board a plane and come back to his life when he felt like it, the way Wes had after he'd retired from the family company. He couldn't move to Coral Canyon at the drop of a hat for a woman, the way Colton had done.

Gray loved his son very much, but he alone knew that his life wasn't entirely his own. "It's fine, Lord," he said to himself. "I don't mean to complain. I love Hunter, and I'd rather he be with me than his mother." He let out his breath, hoping some of the negativity he harbored inside would go with it. A bit of tension released from his shoulders, and he added, "Guide me to what I should do next."

Gray's future was wide open, he knew that. Hunter would keep getting up in the morning and going to school. There would be science fair projects, and math homework he didn't know how to do, and a brand new challenge for both of them—junior high. Multiple classes, dances…girls.

That last one Gray barely knew what to do with himself. His first marriage had been one long fight, and when it had finally ended, he hadn't even recognized himself anymore. He'd tried a couple of relationships since, and both of them had been nothing but disaster after disaster. He should've known he couldn't date in the greater Denver area—at least not anyone who used the Internet or drove down the freeways. His surname was everywhere there, and the two women he'd been out with since Sheila's departure from his life had been after only one thing: Money.

That had hurt Gray, sure. But the worst part was knowing that Hunter had started to bond with Maddie. She'd known it, too, and she'd exploited the boy to get money from Gray for her. He'd never been so angry in his life. And having to explain his failures and shortcomings to a seven-year-old?

Gray hadn't dated in years. Four years, to be precise. Which was why he still hadn't gotten out of his truck either.

Elise would likely be here already. He'd pulled in right at the time they were set to meet, and he'd been sitting in the vehicle for at least ten minutes. She hadn't called or texted yet, but he knew he was probably causing some anxiety in her soul too. And he didn't want to do that.

"Help me," he begged as he got out of the truck. The chill in Wyoming in December was not to be trifled with, and Gray flipped up the collar on his coat to keep the wind off his neck. Someone had cleared the sidewalks, but he had to traverse snow and sleet to get there. His leather cowboy boots kept the dampness off his feet, and he hurried the rest of the way to the entrance of the restaurant.

He'd let Elise pick where she wanted to eat, because he didn't live here and didn't know what was good. By the level of noise and the amount of people waiting inside the reception area, he knew this place must be popular.

Glancing around, he searched for the beautiful blonde who'd first caught his eye at Colton's house. Elise was light everywhere Gray was dark, and he wondered if their opposites extended to other things. He hadn't spoken to her a whole lot over the months, little things here and there. The woman loved memes, and whenever Gray saw one he thought she'd like, he sent it to her.

They talked about Colton and Annie, her work at the lodge, and Bree. He did know she loved to bake and was good at it, and that she could literally cultivate any plant back to life. But most of what he knew about Elise hadn't come from her, but Colton.

Her best friend.

Gray wasn't sure what he was doing, getting involved with her. If things went badly—and Gray had no reason to think they wouldn't—he'd have to deal with Colton.

He couldn't find Elise among the crowd, as she had a way of slipping through the cracks. Still, he'd never had a problem locating her at the lodge or among all the guests at his brother's wedding.

"Hey," a woman said, and he turned toward the voice. Elise stood there, her cheeks pink and those light green eyes making something unhitch in his chest that he hadn't even known was so dang tight.

"There you are."

"Sorry I'm late." She glanced around, nerves pouring off of her. Gray was exceptionally good at reading a person, and he could tell she didn't like this

"Want to go somewhere else?" he asked.

Hope filled those beautiful eyes. "Did you put our name on the list?"

"I only got here myself," he said. "I was looking for you. So no."

"Sure, we can go somewhere else." She turned and left the restaurant, and Gray followed.

"There's a great steakhouse over on March," she said.

"Okay."

"Meet you there?"

"Yep." Gray separated from her and got behind the wheel of his truck again. His heart beat a little faster than it normally did, because now he'd have to coax himself out of the vehicle one more time.

"Make a right turn on Seagull," his GPS said, and he obeyed. But when he arrived on March Street, it didn't go all the way through. "Your destination is on the right."

"But it's not," he said, pulling to the curb and picking up his phone. He was on a residential street, with homes on both sides. No steakhouse. He looked left and right out the windows. Definitely no steakhouse.

But this was definitely March Street. He typed in the search term "steakhouse" and got several results. Of course he would. This was Wyoming, after all, and they raised a lot of beef cattle here.

Frustration started to lick through him as he tapped and studied the addresses. In the end, he had to dial Elise, who picked up with, "I think I lost you."

"I'm on March Street," he said. "There's no steakhouse

here." He swung his truck around to get out of the cul-de-sac. "What's the name of the place?"

"The Branding Iron," she said. "And it's not on March Street. It's on *Marks* Street."

"Shoot," Gray said, embarrassment moving through him powerfully. "I'll be right there."

"Take your time," she said. "They're busy here too. I put our name on the list, and they said forty minutes."

"Oh, wow." Gray's stomach growled as if telling him he better feed it sooner than forty minutes from now. "See you in a sec."

Turned out that, no, he wouldn't see her in a second. He'd somehow navigated clear out north of town, and it took a good half an hour to even get to the steakhouse.

Something here was definitely wrong, but Gray pulled into the parking lot anyway. Easing around the restaurant, his phone started pinging, shooting out at least a dozen notifications for text messages in the space of two seconds.

"I hate the reception here," he grumbled. He was used to lightning-fast Internet and text messages that went through the moment he sent them. His provider didn't operate well in Coral Canyon, and half of Gray's messages spun and spun, never going through at all. "Oh, wow."

He stopped when he saw the crowds of people standing outside the steakhouse.

And the big plume of smoke rising from the roof. When he heard the sirens for the fire engine, he got out of the way and picked up his phone.

He'd been gone from Colton's for over an hour now, and he barely had time to eat with Elise at this point. She'd texted several times about a kitchen fire at The Branding Iron, and that she'd gone somewhere else.

"Be…right…." Gray dictated as his thumbs typed out the letters. Before he could finish the text and send it, he got thrown forward, the horribly loud sound of metal on metal crunching through his whole body, crackling in his ears, and imprinting on his soul.

He gripped the wheel, his phone gone and forgotten, the text not sent. He sucked at the air, trying to figure out what had happened.

An angry man's face appeared through the driver's side window. "You've got to move this." He gestured furiously, and his clothing indicating he was an emergency worker. "Now."

Gray punched the button to roll down his window. "You hit my truck."

"You're parked in a red zone, Mister," the man said. "Now move immediately. We've got two more ambulances coming and another fire truck."

"I am *not* in a red zone." Gray knew better than that, and he got out of his truck, his own anger spiking. "I moved out of the way when I saw the smoke."

"Just move," the man barked, walking away.

"Who's gonna pay for my truck?" Gray called after him, but he didn't break stride or wave or anything.

Gray circled the back of the truck to access the damage, and sure enough, he was not in a red zone. Not even close. Fine, close, but at least ten feet away.

He'd been hit by an ambulance, which had since been backed up. The tailgate had bent inward in the middle, and that whole assembly would have to be repaired. The fender hung off the truck completely on one side, and the whole thing leaned precariously to the right.

He looked up to see if the ambulance drivers were still there, but they weren't. Gray returned to the cab, frantically searching for his phone. He was a lawyer; he knew what to do to protect himself. And billionaire or not, he shouldn't have to pay for damage to his vehicle that wasn't his fault.

He first made sure the date and time feature on his camera was activated, and then he took at least forty pictures ranging from where he was parked to where the ambulance was—and the license plate of it—to the extent of the damage to his truck.

His fingers ached from the cold, and he'd forgotten about everything and anything else but the pictures and the icy chill threatening to overpower him.

He finally climbed into the cab again, but it was as cold in there as outside, because he'd left the door open. His phone rang, and it didn't connect to the Bluetooth and play through the speakers, which only made him more furious.

"What?" he barked at Colton.

Ohhh, Colton. Maybe something had gone wrong with Hunter. The fight left him, and Gray's pulse pounded.

"Where are you?" he asked. "Elise just called me crying."

CHAPTER 2

E lise Murphy had never been so mortified in her life. Not even when Brandt had broken up with her via a text while she sat in the stand before one of his rodeos. She'd driven for two hours to be there, and she hadn't told him she was coming.

The text had jolted her back to reality, not this make-believe place where women as plain and quiet as Elise married bull riding champions. Just one look at Violet Everett confirmed that. She was a country music star with platinum albums. That was the kind of woman a billionaire bull rider wanted on his arm.

Elise sniffled, because she needed to calm down before she got back to the lodge. She drew in deep breath after deep breath, horrified that she'd called Colton to ask him if Gray didn't like her.

"What a mess," she said, her voice cracking and tears

slowly leaking down her face again. She wasn't fourteen. She didn't need to ask her best friend if his brother liked her.

A sting moved through her lungs, making breathing difficult, but she clenched her fingers on the steering wheel and kept the car on the mountain road. This Christmas wasn't nearly as snowy as last, for which Elise was grateful. She didn't like the snow that much, and driving in it especially terrified her.

She'd seen Gray walk into Devil's Tower ten minutes late. She'd followed him after counting to twenty-five, a random number she landed on because if she let herself go higher, she might not have gone inside at all.

He'd barely looked at her, barely said two words to her, and then he'd gotten right back in his truck like he had a checklist to get done that day, and lunch with her was an inconvenience.

She'd listened to her affirmations all the way to the steak-house, and when he didn't come, and didn't come…Elise knew now that she'd started to spiral then.

"But he called," she said to the towering Tetons in the distance. The pine trees stood guard on the sides of the road too, never losing their needles and creating the perfect Christmas backdrop.

The big event had been yesterday, and Elise had skipped the rowdy present-unwrapping in the main living area of the lodge. She did love watching the little children open their gifts, but for some reason, she hadn't been able to face going this year.

She pulled off the road, her car fishtailing a bit when she hit the snow on the shoulder going a little too fast. Her pulse picked up, but the vehicle came to a stop a moment later. With a sense of hysteria moving through her, she dug into her purse to find her phone. Her fingers shook while she swiped and jabbed, finally getting a call to go through to her mother.

"Elise, dear," her mom answered, her voice rich as clover honey. Elise started to relax just with the sound of it in her ears. "How are you?"

"Okay," she said, but her word wobbled. "Actually, not great."

"Not great? I thought you were going out with Gray today?"

"Yeah, me too," she said, her cheeks getting wet again with a fresh set of tears. "It didn't work out."

"Oh, no," her mother said. "You were so excited about it." She sounded genuinely upset on Elise's behalf. "Tell me what happened."

"Maybe I should leave Wyoming," Elise said instead of getting into the story. "Go somewhere warm, where rich people will pay me to design their yards. Put my degree to some actual good use."

"You think that's what you want?" Mom asked. "Eh?" The Canadian came out in her whenever she asked questions, and that "eh" caused a smile to bloom on Elise's face.

She shook her head. "No, though I would like somewhere warm about now."

"Still snowing up there?"

"Not for a couple of days," she said. "It's just really cold now. Clear sky. Subarctic temperatures."

"You could come to Vegas," she said. "I know you're not

working around the lodge right now, while the Whittakers are there."

Elise let the thought roll through her mind, really examining all sides of it. "I could," she said, because she didn't hate the idea. "Let me think about it a little more."

"I'll be here until the third," her mom said. "Plenty of time to shop, get a pedicure, lounge by the pool...Henry has a pool in his backyard, dear. You wouldn't even have to go out in public."

Elise didn't even own a swimming suit, so the shopping trip would have to come before the lounging. She leaned her head back against the rest. "Sounds nice," she said, letting her eyes drift closed.

"What happened with Gray?" Mom spoke with a quieter voice now, and Elise had calmed enough to start the story. She detailed how things had gone at Devil's Tower, and how Gray had gotten lost.

"And then he didn't show up," Elise said. "I texted him and called him, and nothing. It was like he just disappeared. And then smoke started pouring out of the kitchen, and people started yelling and running out of the restaurant. I left, and I texted and called Gray again to let him know to meet me somewhere else."

Elise paused, reliving the frustration at so much silence. She'd thought she craved silence, especially after dealing with the huge crowd at the lodge, then more people in town. Apparently, no one made lunch for themselves on the day after Christmas, as every restaurant Elise had been to that day had been jam-packed.

Even the third one, which wasn't even that good.

She'd stood by the door, literally getting smashed behind it when people went in and out, as if she were invisible. In so many ways, Elise was invisible. She'd *perfected* how to be invisible, and most of the time she liked it.

But not behind a door, and not with Gray Hammond.

"And he never showed up," she said. "Never called. Never texted. I think he saw me at Devil's Tower, and was like, 'Wait a second…I'm not attracted to her.'" She sighed, because sometimes living inside her own head was very hard.

"I'm sure that's not true," her mom said. "Elise, you're a beautiful woman."

"I'm thin," Elise said. "Mom, there's a difference between being thin and being beautiful."

"Sweetie," she said. "I'm sure he didn't run away from you on purpose. Something must've happened."

Elise opened her eyes and looked at the bright blue sky, without a cloud in sight. "I called Colton."

Her mother didn't say anything, which was an indication that Elise shouldn't have called Colton. "He said he hadn't heard from Gray. So whatever happened, he didn't know about it." Elise didn't either. "It's fine. I have spaghetti and meatballs at my cabin, and plenty of ice cream, and I'll be fine."

"You said fine twice."

"Well, it's a two-fine kind of day," Elise said, a smile perking up her lips. "Thanks for letting me vent, Mom. I love you."

"Anytime," she said. "Maybe try calling him from the

cabin? Maybe he was in a place of poor reception. That place is like a pocket for my network. Only works half the time."

"Okay, Mom," Elise said. "I've got to drive now. Love you." She hung up, because she didn't want to get in to the fact that her mother had only been to Coral Canyon once in the last four years that Elise had lived and worked in Wyoming. Once—and that was to help Elise move from Jackson Hole to the lodge.

She continued up the mountain, the road in front of her like a shiny, black snake through the snow. She went past the lodge to an access road only she and Bree used, as it led to their cabin. She parked under the semi-permanent canopy Graham and Eli had erected for her and Bree, as there was no garage at the cabin.

Bree's car wasn't there, which indicated she'd likely gone down the canyon to her boyfriend's house. Another Hammond, this one the oldest and the former CEO of the company that had made all the brothers billionaires.

Elise didn't care about Gray's money. She blinked and she saw him standing in Colton's kitchen, shirtless, pouring coffee. Another blink, and their eyes met through the crowd. Another, and she witnessed him laugh with his son.

He made her feel something she hadn't in a long time, and she'd liked him. He'd been smart and kind, soft but clearly an alpha male. He wore the cowboy hat and the boots, and while Elise had told herself she didn't like cowboys, she now knew she'd been lying to herself for years.

"It's fine," she told herself as she went inside. "Fine, fine, fine." Four fines didn't make anything better, but they did help get her inside and get the plastic container of spaghetti into the microwave.

She put her phone on silent, left it in her room, and changed out of the cute checkered slacks she'd specifically bought for this date. She hadn't worn them except to try them on, and Gray probably hadn't even noticed them.

"It's fine," Elise told herself again. And then again. And then again.

———

THE DAYS PASSED, AND ELISE HELPED CELIA IN THE KITCHEN and stayed out of the way. The Hammonds came up to the lodge on New Year's Eve—the day of the Cupcake Wars—and Elise made a silent escape only a few minutes before they arrived.

She'd texted Gray between Thanksgiving and Christmas about what the Cupcake Wars entailed, and he'd said he'd compete with her. But she found she couldn't handle the noise and crowds in the lodge, and she texted him to say so.

Her phone rang with his name on the screen, and she only hesitated for a moment before she answered it.

"Elise," he said, his voice as smooth as a still lake. "You don't feel well?"

"It's just so noisy at the lodge."

That noise came through the receiver on his phone. "It sure is."

She didn't know what else to say. He'd called the other night too to explain about the fire engines, and getting hit by the ambulance, and all of that. He claimed not to have gotten her texts until hours later, and Elise had just nodded during the conversation.

He hadn't asked her out again, and she certainly wasn't going to ask. Not again.

"I'm going home tomorrow."

"Yes," she said, wondering what she'd thought they could become. He wasn't like Colton; he couldn't just leave Ivory Peaks whenever he wanted. She didn't know Gray well, but she knew he felt a great responsibility for his parents, and she knew his son was nearly twelve and in school.

"Colton says you make a mean chocolate cake," Gray said. "Maybe I could come to your cabin and taste it."

His suggestion gave her pause for a moment, but then his voice reverberated in her ears. *I'm going home tomorrow.*

"I don't think so, Gray," she said. "I'm not up to it."

"Okay," he said, his voice giving nothing away. "I'm real sorry it didn't work out for lunch."

"Me too," she said. "'Bye, Gray." She ended the call and let her hand fall to her side. There was nothing more to say.

———

A COUPLE OF WEEKS PASSED, AND ELISE FOUND HERSELF AT THE courthouse one afternoon, a jury summons in her hand. She really couldn't sit on a jury, as the very thought of having to decide someone else's fate made her sick to her stomach.

But getting arrested for not showing up did too, so she'd put on her checkered pants—might as well wear them for something—and driven down the canyon. The wind whipped at her scarf, and Elise tried to tuck it under her hood and walk at the same time. She stumbled, but righted herself and kept going.

She glanced up to see how far she had to go before she'd find relief from this wind, but her eyes stung.

Ducking her head, she focused on the ground at her feet. As long as there was flat cement, she'd be okay. She'd make it.

A cry filled the air, and Elise looked left to see a blue and yellow awning bumbling down the street toward her. It sent glass shattering when it hit windows on cars, and Elise froze.

Don't stand here, she thought. Or maybe it was the voice of the Lord telling her to move so she didn't get hurt.

No matter what it was, she obeyed, and she darted forward at the same time a huge gust of wind blew into the square, bringing the awning closer and practically lifting Elise off her feet.

She cried out as she fought the wind. She wasn't going to win this battle against Mother Nature, and she hunched her back and faced away from the wind so it would simply push her ahead of the awning.

Push her it did, right into the very solid form of someone else. "Sorry," she said automatically, but her voice got lost in the rush of air.

"Come on," the man said, grabbing onto her with very strong hands. "Let's hunker down here." He pulled her several steps back the way she'd come, and then down to the ground. The wind and chill lessened, and Elise pulled in a breath, feeling like she'd just run a marathon. She had no idea where she was or what they hid behind, other than it was made of bricks.

"Elise?"

She looked up from beneath her hood, that voice making her eyes widen. And when she looked into the dark, gray, stormy depths of Gray Hammond's eyes, time froze.

CHAPTER 3

G ray could not believe he was looking into the light green eyes of Elise Murphy. The woman had been haunting him for weeks. Perhaps she was a spirit? He reached out and touched her face, his fingers sliding easily along her jaw and behind her ear, as if he'd touched her so intimately many times before.

Her mouth dropped open a little, and now all Gray could do was stare at those pink lips. To be fair, Elise's whole face was a shade of pink, because it was mighty cold outside, and she looked like she'd been walking in the chill for a bit.

"It is you," he said, aware of the wonder in his voice. Was God playing some sort of trick on him? Or was this divine intervention in the best way possible? The Lord might as well have picked up a megaphone and shouted at him to *try harder, Gray. Don't let her tell you no. Call her again. Set something up.*

He'd known about his trip to Coral Canyon and this

hearing to address his accident for over a week. He could've texted or called her.

"What are you doing here?" she asked.

Gray dropped his hand, wishing he hadn't lost his cowboy hat in this gale-force wind. He needed it to hide behind in this moment. He easily outweighed Elise two to one—maybe more—but she made him so nervous somehow. Maybe just the innocence in her eyes, or the way she looked at him with such openness. *No expectations*, Gray realized. She had no expectations for him, and Gray sure did like that.

"I had a hearing," he said. "The city doesn't want to pay for my car repairs, but they hit me when I wasn't in a red zone." He knew the law, and he knew he was in the right. So he'd threatened to file a suit against them, and they'd set up this hearing.

"How long have you been here?"

"I got in yesterday," he said. "I left Hunter in Ivory Peaks with my brother. He's getting him to school today and tomorrow. I'll head home on Sunday." Plenty of time to take her to dinner. Before he could get too far inside his head and start to tell himself that it was better things between him and Elise had ended before they'd started, he opened his mouth and let the first words he could think of come out.

"Can you go to dinner tonight?"

Elise blinked, her surprise laid out on her face. "Dinner? Tonight?"

"With me," he said. "To be perfectly clear. I'll come get you, so we don't get separated. We'll be in the truck together, so even if I don't get your texts, it won't matter." Gray had been in plenty of tough situations. Endured dozens if not hundreds of tense court proceedings. He always knew what to say and how to say it.

But now, faced with this beautiful woman, Gray felt like the earth was shaking. He watched the rejection enter her expression, and he quickly added, "Please, Elise. We didn't even get to try last time."

"Maybe there's a reason for that," she said.

"Maybe there's a reason the wind literally blew you into my arms." An alarm on his phone went off, and Gray silenced it.

"What's that?"

"Ten minutes until the hearing." He peered over the top of the wall of the inner courtyard where they'd taken shelter. The awning had gotten stuck against a fence, and he looked to the steps of the courthouse. "Let's make a run for it."

He took her hand in his, rose, and started for the entrance, situating Elise on his right side so his body shielded her from the wind. They made it inside, and Gray exhaled heavily. "Whew. That was crazy."

Elise pushed her hood back and smoothed down her hair. Gray tore his eyes from the cornsilk, telling himself not to stare. "Why are you here?"

"Jury summons," she said.

"Oh, yuck," he said, putting a smile on his face. Elise returned it, and Gray felt like that was a positive move. "So…dinner?" He told himself not to ask again. If she said no, she said no. She could make her own choices, and Gray would have to live with them, even if he didn't like them. He knew that from his first wife, Sheila.

The seconds ticked by, and finally Elise said, "All right,

Gray. I don't want to see what Mother Nature might do next time if I say no."

"You can say no," he said. "If you want to." He really hoped she wouldn't, though.

"I don't want to say no."

A smile burst onto his face. "Great," he said. "I'll pick you up at six?"

"Six would be great." Elise pulled her jury summons out of her purse. "Well, I'm this way."

"I'm that way."

She moved past him with the words, "See you later, Gray," and he twisted to watch her enter the courthouse by putting her purse on the conveyor belt and then walking through the metal detector.

He went down the hall and through a different metal detector to courtroom four, where his hearing was. He wasn't nervous at all, because Gray knew how to put together a compelling case and how to present it in as few words as possible. He didn't think for a moment that he wouldn't walk out of there with his desired result, and the fact that he'd gotten a date with Elise only fueled his confidence.

"Elise," he whispered to himself, grinning. "Thank you, Lord." He tipped his head back and looked up as if he could see heaven from here. He paused and adjusted his suit coat, tugged on his sleeves, and ran his fingers through his hair before he reached for the doorknob.

————

"So they're going to pay?" Colton asked after Gray had brought back lunch and told him the story.

"Yep." Gray picked up another French fry. He had not mentioned Elise, because Colton had badgered him plenty about her over the holidays. After that, he'd gone mysteriously quiet, and Gray had a suspicion that his brother was just biding his time. He finished eating and started wadding up the wrappers and napkins.

"I'm gonna have to wait to run." He tossed everything in Colton's trashcan. "What is there to do here?"

"What do you do at home?"

"Well, I've been going through the house," Gray said. "Every cupboard and closet. Throwing away stuff that's too small or old or whatever. Stuff I haven't had time to even think about in the last decade." He threw Colton a look that didn't really meet his brother's eyes. "And I run. And I help Mom and Dad. Hunter's in school." The hours got filled, Gray knew that.

"We could go to a movie," Colton said.

"What do you do all day?"

"Whatever I want." Colton wouldn't meet Gray's eyes, and Gray knew he didn't do a whole lot.

"You need a job," Gray said.

"That I do, brother." Colton laughed, and Gray joined in. "Sometimes I go up to the lodge with Annie." He shrugged. "I go see what Wes is doing. Oh, I volunteer at the fire station a couple of times a month. I help with snow removal at the community center. And I go out to Springside a few times a week to work in the lab."

"So you do have a job."

"Kind of," he said, reaching for his wallet. "Movie or not?"

"I'm down," Gray said, though he didn't normally go to movies or sit still for hours at a time. But in a movie, he wouldn't have to talk about Elise—or anything—and it would motivate him on the treadmill later that evening.

Wait a second, he told himself. He couldn't run that evening. He had to pick Elise up at six—and he didn't know where she lived.

So he'd text her, and he pulled out his phone to do just that. He tapped and typed, sending the message without thinking where he stood and who he was with. He glanced up to see if Colton was watching him, and his brother looked away.

A little sketchy, but Gray went back to his phone, because he'd only asked her where her cabin was in relation to the lodge, and he wanted to find out where she wanted to go. He got that question sent off, and he shoved his phone in his back pocket.

"What movie do you want to go see?"

Colton looked up from his phone too. "The one I want to see doesn't start until four-ten."

"Oh, okay," Gray said. "So we'll hang out here. Maybe we could go ice fishing."

"Why can't we go at four-ten?"

Gray heard something in his voice, and he didn't like it. He also couldn't lie. He met Colton's eyes, and he knew his brother had seen him texting Elise. The glint in his eyes testified of it, and Gray clenched his teeth together.

"It's about thirty minutes up to Elise's," Colton said.

"And I'd be shocked if she didn't want you to take her to Wok This Way."

"Last time, she suggested Devil's Tower."

"She's not going to want to go anywhere near where you guys tried to go last time."

"Has she told you everything about last time?" Gray asked.

"She hasn't said a single thing." Colton sobered, which led Gray to believe him. "I tried to get her to tell me, and she shut me down and said she didn't want to discuss you with me."

"Ditto," Gray said. "I don't want to talk about her."

"Maybe you could talk about your plan, then."

"What do you mean?"

Colton laughed, the sound happy but also undergirded with a hint of sarcasm. "Come on, Gray. I've known you your whole life, and you—"

"Not true," Gray said. "*I've* known *you* your whole life, but I had two years here without you."

"Oh, jeez," Colton said. "I know you, Gray. You don't do *anything* without a plan."

"Well, I'm going to dinner at an unknown location without a plan," he said, turning away from Colton. His insides quaked a little just thinking about what he'd said.

"Take her to Wok This Way. And tell me how you even set this up. Last I heard, she wouldn't talk to you."

"Also not true," Gray said, walking away from Colton and going into the living room. Colton's house was large and new, and Gray actually really liked it. He had two cushy couches that both faced an enormous TV, and Gray figured they could have their movie right here and the only thing they wouldn't have was the greasy movie theater popcorn. After eating a burger and fries for lunch, Gray couldn't afford the popcorn anyway, not if he wanted to qualify for the Boston Marathon. And he did.

"She would talk to you?"

"We *weren't* talking," Gray said. "Period. It wasn't like I kept calling and texting and she ignored me." He sat on the end of one couch and crossed his ankle over his knee.

"But you are now." Colton sat on the other end of the couch, his expression earnest. Gray knew he just wanted what was best for Gray. Colton wanted everyone to be happy, and Gray thought for a good, long moment about if he was happy or not.

He loved running, and he was happy when he did that. He loved Hunter and even when he didn't want to check homework or meet with his son's teachers, he did it. He had a nice house too, and a nice truck. If he was hard-pressed to answer, he'd say he was happy enough.

And he knew "happy enough" wasn't good enough. He wanted more. He wanted to be blissfully happy, the way Colton was with Annie. The way Wes was with Bree.

Could he find that level of joy with Elise?

He wouldn't know if he didn't try, though his first instinct was to back away slowly, hands up so he didn't startle anything in his life. He didn't particularly enjoy change, but at the same time, he knew for certain that something needed to be modified in his life. And soon.

"Gray," Colton said, clearly exasperated.

"We ran into each other at the courthouse this morning," he said.

"What? Why was she at the courthouse?"

"Jury summons," he said. "And I'm not exaggerating when I say we ran into each other. The wind literally picked her up and pushed her into me."

Colton's eyes widened, and he looked like a child on Christmas morning. "It's fate."

"Oh, it is not." Gray waved his hand. "I don't believe in fate."

"But you asked her out." Colton leaned back and folded his arms, this probably extremely entertaining for him. "Or did she ask you again?"

"I asked her, if you must know," Gray said.

Colton grinned. "I must know," he said in a mock British accent. "And I also must know what your plan is."

"What plan?" Gray asked, hitting each word quite hard.

"Gray, you live in Ivory Peaks. She does not. You have a son, who, I believe, is the reason you haven't been out with anyone in years." He cocked one eyebrow in that maddening way of his, but Gray couldn't deny any of it.

"Hunter likes Elise," he said, his voice definitely filled with a defensive note.

"He liked Maddie too."

Gray jerked his eyes to Colton, who had gone too far.

"I'm sorry," he said.

Gray got to his feet, his chest storming and stinging.

"Gray, I'm sorry."

He shook his head and headed for the stairs, pins and

needles stabbing every organ in his body as he stomped away from his brother.

"Gray."

He paused with his foot on the bottom step. "I love my son," Gray said.

"I know that. I shouldn't have said that. Elise is nothing like Maddie."

"I don't need you to tell me about Elise," Gray said.

"Come back. I'm sorry."

He'd apologized several times, and Gray didn't want to spend the afternoon in the spare bedroom on the second floor. Sighing, Gray turned around and walked slowly back toward the living room, glaring as he sat on the couch.

"I won't ask you anything more about Elise," Colton said, making a cross over his heart as if they were in grade school. He leaned back into the couch. "So. Tell me about your training schedule for the marathon."

Gray blinked at him, thinking it would slowly kill Colton to talk about anything but Elise. And he sort of wanted to watch that, so he launched into all the details about his diet, the sports drinks and tablets he used, and how tonight, he really needed to run seven miles but wouldn't have time.

Colton made a fake snoring sound and let his head fall forward as if he'd fallen asleep, and Gray couldn't help laughing. Colton joined him, and Gray shook his head.

"Just promise me one thing," Colton said. "Don't tell any of this to Elise tonight."

Gray quieted and looked at Colton, sudden nerves moving through him. "What should I talk about?" His mouth felt too dry. "I haven't been on a date in a long time."

"You'll be fine," Colton said, which wasn't helpful at all. "But it might be good to know why you're willing to go out with Elise now, when nothing else has changed with you and Hunter."

"Maybe I have changed," Gray said, but deep in his soul he knew there was no *maybe* about it. "And, you know, uh, Elise isn't like other women I've been out with."

"I can't wait to hear how it goes tonight." Colton looked absolutely giddy, and Gray could only hope it was better than the last time he'd tried to have a meal with Elise.

In fact, he started praying for that simple thing. *Just better than last time, please*, he thought. Honestly, he wouldn't need the Lord's help to make that happen, but he asked anyway.

CHAPTER 4

E lise stood in her cabin, the Broadway musical soundtrack she'd put on chasing away the silence. Bree had gone to Maui with her boyfriend, Wes, and they'd gotten married the very first night they got there.

Elise had been shocked when Bree had called to tell her the next day—only four days ago—but she was happy for her friend. Of course she was. Bree had gone through quite a few difficult relationships in the past few years, and she deserved someone as amazing as Wes Hammond.

She looked at herself in the mirror. "You're going to have to learn how to live by yourself," she told herself in a very stern voice. But she didn't want to. Last fall and winter, when Bree had gone to Vermont to visit her parents, Elise had gone down the canyon to stay with Colton and Annie more often than not. She'd also stayed with Patsy and Sophia a couple of times. She really didn't like being in the remote cabin when it was dark, and during the winter, Wyoming always seemed to carry a bit of darkness in the air.

She shivered just thinking about coming back here alone, but she was determined to do it. She'd locked every door and window last night, double checked them, and then curled into her pillows. It had only taken an hour to fall asleep, and nothing had been disturbed in the snow around the cabin in the morning.

"Two nights in a row," she vowed. "Then three." She wondered if she'd have to live alone now permanently, or if the Whittaker brothers would hire someone else that would need Bree's room. That also brought a round of nerves to Elise's system, because while she thought she was agreeable and likable, it was still hard for her to meet new people. Especially if she had to live across the hall from them.

Someone knocked on the front door down the hall and through the living room, and Elise nearly jumped out of her skin. And it wasn't even dark yet. She pressed one palm over her now-rapidly beating heart and pressed her lips together, the image of Gray Hammond filling her mind.

She couldn't believe he'd asked her out, and she'd started to think she'd overreacted back in December. That only made her feel an increased measure of embarrassment, and she considered not opening the door.

But her car sat in the semi-permanent carport outside, and surely Gray would see it. He was a corporate lawyer, for crying out loud. And he hadn't taken her evasiveness for an answer, and he'd been so handsome and so strong and so....

Elise sighed, because she knew she was already

completely smitten by the tall, muscled cowboy lawyer who liked to run marathons. Elise hadn't run intentionally a day in her life, and panic reared as she considered what they might talk about over dinner.

The doorbell pealed, interrupting her thoughts, and a moment later, her phone chimed. Without looking at the message, she swiped it off the bathroom counter in front of her and headed down the hall. "Coming," she called, everything inside her buzzing with anticipation.

She reached the door and twisted the knob, but it didn't budge. Of course. She'd locked it behind her when she'd gotten back from the lodge. Her fingers felt sticky and unattached to her body as she fumbled with the lock to get it twisted the other way.

A second passed, maybe two, but they felt like years. She grumbled under her breath, finally getting the mechanism to move, and she gripped the doorknob like it was a poisonous snake she needed to strangle into submission. She yanked the door open and looked up into Gray's devilishly handsome face.

He hadn't shaved, and oh, wow, Elise's fingers started itching to touch that face and feel his beard against her cheek as he kissed her. Heat bolted through her body when he smiled and said, "Evening, Elise," so easily. Not a hitch or hiccup in his voice at all. His dark gray eyes slid down to her feet and back to her eyes. "Cute boots."

"Thanks," she managed to say, looking down too. "Patsy gave them to me." She loved the knee-high crocheted boots. "She actually made them. She's a whiz with a needle."

Gray nodded like he cared, and Elise commanded herself to stop talking about someone he didn't know. "Let me get my purse," she said, turning to find it. She always put it in the same spot, so luckily it was sitting on the sideboard she and Bree used for mail, car keys, and purses.

He waited on the front porch, and Elise kicked herself mentally for not inviting him inside. It was cold out there, especially with the sun already down. She joined him, a smile stuck to her face. She didn't need to be so nervous around him.

Just because he was a cowboy-lawyer-god didn't mean he wouldn't like her. At least that was what Bree had texted that afternoon. Elise had been trying to convince herself of it ever since.

"You're not going to wear a coat?" Gray asked, and another dose of heat filled Elise.

"Oh, right." She ducked back inside, calling, "You can come in," over her shoulder. The cabin was small, and it belonged to Laney. She'd built it as a refuge from her ranch just a mile down the road; somewhere she could stay if she got caught in bad weather or she needed an escape for a couple of hours.

It wasn't fancy by any means, and it didn't have a coat closet in the front room. In fact, the house only had one closet, and it was in the hallway, where she and Bree kept their towels, sheets, and coats. Elise ducked around the corner, the distinctive click of the front door closing as Gray came inside echoing in her ears.

Don't freak out, she told herself. *You like him. Big deal. He likes you too.* She practically ripped the door off the closet and pulled out the coat she wore to church. It was a cute little black number that had a cinch in the waist.

She went around the corner and almost ran right into Gray. "Oh, sorry."

He simply smiled at her, took her coat from her hands, and held it up to help her put it on. Elise turned around slowly and put her arm through one of the sleeves. "How are your parents in Colorado?" she asked, trying not to focus on the warmth from his body or the scent of his woodsy cologne. But he'd come inside, and she'd be able to smell that forever now.

"They're okay," he said. "Ames is watching after them and Hunter while I'm gone."

"And Ames is one of the twins."

"That's right."

"Who's the other one?" She pulled her hair above her collar and turned as she zipped up her coat.

Gray gazed at her, a new edge in his eyes now. If Elise wasn't mistaken—and she didn't think she was—it was a heated edge. He licked his lips before saying, "Cy. He's in California. Has a motorcycle shop there."

"That's right. I knew it was a short name. I would've said Ty, though."

Gray ducked his head, that dark, delicious cowboy hat hiding the upper half of his face as he reached out and touched her hand. Elise pulled in a breath, and she thought Gray did too. But he didn't pull his hand back, and a moment later, his fingers slid between hers. "I was thinking we'd go to Wok This Way for dinner." He looked up, a boyish charm in his eyes now. "Sound good?"

"Sounds amazing," she said, her words full of air. "I meant to text you back when you asked, but there was so much going on." Her heartbeat skipped around.

"No big deal," he said. "I figured out how to Google." He turned and led her through her own house, his hand very secure in hers. Elise could hear symphonies playing and fireworks booming, and she couldn't stop smiling. "This place is nice," Gray said when he opened the front door.

"It gets the job done," Elise said, stepping out behind him and turning to pull the door closed behind her. She'd have to let go of his hand to lock it, and she paused, considering just leaving it open.

She and Bree hardly ever locked the cabin. It was only Elise's overactive imagination that had her thinking an intruder would enter while she was gone and be waiting for her in the bedroom closet.

"You don't like the cabin?" Gray asked.

"Did I sound like I didn't?" Elise couldn't just leave it unlocked. She let go of his hand and reached into her purse for her keys.

"I sensed some doubt," he said.

"It's…I don't like being alone at night." She quickly locked the door and turned back to him. "Kind of silly, I know." She tried to smile away the nerves, but they didn't really go.

He nodded. "Hunter doesn't like being alone at night, either."

"Great," she said, being bold and putting her hand back

in his. "You'll probably do better not to compare me to a ten-year-old boy again." She gave him what she hoped would be a flirty smile, and she knew she'd succeeded when he chuckled.

"I didn't mean to do that," he said. "And he's eleven. Almost twelve."

"Got it," she said, leading him to the steps. "When's his birthday?"

"March."

"My birthday is in March."

"I don't see how I'm supposed to *not* compare you two when you're so similar." He nudged her with his elbow. "But I'll work on it."

Elise smiled, and she let him take her to the passenger side of the truck, open her door, and wait while she climbed inside. She'd ditched the checkered pants, and tonight, she wore a pair of black jeans that could've been a second skin with a pale pink sweater. With the coat, though, she was wearing black from head to toe.

As she watched Gray round the front of the truck, her heart pounded. Hunter was almost twelve. That meant Gray had to be a lot older than her. She wondered if that would matter to him. She wondered if he'd dated a lot in the past. She wondered if he'd been able to stop thinking about their geographical differences.

She hadn't.

She'd almost texted him half a dozen times after she'd been dismissed from the jury selection to tell him she couldn't make it to dinner. What was the point, anyway?

Bree had told her that people dated over long distances all the time, and to just give Gray a chance.

He opened the driver's side door and got behind the wheel. "All right. Let's get some heat in this thing." He started the engine and started pointing to buttons. "You can control your air right there," he said. "Make it hotter or colder. You have a seat-heater here. Bottom and back, or just one." He pushed and turned and got his temperature controls where he wanted them.

Elise had never seen so many fancy features on a vehicle before. Of course, she'd been driving the same hatchback for a decade, and she saw no reason to replace it as it still ran great.

Gray backed down the snow-packed lane with the help of a rear-view camera as if he'd done it a thousand times and started down the canyon. "Did you end up on the jury?"

"No, thank goodness." Elise sighed. "What about you? How did the hearing go?"

"I won," he said.

"Naturally." She shook her head, her smile genuine now. "I bet you're used to that."

"I mean, I don't normally do trial stuff," he said. "Or hearings."

"No?"

"Corporate law is much more boring than the TV shows," he said. "I'm not a defense attorney or a prosecutor. I advise executives on what the law is, and I make sure we follow it so people don't sue us." He gave her a fake yawn. "It's all very boring."

"Interesting," she said.

"What is?"

"Did you like it?"

"Oh, yeah," he said, and he seemed so relaxed. "I really liked it." He looked out the window on his side of the truck, keeping his face from her view.

She giggled and tucked her hair, her flirtations likely going unseen as he didn't look at her. She quieted, her stomach cinching slightly. "What are you doing now?"

"Nothing," he said quietly, finally glancing at her. "That's the real problem, not that my job was boring."

"Yeah, because you did it for how long?" Maybe the length of his career at his family's company would give her a hint to his age.

"Twenty years," he said.

Elise nodded and smiled, smiled and nodded, because her panic was about to boil over. "Most people would kill to do nothing."

"Yeah, for a day or two," he said. "Maybe even a week. Not indefinitely."

"I guess that's true," she said.

"Free time is fun when you're busy," he said.

"What do you like to do in your free time?" she asked.

"I'm training for a marathon right now," he said. "So that's helped a little. I spend a lot of time running and dealing with what I'm going to eat."

"I'm surprised you chose Wok This Way," she said. "I'm not sure what you know about the menu, but it's not marathon food."

He smiled at her, and Elise wanted to seize onto that moment and hold it in her palm forever. "And I didn't even run today." He chuckled, the deep sound filling the cab of the truck in a way that sent a thrill down Elise's spine. "It's fine. I'm doing ten miles tomorrow."

"That's incredible," Elise said. "I can't even remember the last time I *drove* ten miles." They laughed together, and Elise felt the last of the tension leave her body. "So, Gray," she said. "How old are you?"

He didn't answer right away, and Elise's guard went right back up. "I mean, I'm not very old, and it just occurred to me that you might, well, you might be a little older than me." She glanced at him, her mouth running away with her again. "I'm only thirty, and you said you've been a lawyer for twenty, and you've got all that sexy silver in your beard, so I'm thinking you're probably, what? Forty-five?"

The only reason she'd stopped talking was because she had to breathe, and in that moment, her mind caught up with what she'd said.

Sexy silver in your beard.

She wanted to disappear. Melt into the luxurious leather she sat on and slither back to her scary cabin-in-the-dark.

"Your math skills are impressive," he said. "I'm forty-four."

Elise nodded, because she didn't dare open her mouth again. She had no idea what she'd say then. Gray reached up and ran one hand over his beard. "I guess my beard does have silver in it." He looked at himself in the rear-view mirror as if he hadn't noticed it before. "You think it's sexy?"

"Oh, dear," she said dryly, hoping to play this off as a

joke. Could she? "Do you really need to fish for compliments?"

Gray chuckled, reached across the console, and took her hand again. "I think you look great tonight," he said. "How's that?"

"Thank you," she said, pleased he hadn't made too big of a deal out of her big mouth. "I think you're very handsome. At least you know what kind of winter coat is appropriate for men your age."

"What does that mean?"

"Have you *seen* Colton's winter coat?"

"Oh, well, Colton. He's always had a bit of a rebellious streak in him."

"Has he? Is that what makes a man wear a puffy coat?" She laughed, and Gray joined her. "I like yours better."

"Noted," he said. He wore a black and navy parka that only made his chest and shoulders seem that much bulkier.

"Tell me something about yourself," she said. "I mean, I told you my birthday, how old I am, that I'm scared of the dark, or maybe scared of living alone. Not sure on that. That I think you're handsome and sexy, *and* my opinion on winter outdoor wear." She grinned at him, though she wanted to staple her lips closed. "And all I got from you was that Hunter is almost twelve and that you're forty-four."

"Hey, I said I thought you were pretty."

"Did you, though?" She cocked her head at him, enjoying this conversation so much. "I believe you said I looked amazing tonight. That could be because this is a cute coat and you like my boots. There's a difference between someone looking good when they get all dolled up to go to dinner and being beautiful."

"Look who's fishing for compliments now."

Elise burst out laughing, eternally grateful this date was going better than the last one they'd tried to go on. She sobered and looked at Gray expectantly, but he didn't say anything.

CHAPTER 5

Gray's muscles tightened and released, and he commanded himself to talk. Elise was waiting for him to say something, and probably something amazing.

"I like to go fishing in my free time," he said, cutting a glance out of the corner of his eye toward her. "Hunter and I just go out to the river or to Ivory Lake, and it's peaceful. We'll stay for an hour or two, catch a few fish, and take them home for dinner. He cleans. I cook."

"That sounds nice," Elise said, her voice quieter and less flirty than before. Gray liked both versions of the blonde woman in the truck with him, and he did find her absolutely beautiful. Stunningly beautiful, and he'd have to make sure he told her before he went back to Colton's that evening.

"It is nice," he said. "I work a lot—or I used to work a lot —and those fishing trips were really important to both of us."

"So running and fishing."

"And with Hunter and my job, that kept my life really full."

"Sounds like it." Elise adjusted her hand in his. "You don't have to tell me, but...what happened to Hunter's mother?"

"She lives in Florida," Gray said, the words just there. They came out easier than he'd thought they would too. For how little he dated, especially. Everyone in his life knew about Sheila, and he hadn't had to explain his situation to anyone in a long time. "We've been divorced almost seven years now."

"And you have custody?"

"Yes," Gray said. "She left the state and hasn't been back. She didn't even contact us for a few years. It's only been the last couple of years or so that she's started calling Hunter again."

"Wow," Elise said. "Really? I can't imagine doing that to my child." She pulled in a tight breath. "I mean, I'm not judging her. Everyone has something they have to deal with, you know?" She squeezed his hand. "I didn't mean to sound like I knew better than her."

"It's fine," he said. "I understand what you meant." Gray sensed in Elise a very caring spirit, and no, she wouldn't leave her son behind without a word, a call, birthday cards, or Christmas presents.

The road flattened as he came out of the canyon, and he made the required turn to get them to downtown Coral Canyon. "Have you lived here long?" he asked. "Grow up here? Anything like that?"

"I'm from Canada, actually," she said. "Prince Edward

Island. My brother lives there with his wife, and my mom… well, my mom started dating last year—this guy in Las Vegas—and I think she sort of lives in both places now."

"That's quite the distance," Gray said. "And climate change."

"Right?" Elise trilled out a light laugh that made part of Gray's soul that had long been dark light up again. He felt like that about Elise completely—that she'd reawakened part of himself that had been dormant for many long years.

"So, what do you think about that?" she asked.

"About what?" He pulled into the parking lot at Wok This Way, noting how there were plenty of parking spaces. Relief rushed through him, because he didn't want this date to be *anything* like the last one.

"About long-distance dating."

Gray flinched, pressing too hard on the brake as he came to a stop in the parking space. He flipped the truck into park and removed his foot from the brake. "Oh."

"I ask a lot of questions," Elise said. "Don't I?"

"A few," Gray said. "Questions I can handle, Elise. I have conducted a lot of meetings where a lot of questions are asked." He turned and smiled at her. He couldn't imagine taking her to dinner tonight and having that be the end of things between them. But what their relationship would look like moving forward, he had no idea.

Slowly, he lifted her hand to his lips and placed a kiss against her wrist. He didn't know why, but he felt compelled to do so, just like he'd felt this insatiable pull to hold her hand in the cabin.

He lifted his gaze and met hers. "I don't know," he said

honestly. "About the long-distance dating. I think...." He exhaled, trying to buy himself a moment to organize his words. "I think I want to get to know you. I don't see this being a one-night thing, where I drop you off tonight and we call it done." He studied her light green eyes, which were so wide and filled with things streaming through them he couldn't quite decipher. "What do you think?"

"I think I know how to video chat," she said.

He chuckled and nodded. "I can do that too." He gave her a smile that felt very flirty on his face. And for him, that was saying something. "So I've now told you my age, what I like to do in my free time, that I'm pretty...what's the word? I'm not *unhappy* about not being a lawyer anymore."

"Lost?" she suggested.

"Not really," he said. "Wes was lost after he retired. I still feel grounded, and like I have a purpose. Maybe I'm just discontent?"

"Ooh, good word." Elise smiled at him.

"So I'm discontent in my career," he said. "And you know about Sheila now, and how old Hunter is. And how old I am—and I feel nothing about the age difference, Elise, in case you were wondering about that."

"I was *just* going to ask."

Gray grinned at her. "I had a feeling." He ducked his head again. "What else? Oh, yes." He looked at her again, right into those beautiful eyes, that pretty face with all that white-blonde hair framing it. "And I think you're absolutely beautiful. Gorgeous." His voice stuck on the last word, and he cleared his throat.

A flush crawled up her neck and stained her cheeks a lovely rosy shade. "Thank you, Gray."

"Oh, and one more thing," he said.

"We haven't even gone inside yet," she teased.

"Yeah, well, maybe if I get this out, we can just do surface stuff while we eat."

"Surface stuff sounds nice." She tilted her head an inch or two and waited.

"It's just—if I mess up too badly along the way, I hope you'll be forgiving," he said. "Just tell me what I'm doing wrong. I haven't dated in a very long time."

Surprise filled those sea foam green eyes. "You haven't?"

"Not for years," he said, swallowing afterward. "I tried a couple of relationships after my divorce, but they were both complete disasters."

"Completely?"

"Beyond," Gray said darkly.

"You or them?"

"Both?" he guessed. He sighed. "I don't know. I just know it was terrible, and I took a break."

"How many years?"

"Five?"

She nodded and faced the windshield. "We all have those disasters, Gray. I haven't dated anyone very seriously for a while either. A date here and there. Innocent flirting." She gave him a smile. "Now, are we going in or what? I'm starving."

Gray smiled too, his own stomach starting to complain about this prolonged conversation in the cab of his truck. "Yeah, let's go eat."

——————

Hours later, Gray stood on Elise's porch while she fiddled with the lock on her front door. He'd had the best night with her, and he was unsure of the next step. Should he ask to see her again tomorrow? He had three more days in Coral Canyon.

Should he kiss her?

He could admit he'd thought about it—several times—during dinner. She made him smile and laugh. She was smart and clever, and there was the whole gorgeousness to deal with too.

"Thank you, Gray," she said, finally turning back to him once the door had opened and golden light spilled out onto the porch. "I'm going to have to talk to Graham about fixing the porch light. I didn't realize it was out." She glanced up at the dark bulb there, and Gray could feel her unease.

"I can come fix it for you," he offered, the words just there, sounding across his vocal cords.

She looked up at him with a perfect brightness of hope in her face. "Really?"

"I'm here for three more days," he said. "I can come tomorrow." He wanted to shrug like it was no big deal, but somehow, he knew it was. And Elise did too. Not only that, but Gray was far too old to play things off as not serious when they were.

He leaned down and took her into his arms. "Thank you for going to dinner with me. That was the most fun I've had in a long time." He swayed with her slightly, telling himself to get off that porch as quickly as he could.

Then he wouldn't say or do something to embarrass himself.

"Me too," she said. "Even if I did think you were being pushy this morning."

He chuckled and stepped back, his heartbeat booming in a way it hadn't in a while. "Maybe I could take you to dinner tomorrow night too," he said. "I swear this will be the only time I ask."

"Mm." She put both palms against his chest, and though he couldn't feel anything but pressure, he sure did like her touch. "How about you come here, and I'll cook? I'll look up marathon-appropriate meals."

A grin filled his whole face. "Deal. What time?"

"Six again?"

"I'll be here," he said.

"Great." Elise tipped up and kissed his cheek. "See you then, Gray." She settled back on her feet before he could truly process what had happened, turned, and went inside her cabin, the door closing behind her.

Gray stood on the porch as the lock clicked, the heat from her lips streaming through his body though she'd only touched him for a moment. "Good-night," he whispered, wondering if he'd ever been this filled with magic before.

He must've been, he reasoned as he went back to the truck and headed back to Colton's. His brother would be waiting up, despite the way he and Elise had lingered at the restaurant until they were closing.

For the first time maybe ever, Gray *wanted* Colton to be waiting up so he could ask about the date. Gray was suddenly out of his depth and needed help.

It was all fine and good to put his mother off about dating. Act disgruntled and disgusted at her questions about his love life and why he didn't want to get married again.

It was easy to tell Colton not to make a big deal out of one date. Easy to roll his eyes when Wes said Gray could do what he wanted, as if Gray *knew* what he wanted.

His date with Elise tonight proved he had no idea what he really wanted. He'd been keeping himself separate from women for years, because he'd thought that was what he wanted. For him and Hunter. For their safety. Because he was perfectly content with being Hunter's dad.

"And that hasn't changed," Gray told himself as he drove, his headlights cutting a path through the darkness on this mountain. "But this date is a big deal."

It was, because Gray genuinely liked Elise. A lot more than he'd even acknowledged. They hadn't mentioned the failed date over Christmas, which suited him just fine. He didn't need to hash everything out about every situation.

He pulled up to Colton's and went inside through the garage, finding a light on over the stove and the sound of his brother's soft snores coming from the couch. He paused next to the island, trying to decide what to do. He could easily sneak past Colton. Did he want to?

He'd want someone to wake him so he didn't spend the night on the couch. Gray's back protested just thinking about sleeping on a couch all night. He tossed his keys onto the counter, where they made a loud clanking noise. He sighed as he unzipped his coat and went into the living room.

"Colt," he said. "You awake?"

"I am," Colton mumbled. "Yes, I am." He sat up, and

Gray tossed his coat over the back of a recliner. He sat down in it and sighed again.

"Bad?" Colton asked. A moment later, he snapped on the lamp beside the couch, his eyes searching Gray's face.

Gray kept his face impassive for as long as he dared, then he let the happiness over that night's date bleed out and curl up his mouth. "It was great."

A smile burst onto Colton's face too. "Yeah, it was."

Gray closed his eyes for a moment, trying to hold onto every individual moment of the last few hours. Of course he couldn't, but it was a miracle he wanted to.

"Wait. Was it really?"

"Yes," Gray said. "It was. She's *amazing*, Colton. I'm so out of my league here."

Confusion pulled across Colton's eyebrows. "What do you mean?"

"I mean, she's witty and fun and clever. I'm a boring, *old* lawyer. Emphasis on old." He'd said their age difference didn't matter to him, and it didn't.

"Oh, come on," Colton said. "You're not that much older than her."

"How old do you think she is?"

"I—she's got to be almost forty, right?"

"Not even close, Colt."

His eyes widened. "Thirty…four?"

"She's straight-up thirty," Gray said. "I'm fourteen years older than her."

"It's fine," Colton said smoothly. "You like her, and she's amazing."

"I do," Gray said. "It's odd, because I do. And she is."

"I'm so glad," Colton said, standing up. "Okay, let's hit the sack. I'm exhausted."

"That's it?" Gray asked, alarm pulling through him.

"Yeah," Colton said. "It was good. Done. What's there to talk about?"

"What about the fact that I live in Colorado? Or the fact that I have a son? Or that I have no idea what I'm doing? When do I kiss her? What do we talk about once I go home? Should I move here? What about Hunter and his school? What about Mom and Dad?" He stood up too, every worry and every question he'd thought in the past several months since meeting Elise streaming from his mouth.

Colton blinked at him several times, his mouth falling open. "Gray," he finally said. "You have never worried about stuff like this. You just act."

"Yeah, well, I don't know *how* to act in this situation, Colton." And he hated that, because he always knew how to act. Always knew what to do. Always knew how to do it.

"You're thinking about kissing her already?" Colton grinned, and Gray shook his head.

"You're right. I should've just left you to get a stiff back on the couch." He started toward the steps and went up while Colton chuckled.

He'd almost reached the top when Colton called after him, "You know what you're doing, Gray. Don't forget to take that leap."

"Whatever," Gray muttered, because instant annoyance clouded his thoughts. He'd had the leap of faith talk with Wes, not Colton, and his oldest brother had obviously told Colton. So they were talking about him.

Great. Just great

Gray went into the spare bedroom where he was staying, removing his shoes and undressing, leaving his clothes on the floor where they fell. At least until morning, when he'd pick everything up, fold it, and place it in his suitcase.

But for now, he fell back onto the bed and looked up at the ceiling. "Help me to know what to do," he whispered. "With Hunter, with Elise, with myself. For Mom and Dad, and everyone who'll be impacted by this potential relationship."

Satisfied with his prayer and that the Lord would continue to direct him the way He always had, Gray closed his eyes and fell asleep, dreaming of Elise and what might happen when he showed up to fix her porch light the next day.

CHAPTER 6

E lise slept in during the winter months, which meant she didn't get to the lodge until after the sun rose and had started to warm the day.

She congratulated herself on staying in her cabin alone for two nights in a row as she made the ten-minute walk to the lodge. "Morning, Graham," she called as she passed the stable where he worked.

He lifted his hand in hello and called, "Hullo, Elise," before getting right back to work. She knew why. No one wanted to be outside in the January chill, even if the sun was visible this morning. The clear weather almost made the air colder, in Elise's opinion, and she ducked her chin into her scarf and kept up her pace to the lodge.

The scent of maple syrup and freshly baked bread filled the lodge, with the hint of cinnamon underneath. Elise unzipped her coat—not the cute black one from last night—

and tried to make sense of the chatter coming from around the corner.

Sophia cooked during the week, and the lodge offered breakfast five days a week. Saturday, Celia came up to the lodge and prepared a big dinner, and Sunday was all about lunch. Elise hung up her coat and unwrapped her scarf, still unable to distinguish any voices she knew.

Since she took care of the grounds, and in the winter, there weren't a lot of flower beds to cultivate or weed, she helped with the fire in the main room, checked the theater room downstairs, and helped with anything else guests needed or that Sophia, Annie, Bree, or Patsy needed.

"Morning, Elise," Patsy said, but by the time Elise looked toward the mouth of the hallway, the other woman had already strode past.

"Morning," Elise said anyway, taking a moment to smooth her hair down after removing her hat. Then she rounded the corner and went into the half of the kitchen where all the food prep happened. Glancing right, she saw the huge dining room table was half-full of guests, and she took in the three griddles on the counter.

"This looks amazing, Sophia," she said, picking up a spatula and nudging it under a piece of French toast. Her mouth watered, and this toast was ready to flip. "Want me to flip this?" She looked at Sophia, who sometimes wanted complete control over her kitchen.

But today, she said, "Sure, thanks," as she lifted bacon off a tray with a pair of tongs.

Elise did as she asked, making sure to tell Sophia how much she liked her French toast, because sometimes Sophia felt like everyone liked Celia's cooking more than hers. It wasn't a matter of liking the food better, as Elise had told her many times. Celia had more time to cook, and she only made two meals a week. Of course her meals were going to be a little more in-depth.

"When you're done there," Patsy said to Elise. "We have the snowshoe group doing their day-long trek, and I need some help with the sack lunches."

"Sure thing," Elise said, finishing with the last piece of French toast.

"All right, everyone," Sophia said, but her voice wasn't anywhere near loud enough to carry over the guest chatter in the dining area. She looked at Elise, who nodded just once. Sophia put her fingers in her mouth and whistled, and that got everyone to quiet down real quick.

The lodge had a speaker system that Patsy used from time to time, but honestly, the only time she needed it was for emergencies—or when the Whittaker family was at the lodge together. There was so many of them, and they tended to spread out, let their kids have free rein in the lodge, and shout everything they said.

Elise loved them, though she'd struggled to find her place among them for a while. Sometimes she still felt completely out of place when the family came to the lodge, but more often than not, she belonged to her friends and they belonged to her.

Sophia went over the food and invited the guests to come get a plate and start eating. A surge started then, but Elise turned her back on the activity in the dining area and moved over to the other counter, where Patsy was slicing the home-made bread for sandwiches.

"Did you make this?" Elise asked, admiring the bread.

"Sophia." Patsy smiled at Elise and nodded to the jar of peanut butter. "I've put what we need on the cupboard there. I think there were six PB&Js."

"On it," Elise said, first finding the yellow paper with the number and type of sandwiches written on it, which Patsy had stuck to the cupboard door that concealed the lunch plates. She picked up a knife and laid out a couple of slices of bread. As she spread creamy peanut butter over one side, she glanced at Patsy.

"So…how was your night at the symphony?"

Patsy's face relaxed into an expression of pure joy. "Amazing." She placed a piece of cheddar cheese over the turkey she'd already put on her slice of bread. "I love live music, and concerts don't come to Coral Canyon very often."

"They will once they get that new music hall done," Elise said.

"I hope so," Patsy said, and she did look hopeful.

"And?" Elise prompted, but Patsy kept her head down. Too bad she'd recently cut off most of her hair and couldn't hide behind it.

"And what?" Patsy finally asked.

"Oh, come on," Elise said, glancing over her shoulder. Sophia was still plenty busy with the guests, not that Patsy wouldn't be able to talk about the new man in her life in front of her roommate. In fact, Sophia probably knew more than Elise. "You and John?"

"He liked the symphony too."

"No, Patsy." Elise giggled and shook her head while she reached for the strawberry jam. "What did he say about your hair? Did he like it?"

Patsy lifted one shoulder in a shrug and sealed the bag with the turkey and cheese sandwich in it. She immediately started laying out more bread. "He didn't mention it."

"He didn't mention it at all?" Elise lifted her eyebrows. Patsy had been so excited to get her hair done, something she claimed she didn't do very often. Her hair had been blonde for as long as Elise had known her, but she'd gotten it colored to make it even blonder and brighter. And it now lay in a cute pixie cut that really accentuated Patsy's delicate bone structure. She was a beautiful woman, only an inch or two taller than Elise, but she knew exactly how to keep the lodge running like a well-oiled machine.

"No," Patsy said, and Elise thought she heard a sniff from the other woman. But when she looked, Patsy was busy spreading mayo and then mustard. Elise didn't know what to say or do, and in the end, she went back to making peanut butter sandwiches.

"Well, he's just…blind," Elise said, because she tried very hard not to judge others or call names. "It's so cute, Patsy. Really."

"Thank you, Elise," Patsy said, and she definitely heard a sniff this time. She put her knife down and slipped her arm around Patsy's waist. Patsy paused in her activity too and leaned into Elise. "I think I'm going to break up with him."

"Over your hair?" Elise looked at her. "Not that I blame you. I—I just—you do what you think is right."

"I bought a new dress, and he didn't say anything about

that either." Patsy reached up and swiped at her eyes. "It's stupid, I know, but I feel like he doesn't even *see* me. Like, he's happy to see me, and we get along great, but he doesn't *see* me."

"Maybe he just needs to be told," Elise said. "Remember how Rose was telling us how she just started telling Liam, 'Look, when I get home from the salon, I need you to tell me how amazing my hair looks, even if you don't think it looks different.' And he did." She looked at Patsy, her eyebrows up. "Maybe?"

"Maybe," Patsy said, reaching for the turkey again. "Or maybe I need to put myself back out there to find someone who'll notice when I cut off ten inches of hair."

"It is hard to miss," Elise said, going back to her sandwich-making too.

"Even Graham noticed," Patsy said, cocking one eyebrow at Elise. "And that man doesn't notice much."

Elise giggled as she finished another sandwich. "You're right about that."

"Excuse me, ladies. Elise?"

She jerked her head up, the sound of that delicious voice so out of place in the lodge. Yet Gray Hammond stood there, holding his cowboy hat in his hand, the silver in his beard extending up into his sideburns and his hair.

She dropped the knife and wiped her hands down the front of her jeans, forgetting she didn't wear an apron. "Gray."

Patsy was staring at Gray too, and he smiled at the pair of them while he put his hat back on.

"Did you get breakfast?" Sophia asked, stepping in front

of Patsy and Elise. "You go around the other side, sir. There's plenty."

Elise took a step to the right to see him better, wondering what he'd tell her. She didn't think French toast, sugary syrup, and bacon were quite the fitness foods Gray was used to, though she couldn't wait for her plate full of carbs, sugar, and fat.

"No, thank you, ma'am," he said, tipping his hat. "I'm not a guest here. I'm just here to see Elise."

"Oh." Sophia twisted to look at Elise, who smiled nervously at her friends. She wasn't sure why. She'd been out with a few other men. First dates…fine, maybe her friends' surprised stares were warranted.

But Gray was a man among men, and every cell in Elise's body knew it.

"Go on, then," Patsy said.

"You needed help with the sandwiches." She glanced at Patsy and then Gray. "I'll be done in a few minutes. You want to wait? You really can eat. I'm going to, after this."

"I'll wait for you then." He fell back a step and then retook it. "Unless you need help in here?"

"Sure," Patsy said, gesturing him forward. "I'll always put a strong cowboy to work." She gave him a smile that only spoke of professionalism and guided him to the cardboard boxes they used for lunches on their hikes and daytrips. She taught him how to fold them and then told him to put a sandwich in each one, a cookie, a bag of chips, and a napkin pack.

He repeated it all to her and got to work. Elise had a very hard time focusing on peanut butter and jelly after that, especially when Gray said, "Shoot," and something fell on the floor.

She looked over to find a jumble of boxes on the counter, none of them made quite right. On the floor lay the box of napkin packages and a turkey sandwich. He looked at Patsy like he didn't know how to pick something up off the floor.

"It's in a bag," Patsy said. "Just pick it up." She glanced at Elise. "Elise."

That was all Patsy needed to say, and Elise put down her peanut butter knife and moved down the counter to the deformed boxes. "Oh, okay. You put the bottom flap in first, and it has to go in second." She pulled on one corner of the box, and the whole thing collapsed. She quickly propped it open again, putting the correct flap in first, and then the second. "See?"

"I actually do not see," he said. "But maybe if you do that, I can do everything else." He seemed flustered, and Elise found him utterly adorable. He went down to the tray of sandwiches and brought it back while she fixed another box.

"How can a super-smart lawyer like you not know how to make a box?" she teased.

"Believe it or not, we didn't learn this in law school."

"You have a son."

"He makes his own lunch," Gray said, sliding her a look out of the corner of his eye.

"Ah, I see." She fixed another box and set it on the counter for him. With that off his task list, he was able to put in the cookies, chips, and sandwiches. "You're here early."

"It's almost nine-thirty," he said. "I ran, showered, ate breakfast, and drove up here."

"What in the world?" She paused and looked at him. "What time did you get up?"

"Five-thirty." He looked at her like that was a completely normal time to get up.

"I have never gotten up at five-thirty in my life." She shook her head, marveling at him. "Okay, that was a lie. In the summer, I get up really early to work in the cool morning hours."

"So you're like a bear," he said.

"Okay, never compare a woman to a bear again," she said, nudging him with her hip. "I mean, honestly, Gray. First I'm an eleven-year-old boy and now I'm a bear?" She was only half-kidding, so when she looked at him, she knew he saw a hint of irritation in her expression. She certainly felt it roaring through her veins.

"I'm sorry," he said. "I just meant you sleep more in the winter. You know, like a bear hibernates."

"I think hibernation is different than sleeping past five-thirty." She fixed another box and set it up for him. "How many, Patsy?" Gray had just been making boxes blindly, but Elise didn't see the point unless they needed them. Storing flat boxes was so much easier than built ones.

"Thirteen," she said, and Elise did a quick count.

"One more." Elise fixed the last box and popped the other three back to their flat state. "Okay, where are you?" Her stomach growled, and she wanted this project done so she could eat breakfast.

"Chips," he said, dropping another cookie into the box she'd just made.

She stepped around him to get the bag of fun-sized chips and began distributing them into the boxes. He put his hand on hers, stilling time as she looked into his eyes. "I'm sorry, Elise," he said. "I didn't mean to indicate you were a bear." He swallowed, his eyes full of sorrow. "You're not mad, are you?"

How could she possibly stay mad at him? Not when he looked so remorseful and had apologized so sincerely?

She shook her head. "It's okay."

"Once we eat, can we go get your porch light fixed? What else do you have to do today? Maybe I could help." He looked at the lunch boxes. "As long as it doesn't require making a box or anything with flaps."

Elise giggled, her irritation completely gone in only a few seconds. "We'll check on the sidewalks, because the wind up here likes to blow snow around," she said. "And I take care of the check-in area to make sure it's clean and ready for guests. In the winter, we check-in at the office, so there's signs we put up. I build a fire in the living room. Stuff like that."

"So stuff I can help with," he said.

"Do you know how to make a fire?"

"I was a Boy Scout."

"That doesn't answer the question," she teased.

He simply smiled and shook his head.

"What?" she asked. "You couldn't make a box out of a template that literally has folds in it."

"Okay," he said, and Elise thought he might be getting irritated with her.

"It's actually kind of refreshing."

"What is?"

"That you're not perfect."

"I can assure you that I'm not."

"It's just that Colton once said that you were all polished and proper. Buttoned up right, I think he said." Elise watched him, and a hint of darkness definitely entered his eyes. "And he's right, Gray. You are perfect, and polished, and proper."

"And you don't like that?"

"I like it," she said quietly, quickly dropping her eyes when he moved his toward her. "I'm just saying that to see you fumble with the boxes was kind of nice." It meant he was human, and not superhuman, and maybe he'd be okay with being with another regular human…like her.

"I'll make sure Colton doesn't tell you anything else about me," he said, and Elise burst out laughing.

"That's what you got out of what I said?"

"One of the things." Gray smiled at her and picked up the napkin packs.

"After all of that, we can go back to my house to do the porch light." She linked her arm through his and let him finish up the lunch boxes. "Thank you for coming to help me with it."

"Everything went okay last night?"

"I'm still alive," she said, though she hadn't liked going into the cabin alone, and she'd almost asked him to come check under her bed and in the closet. But he'd seemed rooted to the spot on her front porch, and Elise didn't need to reveal any more of her weaknesses to him. So she'd hugged him and kissed his cheek and sent him on his way.

Her lips vibrated with the memory, and she stepped away from him. "The lunches are done, Patsy."

"Thank you, Elise," she said. "Leave them there, and when the group comes down, they can take one as they go out the back door."

"Who's eating?" Sophia asked. "The guests are done, and I can start to box up if y'all aren't hungry."

"I'm hungry," Elise said, turning toward her. "And did you meet Gray? I don't think I even introduced him." She looked back at where he stood with the lunches, foolishness filling her. "Gray, these are my friends and co-workers, Pasty Foxhill and Sophia Cooke. Guys, this is Gray Hammond. He's Colton's brother."

Elise beamed at him, though a flicker of discomfort moved through her. *He's Colton's brother.*

He was. He absolutely was. But what was he to her?

He shot her a look that held that exact question, but Elise kept her smile hitched in place.

"Pleasure to meet you," he said to Sophia, shaking her hand. He repeated the words and gesture with Patsy, and Elise grabbed a plate and started putting French toast on it.

Gray took a piece and the cup of coffee Patsy offered, and the four of them sat down to eat together. Patsy carried the conversation by asking Gray about himself, and Elise shot her a grateful look.

Gray would barely look at her, and Elise couldn't help feeling like she'd made a terrible mistake.

CHAPTER 7

Gray stuck close to Elise as she flitted around the lodge, setting up a podium with a tablet on it, building a fire in the living room, and setting out signs. The sidewalks were clear—thankfully—and by the time they got away from the other women working around the lodge, a couple of hours had passed.

Gray didn't mind; he literally had nothing to do that day. He honestly didn't know how Colton could stand the open hours without something to fill them with. He'd have to ask again, because Gray knew he'd run out of things to do soon enough.

He's Colton's brother went through his mind over and over again. Every time he heard those words, his annoyance spiked. But what was Elise supposed to call him?

Her friend?

He wouldn't have liked that either.

"You know," he said as they went past the stable. "I was here last Christmas Eve. I met Patsy and Sophia then."

"Oh, that's right," Elise said, her voice a bit too bright.

Gray didn't want to have a difficult conversation with her or make her feel bad about what she'd said. He'd seen the way her smile had turned plastic as they'd sat down to breakfast. She already knew what she'd said.

So maybe he didn't need to bring it up.

The silence between them felt charged, though, and he didn't like it. "It's great your cabin is connected with a side-walk," he said, cursing himself the moment the sentence left his mouth. What did it even mean?

"Yeah," she said, and Gray started praying to salvage this situation.

All of the differences between them crowded into his mind, and Gray wondered if maybe they were just too oppo-site. Maybe once he went back to Colorado, he wouldn't feel as strongly about her as he did right now.

"I'm sorry about that," she finally said. "That weird introduction. I didn't know...I don't know what we are."

"I don't either," he said, relief flowing through him. "It was fine. A little odd, but fine."

She reached over and took his hand in hers, her gloves a barrier between their skin. "At least I didn't say you were a bear."

He tipped his head back and laughed, all the tension between them gone with that single action. "I'm definitely striking out more than you, Elise."

"Sometimes we all just need a pass," she said.

"So I'll take one for the bear comment," he said. "And the boxes."

"And I get one for the awkward introduction."

"Deal." After that, the conversation flowed again, and she asked him about the farm where he'd grown up while he got to work on her porch light.

"It was a great place," he said. "It still is. Just a little run down." He reached up to take the light bulb out now that he'd removed the cover, but it was stuck tight. He grunted as he squeezed the glass and tried to twist it. "I think this is rusted."

He'd brought out a folding chair to reach the light, not a ladder, and he couldn't get any higher to see better.

"I'll be right back," she said, leaving him on the porch as she disappeared into her cabin.

Gray tried again, but the bulb wasn't moving. And if it really was rusted, maybe he wouldn't be able to put a new one in either. "Come on," he muttered, reaching up with both hands to try to get some leverage on it, grip it more tightly, or something.

All at once, without any warning, the bulb shattered. He cried out. Pain sliced through his hand. Broken glass and other debris rained down on his face.

He instinctively curled into himself, ducking his head and bringing his hands to his chest. The scent of blood filled his nose as he coughed and tried to get the shards out of his mouth.

His head swam, and Gray needed to get off the chair before he fell. A groan came out of his mouth, and he reached to balance himself against the house beside him just as the door opened.

"I broke it," he said, stumbling as he came down off the chair.

"Whoa," Elise said, hurrying out onto the porch. "Are you okay?"

He hadn't looked at his hand yet, because his eyes stung and he wanted them to keep watering so his tears would get out all foreign objects. He blinked and finally closed them once Elise put her hand on his arm.

"Gray, you're bleeding."

"Uh huh," he said stupidly. "My eyes hurt. I might have gotten glass in them."

"Come in the house," she said her voice filled with authority. Gray liked that voice, liked how she took charge, and he let her lead him into the cabin.

"Oh, I don't do well with blood," she said, her voice shaky now. "But I'm okay. I'm going to be okay." She kept muttering under her breath as she parked him in front of the sink. She narrated everything she did, and Gray just went with it. "I've got the sink on. The water is getting warm. I'm going to take care of your fingers first, and then we'll look at your eyes. Can you put your hand in the water, Gray? Put your hands in the water."

Her cold fingers guided his, and the water felt like hot needles against his icy, cut skin. He jerked them back, but she held them in. "I've got to see it," she said. "It's going to be fine. You're okay. I'm okay."

She didn't sound okay, but Gray didn't dare open his

eyes to look at her. "I am okay, Elise," he said. "I just want to be careful. Are you going to pass out?"

"No," she said. "This isn't too bad. Just two fingers—your pointer and your middle finger. The cuts don't look too deep. Let me go get some Band-Aids." She left him standing in front of the kitchen sink, and Gray opened his eyes enough to see his fingers. Blood dripped into the sink, and he picked up the rag there. Pressing it to his fingers, he shimmied his way out of his coat and bent over the sink.

If he could just splash some water on his face, he could be sure he wouldn't be inhaling light bulb filaments or broken glass. With his two good fingers and his thumb holding the rag over his two injured fingers, he used his free hand to washed his face. He opened his eyes and splashed water right into them, which stung.

But it also convinced him he wasn't going to scratch a retina with a piece of glass.

Elise returned and said, "Towels. I have towels." A moment later, she held one to his face, and he let her pat it dry. She took over with the rag and the towel, bandaging up his fingers a few moments later. "There."

She looked up and met his eyes, and Gray felt sure he'd entered the presence of an angel. "Thank you," he said.

"I need to sit down." She moved over to the kitchen table and took a seat, closing her eyes and breathing in deeply. Gray joined her, though he didn't think he'd pass out. He'd seen plenty of blood before, too.

"Once, when Hunter was a little boy," he said, hoping a story would calm her further. "He was riding his scooter in the parking lot at HMC. That's the family company.

Hammond Manufacturing. Anyway." Gray took a deep breath. "He was maybe six or seven. Sheila had already left, and I had something I had to do at the office one weekend. Hunter's so great, and he didn't mind coming to the office with me, especially if I let him ride his scooter. So he was, and I was busy doing who-knows-what."

He could still see his son's face though, even if he couldn't remember what he'd been doing at HMC. "The next thing I know, he's getting off the elevator just shrieking. Positively shrieking, and there's blood all over his face."

"Oh, dear," Elise said, her eyes opening and focusing on him.

Gray reached across the small, round table and took both of her hands in his. "Yeah, that was about my reaction. I hurried to him and got him in the kitchen at the office there to see what was going on. Through his tears, he told me he'd run into a parked truck on his scooter, and though he was wearing a helmet, he had this big gash on his chin. So I took him to the ER, and he got five stitches."

"Wow. I've never had stitches."

"Never?"

"Nope." Elise shook her head, her eyes wide, but the color coming back into her face.

"I've had them a few times," he said. "Once, I got this fish hook stuck in the back of my bicep, and it ripped out a great big chunk." His arm twinged in phantom pain, as if it could remember that. He chuckled. "Anyway, Hunter was fine. We had to call the guy who owned the truck and tell him, because Hunt had dented it."

He shook his head again, that memory of that terrible

thing actually not so bad now, all these years later. "And let me tell you, that was a day that I felt like the biggest failure of a parent."

"No," Elise said, turning her hand and aligning her fingers with his.

"You think I'm perfect, Elise, and I have a thousand more stories like that to illustrate I'm not."

She nodded. "I know that, Gray. I do. We all have stuff about ourselves we don't like. Mistakes we've made."

"That's right."

"To me," she said. "From the outside, and as someone just starting to scratch the surface of Gray Hammond, you're pretty darn perfect."

Warmth filled Gray, and he let himself smile at her. "I could say the same thing about you."

"Oh, really?" She cocked both eyebrows at him. "Which part did you like better? That I'm afraid to sleep alone in my own cabin, or that I almost fainted at the sight of blood?" She shook her head and laughed, and he liked that she didn't take herself too seriously. "You're a little intimidating, Mister Hammond, with your law degree, and your perfect poise, and your marathon body."

"Oh, so me shattering a light bulb in my face and not being able to make pre-scored boxes is just forgotten now?"

She laughed again, and Gray joined her this time. He lifted her hand to his lips, and everything sobered between them. Gray looked at her, really looked, and his heartbeat started sprinting in his chest. "I like you, Elise Murphy," he said. "Do you really think we can keep getting to know each other when I go back to Colorado?"

"I hope so," she whispered.

And hope was all Gray needed in that moment. "Me too," he said. "Now, we still have that porch light to take care of."

––––––––

LATER THAT NIGHT, COLTON ONCE AGAIN SNORED ON THE couch when Gray finally returned from his evening at Elise's cabin. She'd made an enormous pan of chicken enchiladas, half of which Gray had brought home for Colton and Annie at her insistence.

"Hey," he said as he nudged Colton's foot again. "I'm back.'

"I'm awake," his brother said, bolting to a sitting position. "I'm up. I am."

"Elise sent chicken enchiladas."

"Sweet." Colton got up and followed Gray into the kitchen, got out a plate, and peeled the foil off the pan.

"You're having one right now?"

"Why wouldn't I have one right now?" Colton peered at his brother. "And if you'd just wait one more hour in the morning, I'd go running with you."

"You would?"

"You'll be faster than me, but that's okay. When I went last summer, Wes had to ride a bike to keep up with me." Colton put three enchiladas on a plate and turned to stick them in the microwave.

"I don't run outside often," Gray said. "I don't know how

fast I'll be." He looked down at his bandaged fingers. "I can wait another hour."

"Perfect." Colton faced him again. "So? Dinner tonight? All alone at her place. Good? Bad? Kissing?"

Gray rolled his eyes, the very thought of kissing Elise sending his pulse into a frenzy. Yes, he wanted to kiss her. So part of that pick-up was due to anticipation. The other ninety percent was because of fear.

"Dinner tonight was great," he said. "We get along great, Colt."

"Two greats," Colton said. "Must be *great*." He grinned and pulled a fork out of the drawer. "And?"

"No kissing." Gray almost reached up and touched his cheek, but he stopped himself in time. Elise had kissed him there again, and he'd asked to see her the following day too. "Is this stupid? I'm leaving on Sunday."

"I left Coral Canyon."

"It's not the same, Colt."

"I know." For once, his brother didn't try to make a joke or act like Gray's situation was the same as his. "I don't think it's stupid. You have a phone. You can see how it goes." He turned to get his enchiladas out of the microwave. "I actually think it's a good thing for you to have some distance from the relationship in another day."

"Why's that?"

"Because your natural instinct is to squash it. I can see it on your face." He faced Gray again. "Tell me I'm wrong."

Gray just shook his head, because he couldn't tell Colton that.

"This way, instead of killing it and breaking up with her because you're afraid you'll fall for her, you can go home, do your Dad thing. Deal with Mom and Dad. Run with Ames. And keep talking to Elise. See if it really had legs to stand on."

"And what if it does?" That was the thing Gray was most scared about. He looked at Colton, letting his fear and anxiety march across his face.

"Then you can make a plan," Colton said. "You like plans, Gray."

He nodded, because he did like making a plan. Even if he had to abandon it halfway through, he liked knowing he'd thought through a situation to an acceptable end.

Problem was, he could not see how things with Elise would end, and whether or not that would leave him—and Hunter—in peril.

"Plus," Colton said. "This way, you keep Hunter on the sidelines for longer." He waved his fork in the air like making a checkmark. "You do what you want to do when it comes to him and women. You protect him."

"Do you think he needs to be protected from Elise?"

"Heck, no," Colton said. "But I think *you* think that, and this way, you can do that."

Gray nodded, because even if he didn't want to admit it, Colton was right. In fact, long-distance dating sounded like a really good idea for Gray, and he clapped his brother on the shoulder and said, "Thanks for waiting up for me, brother."

"Anytime."

Gray went upstairs, but tonight, instead of collapsing in bed and thinking about Elise, he dropped to his knees and began to pour his heart out to the Lord.

CHAPTER 8

E lise thought whoever had decided to serve pizza through a drive-through window was a genius. She was glad she didn't have to get out of the car, because as it was, the wind tried to steal the two boxes of pizza from her as she took them from the teen handing them to her through the window.

"Thanks," she said, smiling at the girl. She drove happily on her way, knowing the way to Colton's house as if it were her own. She'd stayed in her cabin for the third night in a row, and she was beginning to think she could definitely do it for a fourth night.

Before she knew it, a week would've passed, and then a few days later, Bree would be back.

"Bree's married," Elise told herself as she made the turn onto Colton's street. She saw Gray's dark brown truck in the driveway, and her heartbeat skipped around happily. He'd enjoyed dinner at her house last night, and she'd been glad to cook for him. Then they'd sat on the couch and talked about why they lived in a state where it snowed, and where they'd go if they could go anywhere.

Elise knew Gray had the money to go anywhere he wanted, and she'd been somewhat surprised by his confession that he wanted to visit a rain forest and then maybe a beach. "Maybe?" she'd asked him.

"I don't really care to travel," he said. "It was Wes who wanted to see every state." Gray had shrugged then, and Elise found him so attractive when he was relaxed. When he took his cowboy hat off to eat and chat. When he didn't have his shirt buttoned all the way to his throat.

He'd been relaxed and casual in her cabin, but never once did he do or say anything improper. They'd talked about Hunter only a little bit, and Elise had initiated that brief conversation about what Hunter liked to do in his free time.

Gray had said Hunter liked to work the farm and fish, and Elise had taken that to mean the apple hadn't fallen very far from the tree.

As she pulled up to the curb, her phone rang, and Elise picked it up from the cup holder to find her mother calling. "Mom," she said after she'd connected the call.

"How are you, Elise?"

"Good," she said, glancing toward the brand new house Colton had purchased in this new neighborhood. No one had come out to get the pizza, and she wondered if she should run it in and then continue her phone call. "What's going on?"

"I have some news," her mom said, and Elise heard the

excitement in the words. She tensed, because she had a suspicion of what her mother was about to say.

"Henry asked me to marry him, and I said yes!"

"I knew it," Elise said, smiling. "That's great, Mom." She'd definitely have to go to Las Vegas and meet Henry, probably before the wedding. She had the distinct thought that she should go in the next couple of weeks, because she didn't have a lot of work in the winter. "When's the big day? Wait. You're not running off to one of those twenty-four-hour chapels in Vegas, are you?"

"Of course not." Her mom laughed. "Henry has three kids, and he's talking to them about their schedules. One of his sons is a big lawyer in Washington D.C."

"Summer? Fall? It'll be in Vegas, I'm assuming."

"Yes," she said. "Here. I'll be moving, and I'm not looking forward to that, let me tell you."

"But it'll be worth it," Elise said.

"Yeah," her mother said, a hint of sadness entering her voice. "You'll come, right?"

"Mom," Elise said. "Of course I will. I think I should come meet Henry really soon, too. Don't you think?"

"I would love that," her mother said. She'd invited Elise over Christmas too, after the disastrous date with Gray, but Elise hadn't gone. When her mother had questioned her later, Elise had admitted she couldn't afford the plane ticket. So she wasn't surprised when her mom said, "I'll get you a ticket. Any day that works? I know you don't have a lot of work in the winter."

"Let me talk to Graham," she said. "I'll get back to you." Who she really needed to talk to was Patsy, so she congratulated her mother one more time. Added, "I love you, Mom. I'm so happy for you," and ended the call.

She immediately texted Patsy to ask her when she absolutely needed Elise at the lodge for over the next couple of weeks.

Are you going somewhere? Patsy asked.

My mom got engaged, Elise told her. *I need to go to Vegas to meet him.*

Her stepfather. Elise shook her head, the thought entirely wild. Henry wouldn't really be her stepfather anyway. She didn't live at home, and she didn't spend much time with her mother, not since coming to the US, at least.

But her mom would be in the US now, and perhaps Elise should make a better attempt to see her more often. They talked a lot, and that seemed to be enough for the both of them.

Wow, that's amazing. Good for her. A moment later, Elise got another text from her friend. *Anytime will be fine, Elise. There's nothing on the calendar until Valentine's Day.*

Right, Elise sent back, and she got out of the car, circling it to collect the pizza. Her thoughts rotated around Valentine's Day at Whiskey Mountain Lodge, which was quite the affair. Nothing like Christmastime, that was for sure. But Patsy had designed a "romantic retreat" this year, and she needed everyone to make the weekend what she'd advertised it to be. They'd sold out their rooms in fifteen minutes, which had prompted Patsy to start thinking of other special events she could do at the lodge, especially in the winter.

Elise hadn't been looking forward to the Valentine's Day celebrations at the lodge, but she wondered now if she should—or even could—invite Gray back to Coral Canyon in a month's time to go to dinner with her.

The idea bit into her brain and started to grow. She let it do that while she rang the doorbell, and as she smiled at Gray when he opened the door. "Hey," she said, handing him the pizza boxes. "Smells like Annie's been baking."

"All morning," he said. "And let me tell you, I need to get back to my regular life. All this banana bread for breakfast and pizza for lunch is really going to slow me down."

Elise could only smile at him. "I'll bet. You still have four months before the marathon." He'd told her in depth about his desire to run the Boston Marathon next year, and that meant he had to qualify and apply. He was running his first qualifying marathon in May, and he had until September, when applications were due for Boston, to get a qualifying time.

She suspected he'd qualify on his first try, and she'd already started thinking of how she could congratulate him.

She stepped past him and into the house, slightly nervous to be spending the day with Colton and Annie. They were married, after all, and Elise wasn't even sure if Gray was her boyfriend. He hadn't kissed her, and Elise started to panic a little bit.

Did she want him to kiss her before he left tomorrow morning? Would it make things harder or easier for them going forward with a long-distance relationship?

"Did you run already this morning?"

"I did hill training this morning," he said. "There are great hills here."

"He almost killed me," Colton said, and Elise turned

toward her best friend. "Hey, friend." He hugged her, and she expected him to whisper something about his brother. So when he didn't, she stepped back in surprise.

"Hey, Annie." She hugged her friend too and sighed as she settled onto a barstool in the kitchen.

"How are things up at the lodge?"

"Busy, funnily enough," Elise said. "I think the lack of snow this year has people traveling more."

"Lack of snow?" Annie laughed and looked out the back windows. "There's tons of snow."

"But it's already on the ground," Elise said. "And people love skiing and snowshoeing, and they're coming here to do it." Elise shrugged. "All I know is what Patsy tells me, and she says our bookings are up."

"It's good for me," Annie said. "I send Donna up on the weekends."

"Yes, I saw her this morning. Listen, I wanted to talk to you about planning something for Bree."

"Oh?" Annie looked at her and then focused back on chopping the lettuce for a salad.

"Yeah, not a bachelorette party or anything, but a celebration for her and Wes."

"Wes has already talked to my mom about doing something in Ivory Peaks," Colton said, joining Annie on the other side of the island. "So we'll have to go down there at some point for that."

"Do you know any details?"

"Not even one," Colton said. "Only that Wes called yesterday to say he wanted to have a family party to celebrate his wedding once he and Bree got back."

Elise was glad that would happen, but that didn't include Bree's friends here in Coral Canyon. She had friends at the employment office where she'd worked last year, and all of her friends at lodge.

But she didn't want to intrude on the Hammond family plans, and perhaps she could just talk to Bree about having a girl's night once she and Wes returned to Coral Canyon and their lives settled down.

She glanced around to find Gray, but he'd disappeared. She'd spent plenty of time with Colton and Annie, so she wasn't nervous. At least not until Annie said, "Colton tells me precious little about you and Gray. What's going on there?"

Elise stared at her, quickly switching her gaze to Colton's. "Hey, you heard her. I say precious little."

"That's because Gray doesn't tell you anything."

"Sure," Colton said, his smile never wavering.

Elise didn't know what that meant, and she really hoped it meant Gray didn't tell his brother anything. Everything suddenly seemed knotted, and she couldn't believe she'd gotten involved with Gray. She'd known it would be messy and could potentially impact her friendship with Colton. And she didn't want to lose his friendship. He felt like a brother to her, and she needed that here in Coral Canyon, especially now that Bree had gotten married.

In that moment, Elise realized that Bree getting married, while wonderful, was going to be very hard for her. She felt like she'd lost her best friend already.

"We're ready," Annie said. "If you're not going to say anything about Gray."

"Nothing to say," Elise said. "We're getting to know each other. That's all."

"Do you like what you've learned so far?" Annie asked.

"Yeah, sure," Elise said, deciding she could admit that. She couldn't quite look at Colton though, and while she'd been nervous to spend the day as a couple of couples, she really wished Gray were here so these questions would stop.

"I'm glad," Annie said, smiling at Elise. "Now, Colt, we need to talk about Valentine's Day, because I'm almost positive Mitchell is going to propose to Em, and I don't want to miss it."

"On Valentine's Day?" he asked. "We're going on that cruise."

"I know, that's why I'm bringing it up."

"Maybe I should talk to him," Colton said.

"Maybe they should come on the cruise with us."

Elise could tell they'd had this conversation before, because Colton's eyes flashed but he said nothing.

"Sorry," Gray said, breezing back into the kitchen. "That was Hunt."

"Is he surviving Ames?" Colton asked, not the only one grabbing onto Gray's appearance.

"Barely," Gray said with a wry smile. Elise remembered the more eccentric younger brother, who'd worn a top hat to Colton's wedding. "But no. Ames and Hunter get along great."

"Everyone gets along great with Hunter," Colton said, and Elise watched the two brothers enter a staring contest, neither of them blinking.

"Enough," Annie said, but Elise had obviously missed

something. A new kind of awkwardness descended on the kitchen, and Annie elbowed Colton. "Say grace, Colt, and let's eat."

"All right," he said, finally looking away from Gray. Elise watched him, but he didn't look at her at all. He didn't wear his cowboy hat that day, so he didn't need to remove it to say grace, and Elise closed her eyes while Colton said a quick prayer.

Thankfully, lunch was a much easier affair, without cryptic conversations she didn't understand. Still, when Gray asked, "Would you like to take a walk with me?" Elise practically jumped to her feet.

"Sure." She got bundled up again, making sure she had her hat, gloves, scarf, and coat before following Gray out the front door. He took her hand in his before he even went down the steps, and she heard a soft sigh come from his mouth.

She enjoyed being with him, even on a chilly afternoon. He made her feel warm from the inside out, and she finally said, "What's wrong?"

"Nothing," he said. "Other than my nosy brother."

Elise smiled, but she didn't argue with him. "He can ask some point-blank questions, that's for sure." She squeezed his hand. "Oh, I have some news."

"Oh?"

"My mother got engaged," she said. "So that's exciting."

"Wow, good for her," he said. "Are you really excited?"

"I haven't met him yet," Elise said. "But yes, I'm excited for her. She's been dating him for a long time."

"How long?"

"Just over two years."

"And they're in the long-distance relationship, right?"

"Right."

"So maybe there's hope," Gray said.

"There's always hope." She looked up at him. "Right? I sometimes feel like I live by hope alone."

"I feel like that a lot too," he said.

Elise turned the corner with him at her side and strolling with him on a Saturday after lunch felt so right. So perfect. So peaceful.

The idea she'd let take root in her mind before she'd gone inside Colton's house grew and swelled, and she took a breath. "What do you think about coming back up here for Valentine's Day?"

"Valentine's Day?"

"There's a big thing at the lodge," she said. "That weekend. So I have to work, but maybe a couple of days before. Or after. I don't know." She wished she'd given herself more time to think this through. "I know you have Hunter, and it's fine. I was just thinking out loud, and you know, Colton and Annie's house will be empty, and I thought it would be an easy time to come."

"Breathe, Elise," Gray said with a chuckle.

Elise knew he didn't mean for the comment to hurt her feelings, but a sting still moved through her. "Sorry."

"Don't be sorry. Thinking out loud is fine." He looked at her, and he was easily the best-looking and kindest man she'd ever been out with. And not really a cowboy, despite the hat and boots he seemed to wear everywhere.

Not when he's running, she thought, and she wondered

what he looked like when he ran. In the summer, did he wear a shirt?

An image of his naked torso flashed through her mind, because she'd seen him standing in Colton's house, shirtless, months and months ago.

"I'll look at what's going on with things in Colorado, okay?" He glanced at her, and Elise felt her time with him slipping through her fingers like smoke.

"Can't ask for more than that," she said, but she wanted more.

She wanted to kiss him. "Gray?" She slowed and paused, and he did too.

"Mm?" He seemed distracted, and she waited for his attention to come back to her.

When he finally looked fully at her, Elise employed all of her bravery. She smiled up at him and slid her hands up the front of his coat. She wasn't sure if she should ask to kiss him or if he would get the hint, and her heart pounded in her throat, then against the back of her tongue.

"Elise?"

"What time are you leaving in the morning?" she asked.

"Early," he said. "It's a rest day, but I'd love to be home in the afternoon so I can get Hunter, see my parents, and still be home early, as Hunt has school the next day."

"So I won't see you."

"I don't think so."

"So maybe you—maybe I could kiss you goodbye right now?" Her whole head throbbed with her pulse, and that only amplified with every second Gray looked down at her.

She'd never felt so foolish, and her calves started to

scream at her to settle back onto her feet fully. She did, saying, "It's fine, Gray. I feel so stupid."

She'd taken one step when he pulled her back, swept her into his arms, and leaned down to kiss her.

A squeak came out of her mouth, and then she melted into his touch, the taste of him, the absolute strength of his arms as he held her on the street and kissed her.

CHAPTER 9

G ray hadn't kissed a woman in years, and as he did so with Elise, he sure hoped he remembered how. She didn't complain or pull away, and Gray figured he was doing a decent job.

Kissing Elise only increased the magic between them, and while he'd definitely thought about kissing her, he hadn't planned to do it before he left tomorrow. Now he wondered why. Now he wondered how he could've driven all the way home without this memory securely in his mind.

He could've kept kissing her, but something in his mind told him he was standing at the end of the street where his brother lived, and he better get control of himself. He hadn't been aware of the hammering of his heart until he pulled back, and he opened his eyes, hoping to get a favorable response from Elise.

She still had her eyes closed, a small smile on those very

kissable lips. Those eyes opened and met his, and she giggled.

He didn't know what to say either, so he tucked her against his side and headed back to Colton's. He'd needed an escape, because Colton could annoy him with a simple statement—like the one he'd made about Hunter getting along with everyone.

"Wanna go to a movie this afternoon?" he asked.

"That would be great," Elise said. "I don't know why, but I feel kind of weird hanging out with Annie and Colton."

"Praise the Lord," Gray said. "I feel the exact same way." They laughed together, and Gray felt lighter than he had since Sheila had walked out on him and Hunter, making him a single dad and the subject of gossip around Denver for a good solid year.

"Why is that?" she asked.

"I don't know," he said. "Maybe because they're not really agreeing about their cruise right now. Maybe because Colton says stuff he shouldn't. Maybe because they're married and we're...."

"Not," Elise supplied for him, and Gray thought that fit pretty well.

"Yeah," he said. "Not." He wanted to ask her what they were, but he decided he didn't need a label right now. In fact, it might make things more complicated for him. So he kept his mouth shut and went back to Colton's, where he told his brother that he and Elise were going to the movies for the afternoon.

"Wait, what?" Colton looked up from his phone. "The movies?"

"You're not invited," Gray said.

"Gray," Elise said quietly, and he glanced at her. She wore compassion in her eyes, and Gray looked back at his brother.

"No offense," he said. "But Elise and I just want to spend our last few hours together alone." He knew that would appease his brother, and sure enough, a smile spread across Colton's face.

"Oh, all right," he said. "I see how you are."

"Sure, you do," Gray said, grinning at Colton. He'd been talking with Colton a little bit at the end of every night, but he knew he wouldn't be admitting to the kiss that had just happened down the street. Oh, no, he would not.

———

"Hey, I'm here," Gray called the next afternoon, after many long hours of driving.

"Dad!" Hunter came tearing around the corner from the kitchen of Ames's house, followed by Ames himself.

Joy burst through Gray, and he received his son into his arms with a smile and a laugh. Even a couple of years ago, Gray would've been able to scoop the boy right into the air and hold him on his hip. But Hunter really was getting older now, and Gray just hugged him tight.

"Were you good for Uncle Ames?"

"He was practically perfect in every way," Ames said, waiting his turn a few paces away. Gray released his son and stepped over to his brother. Ames grinned as he hugged Gray, patting him on the back.

"Thank you," Gray said, and he needed to find something to do for his brother. Because this would not be the last weekend Gray asked him to take Hunter. He'd often relied on his parents if Gray had to go out of town for work or to watch the boy while he went out on a date. But the dates had dried up years ago, and Gray was worried about his parents' age and leaving Hunter with them.

But he didn't need to bring up a romantic Valentine's Day weekend with Elise with his brother right now. Maybe things would disintegrate between him and Elise in the next few weeks, and he wouldn't have to mention it at all.

As he stepped away from Ames, a replay of the kiss he'd shared with her yesterday blared in his mind. He'd definitely do what he could to keep the relationship going, and that meant another long drive north in just a few weeks.

"Have you guys had dinner?" he asked.

"It's four-ten," Ames said.

"So that's a no," Gray said. "Maybe I'll call Mom and see if she'd like me to bring dinner out." He raised his eyebrows at his son. "Or did you guys go over there after church?"

"We didn't go to church today," Hunter said.

Gray worked hard not to look at his brother. "Oh," he said. "Right." He'd forgotten that Ames wasn't the most faithful of sermon-goers. He believed, Gray knew that. He had faith. He claimed as a cop, he had to have more faith than the rest of the brothers, or he'd never go to work.

Gray had gotten so used to rolling his eyes at the things Ames said, that he hadn't really taken his brother seriously. He finally glanced at Ames. "So should I call them?"

"If you're buying dinner, I'm in," he said.

Gray shook his head, his smile quick to appear. "I'll call Mom." He stepped away to do that, and quickly made plans with his parents. "All right, Hunt. Pick what you want, and remember that Grandma doesn't like spicy stuff."

Just being reunited with his son had settled something in Gray that had been seething in Coral Canyon. He wanted to say it was being back in Colorado—back home—but he knew that wasn't the root of the issue.

He had family in Coral Canyon too. Colton lived there, and Wes had bought a house too. If Gray moved there and took his parents with him, there'd be more Hammonds in Coral Canyon than Colorado.

The issue was Hunter and where he'd be the happiest. So while Gray was glad his brothers had been able to sell their penthouses and homes and make the move in their lives that made sense to them, he wondered if he had the same luxury.

"Five Brothers," Hunter said, and Gray's mouth watered though he'd had a burger for lunch. He'd skipped the fries, but he wouldn't be able to resist the twice-fried sweet potato fries at Five Brothers—with the garlic aioli dipping sauce.

"Perfect," he said. "I'm ordering now, and we'll pick up on our way out of town." He started swiping, putting in what he and his son wanted. "What do you want, Ames?"

"Let me see."

Gray handed him his phone and went to sit beside his son on the couch. "Did you really get all your homework done?"

"Yes, sir."

Gray smiled at Hunter. "And how's the farm?"

"About the same." Hunter looked back at Gray with the

same eyes Gray saw when he looked in the mirror. "Grandpa came out and helped, and he's still really strong, Dad."

"Is he? What did he do?"

"He lifted the hay bales right over the fence as if they weighed nothing."

"Wow," Gray said, impressed. "I bet he was still glad to have you there to help."

"He was," Hunter said. "They sold two more horses."

"Yeah, Grandpa called me on the way back today and told me."

Hunter nodded, and Gray let his thoughts wander down a path where his father sold the farm that had been in the Hammond family for generations. He simply couldn't see it happening. He could see himself working it, and his throat narrowed.

"What if we worked the farm full-time?" he asked, glancing at Ames to make sure he was still involved in the food ordering app.

Hunter looked at Gray, his eyebrows up. "Full-time?"

"What if we moved out there?" Gray continued. "And I worked the farm now that I'm not at the company. And you did too, and then went to school and all that." He gave his son a gentle smile. "That's what I did when I was your age, you know. I fed the chickens and horses before school and after school. Worked all summer." Gray had had a childhood full of work, from sunup to sundown.

"Would I have to change schools?"

"Most likely," Gray said. "We can wait until the end of this year."

Hunter didn't like that answer, as his frown pulled down his eyebrows and he ducked his head. He wouldn't say anything until he knew exactly what to say. Gray knew, because he'd had plenty of real conversations with his son.

"You don't want to."

Hunter shook his head.

"Maybe I can find out if we can keep you at the junior high you'd be going to next year," Gray said. "And drive you in."

Hope filled his son's face when he looked up, and Gray had his answer. To a lot of questions, really, including a very sensitive one about Elise and making a move to Coral Canyon at the end of the school year.

His heart felt like it was sinking, sinking, sinking, and he couldn't do anything to save it.

"Done," Ames said, handing the phone back. "And you got a few texts. I just swiped them away."

"Thanks," Gray said, the word laced with misery. If Ames or Hunter heard it, they didn't say anything. "What do Grandma and Grandpa like from Five Brothers?" He looked at Hunter.

"Grandpa likes the Surf Rider," Hunter said. "With avocado. I think Grandma gets the Tropical Surf Salad."

"That sounds right," Gray said, making the choices quickly and checking out. "Twenty-two minutes." He got up, his back protesting. He'd run the hills a lot yesterday, and he felt like he needed one more day of rest from his marathon training.

But he was less than four months out from the Colfax Marathon, and his schedule required six days a week of running. Tomorrow, he was supposed to do six miles at an easy pace. He could, and he would. Sleeping in his own bed tonight would help tremendously.

"We're at least that far out, so let's get loaded up. Are you packed?"

"Yes, sir."

"Go get your bag then." He watched Hunter head toward the hallway and go down it, a smile singing in his soul.

"He is the best kid," Ames said. "I still can't believe you make him call you sir."

"I don't," Gray said. "He just does it."

"Yeah, well, I told him while he's here, he doesn't have to do it."

"Your choice," Gray said, shrugging. "I don't care either way." He looked down at his phone, remembering the texts Ames had mentioned.

He hadn't had time to swipe before Ames asked, "Who's Elise?"

Gray's head shot back up; his pulse sprinted instantly. "What? Who?"

Ames grinned and folded his arms. "Yeah, exactly. Who's Elise?"

"No one," Gray said even as the heat licked its way through his core and into his face. He focused back on his phone, navigating to the texts. Sure enough, Elise had been the one to text while Ames had been putting in his order.

Hope you made it back okay.

Let me know when you do.

Miss you already!

He groaned inwardly, because that last text—while it made Gray's whole day brighter—was the one that negated his claim that Elise was "no one."

"Do you have a girlfriend, Gray?" Ames asked, not about to let this go. Ames never let anything go. He said blunt things, and he asked hard questions. Gray had always admired that about his brother—until now.

He looked up, glanced at the hallway, and met his brother's eyes again. "Swear to secrecy," he said.

"Oh, come on. We're not eleven."

"I have a son, and Mom will ask. Swear it, or I'm walking out and you can drive to pick up your own dinner."

Ames's expression changed from a teasing, playful glint to a serious one. "Fine. I'll swear it."

"If you don't before Hunt gets back, deal's off." Gray lifted his chin.

"You're kind of a tyrant."

"I'm sure he'll be back any second." And Gray wasn't saying a word about Elise to Hunter. Not right now. Not yet.

"I said I'd swear it."

Gray just waited, and Ames rolled his eyes. "Fine. I swear that I will not repeat what I'm about to hear to anyone. Not my twin, not my mother, not any of my brothers. No one." He even reached up and made a locking motion in front of his mouth. "Happy now?"

"Yes," Gray said. "And the answer to your question is yes. And no, I don't want to talk about it right now, and no, you can't ask me any questions in front of Hunter or Mom and Dad, and yes, Colton knows, and yes, you're only the second person who knows."

Hunter came around the corner. "Got it," he said. "I couldn't find my tablet charger, but it was in the bathroom."

"So you got it?" Gray asked, moving seamlessly from one conversation to another.

"Yep."

"Great." He took his son's bag, let his eyes linger on Ames, where entire conversations were had and acknowledged, and then turned toward the front door. "Let's go then."

CHAPTER 10

Ames Hammond pulled a pair of jogging pants over his skin-tight lycra running leggings, because it was freezing outside. He normally went to the gym to work out in the winter, but Gray had talked him into their outdoor spring, summer, and autumn runs together while he trained for a marathon.

Ames had protested, claiming he couldn't run ten miles when he hadn't been training the way Gray had, but in the end, if he wanted to talk to his brother, it would have to be while they did a five-mile run together.

Gray had told him to walk the five miles home, but Ames couldn't do that and not freeze to death, so he'd run the whole ten miles.

It would only be nine-point-four anyway, as Gray lived 4.7 miles from him. He'd said he'd drop Hunter at school, go home, change, and start his first leg of the run. Ames would meet him outside, and they'd run the 4.7 miles back to Gray's house. That would be his ten miles, at which point, Ames would return home, finishing his ten-mile run alone.

So they ran together for half of their distance, and Ames had loved doing it in the warmer months. He'd gotten to know Gray better over the years once their mutual love of working out had been discovered.

Ames just didn't normally keep up the training in the depths of winter. True to his vow of secrecy, he'd said nothing more about Gray's girlfriend in front of their parents, Hunter, or to Gray at all. Not in person, and not via text.

Ames respected the other brother's boundaries, and he'd talk to Gray about Elise this morning.

A sense of awe filled him that Gray had started dating again. First, that Ames didn't know. Second, that Colton did. And third, that Gray would even do it in the first place. He'd been so anti-dating and anti-marriage for so long, and Ames had started to rely on his brother's single status as a shield for himself.

But if Gray got married again....

Ames cut off the thought, bent to get his socks out of the bottom drawer of his dresser, and grabbed his shoes on the way out of the bedroom. The room across the hall from the master suite felt strangely empty now that Hunter wasn't there, and Ames paused to look inside. He'd need to strip the bed and do the laundry to get the bed ready for the next guest.

No one stayed with Ames anyway, so there was no hurry. In fact, the next person who'd likely stay with him was

Hunter, so he'd be back in that same bed, with those same sheets.

In order to keep up with Gray, Ames swallowed his vitamins with a few big gulps of a Monster energy drink. He'd have to go to the bathroom during the run, but he could use Gray's house at the midway point. Heck, maybe he'd get Gray to drive him home.

With that as a plan, Ames chugged the rest of the Monster and looked up at the ceiling. "Bless me not to die today."

It was a prayer he offered to the Lord often, because Ames strapped a gun around his waist and went to work five days out of seven. Danger was an implicit part of his job, and he didn't want to die before the age of forty.

Not after forty, either, but that was the benchmark he was using for now.

He wondered briefly if he should be using a benchmark like *before he got married and had kids* or *before he'd made his dad proud.*

His dad was proud of him already, Ames knew that. The man simply held such high standards and being a police officer felt like it ranked really low on the list. With one brother a CEO, with an advanced degree in business and economics, another a high-profile corporate attorney, and another with scads of scientific credentials to his name, Ames often felt like a sore thumb in the family.

His only saving grace now was Cy, the youngest of the Hammond brothers by five minutes. He, though, owned a massive custom motorcycle shop in California, where he built bikes for the rich and famous as well as rides for disabled veterans and others who'd served in the military. He'd taken his two billion and done something. Make more of himself. Did a lot of good in the world.

Ames had bought a couple of motorcycles from Cy, and he had two classic cars in storage in addition to the two trucks parked in his driveway. He'd gone to school too, but only for a year before transferring to the police academy. His big plan had been to get a criminal justice degree, but he never had.

He never had applied to a lot of things in Ames's life.

He pulled his shoes on and said, "Come on, Georgia. Gray will be here soon." He got down the leash for the German shepherd, but he wouldn't need it. The dog ran with him a lot, and she knew to stay right by him no matter what distractions came her way.

She was a police dog, and she and Ames had bonded instantly. He did everything with the dog, from sleep, to shop, to train, to traffic stops. He gave her a healthy scrub before he opened the front door and went out onto the porch. She followed him, waiting at the top of the steps for him to go down.

He adjusted his hat so it covered his ears more fully and pulled on his gloves. "All right, Gray," he muttered into the bleak sky. "Where are you?" He better hurry up—and he better be ready to answer questions about the mysterious Elise who'd texted him yesterday.

"Let's go," he told the dog, going down the steps. He paused at the bottom and started stretching, feeling his muscles yawn and start to wake up. Several minutes later, Gray came running toward him, lifting his hand.

He was moving fast, and Ames knew he was about to punish his body severely. "All right," he said to Georgia. "Right side."

She moved where he wanted her, and he got himself going so he could join Gray stride for stride as he rounded the half-circle of the cul-de-sac where Ames lived.

"You're going to kill me," Ames said, his lungs already protesting against this rigorous movement.

"This is an easy pace," Gray said, barely winded. "I'm not doing a marathon pace."

"I haven't run in two months."

"Colton kept up with me," Gray said. "I'm sure you can too."

If Gray knew that mentioning what Colton could do that Ames couldn't would light a fire in Ames's gut, he wouldn't have said it. But Ames hated being compared to any of his brothers, but Cy and Colton were the worst.

He struggled to find his rhythm as they left the neighborhood, but after the first mile, his lungs remembered how to breathe, and his muscles had remembered how to propel his body down the street in a nice running stride.

"There you go," Gray said, shooting him a smile.

"Found it," Ames said, proud of himself. "So can you talk at this pace?"

"Sure," Gray said, everything about him so smooth. He really was the most polished brother, with always the right thing to say and always the right clothes in the right place. He knew so much, but he never acted like he was the smartest of them all. He was kind and respectful, and the reason Hunter called his father "sir" was because Gray commanded respect—and usually got it.

"Is Elise your girlfriend?"

"Yes," Gray said.

"And how did you meet her?"

"You've met her too," Gray said. "She's Colton's friend in Coral Canyon."

"She lives in Coral Canyon?"

"Yes."

Ames tried to get a sense of how Gray felt about that, but his brother was all buttoned up, as usual. "That's all I get? I'm out here in the sub-arctic temperatures, running, and I get 'yes'? Come on, man."

Gray smiled, and a stride or two later, a chuckle came out of his mouth. He evened out his breathing, never breaking his pace, and said, "I don't know how I feel about it."

"Are you going to call? Text?"

"All of that," he said. "She called last night after Hunter went to bed."

"So we're not involving Hunter in this."

"*We're* not doing anything." Gray gave him a look. "*I'll* figure it out."

Ames nodded, because he knew the smothering feeling of having a bunch of people in his business. His mother was definitely the worst culprit when it came to meddling, but Colton did a ton, and for Ames especially, so did Cy. He always seemed to know better than Ames what Ames should do with his life. He couldn't count how many times he'd told Cy that just because they were identical didn't mean they were the same.

Wes stayed out of everyone's business fairly well, as did Gray. In fact, Gray was the best at it, probably because he wanted the same treatment in return.

"Do you have a picture of her?"

"I actually don't," Gray said. "You don't remember her?" He glanced at Ames. "Petite, white-blond hair, real slim, light green eyes?" He sucked at the air, and Ames wondered if it was just from all the words he'd strung together. "She never strayed far from Colt."

"I don't remember her at all."

"I haven't been able to get her out of my head," Gray said. "Even back then, when we first met…." He let his voice trail off, and Ames focused on the rhythmic sound of his breathing, the pounding of their feet on the cleared pavement.

Ames knew what it was like to have someone hovering in his head he couldn't get rid of. That would be Angie Lawson for him. He hadn't spoken to the brunette in at least a year, and yet, there she still was. He could picture every eyelash, the deep, red lipstick she favored, the little black dresses she'd worn to every dinner.

He'd had her, and he'd messed up. Last he'd heard, she'd started dating someone else, and that guy hadn't been too cool for her, hadn't wasted his time, and hadn't made her doubt herself. Ames was fairly certain she was engaged now, but he'd blocked her and most of her friends from social media for his own sanity.

It was never fun to look back on his mistakes, that was for sure. Just like he shouldn't have given up long-distance running when the weather turned cold. He preferred to lift at the gym in the winter, because all of his friends at the fire station and on the force dominated the weights.

He didn't ask anything else during the run, because he didn't need to know more. Finally, Gray's house came into view, and relief sagged through Ames's muscles. Gray had started to slow down about a half-mile ago, and he slowed even further. About a half a block away, he began walking, his breathing going in and out smoothly. "Not bad, right?" He gave Ames a smile.

"I'm not running back," Ames panted. "I've got to use the bathroom, and then you can drive me."

"Drive you?"

"What else have you got to do today?" Ames challenged.

Gray said nothing, and that answered the question. "Exactly," Ames said, his legs starting to cramp. "I'm dying."

"You're so dramatic."

"Do you have those cell salts?"

"Yes," Gray said. "I'll doctor you up, and you can make breakfast while I shower, and then I'll drive you home." He paused in his driveway. "Not working today?"

"Not until four," Ames said. "I'm on the night shift for the next few weeks."

"Ah." Gray stretched, and Ames followed him, because Gray knew how to cool down after a run. A few minutes later, his bladder didn't care about cooling down, and he left Gray in the driveway in favor of the bathroom.

When he came out, Gray had entered the house too, and he'd put Ames's favorite band over the speaker system. "Come drink this," he said, indicating the tall glass of cloudy liquid on the counter. "And take some painkillers."

"Thanks," Ames said, reaching for the glass and the pills. He downed it all, his chest still stitching with pain. But he put a smile on his face. "I've got to get back on the treadmill for longer than two miles."

"Yes, you do." He grinned. "Hey, I wanted to ask you about your schedule next month."

"Yeah?"

"Yeah, uh, Elise invited me up to Wyoming for Valentine's Day." His face started to turn red, and Ames marveled at that. Gray never got embarrassed. Well, almost never. "Not really Valentine's Day. I mean, close to it. She has to work that weekend, and I thought I'd go maybe during the week, but I know that's harder for you and Hunter, and I don't know, if you're on nights…."

Ames had never heard Gray say so many run-on sentences before. It took a few moments to process everything, catalogue it as his brother's nerves, and enjoy that Gray was flustered over this woman. Legit flustered.

"I'm on nights until February sixth," he said. "It's not hard to have Hunter during the week, Gray. He goes to school. I go to work. We come home."

"It's just that Mom and Dad are getting older, and then I'd have to explain everything to Mom."

"I know," Ames said. "I get it. It's fine." He turned to fill up his glass with plain water from the sink. "So what will you tell them? Why do you need to go up there again?"

"I don't know."

"She'll know you're gone."

"Yeah, she will." He looked miserable, and Ames didn't want to add to that.

"Be straight up with me, Gray," he said anyway. "Are you going to move up there?" Ames hated the snakes writhing in his stomach, but they'd been there since Gray had said his girlfriend lived in Coral Canyon.

"I don't know." Gray bent his head and raked both hands through his hair.

"I don't want you to move up there," Ames said, which brought Gray's head up. His eyes filled with questions.

"Why not?"

"Because then I'm here by myself," Ames said. "And Mom and Dad need a lot of help, and I can't do it alone." That was a valid reason, but not the only one. "I don't want to live here by myself. The best part about Colorado was that we were all here, and now there's more of us somewhere else than here."

Gray nodded. "I hear you. I doubt Dad will ever sell that farm. I'm thinking about buying it and taking it over. They can live in the granny house, and Hunter and I will take the homestead."

"So maybe Elise would move here."

"Maybe I should see if we'll have a relationship that lasts longer than a weekend," Gray said with a smile. "Maybe you're getting way too far ahead of yourself."

"And maybe a man likes to have a plan." Ames lifted his eyebrows, silently daring Gray to contradict him. If there was something the two of them shared, it was their love of plans and checklists.

Gray laughed, got up, and embraced Ames. "Love you,

brother. As soon as I know anything, I'll let you know." He nodded toward the fridge. "Find something for us to eat. Low fat, low sugar. I'm going to go shower."

"Low fat and low sugar foods aren't worth eating," Ames called after his brother, but Gray just laughed and continued toward the doorway that led to the master suite.

Ames watched him go, a storm moving into his soul. Things were changing, and Ames did not like that.

"Focus on what you can control," he muttered to himself. And he could control how soft the scrambled eggs were, so he got down a pan from the rack above the island and set about making breakfast.

CHAPTER 11

E lise's phone beeped at her, and a notification came up on the screen. Fifteen percent battery left, and it wasn't even noon yet. She smiled as she got up off the couch at the cabin and went down the hall to her bedroom to get her charger.

Bree and Wes were coming home from Hawaii that day, and Elise had said she'd then help her best friend pack up what she needed to move into Wes's house down in the valley. Bree would be back the next day and over the course of the next couple of weeks to really get all of her stuff out of the cabin, and that brought a slip of sadness to Elise's soul.

But she'd been sleeping in the cabin alone for eleven nights now, and every one got a little bit easier. Colton had suggested she get a dog—a little one—because they liked to bark if they heard anything at all.

Elise had resisted, because the last thing she needed was a little dog yapping because the ice maker in the freezer churned out its cubes and made some clunking noise. Then she'd think there was an intruder, trying to tap-clunk-bang their way into the cabin.

She may or may not have already thought that because of the noise the ice maker made. Adding a barking dog to the mix would only frighten her more. She'd told Colton she was fine, and that she didn't need him to solve all of her problems for her.

"I have nothing else to do," he'd said, and Elise had picked up on that more than anything else they'd talked about recently. She'd suggested he get a job, but he wanted to put it off until after Wes came home, because then there would be the moving, the family celebration, a trip to talk to his parents about selling the farm, all of it.

Elise plugged her phone in out in the living room and went back to her texts with Gray. He didn't have a job during the day either, and every morning after his workout, he texted her how far he'd gone and his time.

Marathon speed today, he'd sent earlier. *Half-marathon distance.*

She had no idea how on earth someone ran thirteen miles without stopping. And she had no idea what marathon speed was. But Gray did, and he'd seemed very pleased with his time. An hour and forty minutes.

He'd run down a road for an hour and forty minutes.

She felt like he existed on a different planet. One made of muscles and protein and determination. One where she would never be able to visit.

He'd told her he was resting tomorrow, and then he'd asked her what she was doing that Monday morning.

Elise didn't have much to do, but she hadn't wanted to tell him she'd been working on a recipe for blue corn pancakes, or that looking through an online catalog of tulip bulbs had brought her an hour of joy.

They both seemed so lame compared to what Gray did with his time. Raising a son. Training for a marathon.

She shook her hair over her head and told herself she was worthy of a man like Gray. Because she was. She normally didn't doubt herself so much, and she wasn't going to start now just because he was built, and beautiful, and a billionaire.

If one wanted to send you flowers, he'd said while she'd been gone to get her charging cable. *What would be an appropriate kind?*

Elise smiled down at her phone, the back of her neck sending a shooting pain down her back. She'd been texting with Gray so much over the last week that she had physical ailments now.

All flowers are acceptable, she typed. *But all women love roses.* She sent the text, hoping she was authorized to speak for all women.

Most women, she amended, giggling quietly to herself. She leaned back into the couch to give respite to her neck and held the phone above her head, continuing the conversation with her boyfriend.

She'd told no one about kissing Gray on the street, and he'd said nothing more about coming to Coral Canyon for Valentine's Day. She didn't need to know right now; she simply *wanted* to know.

He called her each evening after his son went to bed, and

Elise decided she'd ask him that night, when she could hear his voice and judge his mood more easily than through a text.

He finally said he had to go get something done that day, and Elise said good-bye. She sighed happily, gazing up at the ceiling. She should probably go get something done too, so she got up and left her phone on the armrest of the couch. In the kitchen, she pulled out her design notebook and turned it over and then flipped it around, so the back cover was now the front.

She opened the first page, the dress she'd sketched there bringing a balm to her weary soul. She'd told no one—not even Bree—about her secret desire to be a fashion designer. That wasn't entirely true. She didn't really want to be a fashion designer. She just wanted to design dresses for herself.

She'd started with a simple pattern that only had cinching on the waist, and she'd made the dress out of dark green fabric, big, black buttons on the bodice, and precise stitching. She received compliments on it every time she wore it to church, as she knew the fabric brought out the color in her eyes, making her appear less washed out.

Elise picked up a pencil and migrated over to the dining room table, flipping pages to get to the latest design she'd started to pull out of her head. She always worked in a slow, methodical way on her sketches, and then she'd wander the fabric store for hours, trying to find exactly the right fabric to bring the dress to life.

This one, though, she already had a fabric in mind. She'd seen it a few months ago, but she hadn't bought it, a fact she lamented now. The store in Coral Canyon didn't always carry the same fabrics for very long, and Elise thought she should probably get down the canyon and get it if she wanted to make this dress.

She still wasn't sure what length to do the skirt, and she'd drawn several figures of the lower half of the dress, trying to get it just right. She didn't like the look of mid-calf, but she didn't want anything higher than the knee. Making a maxi dress out of this fitted upper half didn't feel right either.

Elise didn't normally wear skin-tight dresses—she wasn't going to clubs or parties—but she loved the feel of the fifties dresses—cinched waists, fitted bodices, fun scooped neck-lines, and a flared skirt.

Her fingers moved, and she adjusted the neckline, and drew long, quick strokes for the skirt, ballooning it out as if it would fall to her knee in the traditional fifties style. But she took it all the way to the floor, and ended up with a ballgown.

The black fabric with bright red cherries on it wouldn't do for a ballgown. Would it? And where would Elise even wear such a dress?

She didn't worry too much about those questions as she sketched. She just let her mind wander and her fingers roam free.

Before she knew it, the light outside shifted, and Elise looked up from her notebook. Her stomach growled, and before she could check the time, her phone rang in the other room. She left her notebook and pencil in the kitchen and went to answer the call.

"Bree," she said into the phone. She laughed immediately afterward. "Where are you? Did you land? On your way back?"

"Yes," Bree said, and it was so, so good to hear her voice. Elise couldn't stop smiling, though the pinch in her chest was very, very real. "We're in town already, actually. We're getting lunch. Have you eaten?"

"Not yet," Elise said. "Where are you?"

"The Souper Bowl," Bree said. "And can I just tell you how amazing it is to be back where there's not one-hundred percent humidity?"

Elise laughed again. "Yeah, just don't breathe in too deeply through your nose. Everything might freeze together."

Bree laughed too, sobering enough to say, "I think you like the combo with the clam chowder and the deluxe grilled cheese."

"That's it," Elise said. "White bread. I'm not a health nut." Of course, she thought of Gray. She wondered if the man even ate bread at all, and she added it to her list of things to talk about with him that night.

"We'll be up in about a half an hour," Bree said.

"Sounds good." After she hung up, Elise went back into the kitchen, marked her place in the notebook, and slid it back into the drawer where she kept it. The pencil went in with it, and she got busy hanging up the *welcome home!* signs and setting out the banana cake with maple frosting she'd made for Bree's and Wes's return.

She was determined to put on a brave and happy face for her friend, so the moment Bree walked through the door,

Elise shouted, "Welcome home! You're back!" She rushed forward and grabbed onto Bree, who looked so tan and so healthy and so happy.

They laughed together while Wes brought in a small carryon-sized bag and closed the door behind them. He wore a smile too, and Elise pulled away from Bree. Her eyes widened as she looked into Bree's dark ones. "Can you believe you're married?"

"It's kind of surreal," Bree said. "To be honest." She gave Wes a smile but kept her attention on Elise. Her smile slipped as she leaned closer. "Are you okay? Really?"

"Eleven nights," Elise whispered. "I'm okay."

"Maybe someone will come live up here with you," Bree said.

Elise shook her head. "Who would do that? Why would I want them to?"

Bree didn't say anything, but Elise actually appreciated the worry in her eyes. It meant she cared about Elise and wanted her to be comfortable and happy. "Oh, I got you something." She practically bounced over to the suitcase by Wes's side, and Elise finally allowed herself to look at him.

Gray's brother.

He was older and sported more gray hair. But he had the same dark eyes, the same sloped nose, the same power emanating from those Hammond shoulders. "How are you, Elise?" Wes asked, his voice filled with only kindness.

Her heart flipped over, because he even sounded like Gray a little bit. "Good," she said, stepping over to him and giving him a quick hug. "How was Maui? Your fiftieth state."

"I really liked it," he said. "Bree…not so much."

"My hair was a rat's nest the whole time," Bree said, her back to Elise as she dug through the suitcase. "And it rained a lot, as if there needed to be *more* moisture in the air." She exchanged a look with Wes and then turned to face Elise. "Surprise."

She held out both hands, each of them clutching something. The first item was a giant bag of caramel macadamia nuts. Elise took it, her eyes widening. "These look amazing."

"They are amazing," Bree said. "When I tasted them, the first thing I said was, 'Elise would love these. I'm getting her the biggest bag I can find.' And I did." She radiated happiness in a way Elise had never seen before, and she actually got a little teary-eyed at the pure spirit Bree brought with her.

"Thank you," she said, her voice catching on the last word.

Wes's phone rang, and he said, "It's Gray, baby. I'll be right back."

Elise couldn't help watching him walk into the kitchen, saying, "Gray, my brother. How are you?" He laughed heartily, and Elise really wanted to know what Gray was saying to his brother. She wasn't sure why. They'd agreed to see each other, and they'd both talked to Colton about staying out of their business. Surely Gray wouldn't call Wes and tell him everything within an hour of Wes being back on the mainland.

Would he?

"Elise," Bree said, and she shook the thoughts out of her head. "I got you this too." She handed her a packet of reddish-orange powder. "It's pineapple seasoning, and it's amazing. You know how you're always saying pineapple is too one-note? This makes it like, ten-note." She beamed at Elise, who took the package of powder and looked at it.

"Oh, and don't worry about not having fresh pineapple," Bree said. "You'll be getting one in the next day or two. Or maybe two. I think we had two shipped."

"You shipped pineapples from Hawaii to Wyoming?"

"Yep." Bree turned back to her bag. "Now come help me empty all of this and get a few things for the next few days." She zipped her suitcase and looked at Elise again. "I feel really bad leaving you up here."

"I'm okay," Elise said. "Honest. And I made that banana cake you love, and I'm starving, so where are the soups and stuff?"

"Wes'll get them in a minute," she said. "And then we'll eat." They started down the hall together, and Elise was just about to ask her another question about moving in with Wes.

But he said, "Elise, you and Gray are dating?" and that made everything in her life come to a screeching halt.

Her footsteps.

Her breathing.

Her pulse.

CHAPTER 12

Gray glanced at his phone, expecting it to be Wes again. They'd just spoken for a few minutes, but Wes had said he'd call him back later, once he'd made it back to his house with his new wife.

Gray could scarcely believe Wes had gotten married on a beach in Maui, without anyone there to witness it in person. He supposed watching a live feed of the wedding counted, and Gray had asked Mom if she'd minded. She said she hadn't, and in Gray's experience, Mom said what she really thought.

But it wasn't Wes's name on the screen.

Elise.

His heartbeat tripled, and he glanced up to see where Hunter was. He'd just picked his son up from school, and he couldn't talk to Elise right now. He swiped the call toward the red button, and it stopped buzzing. His nerves didn't though, especially when Hunter came out of the bathroom and said, "Dad, can I make a grilled cheese sandwich?" and Gray's phone started ringing again.

Elise again. Something was afoot.

"Sure, son," he said. "I have to take this, okay?" He didn't wait for Hunter to acknowledge him. A grilled cheese sandwich would give him ten minutes alone. He practically ran into his bedroom and closed the door, quickly swiping the call on so it wouldn't go to voicemail.

"Hey," he said, feeling out of breath and more than a little frantic. "What's up? Why are you calling in the middle of the afternoon?"

"Why am I calling in the middle of the afternoon?" she echoed. "Let's start with a different question—why did you tell Wes we were dating? I thought we weren't telling anything like that."

Gray's face felt so cold. "I didn't...tell him." He closed his eyes in a long blink, because his brother wasn't stupid, and he'd obviously read something into Gray's words.

"Yeah, you sound real sure of yourself," Elise hissed, and she sounded like she'd stuffed herself in a closet to make this phone call. "They're here, and I told Bree I'd help her pack. So I'm walking down the hall with her, and there's Wes—fresh off the phone with you, for the record—and he's all, Elise are you dating Gray?" She made her voice deep on the last sentence, and Gray actually smiled.

"That was a great impression," he said.

"Gray."

"What did you tell him?"

She groaned, and Gray had a feeling he wouldn't like the

answer. "I told him of course not, and I scampered down the hall and into my room. This is a disaster."

"It's fine," Gray said. "Just go out there and admit it."

"Admit it?" Her voice went up in pitch. "Then I'm going to look like a liar. I *am* a liar. What did you say to him?"

"I knew he'd gotten in," Gray said. "So I just called to see how the trip was. He said it was great; I asked him if he was loving married life; he said yes." Gray exhaled, because he still held a bit of trepidation about getting married again. What would Hunter say? Would he really like Elise if she were his step-mother?

"And then I asked about the celebration he wanted to have, when that might be."

"And?"

"He said close to Valentine's Day, Elise. He mentioned something about how Bree wanted to plan something amazing, and she wanted to come meet my parents before the actual celebration so when they had the party, that wouldn't be the first time."

She said nothing, which prompted Gray to keep talking. "So I told him I might have plans close to Valentine's Day, and that got his questions going, and I said I had to go, but he's not stupid."

"No, he is not."

"He knew about the...thing over Christmas." Gray leaned his head back into the hard door behind him. "And apparently, he and Colt were going to stage some sort of intervention on me when he got home from Hawaii, and anyway, I told him nothing. He's just really smart."

"And now I have to tell him."

"Does it really need to be a secret?"

"Gray," Elise said, her voice placating but strong. "You're the one who wanted it to be, and I quote, on the down-low. Remember?"

"Yes," he said, and he knew why. If everyone in the family knew about his crush on Elise, they'd talk about it. And that meant Hunter would find out.

Gray sighed. "Elise, I'm going to talk to Hunter right now. He should hear about us from me."

"I agree."

"I didn't mean to be secretive," Gray said. "I'm just... overprotective of him."

"Ah," she said. "At least you're being honest now."

His defenses went up and so did his eyebrows. Then they immediately pulled down into a frown. "What do you mean?"

"You said you wanted time to see how things went before you told Hunter," she said. "To *protect* him. But really, you're *over*protective of him."

Gray pressed his teeth together, not knowing what to say. He wasn't sure if he liked that Elise had picked up on that nuance, or if he'd prefer she didn't. He also wasn't sure if he liked that she had put him in his place, when he was so used to doing that to others.

"Yes," he finally admitted. "I'm overprotective of him, because of something that happened in the past."

"Dad?" Hunter asked through the door.

"I have to go," he said, practically jumping away from the door. "Can we talk tonight?"

"I literally have nothing else to do," Elise said, and while her acidic voice scorched his ears, he simply said, "Great, thanks. Talk later," and hung up.

He pulled open the door to find Hunter walking away from him. "Yeah, bud?"

"The bread is moldy."

"Okay, let's go get some more." He smiled at his son like he hadn't just had a semi-argument with his hidden girlfriend in another state. When Gray thought about Elise like that, in those terms, his stomach swirled and stormed. He had to talk to Hunter about dating.

"Hunt," he said as he swiped his keys from the hook by the garage door. "I need to talk to you about something." He went first into the garage, trying to gather his thoughts. He reminded himself that he'd had plenty of adult conversations with Hunter. About his mother. About girls. About sex. About being a good person and making the right choices, even if they weren't popular.

He could tell his son about his girlfriend.

Still, he waited until they'd both gotten in the truck and he was backing out of the garage. "While I was in Coral Canyon this last time," he said, his voice scratching a little. "I ran into Elise Murphy." He shot a nervous look at his son. "Do you remember her from Uncle Colton's wedding?"

"Yeah, I think so," Hunter said. "She helped with the music with us, right?"

"Right," Gray said. "Well, I...went out with her while I was in Wyoming, and we're...." He swallowed, mentally commanding himself to just say the dang word. "Dating. We're dating now. I'm seeing her. She's my girlfriend."

He'd said so much more than just one word. Nervous, he

looked at Hunter. "Is that okay? I mean, how do you feel about that?"

Hunter looked at Gray, his face open as he contemplated what Gray had said. "I think it's great, Dad," he finally said. "I told you it was okay for you to date."

"I know," Gray said. He didn't need his son's permission to date. "But it's just me and you, and I don't want you to think she's more important. Or that—well, I don't know what you think. I need you to tell me."

"I don't think anything, Dad. If you like her and want to go out with her, you should."

Gray looked at his son, sure there was a trick going on. "Yeah?"

"Yeah." Hunter looked out the window on his side of the truck. "And what if I liked a girl, Dad? What do you think I should do?"

Gray dang near slammed on the brakes, his immediate reaction to demand who in the world Hunter could possibly like. Thankfully, he didn't, and he reminded himself that Hunter would be twelve in only six weeks. "Well, it depends," he said, his voice very cool. "Does she know you like her?"

Hunter shook his head no.

"And you don't just want to tell her," Gray mused. "Because you're in sixth grade, and that's weird. So...." He honestly had no idea what advice to give his son. No one had written a pamphlet or a manual on how to talk to your son about his first crush.

Gray panicked a little, thinking maybe this wasn't

Hunter's first crush. Maybe Gray had missed that in his own busyness or his own personal relationship with Elise.

"Valentine's Day is coming up," Gray said, seizing onto the idea as he passed a billboard advertising a dozen red roses for twenty bucks. "Maybe you could get her something. A stuffed animal or something."

"Do girls like stuffed animals?" Hunter asked.

"I honestly have no idea," Gray said, looking at Hunter. The tension in the truck broke, and Gray chuckled with his son.

"What did Mom like?" Hunter asked, and the honesty in his voice struck Gray's heartstrings.

"Mom liked chocolate," Gray said, sifting quickly through his memories for some good ones of Sheila. "And expensive jewelry. And a dinner she didn't have to cook." Not that Sheila had ever done a lot of cooking. "So I'd put chocolates on the counter in the morning when I left for work, and I'd send something to her during the day—earrings or something—and then we'd go to dinner that night."

"Did you take me?"

"Not usually, bud. You'd go stay with Grandma and Grandpa on Valentine's Day."

"Are you going to go back to Wyoming to see Elise for Valentine's Day?"

"I haven't decided yet," Gray said. "Uncle Wes might do his wedding celebration close to that time, and maybe Elise will come down here." He glanced at Hunter. "What do you think of that?"

Hunter shrugged. "It's fine with me, Dad. Honest."

Gray turned into the parking lot at the grocery store, and he told himself not to look at Hunter. To play it cool. "So what's this girl's name that you like?"

"It's no one, Dad," Hunter mumbled.

"Oh, it is too," Gray said. "I'm not going to know who she is or anything."

"Yeah, you know who she is."

Gray pulled into a parking space and looked at Hunter with surprise streaming through him. "I know her?"

"Her family goes to church with us."

"There's a lot of people who go to church with us."

"Her dad is the preacher," Hunter said, looking away. The tips of his ears turned red, and Gray wanted to gather him close and tell him that liking a girl was normal. Natural. Kind of exciting.

"Molly Benson?" Gray guessed, because the Bensons had four daughters, but only one close to Hunter's age.

He didn't nod. He didn't deny it. Hunter just got out of the truck and said, "Let's go get the bread, Dad."

Gray scrambled after his son, reaching him and slinging his arm around his shoulders. "She's cute, bud. You don't need to be embarrassed."

"I'm not embarrassed," Hunter said.

"Oh, well, good."

"But if you embarrass me in front of her...." Hunter shook his head and didn't finish.

"How can I embarrass you in front of her?"

"You say stuff, Dad."

"I do not," Gray said.

"You will," Hunter insisted. "Next time we go to church,

you'll be like, 'hey, Molly, that's a pretty dress,' or some-thing, and then she'll look at me like I'm the creeper."

Gray burst out laughing, though had he known talking about girls would get his son to say so much at once, Gray would've done it earlier. "So I can't tell a girl her dress is pretty?"

"No," Hunter said. "You can't." He gave Gray a glare. "Just forget it, okay?"

"Yeah," Gray said. "Okay." They went inside and got the bread, along with a few other things, and soon enough, they were back in the truck, headed home.

"Maybe she'd like chocolates too," Gray finally said, as if their conversation hadn't stopped at all.

"Yeah," Hunter said. "Maybe."

"I'll get you some cash," Gray said. "And I'll drop you off at the pharmacy, and you can get her what you want." He looked at Hunter. "Okay?"

Hunter nodded, though he still didn't seem super happy. "Okay, Dad. Thanks."

"Okay." For once, Gray felt like he'd just scored a major parenting win, and he smiled to himself. "Now help me make a plan for what to get Elise for Valentine's Day. She *does* know I like her, by the way."

CHAPTER 13

E lise stewed in her emotions all afternoon and well into the evening, despite being surrounded by her friends. After calling Gray and practically getting hung up on, she'd marched across the hall and helped Bree pack a bag.

She had not answered Wes's question, and Bree looked at her with questions in her eyes. "I don't want to talk about it yet," Elise had said.

"Fair enough."

Even packing a couple of suitcases for Bree had taken a toll on Elise, and she felt fragile inside and out. One wrong gust of wind would shatter her carefully placed smile. One wayward look from Colton would bust her wide open.

So it was a real shame when she loaded up in her sedan and followed Wes and Bree over to Colton's house for dinner. Annie had apparently made a big feast to welcome them home, and while Elise normally loved eating what

Annie made, tonight she only felt like a fifth wheel, bumping along behind her friends.

But she made it through the meal with that fake smile on her face. She contributed to the conversation, though every buzz of anyone's phone sent her heartbeat into aftershocks. If anyone noticed how she flinched with every text sent or received, they didn't say.

"All right," she said as Annie got up to put on the coffee. "I have a long drive." She stood and smiled around at everyone. So happy. Happy-happy Elise. "Thanks for dinner, Annie."

"Oh, you can't go yet," Colton said. "We haven't heard anything."

"Nothing to hear," she said over her shoulder, quite coldly too. If she was lucky, Gray would wait to call until she was in the car. The clock ticked closer to nine, and she hadn't realized how late it had gotten.

"I can tell you've been smiling this plastic grin at me for hours," Colton said. "What's wrong?"

"Nothing." Elise practically growled the word. She continued into the foyer to get her coat. The little black number reminded her so much of Gray, and she felt like she was cinching herself into the coat, strangling off all her air.

"It's Gray," Bree said, following them too. "I know it's Gray, Elise." She looked at Colton, and they were the two best friends Elise had ever had. "Wes talked to him when we got back. Wes said he didn't come right out and say he was dating Elise, but that was definitely the vibe Wes got. So he asked her about it." Bree cast a look at Elise. "She clammed right up and scurried into her bedroom for a few minutes."

With every word she said, Elise lost a little bit more air. "I'm standing right here," she said. "I hate it when you guys talk about me like I'm not even here." She sucked at the air, needing to get outside right now.

She yanked open the door, the blast of cold hitting her in the face and practically knocking her backward. Undaunted, she continued outside anyway. She couldn't breathe too deeply out here, or she could get brain freeze—or solidify her lungs in a single breath.

"Elise," Colton said. "Would you just wait?"

"I told you the rules when it came to Gray," Elise said. "We're fine. I'm not talking about him."

"Ah, so there's a *we're*," Bree said, clearly still following Elise as she went down the steps.

She spun back to the two of them, and Colton nearly ran into her he was so close. "And I told you not to talk to him about me too, remember?"

"Yes, ma'am," Colton said automatically. "I just…you're upset, and I don't like it when you're upset. It upsets me." He placed both hands over his heart. "Let us help you."

"You can help me by staying out of my personal life," she said. "If I want or need your help, I have your number." She glared at him, and then switched that look to Bree. She didn't want to have anything between her and Bree, though. The woman had literally been Elise's savior when she'd first arrived in Coral Canyon.

She deflated and sighed. "Can we just…can you guys just let me deal with this? I promise I'm not some fragile flower that can't do anything." She felt dangerously close to crying, and she did not want to be nasally when Gray called. She had a feeling she'd need to have all her wits about her, and her sternest voice in place too.

Bree nodded and enveloped Elise in a hug. "We really do love you and want to help," she whispered.

"I know." Elise thought the best way anyone could help would be to offer her a room for the night. Just the thought of driving through the darkness back to the cabin made her queasy. She shouldn't have agreed to dinner. She shouldn't have stayed so late.

Bree stepped back, and Colton took her place. "If he hurts you, Elise, just tell me. I know where he lives, and I'll take care of him." The fierce protectiveness in his voice made Elise's defenses crack, and she held onto him for too long. Then longer.

Finally, when she thought she might not cry or break when she stepped back, she released him. She could only nod, and then she turned and got in the car. It was far too cold to stand around outside conversing, that was for sure. Yet Bree and Colton stood at the end of the sidewalk, sans coats, while Elise backed out and drove off.

She kept both hands on the wheel as she drove, the heater blasting to warm the interior of the car. She stared straight ahead so she wouldn't imagine being swallowed whole by the absolute darkness around her.

Up, up, up the canyon she went, and Gray didn't call. She'd just pulled into the carport when her phone rang, and she hurried to put the car in park and reach for her phone. Gray's name sat there, and Elise cleared her throat before swiping on the call.

"Hey."

"Elise," Gray said, and how he could say her name with so much power and grace baffled her. He made her feel like a queen, even from across so much distance, and with so much unsaid between them. "I'm sorry I had to run earlier. Our bread was moldy."

"Definitely an emergency," she said.

Gray sighed. "Not really, but it kind of felt like it at the time."

Elise turned off the car and got out. The cabin stared back at her with dark, soulless windows, and she cursed herself for forgetting to turn on a light inside. "I just got home, and I forgot to leave a light on."

"Ah," he said. "Well, I'll stay on the line in case something happens."

"Not helping," she said, her steps slowing. Had she heard another footstep crunching in the snow? She glanced around, but only blackness stared bak.

"The porch will activate, sweetheart," he said. "Keep going."

How he'd known she'd slowed, she didn't know. But urged on by the kindness in his voice, she took another step. When she reached the bottom of the steps, the porch light kicked on, flooding the area with bright light.

She actually flinched, pulling in a breath and holding it tight.

"There you go," Gray said. "Just go inside. The lights are right by the door. There's no one there, Elise."

"I don't even think I locked it," she whispered. "There was so much going on. Wes and Bree were in and out...." She let her voice trail off, hating this weakness in her. Her heart pounded, and she took the stairs quickly, using her adrenaline to propel her through the tasks. If she could just make it inside, lock everything down and flood it all with light, she'd be okay.

The front door was not locked, and that only sent her heartbeat into a tizzy. She snapped on the lights, scanning the living room quickly. "No one here," she said, stepping inside fully and closing the door behind her. "Door locked." She twisted the lock. "I'm going into the kitchen."

"I'm right here," Gray said patiently, and Elise cleared all the rooms with his soothing, supportive voice on the other end of the line.

"All right," she said. "I'm in my room. Doors locked. I think I'll survive the night." She let out a shaky breath, wishing it could be a fun, easy, flirty laugh. "I'm sorry, Gray. I'm such a baby."

"You are not," he said. "You live out in the middle of nowhere. It's fine to be afraid." He cleared his throat. "In fact, that's the reason I've done a few things with you. I'm afraid."

Elise paused in removing her shoes. "You are? Of what?"

"Of messing up as a dad," he said. "Of having this relationship with you when it might not be what's best for Hunter, because *I* want it so badly."

Elise didn't have children, and she didn't want to tell him what he should or shouldn't do as a father. That wasn't her call to make. So she just waited while he stayed silent on the other end of the line. She could imagine him in the room with her, a tortured look on his face as his chest rose and fell, as his mind spun to find the traction it needed.

"My last girlfriend," he finally said, his voice a tad lower and definitely without as much emotion. "Her name was Maddie. She was everything I thought I wanted. Everything I wanted for Hunter. He really liked her too. They got along really well."

"Okay," Elise said, just to have something to say. Was he still hung up on Maddie? He'd said he hadn't dated in years.

"Turned out, she was only using us. Both of us. For money. She wanted my money. She actually used my son to steal from me, and then laughed at him when everything came out." Gray's breathing came through the line. "I'm still very angry about it, and I need to work through that. I know you're not like her, Elise. I know that. But I have not dated since her, because my son is an amazing human being, and he deserves to be treated as such."

"I agree," Elise said, her heart wailing for Gray.

"He thought he was doing something that would make her happy, because he loved her." Gray's voice broke, but he continued with, "I will not put my son through anything remotely close to that again. He went to therapy for a year, and he's doing really well now."

"I understand," Elise said gently. "I'm fine with what we had going, Gray. Honestly, I am. I thought we weren't telling anyone about us, so I was surprised when Wes seemed to know."

"I don't know what Wes heard," Gray said. "I did *not* tell him we were dating."

"I believe you."

"I'm overprotective of Hunter."

"As you should be."

"But I did tell him about us."

Elise's eyebrows went up, and she thawed from her frozen state. She kicked off her shoes and asked, "You did?"

"Yes," Gray said. "He said he's okay with me dating. Honestly, he is." He made his voice sound different on the last few words, as if mimicking his son. He chuckled. "We brainstormed what girls like to get for Valentine's Day tonight, and I think it's a fairly decent list."

"Okay, let's hear it," she said.

"Okay," he said. "We're open to feedback. Hunter has this girl he likes—I just found out tonight, believe it or not. And I kind of have this woman I have a big crush on...." He let the words hang there, and Elise could only smile to herself locked in her bedroom.

Gray cleared his throat. "Okay, so we've got flowers. Chocolate and-or candy. Stuffed animals. Scented candles. Perfume. Jewelry. Cards."

"Hmm," she said, falling into a flirtatious tone pretty easily. "I think for a twelve-year-old girl...getting a card and a flower is pretty special. Maybe the candy. Girls of all ages definitely like candy and-or chocolate."

"Noted. What do you think about the stuffed animal idea?"

"Here's the thing," Elise said. "Women aren't like men. For men, bigger is better, right? Big truck. Big cowboy hat. Big ego." She shook her head. "No. Women like small. Think of how we coo over baby animals on social media. Tiny ribbons and bows and stationery. Little things are cute. Little things are *adorable*."

"I'm taking notes," Gray said. "Keep going."

Elise giggled. "So for Hunter and his girl, go with a baby stuffed animal—not too big—with a tiny little bow, and hey, a tiny card would be amazing too. Tiny bag. All of it little. Girls *love* little things."

"Candy or no?"

"Sure," she said. "Get one of those mini assortments you can find at the corner stores. It'll fit in the tiny bag."

"Got it."

"As for more adult women...." She thought for a moment. "I mean, it depends on the person."

"What might you get for someone who doesn't like living alone but has to do it? Who has a boyfriend in another state she can't see all the time? Who sometimes makes mistakes and makes her angry and just wants her to know he'd be there if he could?"

Elise's eyes and nose began to burn with unshed tears. Gray had said exactly the right thing, and she did wish he was here with her with all the energy of her soul.

"Elise?"

"I'm thinking," she said, her voice thick. She wiped her eyes and took a big breath, trying to steady her emotions. "For someone like that, I think you should get her a dog."

"A dog?"

"Not a stuffed one," Elise said. "But a big dog who'll protect her and warn her if something is happening. Who can sort of act like the boyfriend when he can't be there."

"But what if this woman has already vetoed the idea of a dog?"

"Maybe ask again," she said, smiling even as a tear leaked out of the corner of her eye. She sniffed and wiped it away. "And for the record, I was not angry. I was frustrated at the situation and where I found myself inside it."

"I know that," he said quietly. "Though I wouldn't blame you if you'd been angry."

"I miss you," she whispered, leaning her head back and closing her eyes. She missed him so much. The distance between them felt so great, and so wide, and yet she could feel him right beside her too.

"I miss you, too," he said.

Elise started thinking about her life in Coral Canyon, and what it might look like if she transferred most of it south to Colorado. She didn't have any real ties to this town or the lodge. Yes, it was the first place she'd felt loved and accepted. The first place of her adult life that had felt like home. But she felt like that with Gray too.

"Is bigger better with adult women?" Gray asked. "For dogs, specifically. But also for flowers and chocolates and all of that."

"Yes," Elise said. "In this case, bigger is better for adult women."

"Got it," he said. "Let's talk about Valentine's Day."

"Okay."

"Wes said he might have a celebration down here close to them so our parents don't have to travel. Would you come to that?"

"It depends on when it is. We have a big thing at the lodge."

"Yeah, I remember. I highly doubt Bree would plan it when her friends couldn't come."

"Unless she's going to do something up here too," Elise

said. "But that doesn't sound like her. She doesn't like the spotlight too much."

"So I guess we'll wait and see what they do," Gray said. "Before we make any plans."

"Okay," Elise said.

"Follow-up question," Gray said, and Elise heard the lawyer in him.

It made her smile, and she said, "Go ahead, counselor."

Gray paused, then burst out laughing. Elise basked in the sound of it for a few moments before she joined in.

"That was great," Gray said. "I'll try to be less lawyer-like."

"I enjoyed it," Elise said, teasing him.

"How would you feel about meeting Hunter in an official girlfriend capacity?"

"I feel fine about that," she said.

"Just fine?"

"Great." She'd met Hunter before, and he really was a great kid.

"It's different as soon as you're the girlfriend," he said. "Trust me on that."

"Okay."

"I'm not saying it'll happen right away," Gray said. "We might still go off on our own and keep him isolated from the relationship. I'm going to see how I feel about it."

"It's your call," Elise said. "And I respect whatever decision you make."

"It's not a personal thing against you," Gray said. "It's more like…unchartered ground I need to figure out how to navigate."

"I'll try not to take it personally," Elise said, though she knew she'd already started to take it as such. *Why can't Gray just introduce me to his son? He's already told Hunter that we're dating. What's the big deal?*

She pushed those doubts and worries away, because she knew that it really wasn't about her. No, this thing with Hunter had everything to do with *Gray*, and what he'd missed last time with Maddie that he was determined not to miss again.

"Can we video chat tomorrow night?" Gray asked. "I want to see you."

"Yes," she said. "That sounds fun." The call ended, and Elise sighed a happy sigh as she gazed up at the ceiling. "Thank you, Lord," she prayed. "Bless each of us with clear minds and open hearts to know what to do and what not to do. Especially bless Gray with this as he tries to know what to do for his son."

Elise changed into her pajamas and stole across the hall to brush her teeth. Back in her bedroom with the door locked again, she noticed a flashing light on her phone.

Gray had texted: *What breed of dog might a woman in the woods like to have? This kind?*

He'd sent a picture of a great big hairy beast that looked like a Sasquatch with four legs. Elise giggled and sent back *Definitely not. Too much hair. A woman in the woods who's very busy in the summertime needs a non-shedding dog.*

Non-shedding. Writing that down now....

Elise felt herself falling in love with this man though he was miles from her. She was as excited as she was afraid, because she'd felt like this before, and that relationship had ended so poorly.

Don't make me go through that again, she prayed before climbing into bed and picking up her phone to text with Gray some more.

CHAPTER 14

Wes woke up, the peach scent of Bree's shampoo in his nose. A smile crossed his face as the sound of the shower met his ears. He sure did like waking up with Bree, and he couldn't believe she was his wife.

"Thank you, Lord," he said, rolling over in bed and groaning. He took a moment to stretch his arms high and lean toward the wall, pressing one palm against it and pulling the muscles in his side. He repeated the action on the other side, finally standing up and padding into the bathroom.

Bree had wrapped herself in a towel and stood at the sink.

"Hey, pretty lady." Wes pressed his lips to her temple and trailed his hand along her waist. She smiled at him with foamy toothpaste in her mouth, and he continued into the bathroom. When he finished, he came out and picked up his own toothbrush. "What are we doing today?"

"I have to go to work," she said.

"Are you going to quit?"

"I'm still thinking about it."

Wes wanted to argue with her, but he didn't. Bree loved her job at the lodge, and she wasn't working at the employment office anymore. Wes had agreed to stay on as a business consultant for the lodge, but he wasn't the butler anymore. Graham had hired someone else, and apparently, he practiced his comedy routine with the guests when he checked them in and out, and he made a lot in tips.

Wes went into the kitchen and made coffee while Bree continued getting ready. When she joined him, he had toast and eggs in front of him, and he got up to make more. "Eat mine, love," he said.

"Just toast and coffee," she said, picking up one slice of toast. He put two more pieces of bread in the toaster and watched her doctor up her coffee with cream and sugar. She wore a tight pair of jeans and a pair of boots that went halfway up her calf.

"I'm going to call my mother this morning," Wes said. "Can you talk to Patsy about a good weekend or a couple of days to go to Ivory Peaks?"

Bree turned toward him and lifted her mug to her lips. "Not for the wedding celebration, right?"

"Just to meet them," he said. "Just me and you."

She nodded and sipped. "I'll talk to her."

"Thanks." His bread popped up, and he turned to butter it. "And when do you want to go get the rest of your stuff from the cabin?"

"I don't know," she said with a sigh. "We don't need the

furniture here, and it just makes me sad to go there. I hate that Elise is there alone."

"I know you do." Wes left his buttered toast and turned to Bree, easily wrapping her in his arms. "She seems okay, though."

"I think Gray helps a lot."

"Gray is extraordinarily good with supporting someone," Wes said. "That's true."

"You know, she told me once she'd never go out with one of Colton's brothers."

"Did you ever make that same promise?"

"No." She gazed up at him with a smile on her face. "Colton handed me the phone before I even knew he had brothers, and then you started talking, and the rest is history."

Wes laughed. "History, right."

Bree kissed him, and that was one way to get him to stop laughing. He kissed her back, this beautiful, wonderful wife of his. "Remember, I have therapy this afternoon," she murmured. "Four o'clock."

"I'll pick something up for dinner."

"No meat for me," she said. "I used to be semi-vegetarian, and I want to get back to that."

"Semi-vegetarian? Why have I never heard of this before?"

She just smiled and shook her head. "I don't want red meat. Chicken is probably okay."

"So a chicken salad or something."

"Yes," she said. "The pizza parlor has great salads, so you can get something you like too. Win-win."

"Win-win," Wes repeated as Bree stepped out of his arms. "Okay."

She picked up the second slice of toast from his plate and took her coffee with her. "See you later."

"Bye." Wes stood against the counter and listened to the door close behind Bree. The garage door rumbled up and then down, and Wes was alone in his house. He tossed out everything he'd made for breakfast, because it was cold now. He remade it all and sat down to eat, wondering what Colton was doing that day.

He texted, and Colt said he was going to Springside to assist in the lab. Wes called his mother next, comforted when she picked up with, "Wes, dear, hello."

"Hey, Mom," he said, smiling at the sound of her voice. "How's Dad?"

"Oh, he's doing far too much on the farm," Mom said with a sigh. "Yesterday morning, he went out and he never came back in. About eleven, I realized how late it had gotten, and I called him. He said he was in the stables, trying to catch his breath. He almost passed out." She clicked her tongue, and Wes could see her shake her head.

"He should call Ames." Gray had given everyone an update on their parents, and everyone—except them—seemed to know it was time for them to move off the farm.

"Ames has a very busy job," Mom said.

"Gray then."

"Gray has Hunter, and the man runs and trains for hours every day."

"Mom, the two of you can't manage that farm."

"We're doing fine, honey. How was Hawaii?"

"Amazing," Wes said. "You'd love it there, Mom. We should go." The weather had been a bit humid for his liking, but there was nothing better than the bright sun and the tropical greenery. The sand, the surf, the waves. Wes had loved all of it, even when it rained.

"Heavens," his mother said. "I don't even own a bathing suit, Wes."

"Then you go to the store and get one, Mom." Wes chuckled. "You've traveled before."

"Not for a few years now."

"I'll talk to Dad," Wes said. "You two should go for your anniversary. You'd both love it."

"That's not a bad idea."

Wes knew it wasn't a bad idea. He also knew they wouldn't go. "I want to bring Bree to meet you. When's a good time?"

"Oh, about anytime, I suppose," Mom said. "No, Grams, let me." With her attention divided between Wes and his grandmother, Wes didn't want to stay on the line.

"Bree's asking her boss today," he said. "And I'll let you know."

"Sounds good, dear."

"All right, I'll let you go. I love you, Mom. Tell Dad hi and that I love him too."

"You don't want to talk to him?"

No, Wes didn't particularly want to speak with his father, so he said, "I have to deal with something. I'll call him later." He ended the call, and he decided he better not make a liar out of himself. So he tackled the dishes, "dealing" with them and getting the pan washed and the plates loaded into the dishwasher.

———

TWO WEEKS LATER, ON A TUESDAY MORNING, HE ONCE AGAIN woke to the scent of Bree's shampoo as she showered. Wes got out of bed much faster this time, and he got ready in record time, tossing his deodorant into his bag after he'd used it.

He and Bree were going to Ivory Peaks today, and a certain level of giddiness accompanied Wes while he made coffee and gathered chargers for his phone and laptop. Bree brought only coffee this time, and she asked, "Can we buy breakfast on the way?"

"Sure," he said. They got on the road, and Wes felt like he needed to prep her a little bit. His mother was a special woman, and while he loved her, he also knew how to handle her.

"So my mother…." he started, glancing at her.

"You've told me she'll ask about having kids."

"That she will," Wes said, nodding. "And she always has something to say."

"Reminds me of someone else I know," she said, shooting him a look.

"Hey," Wes said, though he wasn't really offended. "I say what needs to be said."

"Maybe she does too."

"She wants to know everything," he said. "It can get really tiring."

"So she's like Colton."

Wes blinked and then burst out laughing. "I suppose so."

"I know how to handle Colton," Bree said. "I'm going to be fine."

"I know you are," Wes said. "Are you excited to meet them?"

"Yes," she said, reaching for his hand. "And what about you? Excited to spend more time with my parents?"

"Definitely," he said. "When are we making that trip?"

"I don't think we will," she said. "Unless you're dying to. And Wes, I think we should have the wedding celebration in Coral Canyon." She looked at him, and Wes was glad the Wyoming highways were so sparsely driven. Then he could look at Bree without fear of hitting another vehicle.

"Oh?"

"It's too hard for me to take off a lot of work," she said. "And I want all my friends from the lodge to be there, and they can't all take the days off. The Whittakers won't have anyone to work the lodge at all."

"Good point."

"I'm toying with the idea of having it *at* the lodge. You can rent space for special occasions."

Wes's eyebrows went up. "I thought the lodge was booked all summer."

"It's February."

"Is there a time we could do it?"

"We just need a day where the basement rooms aren't booked," Bree said. "Then we can use the basement and the kitchen."

"You want to have our wedding celebration in the basement at the lodge? I don't know, Bree. Our house is nicer."

"Yeah," she said. "You're right."

"Or we could rent somewhere in town if you don't want to clean up afterward."

"Now that life has settled down a little, I can look into this when we get back."

The time passed quickly, and they talked about their trip, about her parents, his brothers, and many other things. Before he knew it, he was turning onto the dirt lane and driving past the trees, the farmhouse coming into view.

"Here we are."

"And you grew up here?"

"Yes," he said, easing the truck to a stop.

"It's beautiful. Reminds me of Coral Canyon."

"It does, doesn't it?" Wes unbuckled his seatbelt and reached for the door handle. "She's standing in the window. Let's go."

Bree giggled as she got out of the truck, and Wes left their bags in the back and instead, latched onto Bree and led her toward the house and up the steps. Mom had the front door open early, and she framed herself in it.

"Mom," Wes said, smiling. He released his wife's hand to hug his mother. She seemed as healthy and robust as ever, and he stepped back. "This is my wife, Bree Richards. Well, she's a Hammond now." He beamed at her, and Bree smiled politely at his mother.

"Yes, she is," Mom said, grinning from ear to ear. "Who would've known Wesley would ever get married?"

"Mom."

His mother ignored him and embraced Bree on the front

porch. Watching them made Wes's heart happy, and he turned as his father emerged onto the porch.

"Hey, Dad." He hugged him too and introduced Bree to the formidable Christopher Hammond. They all went inside, where Bree met Grams and Mom started working in the kitchen, getting dinner out of the oven while she talked and talked about how she'd waited for her sons to get married.

Wes met Bree's eyes and rolled his, but Bree seemed utterly charmed by his mother. Or his mom was utterly charmed by her. No matter what, they got along great, and that was all that mattered to Wes.

"Now if we can just get Gray married again," his mother said. "That man. He's as stubborn as the day is long."

"He sure is," Wes said, not daring to look at Bree for fear he might start laughing. "I'm sure Gray will do what's right for Gray, Mom."

"He's been out here a lot the past couple of weeks to help with the farm, and he seems so happy." She frowned, as if Gray's happiness was upsetting to her. "I'm afraid that if he's happy, he won't be looking for someone."

"I'll be sure to tell him you're upset he's happy," Wes said dryly.

"Oh, you." His mom swatted at him with the oven mitts.

"Me?" Wes put his hand over the spot where she'd whacked him. "Mom, I think you're the one with the issue, not Gray." He finally looked at Bree, who wore a small smile as she put silverware at the four places on the table.

"Sometimes true love takes a long time to find, Mom," Wes said, glad when Bree looked up and met his gaze. "That's all I'm saying."

CHAPTER 15

G ray pulled up to the farmhouse on the east side of
Coral Canyon and peered at the blue truck in the
driveway, then the white shutters outlining the front
windows. This was it, the address he'd been given by a man
named Mathias.

He got out of the truck, glancing at the flowers and
chocolates he'd already picked up in town. Now, he just
needed to get the last part of his Valentine's Day gift for
Elise.

He wasted no time going up the sidewalk to the front
door. Though another month had passed since his last trip to
Coral Canyon, Mother Nature was still dumping snow on
the mountain town, blowing wind down her streets, and
sending temperatures that didn't get above freezing.

He knocked, which set off a round of barking behind the
door. Thankfully, it didn't take long for someone to open the
door, and a man there said, "You must be Gray."

"Mathias?"

"In the flesh." He stood back and gestured for Gray to come in. He did, nodding to the man as he went past. "I've got your pup ready to go. My daughter bathed him this morning, and we've got a bag of food for you, a blanket from the kennel, and his papers."

"Great," Gray said. He paused and took in the living room, which was filled with dogs. Two big ones gazed at him from the couch, one of them finally getting down to stretch before he came over to sniff Gray. He moved slowly, and Gray found himself smiling at the black lab.

"Hello," he said to the dog, bending down to pat him. "You must be Pyne."

"Yep, and that's Daisy on the couch."

Gray looked at the gorgeous silver poodle, but she seemed to know she was a princess, because she stayed put.

"Yours is right here."

Gray turned and took the silver labradoodle, who had the cutest face he'd ever seen. "Oh, wow," he said. "Aren't you even cuter in real life?" He'd done all the work of getting this dog through an online listing, texts, and phone calls.

"What are you going to name him?"

"He's for my girlfriend," Gray said, glancing up from the puppy's face. "I'll let her name him."

"Good idea." Mathias signed a paper. "This says you're taking the puppy. It's got the price on it, and states that he's been to the vet twice now, has been dewormed and had his dew claws removed."

"All right."

"We stand behind our pups," Mathias said. "Take him to the vet in the next seven days. If there's something wrong, don't hesitate to call me. We'll make it right."

Gray looked back at the puppy, wondering what could possibly be wrong with him. He said, "All right," anyway. He took the paperwork, the bag with food, and the blanket, and followed Mathias to the door. With the puppy in a crate on the floor in the backseat, and everything else ready to go, Gray pulled out his phone and sent Mathias the rest of his money.

"Thank you," Mathias called from the front porch. He lifted his hand in a wave, and Gray set his sights on the canyon on the other side of town. The pup whined, and Gray's heart went out to him.

"It's okay," he kept telling him, and the dog would calm for a few minutes. He finally arrived in front of Elise's cabin, spotting her car in the carport. So she'd be here or at the lodge. He hoped here, because he knew she hadn't forgotten to lock up since the day Wes and Bree had come home from Hawaii.

He gathered the dog into his arms, as well as the flowers and chocolates, and headed for the front door. The puppy whined as he reached for the doorbell, and he shushed him.

"Coming," Elise called from inside the cabin, and Gray's pulse increased.

"It's Gray," he said, leaning toward the door.

Elise opened it a moment later, her eyes wide as she took him in, her eyes sweeping the dog in his arms and the assorted things he carried.

"Happy Valentine's Day, Elise." He handed her the dog,

and she cooed and giggled as he licked her face. Gray couldn't help the happiness filling him, and he smiled at his girlfriend and her new puppy. "I couldn't help myself." He held up the chocolates and the flowers.

"Of course you couldn't." She nodded as she turned. "Come in."

He followed her inside, closing the door behind him.

"He's so cute," Elise said, still holding the dog. "What breed is he?"

"He's a labradoodle," Gray said. "A sort of rare one—silver."

"I love him." She glanced up. "Thank you so much, Gray."

"I've got a bunch of stuff for him in the truck. Let me grab it."

"In a minute," Elise said, finally putting the dog down. She came toward him, reached up and cradled his face in her hands. She searched his face, and Gray couldn't look away from her either. She made him feel cherished, and he hadn't felt like that in many, many years.

"You're here," she finally said.

"I'm here." He smiled at her and took a deep breath of her, hoping to commit the soft, floral scent of her to memory. "It's been a while."

"Too long," she said.

"I'll come more often," he said, finally leaning down and touching his mouth to hers. This kiss was so much more than the one they'd shared on the sidewalk, though that one had been amazing and life-changing for Gray.

He knew Elise better now from all their conversations.

She knew more about him, and still liked him, something that was marvelous to Gray. He took his time kissing her, and she didn't urge him to go faster, nor did she pull away until he'd finished.

He leaned his forehead against hers and swayed with her, pulling in deep breaths through his nose. This moment was sweet and special, and Gray never wanted it to end.

"I've got dinner in the oven," Elise finally said.

"Sounds good," Gray said. "Let me go get the rest of the stuff for the pup. What are you going to name him?"

"I don't know," Elise said, grabbing onto Gray's coat collar and hauling him back toward her. "Seriously, thank you, Gray." She kissed him again, and Gray felt himself slipping toward being in love with her.

When he realized how hot he was, he pulled away and ducked his head. "I'll be right back." He headed out the front door while Elise cooed at the puppy, and once the door was closed, Gray took a great, big breath and muttered, "Keep your cool, Gray."

He hadn't had to give himself a pep talk since law school and then his first couple of hearings and meetings with other billionaires. Somehow, Elise was on the same level as them, and he knew it had everything to do with that kiss she'd just given him.

And the gashes still on his heart.

Oh, and his son, whom he'd once again left in Ames's care for this quick, three-day trip to Coral Canyon.

Valentine's Day was actually on Friday, but Gray would be back in Denver a full twenty-four hours before that.

He collected the dog kennel, as well as the extra bag of

food and the bowls he'd bought in Colorado, and turned back to the cabin. It felt like something out of a fairy tale, with icicles dripping from the eaves and the windows lit up with yellow, cheery light.

Elise appeared in one of those windows, that special silver puppy in her arms, and Gray definitely felt like he'd entered another universe. Maybe in this one, dreams could come true and he'd get the happily-ever-after the couples did in those fairy tales.

His heart beat strongly in his chest, and he gave it another minute to stitch together one of his open wounds before he headed back to the cabin. He didn't knock this time, but went straight in. "Dog accessories," he said. "In the kitchen?"

"Yes, please," Elise said, moving parallel with him as he went down one side of the living room and she traversed the other. Gray put the kennel on the floor by the table, and the food and water bowls next to that.

He set about filling the bowls with food and water while he said, "So that kennel is adjustable. It should be barely big enough for him to turn around in. Then he'll learn to go outside to use the bathroom."

"Got it," Elise said.

Gray set the bowl full of water on the floor and opened the bag of food the breeder had given him. With that bowl full, he didn't have anything to occupy his hands—except Elise. He looked at her again, and she smiled from the puppy to him.

"You look different without your cowboy hat," she said.

Gray reached up automatically to touch his head, though he knew he wasn't wearing his hat. "I packed it," he said.

"I'm surprised you don't sleep in it." She giggled and put the puppy down on the floor. "I think I'm going to name him Hutch."

"Hutch?" He watched the puppy toddle around as if it couldn't walk. But he knew it could. It was probably just in shock after being removed from his mother and all his brothers and sisters. He finally made his way over to the bowls and started to sniff. "Does that have some significance?"

"Not really," she said. "I just like that name for a dog."

"It's a good, strong name," he said, sticking his hands in his pockets so he wouldn't run them through Elise's silky hair. "He's gonna be big, Elise. Sixty pounds, I think. At least."

"That's okay," she said. "I signed up for some online dog training, and I've been watching the videos already."

He pulled his attention from the puppy and looked at her. "You must've had a lot of confidence in my ability to find you a dog."

"I have confidence in your ability to do anything," she said, stepping closer to him. She ran her hands up his chest. "You gonna take your coat off and stay a while?"

"Yes." He cleared his throat and shrugged out of his coat, draping it over the back of one of the chairs in the kitchen.

"Good." Elise moved over to the sink and washed her hands. "You should know how terribly hard it is to find a good Valentine's Day gift for someone who doesn't eat sweets and has a marathon to run in only two months."

"I told you I didn't need anything." He'd told her a bunch of times, in fact.

"Right," she said. "And I told you I wanted a puppy, and not only did you show up with that, but all the accessories said puppy needs. And flowers. And chocolate." She turned to face him, and Gray couldn't help smiling.

"You made dinner."

"Yes, let's hope it's not burnt." She picked up the oven mitts on the counter and turned to the oven. She bent over it as the scent of garlic, ham, and cheese came out, and then she produced the most beautiful pizza Gray had ever seen.

"Wow," he said, going to stand next to her at the stove. "It looks delicious."

"Ham, garlic, and pepper Alfredo," she said. "I made that from scratch, I'll have you know." She looked at him, her eyes full of hope and joy. "It's Celia's recipe, and she's an excellent cook." She looked back at the pizza. "Not too burnt."

"It's not burnt at all," he said, his stomach rumbling. "I'm starving."

"My gift first," she said, holding up the oven mitts in a universal sign of *stay here, Gray*. "Give me a second." She hurried out of the kitchen, and Gray took a seat at the table and watched Hutch.

"What is it?" He bent and picked up the dog, who snuggled right into his chest. "Did she tell you while I was outside?" He did like this dog, and he considered—again—getting a dog for himself. Over the past few weeks as he'd done his research and then started looking for a puppy for

Elise, the thought of getting one for him and Hunter had crossed his mind many times.

He wanted a dog who would run with him, and the golden retriever and Labrador breeds would make great running partners. He hadn't pulled that trigger yet, because he was already asking Ames to watch Hunter while Gray left town. He couldn't ask him to dog-sit too. Ames already had dogs he brought home from the police station, and Gray knew his brother wouldn't like taking care of a puppy.

He half-wondered how Elise was going to do it. There was way more snow up here than in Denver, and she'd need to take Hutch out a few times each night in the beginning. She'd said she wanted the dog, and Gray had asked her several times if she was sure. He'd cited the potty training and the leash training and all of that, and she'd said she could do it. That she *wanted* to do it.

"All right," Elise said, reappearing in the kitchen doorway. "Close your eyes."

"Oh, boy." Gray chuckled as he set Hutch on the floor, straightened, and dutifully closed his eyes.

"Remember, you're *very* hard to shop for," she said. Her voice came closer, and the other chair at the table scraped as she sat down. "Okay, open your eyes."

He did, turning toward Elise and finding a plain wooden box on the table. It wasn't wrapped, and someone had clearly made it by hand. "What's this?" he asked, reaching for it. "Did you make this?"

Her laughter filled the kitchen, and she said, "Gray, do you really think I can make a box like that?"

"I don't know." He smiled at her. "Where'd you get it?"

"I bought it at a craft fair," she said. "Boutique. Whatever you want to call it." She nodded to it. "Open it."

Gray admired the handiwork for another few seconds. The box wasn't very big, probably about six inches wide and five inches tall. It was fairly deep though, probably a foot long. The lid had been sectioned into two, with a smaller one at the front, and a much bigger one that took up the back two-thirds of the box. It had been stained a beautiful reddish-brown, where all the grain of the wood shone through in a darker brown.

He lifted the lid on the front third of the box and peered inside. It held note cards—a whole bunch of note cards, and his curiosity had him reaching inside to see what they were.

He pulled out a decent chunk of cards and read the first one.

"Run when you can, walk if you have to, crawl if you must; just never give up." -Dean Karnazes.

He looked up, his admiration for Elise growing by the second. She said nothing, to her credit. Gray looked back at the running quote, noting that she'd illustrated it by hand. Done only in black pen, she'd drawn a pair of running shoes, one perched on top of the other, as if he'd just kicked them off his feet after a long run.

Gray put the top card on the table and looked at the next one.

"The miracle isn't that I finished. The miracle is that I had the courage to start." -John Bingham

She'd hand-lettered the words FINISH LINE in that same black pen, and put bright yellow lines around it, as if it had been bathed in light from heaven.

"Elise," he said, his voice choked with emotion.

"I put them in order from today until the day of the Colfax Marathon," she said. "The most inspiring quotes. So when you get up and you don't feel like running, you can read one, put those shoes on, and get out the door."

He looked away from the cards and at her. She wore a fair bit of anxiety on her face, probably hoping for a good reaction from him. Gray knew she'd worked hard on this, and it was the single best thing anyone had done for him.

He swallowed and shook his head. "You are amazing. This is fantastic."

"Yeah? You like it? Remember—you're very hard to—"

"I love this." Gray put the cards down and closed the distance between them, kissing her again. He wanted to say *I love you*, but he didn't dare, because it felt silly to say that so soon after their relationship had begun. "Thank you," he whispered against her lips. "Thank you so much." He kissed her again, not allowing himself to get too hot like last time. Then he went immediately back to the cards.

"You drew on every one."

"Yes," she said. "Remember how I said I have a lot of time in the winter?"

He glanced at her and read the next card. "*The point is whether or not I improved over yesterday. In long-distance running the only opponent you have to beat is yourself, the way you used to be.*" -Haruki Murakami

Gray thought that last one could be applied to life—he just tried to do better every day over the day before. He cleared his throat and put the cards back in order. "I don't want to look at them all right now." He put them back in the box. "There's way more than sixty here."

"I kind of got carried away," she said. "But once you do Colfax—and qualify—you can save the others for when you're having a bad day while you prep for Boston." She tapped the top of the box that was still lidded. "You've got to open this."

Gray fitted the lid back on the front part of the box that held the cards and removed the lid on the back. It was empty inside, but she'd put little flags on the lid itself, and he quickly realized they were reminders.

May 21 – Colfax Marathon – qualify!

June – Don't quit running!

July – Run in the 5K at the Coral Canyon Fourth of July celebration!

Gray grinned and started to chuckle. "I see what's happening here."

August – Get your Boston application ready!

September 9 – Apply to run in Boston!

End of September – Get notified of acceptance to run in Boston!

October – Only 6 months until Boston (and cake)!

November - Don't stop running yet!

December – Take your training indoors!

"You mean my overuse of exclamation points?" Elise giggled as she smoothed down one of the colorful flags. "Yeah, I got a little excited. But 'take your training indoors' seemed pretty lame with just a period."

Gray looked away from the reminders, her confidence in him astounding. "I haven't even qualified yet."

"You will, Gray." She shook her head, her smile in place. "You know you will."

"I don't know that."

"Well, I know it," she said. "So just go with the flags, okay?"

"Okay." He looked at the empty box. "What do I put in here?"

"Your bibs, your registration card, the email you'll get when you qualify for Boston. It's like a keepsake box for this next year of your running life."

Gray put the lid back on the box. "This is literally the best gift I've ever gotten."

"Please," Elise said, scoffing. "Your parents gave you two billion dollars when you turned twenty-one. This is a box with some note cards in it."

Gray looked at her, hoping he didn't come across as too intense. "Elise, this is so much more than that."

She tucked her hair behind her ear and glanced over to the stove. "You really like it?"

"I love everything about it," he said. "And I'll get to see your handwriting and your drawings everyday. It's perfect. Amazing. And it really is better than the two billion." He meant it too, and her gaze finally flickered back to hers.

"I'm glad you're here," she whispered.

"Me too, sweetheart." They stood up together, and Gray gathered her close to his heart and held her tight. He had no idea what the future held for them, but in that moment, he had to believe that they'd be together. He hadn't felt this strongly about anyone since his ex-wife, and he'd just known with her too.

"Okay," Elise said several moments later. "Let's eat, because I just felt your stomach growl, and that is just not okay."

He laughed then, the mood lightening between them. The distance and the long drive were both against Gray, but he was determined to find a solution they could all live with —him, her, and Hunter.

He didn't know what that looked like yet, but he would figure it out. Oh, yes, he would.

CHAPTER 16

Bree scurried around the kitchen, putting out napkins and the fancy paper plates Wes had bought at the store. Annie, Elise, Sophia, Patsy, and Celia had been in the kitchen with her for the past hour, each of them cooking up something for the wedding celebration that was about to begin.

As if on cue, the doorbell rang, and all six women looked toward the front door.

"I'll get it," Wes said. "I think it's my family from Ivory Peaks." He'd offered to help several times, but Bree kept shooing him out of the kitchen. She'd finally texted Colton to get over to her house so he could entertain his brother, and Colton had done exactly that.

The men had been hanging out in the living room, something playing with a low volume on the television while the women worked in the kitchen.

Her stomach swooped at the sound of more voices, but

she reminded herself she'd met Wes's parents. They were lovely people, and she'd enjoyed her time in Ivory Peaks with them very much. They both liked her too.

Only she knew there was more to her swooping stomach than just nerves.

"Mom," Colton said. "Dad." He got up to hug them both, and Bree watched their exchange with fondness.

She wiped her hands on her apron and left the kitchen. "Chris," she said to Wes's father. "Welcome. It's so good to see you." She hugged him and then turned to his mother. "Hello, Bev. How was the drive?"

"Just fine," the woman said. "We rode with Ames, and he's *such* a good driver."

"Oh, he's just average," Colton said. "Don't let her fool you. She just thinks he's the best because he doesn't speed."

"I've ridden with Wes," Bree said with a smile for Bev. "Ames is surely better than that."

"Hey," Wes said, slipping his hand around her waist. "I heard that."

"I wasn't trying to keep it a secret."

"Everyone knows you're the worst driver of all of us," Ames said, joining the group.

Bree smiled at him. "Hey, Ames." She gave him a quick hug too. "Thanks for driving."

"Hey, I drove too," another brother said, and Bree turned to Gray.

"Of course you did." She hugged him hello too, dying to know how things were going between him and Elise. Her best friend had been fairly tight-lipped about the relationship, and Bree knew she got more information than Colton.

And that Colton was dying a slow death because of it. "Welcome. Where's Hunter?"

They'd all come out to the farmhouse while Bree and Wes had been there, and she did like his family very much. She'd definitely hit the in-law jackpot with the Hammonds, and she found the boy and hugged him too. "How did your dad do with the drive?"

"Just fine," Hunter said. "Felt like it took forever, though."

"That's because we were behind Uncle Ames," Gray said. "And he drives *so slow*."

"I was going the speed limit."

"Not the whole time," Gray said with a cocked eyebrow. "We could've shaved *at least* an hour off that drive."

"You didn't have to follow me." Ames shot him a dirty look.

"And trust me, on the way back, I won't." Gray grinned at him, clearly not fazed by Ames's sharp eyes. Bree kind of was, though. He was a cop, and she wouldn't want to cross him.

Gray stepped away from the group and toward the kitchen, and Bree tried to focus on the conversation at hand and watch him at the same time. She completely failed, because she didn't hear a word anyone said. Instead, she saw Gray start a conversation with Elise that had them both smiling in a way Bree had only seen a couple of times before.

He didn't touch her; she didn't touch him. They didn't sneak off together. But they clearly had the air of two people who liked each other very much, and Bree's heart leapt with happiness for the two of them.

"They look happy, don't they?" Colton asked, his voice right at Bree's ear and barely loud enough for her to hear.

She didn't flinch or look at him. "They sure do."

"Do you know anything else?"

"She hasn't said much in the past couple of weeks." Bree knew Gray had come for Valentine's Day, and that according to Elise, it had been "the best few days of my life."

Six weeks had passed since then, and to her knowledge, Gray hadn't come to Wyoming, and Elise hadn't gone to Colorado. "Their self-restraint is astronomical," she whispered. "I mean, they haven't seen each other in a long time."

"He'll get her to go get something from the truck with him," Colton said. "Twenty bucks."

"I'm not betting against you." She elbowed him. "For all I know, you told him to do that."

Colton chuckled and didn't deny it. "Oh, look, she's taking him outside to see her dog."

Bree watched Elise open the back door, where a fit of barking started. Gray stepped out with her as Elise's silver labradoodle came bounding up to her.

The doorbell rang again, and Bree turned toward it. "I'll get it," she said. "It's probably the Whittakers." With Wes's family already here, she wasn't sure who else it would be.

She opened the front door, and sure enough, Graham and Laney stood there with their kids, Bailey and Ronnie. "Come in," Bree said. "Thank you for coming."

April had just begun, and a lot of the snow had melted. Some stubborn patches stuck to the grass in shady spots, and Mother Nature would likely blow at least one more storm through Coral Canyon before she gave way to springtime. But at least it wasn't the bone-chilling cold of winter.

Graham stepped inside and hugged Bree. "We wouldn't miss it." He took his family into the living area, but Bree kept the door open as Andrew and his family came up the sidewalk.

More hugs, and Bree took their youngest from Becca, saying, "I've got a cookie for you Glen. You stay with me."

She'd just started to close the door when Elise said, "We're heading out, Bree. Gray brought all the rolls, and we need to get them from his truck."

"Okay." She held the two-year-old on her hip as Elise and Gray went out onto the porch, their fingers twining together. She leaned into him, and Gray placed a kiss on her temple. Colton had been right. Bree closed the door and hoped they'd get a few minutes of privacy before more people showed up.

Over the course of the next twenty minutes, the house continued to fill with children and adults as Beau and Eli arrived with their families. Then Rose and Violet showed up, and with their triplets and twins, the sound of high-pitched children's voices made Bree a little weepy.

Her parents arrived next, and Bree hugged them for several long seconds at the front door. "Thank you for coming," she said. "I know it's a long way."

"We have nothing else going on," her dad said. "This sure is a nice house, Bree."

"Thanks," she said. She'd had nothing to do with the house Wes had bought in Coral Canyon when he'd come last year. But she did like the house, because it had plenty of space, big windows, and a cozy feel to it.

Elise and Gray still hadn't come in with the rolls, and Bree cast one more look over her shoulder before closing the front door. "Straight back, Dad. Go say hi to Wes." They'd met him at the lodge when Bree had first gotten him back into her life. They'd gotten along well enough, though Bree still suspected her parents would've liked to have been present for the actual wedding.

"Are we all here?" Wes asked, glancing around. "Yes, there's Bree's parents." He wore a bright smile as he came over and greeted them. "I was just looking for you guys. You made it." He hugged them both too, and Bree's heart grew and grew and grew.

She hoped it would keep growing, because she needed the room. She looked around at all the people who meant so much to her, and tears filled her eyes.

"Is everyone here?" Wes asked, putting his arm around her shoulders.

"Elise and Gray are outside," she said quietly. "But other than that, yes."

Wes said, "Cy's not. I'll call him. Put Colton on Gray and Elise."

She nodded and deftly wove through the crowd to where Colton hovered near the cupcakes—big surprise. She leaned in close and said, "That thing about them sneaking out to the truck? They did, and they're not back."

"And we're starting?"

"As soon as Cy gets here," Bree said. "Wes went to call him."

Colton nodded. "Let's see how long that takes."

Bree turned to Celia and asked, "And we're ready to eat?"

"Yes," Celia said, grinning. "This is so great, Bree. We should have celebrations like this more often."

"More often than Christmas?" Bree giggled and shook her head. "You're crazy. Besides, I'm pretty sure you feed most of these people every Sunday."

"And more," Sophia said. "With the guests."

"Exactly."

"This is different, though," Celia said. "There's so much *energy* here."

The house was full of good vibes, and Bree did like it. She could barely believe everyone fit, but they seemed to, and Wes and Colton had set up chairs and tables for everyone to eat as well.

"Cy's here," Wes called, and the last Hammond brother entered the fray. There was much back patting and welcoming as Colton slipped out the door and into the garage. Bree barely had time to meet Wes's eyes before he said, "Okay, we're ready to start. Everyone quiet down."

She went to his side, clasping his hand in hers. Colton slipped back inside, with Elise and Gray right behind him. Gray moved to stand beside his son, and Elise hustled back into the kitchen, put down a few bags of rolls, and then stood halfway behind Celia.

The noise level decreased, and Wes smiled around at everyone. "We're so glad you could all be here with us." He lifted Bree's hand to his lips and kissed her wrist. "We got married on the beach a few months ago, with just the preacher there. It was great and all, but we wish you could've all been there." He cleared his throat and looked at Bree.

She hadn't written a speech, and she just had one thing to say. "Yes, thank you for coming. Family is so important." She looked out at everyone, finding her mom and dad. A rush of love filled her, because they'd forgiven her so readily. "We have a ton of food, and it's all amazing, because we have some of the best chefs here who've been cooking all morning."

Her hand in Wes's tightened. Her courage almost failed her.

"I just have one thing to say before we say grace." She swallowed, very aware of every eye on her. Well, some of the kids probably didn't care anything about what she was saying—or about to say.

"I'm thrilled to announce that Wes and I will be parents soon."

Nobody moved. Nobody spoke. It was as if a bomb had been tossed into this giant room with two very loud families, and everyone was staring at it to see if it would indeed go off.

Then Wes said, "We will?"

Bree nodded, tears pooling in her eyes and escaping down her face.

He laughed and lifted her right off her feet. Cheers went up, and congratulations started going through the crowd.

Wes finally put her down and looked right into her eyes. "When, Bree?"

"By Thanksgiving."

"Praise the Lord," he whispered. "I love you." He kissed her amid all the chaos, and Bree experience a sweet, pure form of joy.

Then Colton said, "Okay, I'm gonna pray, and then we can eat and find out more about Bree's pregnancy. Does anyone object?"

No one did, and Bree squeezed Wes's hand tight, tight as Colton said grace over their wedding feast.

CHAPTER 17

Elise looked left and right, right and left, the streets in downtown Denver so confusing. She hadn't been in a city this big in many years, and her blood pressure felt like it might pop through her veins at any moment.

"I think it's this way," she muttered to herself, realizing she was now going the wrong way down a one-way street. "Shoot." She veered off onto another street—more like an alley, really—before anyone could see the bumbling fool from out of town trying to find their way around.

She pulled in a breath and brought the car to a stop. "Please help me," she prayed. She'd dropped Hutch off at Colton's house and left Coral Canyon yesterday, and she'd stayed in a tiny town about six hours from Denver before getting an early start on the rest of her trip this morning.

She couldn't just call Gray and ask him, because he didn't know she was coming. They'd talked last night, and

Elise had asked him more questions about the marathon. Where was it? What time did it start? When would he finish? Would he have his phone with him so she could text him motivational messages?

He'd laughed at that last one, and if there was anything better than Gray Hammond's laugh, Elise didn't want to know about it.

She had not breathed a word about her trip to anyone except Patsy and Graham, and they'd both sworn they wouldn't say anything to anyone. Not telling Bree had been extremely difficult, but she was married to Gray's brother, and Elise simply didn't want him to know she'd come to watch him cross the finish line—hopefully with a Boston-marathon-qualifying time.

"Okay." She took a deep breath and picked up her phone. "I need to get to the Sheraton." She'd chosen the hotel because it was a familiar brand, and it happened to be located right downtown and only two blocks from the marathon route and Colfax Avenue. Apparently a lot of people gathered at the Civic Center Park to watch the runners, and Elise wanted to be there for Gray. Even if she was just a tiny voice among thousands, she wanted to be there to cheer specifically for him.

She didn't dwell on the fact that she'd done something eerily similar for Brandt, and he'd broken up with her while she watched from the stands. He hadn't known she was coming to his rodeo finals—she'd wanted to surprise him.

She'd told herself over and over that Gray wasn't Brandt, and their relationship was on very sturdy ground. Gray wasn't going to break up with her.

Her phone rang, and she jumped. She picked it up and saw Gray's name, and she stayed right where she was though she'd been about to pull out and get herself to the hotel. "Hey," she said.

"Hey." He wore a smile in his voice. "What are you doing today?"

"Uh, not much," she said, and she hoped it wasn't a lie. All she'd done was drive today, and that wasn't much. Right? "What about you? How'd your run go this morning?"

"It was great," he said. "Easy four miles, with five minutes at race pace."

"Ah," she said. "Race pace." She knew all about the time he needed to beat to qualify for Boston, as she'd had plenty of time this winter to look things up on the Internet. Now that spring had arrived in Wyoming, though, Elise had been working a lot more. Her business picked up in the spring, and she had half a dozen clients booked with Two Green Thumbs, her licensed landscaping and lawn care business, that relied on her to come every week.

"You're not working in someone's yard right now, are you?"

"No, sir," she said.

"Have you got a second?"

"Sure." She glanced out the window, and while the alley would terrify her in the dark, it seemed fairly benign in the light of day. "What's up?" She made sure her doors were locked just to be safe.

"I know I'm coming for the Fourth of July," he said. "But it's been a while since we've seen each other."

"Yeah," she said. Bree and Wes's wedding celebration

was almost two months old now. She'd spent an amazing half-hour with Gray tucked around the side of the house, giggling and talking and kissing. He'd only been in town for the weekend, and while she'd also gotten to go to dinner with him later that same night, it hadn't been a very long visit.

They spoke on the phone almost every day, and they definitely communicated via text every day. They did video chats often, and while Elise got to "see" him, it definitely wasn't the same as holding his hand, smelling the musky scent of his cologne, or kissing him.

Elise had fallen for Gray, that was for certain. They hadn't talked about Hunter again, and they hadn't discussed what their future might look like at all. Right now, they were simply living in the present, and while Elise enjoyed it, she was ready for some harder conversations.

"I know you're busy," Gray said. "I was thinking I'd come next weekend. It's Memorial Day, and Hunt will be done with school."

"Right," she said. "Are you going to bring him?"

"What do you think?"

"Honestly, Gray?"

"Always honestly, Elise."

"I think it's time to include him in our relationship," she said. "I know that makes you nervous. It makes me a little nervous too. But...I don't know. He knows we're dating. It's silly to pretend we're just friends in public and then sneak off behind the garage to kiss each other."

"I was hoping you'd say that," he said, a measure of relief in his voice.

"You were?"

"Yeah," he said. "I think I'm ready for Hunter to start to build a relationship with you too."

"Wow," she said.

"You thought I was going to argue with you."

"Yeah, a little." Elise gave him a light laugh. "You really think you're ready?"

"Yes," Gray said firmly. "And I think he's ready, and I guess I was hoping you'd be ready too."

"I'm ready," Elise said, even though she wasn't sure what she needed to be ready for. Hunter was a great kid, and she'd always thought so. At the same time, her mind blanked as to what they might be able to talk about.

"Great," Gray said, that smile back in his voice. "So next weekend. I think we'll drive halfway on Friday. Hunt only has half a day of school. So we'll be there Saturday."

"I'll try to get all my clients done early," she said. She'd already taken this weekend off, and she'd asked a friend who also owned a landscaping company to help with the yards she couldn't do. She couldn't take next weekend off too.

"Great," Gray said again. "See you then."

"Okay." The call ended, and Elise leaned back against the headrest. "He probably won't come next weekend," she told herself. "Not when you show up at the finish line."

But he might, and Elise should be ready for that. "Deal with it later," she told herself, checking her blind spot, though no one had come down this alley in all the time she'd been sitting here. "Get to the hotel."

By some miracle wrought by God, Elise managed to navigate the narrow, downtown streets to the Sheraton, and she paid for valet parking and went inside. The hotel was simply huge, and thankfully, she got a room in the main building so she didn't have to cross the street to the other half of it.

She collapsed onto the bed and looked up at the ceiling, her mind whirring and her heart beating double-time. She'd done it. She'd made a hotel reservation, driven the nine hours from Coral Canyon to Denver, and tomorrow, she was going to watch her boyfriend run a marathon.

———

The following morning, Elise woke before her alarm. She hadn't slept well at all, because today was race day. She couldn't imagine how Gray had slept at all, but she hoped he had. She dressed quickly and went downstairs, grabbed a to-go cup of coffee from a shop on the corner by the hotel, and proceeded to walk to the park. She had to cross Colfax to get to it, and it felt like the party was already in full swing.

People had signs and their faces painted, and some wore huge, brightly colored wigs. The energy pouring out of the city was infectious, and Elise grinned around at everything happening. She'd heard on the news last night that there were over twenty thousand runners in today's marathon, and that set a new record for the event.

She felt proud and excited to be part of it, even if it was just to jump up and down and scream for Gray. She hoped she'd recognize him on the course. She'd never watched a marathon live, and she had a feeling he'd be running fast.

When they'd talked last night, he said his goal was to

complete the twenty-six-point-two miles in under three hours. "For my age range," he said. "I have to beat three hours and ten minutes to qualify for Boston."

"You can do it," she'd told him. She'd asked how they kept track of so many people's times, and he told her he had a tracker in his bib. It would activate when he crossed the starting line and then the finish line. It would record his time, and he'd get a preliminary time that day, and an official time a few days later.

After she watched him run by here, Elise planned to walk the couple of miles to City Park, where the race started and ended. She should have time, as Civic Center was within the first three miles of the marathon. Gray probably wouldn't even be sweating when he ran by her the first time.

She shivered in the shade, as the sun wasn't quite up yet. The marathon started at six a.m., and Gray was in Group C. She wasn't entirely sure what that meant, only that he wouldn't be one of the very first to run past Civic Center Park.

She wandered down the sidewalk, toward where a group of colorfully dressed drummers were filling the air with a nifty beat. She sipped her coffee and smiled at them and kept going. She found a spot where she had an excellent view of the entire road, and she took up residence there.

Quickly, because she'd forgotten in her haste to get to the park and get a spot, she pulled out her phone and started a text to Gray. *Race day! You're going to crush it. Run fast!* She added a heart to the end of the message and sent it without second-guessing herself.

The heart didn't mean she loved him, but...did she?

Elise thought she'd been in love with Brandt, but he obviously hadn't felt the same. Did she love Gray? On some level, she did. What she didn't know was if she was *in love* with him. She knew she sure liked talking to him. She admired him. She liked the way he spoke to her with respect and kindness, and he never made fun of her fears.

Thanks! he sent back. *Nervous. Gonna run it off. Haha.*

She grinned at his lame joke, even liking that, and focused on the street again. She should be able to see him coming for quite a while, as this was a straight-away on the course. *Please bless me to see him,* she prayed. She wasn't sure if she wanted him to know only three miles in that she'd come, but at the same time, she did. Then he'd know she would be at the finish line, screaming for him to finish strong.

Her phone chimed at six a.m. and she swore she could hear a swell of cheering from down the road. The first group should be on their way, and she figured she had twenty or twenty-five minutes before she'd see anyone.

She threw her empty coffee cup away and quickly used a portapotty before resuming her post along the fence facing Colfax. Cheers started at the end of the park, and she tipped up onto her toes and craned her neck to see down the street.

Runners were coming, and they looked so athletic in their short shorts and tank tops. They had muscles for days, and this twenty-six miles weren't the first they'd run. Men and women started getting closer to her, and so many of them wore sunglasses.

Elise panicked. If Gray was wearing sunglasses, how would she recognize him? She should've asked him to video himself running so she could see what he wore and how his gait looked, or at least what his race attire looked like, or what his bib number was.

She gripped the fence and kept watching, trying to look at every single person. Runners of all shapes and sizes kept going by, some of them so fast.

Someone came over the loudspeaker in the park and said, "We won't see the pacing teams for a few minutes, as our first one keeps people on track for a three-hour, fifteen minute marathon." The man kept talking, but Elise stopped listening.

Gray wanted to run faster than that.

She concentrated harder, her eyes sweeping people close to her and moving farther back. All at once, there he was.

Running fast—wow, so fast—and wearing a pair of navy shorts and a pale yellow tank top. He was wearing sunglasses, but she knew those shoulders and that beard and everything about him screamed Gray.

"Go!" she yelled without thinking. She jumped as if Gray could see or hear her. "Yay, Gray!" He got closer, and he was ultra-focused, not looking left or right. He wouldn't see her. He couldn't hear her. She whooped and yelled his name again.

She knew the moment he looked over and saw her. His stride faltered, and she yelled, "Go! Run fast, Gray!" as she waved both hands above her head.

His face broke into a smile, and he did exactly what she said. He waved as he ran fast past her, and Elise felt warm from head to toe.

She watched him until she couldn't see him anymore,

and then she sighed. "Go, Gray, go," she whispered to herself, hoping her presence here was motivating for him.

Now she just had to get to City Park and wait a couple of hours to know.

CHAPTER 18

G ray wanted to quit at mile nineteen, the same way he always did. He wasn't about to slow down, though.

Elise is here, he thought. *Elise is here. Don't you dare quit. Elise is here.*

He held onto the thought, because the mental game at mile twenty always caused a struggle with him. After that, it was *five more miles.*

Four more miles.

Three more miles.

And three miles was nothing to Gray. He could run three miles in his sleep, and he couldn't wait to cross the finish line, find Elise, and hug her tight.

He could not believe she'd come to watch him run. That made his smile, and the next mile passed in a blur.

One more mile.

He was almost there, and he felt himself picking up the pace. He glanced at the watch on his wrist, surprised to see he'd just barely passed two hours and fifty minutes. If he could get this next mile done in under ten—and he could—he'd make his goal.

And he'd qualify.

The noise of City Park entered his ears, and Gray focused on it. He used the energy of the crowd and the beat from the drums to continue his rhythm. The moment he entered the park, he started looking for Ames and Hunter, then Elise.

"Go, Dad!"

He waved to Hunt, smiling for all he was worth. He was going to qualify for Boston. Gray couldn't believe it, though he'd worked hard for this over the course of the last eight months. He not only was going to qualify, but he was going to beat the men's time in his age group by over ten minutes. That would allow him to register early for Boston, and he'd most likely get in.

He couldn't see or hear Elise, but the finish line was within his view now. Thousands of people screamed and cheered, and Gray stayed right in the middle of the course, wanting to get the best time he possibly could.

So he focused, and he ran as fast as he could push himself, all the way across the finish line.

There was no fanfare for him. Hundreds of others had crossed the line too, and more streamed over it behind him. With so many running this year, that was to be expected.

"Gray!"

He turned toward the magical sound of Elise's voice, his chest expanding and collapsing so quickly as he pulled in breath after breath. He still managed to say, "Elise," and jog toward her. She laughed as he lifted her off her feet and spun her around.

"That was incredible," she said, bracing her hands against his shoulders. "Absolutely incredible." She looked down on him, and with the sun highlighting her nearly-white hair, she looked like an angel straight from heaven.

He set her on her feet, still trying to catch his breath. She ran her hands down the sides of his face. "Look at you. You're just amazing." She beamed up at him. "Watching you run is crazy."

"You're here," he managed to say.

"Yes, Gray." She laughed again, and Gray wanted nothing more than to kiss her.

"Dad," Hunter said, and Gray fell back a step automatically.

"Hunter," he said, taking a few steps to crush his son in a hug too.

"You did great, Dad," Hunter said. He held up his phone. "I clocked you at two hours, fifty-seven minutes, and twenty-nine seconds."

"Incredible," Ames said. "I knew you were going to crush it." He also took Gray into a hug and slapped him on the back. "Elise came?" he whispered in Gray's ear.

But there was so much going on, from music to people cheering, to more runners joining the fray.

"Let's go over to the meadow," he said, his breathing starting to quiet. "And I need something to drink."

"I'll get you a Gatorade," Hunt said, jogging off to one of the nearby drink stands.

Gray turned toward Elise and extended his hand for her

to hold. She easily took it and fell in step with him. "You remember my brother, Ames," he said.

"Of course," Elise said, peering past him to Ames. "Nice to see you again, Ames."

"You too, Elise. I didn't know you were coming."

"Neither did I," Gray said, squeezing her hand. "You're a sneaky one."

"You liked the surprise, though, didn't you?" she asked, a teasing quality in her voice.

Gray had liked it, yes. He'd been shocked to see her standing in Civic Center Park, but thrilled at the same time. He'd wanted to rush over to the fence and kiss her, but she'd told him to run, and run fast.

"I'm definitely glad you're here," he said, reaching for the bottle Hunter was bringing him. He'd been planning to take Hunter fishing this week—their first trip of the spring—and talk to him about Elise before they made their weekend trip to Coral Canyon.

But now….

He drank and drank, buying himself some time. Finally, he said, "Hunter, this is Elise. You remember me telling you about her?"

Hunter's eyes lit up, and Gray thought perhaps he really didn't mind Gray dating. "Yeah, sure, Elise."

"Elise," Gray said. "My son, Hunter."

"Oh, I know who you are," Elise said with a big grin. She stepped right into Hunter, who was already taller than her, and hugged him. Hunter wore pure surprise on his face, and then he relaxed into the hug. Seemed to enjoy it, even.

Gray sure did like watching the two of them embrace,

because he'd always wanted someone who wouldn't be different around Hunter. Gray raised his eyebrows as he grinned at his son, and Hunter just smiled back.

Elise stepped away and looked at the three of them. "So what do we do now?"

"I have to turn in my bib," Gray said, heading toward the official's tent. "I'll check my unofficial time, and then we can do whatever. There's a big party here in the park. We can go to lunch."

"We were going to go out to the farm," Hunter said.

"We can do that too." Gray almost lost the ability to swallow, though, because if they went out to the farm, he'd have to introduce Elise to his parents. As his girlfriend.

It's probably time to do that anyway, he thought as he handed over his bib. Though he probably should've started with *telling* them he had a girlfriend before he just showed up with one.

A man under the tent handed him a paper with his unofficial time, as well as his bib number so he could look up the official time on the website in a few days. He handed it to Hunter and asked, "Will you put this in the backpack, Hunt?"

Once his son took the paper, Gray looked at Elise, his eyebrows up again. "What do you think, Elise? Do you want to go out to the farm?"

"Sure," she said easily, and he didn't think she quite understood.

"Oh, boy," Ames said. "Elise, my mother and father live on the farm." He glanced at Gray. "And judging by the way my brother's face has turned all white, he either needs something to eat really fast, or he hasn't even mentioned you to our dear mother." Ames looked at him with nothing but pure joy and absolute knowing in his smile.

Gray lifted the Gatorade bottle to his lips again, finishing the rest of it before speaking. "First up is eating. I'm famished. Second...yeah, I better text my mother and let her know my girlfriend is in town."

"Or that you even have a girlfriend," Hunter muttered.

"Hey," Gray said. "I keep your secrets." He glanced at Elise, wondering what she thought about him keeping her all to himself. She wore a sunny expression, and he hoped that it wasn't fake. In his starving state, he was having a hard time thinking about anything but getting something to eat.

"Food first," Ames said. "You text Mom, and I'll find us somewhere to get a lot of carbs."

"Let's go to The Counter," Hunter said. "It's around here somewhere, right, Dad?" He looked around, as if the restaurant would magically pop up.

"Other side of twenty-first," Gray said. "It has a killer cheddar burger."

"Deal," Ames said. He frowned at Gray. "Did you text Mom?"

"In the last five seconds? No. Leave me alone." He glared at Ames, softening his gaze when he looked at Elise. "Do you have a car? Did you walk down here?"

"I walked," she said. "I'm staying at the Sheraton, which is right by Civic Center Park."

He nodded and looked at Ames. "So we're all with you, Ames. I don't know where you parked, so lead us out."

His brother started weaving through the crowd, and Gray followed. He did manage to ask Hunter for his phone, and he did text his mother that they'd be coming out to the farm in an hour or two.

That's great, his mom sent back. *How was the marathon?*

Great, Gray said. *I'm pretty sure I qualified.*

That's great, Gray. Will you stay for dinner?

Leave it to his mother to not get what a huge deal it was to qualify for the Boston Marathon. It was only something Gray had been working toward for the past eight months. But really, would he stay for dinner?

Yes, he sent, because he might as well stay for dinner. *And Mom? My girlfriend is coming with me.*

His phone rang in the next beat of time, and Gray chuckled as he answered his mother's call. "Hey, Ma."

"Don't you dare tease me, Gray Hunter Hammond. You have a girlfriend?"

"Yes, Mom. She came down to watch me run." He shot a look at Elise, who just smiled at him and kept walking. He'd looked at her cards and drawings every day since Valentine's Day, and he missed her powerfully.

"Well, I'll be." When that was all she said, Gray knew he'd really surprised her. His mother always had something to say, and it sure was nice to stump her for once. He chuckled as Elise moved up to walk beside Hunter. She asked him something, and Hunter seemed to light up as he turned toward her to answer.

Gray fell back another step, and not just because of extreme hunger. He felt like he existed on one side of a pane of glass, and Elise and Hunter on the other. He couldn't hear them, but he could see them. Watching them interact was like a warm blanket on a cold night, heating his soul in places he hadn't realized it had caught a chill.

In that single moment in time, when Elise laughed and Hunter joined her, Gray could see her as his stepmother. He could see the three of them as a family.

"Gray?" his mother asked.

He shook himself out of the fantasy and blurted, "Yeah. Yeah, I'm here."

"I'll get some dough rising," she said. "I'm so excited to meet your girlfriend."

"Thanks, Mom," Gray said, and he ended the call. He was excited to introduce Elise to his parents as the woman he was dating. He was. He just happened to be a bit terrified of the huge steps they were taking too, though he told himself he was ready.

He was.

Wasn't he?

─────────

A COUPLE OF HOURS LATER, AMES FINALLY TURNED OFF THE highway and onto the dirt lane that led to the farmhouse. He'd refused to drive even a mile over the speed limit, and Gray's patience was at an all-time low.

"Here we go," he said as he looked around the bucket seats of Ames's truck. "The house comes into view...here."

Ames passed the trees, and the farm and the farmhouse spread before them.

"Wow," Elise said. "Look at all of this. It's beautiful." She looked at Gray with wide eyes and squeezed his hand.

They'd had a great lunch, where he'd eaten a lot of French fries, his whole burger, and a chocolate chip cookie. She'd conversed effortlessly with Ames and Hunter while Gray got his brain cells working again, and he sure did love having her in his life.

"I grew up in this house," Gray said. "All of us boys worked this farm. Hunt and I work out here quite a bit these days."

"I do too," Ames said.

Gray needed to talk to Elise about the idea of him buying the farm, moving his parents into the granny house, and living out here.

"I love it," she said.

"Yeah?"

"Oh yeah. I love farms and ranches and small towns."

"That's why you're in Coral Canyon," he said, looking at her.

"Sort of," she said, looking away.

"I sense a story," he said quietly.

"There's a story," she said. "I'll tell you later."

"Maybe we can take a walk around the farm this afternoon."

"I can't believe you can even walk at all." She met his eyes. "You ran twenty-six miles this morning."

"In under three hours," Hunter said, looking at Gray with admiration in his eyes.

Gray grinned at him while his feet reminded him with a twinge of pain. "It'll be a short walk."

Ames brought the truck to a stop, and they all started getting out. Before Gray could close his door, his mother called hello from the porch, and a sigh moved through him. Instead of a walk around the farm this afternoon, he really needed a nap.

"Grandma," Hunter said, running toward the porch. His mother hugged Hunter tight and said something to him. He nodded and headed into the house, probably to get his grandfather from the office.

"Hey, Ma." Ames hugged their mother, and Gray took Elise's hand as they walked up the steps toward his mother.

"Mom." He hugged her too, feeling her anticipation way down deep in his own bones. He stepped back and faced Elise. "This is Elise Murphy. Elise, this is my mother, Beverly."

"You can call me Bev," she said. She pressed one hand over her heart, practically breathless. "Look at you. You're so pretty, and who knew Gray would ever bring home another woman?"

"Mom, you're embarrassing me."

She didn't even look at him. "You're forty-four. You don't get embarrassed."

"It's wonderful to meet you, ma'am," Elise said, reaching for her hand. "Gray has a lot of good things to say about you, your husband, and this farm. I'm so pleased to be here."

"How old are you, dear?"

"Mom," Gray said, his irritation rearing. "You don't have to know everything up front." He shook his head as he looked at Elise. "I should've warned you better. You don't have to answer that."

"Where did you two meet?"

"You've met her too," Gray said, a brick of dread settling in his stomach. "She lives in Coral Canyon. She was at Colton's wedding and at Wes's celebration."

"She lives in Coral Canyon?" Mom looked at him, surprise mixed with fear. "Are you going to move there too?"

"I don't know, Mom." Gray looked away from Elise. Bringing her here without prepping both of them was a mistake. Heck, *he* wasn't even prepped for this conversation.

"Gray," his father said, and Gray turned with relief. "Hunter said you had someone for me to meet." His eyes flicked to Elise, and shock moved through his expression too. "Oh, I see you do."

Gray wanted to march Elise down the steps and take her back to his house. He could order pizza and put on a movie and fall asleep to recover from the morning he'd had. Instead, he said, "Dad, this is my girlfriend, Elise Murphy."

"Girlfriend?" His father's voice could've called dogs. He recovered quickly and said, "Of course. I'm Chris Hammond. Welcome to the farm."

The funny farm, Gray thought, and he wondered what he'd been thinking bringing Elise here, especially when Hunter said, "Dad, Grams said she needs help getting to the bathroom, and she wants you to do it."

CHAPTER 19

Elise had a whole conversation with Gray as he hesitated for a moment. She found it entirely unfair that he could look twice as handsome while blushing, and she lifted her hand as a way to tell him to go help his grandmother. She'd be fine.

But one look at Bev and Chris, and Elise wasn't so sure. They were sizing her up big time, and she didn't feel like she'd pass.

"Grandma," Hunter said, and that caused Bev to turn. "Dad says we shouldn't make Elise stand on the front porch." He came toward the three of them, and he smiled at Elise. "C'mon, Elise. I'll let you in."

"I didn't say she couldn't come in," Bev said, turning to follow them. "Did I say that?"

"No," Chris said. "But we *were* just standing on the porch, and we don't need to heat the whole farm."

"The heater isn't even on," Bev said. "We're in that weird

weather zone where we don't need the heater or the air conditioner."

Elise sure did like listening to the two of them converse back and forth, but she really liked going with Hunter into the kitchen, where he asked her if she wanted something to drink. "Just water if you've got it."

"Grandma has these really awesome flavored lemonades," he said. "Colton likes the guava one. My dad's favorite is the mango. I like the raspberry." He pulled one of those out, and the bottles looked really fancy. Much bigger than any bottle of lemonade Elise had seen before, with textured glass on the neck, and a wide mouth with a bulky silver cap.

"What other flavors do they have?" She joined him in the kitchen. "And what else do you know about your uncle Colton?"

Hunter looked at her, his eyes wide and innocent. Elise grinned at him. "He's always teasing me about something," she said. "I'd love to get some dirt on him."

A hint of mischief entered Hunter's expression. "This is a good one, then." He leaned a little closer, as if they were conspirators about to share trade secrets. "He's afraid of ducks."

Elise burst out laughing, tipping her head back and really letting the sound out of her throat. "Ducks, wow," she said, still giggling.

Hunter finished laughing too. "And geese. He basically doesn't like birds." He took out another bottle. "Strawberry. I think that's all she's got."

"Understandable about the birds." Elise took the bottle. "Strawberry is great."

"So Elise," Chris said, and she turned away from Hunter and the fridge. "What do you do in Coral Canyon?"

"I work at the lodge where Colton and Annie met," she said. "And Bree and Wes, I suppose. And I own a landscaping company."

"Ah, good for you." He smiled, and the gesture seemed genuine. "I suppose you're fairly ingrained into society?"

Elise blinked and handed her drink back to Hunter, because he held the bottle opener. He popped the top on her lemonade and gave it back to her. She took a drink, wondering if she could guzzle the whole thing as she tried to come up with an answer.

She wasn't even sure what "ingrained into society" meant. No amount of drinking would buy her the ability to Google that and figure out what he was asking. She set her bottle on the counter. "I'm not sure what you mean."

"He's wondering how mobile you are," Bev said, and Elise felt like she needed a master's degree to talk to these people.

She looked at Hunter, silently begging him for help. He just shrugged and went around the island to the table. She wanted to go with him, but she faced Gray's parents again. "I have a car," she said, sudden realizations hitting her. "Gray and I haven't decided what to do about the distance thing."

The distance thing. She wished a tornado would strike the house and suck her up into the funnel. But here in the Rocky Mountains, there wasn't going to be any tornado to save her.

"So you're not very serious," Chris said.

"Dad," Gray said. "What are you asking her?" He'd just re-entered the living area, a very old woman on his arm. "Elise, come meet Grams."

"Excuse me." Elise kept a plastic smile on her face while she ducked around Chris and Bev. She knew what they were asking. If she and Gray were serious, why hadn't they talked about serious things? Why didn't they have a plan for their future?

Very good questions, in Elise's opinion.

"Grams," Gray said, holding her hands to steady her while she sat in a recliner. "This is Elise Murphy. We're dating." He smiled at the old woman and tucked Elise against his side. "Elise, this is my grandmother. My father's mother, Opal."

"Opal, lovely to meet you," Elise said, feeling her smile change into a real one.

"You too." Opal looked at Gray, and then back to Elise. They looked at each other and back to her. "I like her, Gray."

"You do, huh?" He chuckled and sat down on the nearby couch. Elise joined him, perching right on the edge of it. "She said five words to you, Grams. What do you like about her?"

"Oh, you boys. You just think I'm old, but when you get to be my age, you have a feeling about a person."

"Is that right?" Gray asked. He looked at Elise. "I hope I live to be ninety-eight."

"Are you ninety-eight?" she asked Opal.

The older woman practically puffed up. "That's right. And these boys are going to be the death of me."

Elise giggled and reached out to hold Opal's papery

hand. "Tell me about Colton. What does he do to drive you to the edge of death?"

"Oh, he's the worst one."

"I don't think so, Grams," Gray said. "Wes got married in Hawaii on a whim."

"It wasn't a whim," Elise said, meeting his eye. "They were in love."

"Oh, so romantic," Gray said dryly.

"You're not romantic?" Elise asked, releasing Opal's hand. "Come on, Gray. You bought me a dog for Valentine's Day."

"You've been dating since Valentine's Day?" Bev asked, and Elise practically got whiplash she turned toward his mother so fast.

"Yes, Mother," Gray said, glancing at Ames, who sat on the opposite couch.

"You haven't said one word about her." Bev looked like he'd betrayed her in the worst way possible, her dark eyes wide and shocked. She actually pressed both hands to her chest as if her heart was having trouble. No wonder Colton was so dramatic. Elise couldn't wait to tease him about that either.

If she survived this visit with Gray's parents.

"We were keeping things quiet," Gray said without an ounce of apology. "Remember how we've talked about how I'll handle my love life the way I see fit, Mom?"

"Bev," Chris said, arriving on the scene. "Don't badger the boy. This is why he doesn't tell you things."

"And I'm forty-four," Gray said. "I'm not a boy." He

wore a smile though, and he put his arm around Elise. "Who wants to know how the marathon went?"

"Oh, the marathon," his mother said, her voice growing animated. "I completely forgot about that. Tell us about it."

"I wish I could forget about it," he said, groaning. "My legs are dying." He looked into the kitchen, where Hunter sat at the table, looking at something in front of him. Elise assumed it would be his phone, though she hadn't seen the boy with a device. "Hunt? Can you get me some painkillers?"

"I can get them," Elise said, jumping to her feet. "Hunter, point me in the right direction."

He got up, and she saw he'd been working on a cross-word puzzle. "They're next to the stove." He pointed to the skinny cupboard between the stove and a corner lazy Susan.

Elise opened it, asking over her shoulder, "Do you like crossword puzzles?"

"Yeah," he said. "Grandpa keeps a book here for me, and I try to do one every day." He ducked his head, as if embarrassed of this particular hobby. The mannerism was so much like Gray, and it caused affection to swell in Elise's heart.

She got down the bottle of painkillers, but instead of taking them straight over to Gray, she detoured to the table, where Hunter had retreated. He'd finished about a quarter of the puzzle, and Elise looked at it over his shoulder. "It's okay to have something you enjoy doing," she said quietly.

He looked up at her. "What do you do?"

Elise swallowed, because she hadn't even told Gray about her sketching obsession. She had used it on all of his motivational running cards, though.

"I like to sketch dresses," she said. "But shh. It's a secret."

Hunter searched her face. "Is it really?"

She nodded and looked over her shoulder. Everyone in the living room was watching her, and she couldn't judge their expressions in only a moment. "It really is, Hunter," she said. "You're the only person I've told."

"Not even my dad?"

She shook her head. "So don't tell him, okay?"

"Okay," he said, glancing over to Gray too. "Are you embarrassed about the sketches?"

"No," she said. "They're just...personal. I don't show them to anyone, and I haven't told anyone about them. Sometimes it's nice to have something that's just yours." She wasn't sure how much he'd understand about this, because he was only twelve. So she patted his shoulder and said, "Good luck with this one, Hunter," and turned to take the pills to Gray.

He finished his story about the marathon and swallowed a few pills. "If I sit here for a few minutes, I'll recover enough to take you on a tour of the farm." He indicated she should come sit next to him. She did, stepping past his father to do it.

"That sounds fun," she said.

"How familiar with farms are you?" Gray asked, grinning at her. He took her hand in his, and she really liked having their relationship out in the open.

"Not very familiar," she said. "But there are horses at the lodge. So I'm familiar with the smell."

Bev laughed, and Elise was glad she'd been able to cause that. The conversation continued, and she told Gray's parents about her childhood in Prince Edward Island, and her mom and her brother.

"Oh, Gray, my mom's getting married at the end of August. I guess Henry's parents won't be able to travel until then."

"End of August. If you know the dates, let me know, and I'll put them on my calendar."

"She texted me yesterday, while I was driving." Elise pulled out her phone and started tapping. "August... twenty-first." She looked up, and Gray tap-tapped to add it to his calendar.

"Got it." He smiled at her, and Elise experienced a very surreal moment between the two of them. They sat there, making plans for months down the road, putting events on their calendars, as if their lives were so intertwined already.

"Where's your father, Elise?" Bev asked.

Elise's smile slid right off her face. The question was innocent enough, but she hated answering it. "Uh, I'm not sure," she said. "I don't know him at all."

"Oh." Bev looked at Gray and then Chris. "I'm sorry."

"It was always just me, Malcolm, and Mom," Elise said. "I think he lives in Canada, but we never saw him growing up or anything."

"Interesting."

Elise didn't see what was interesting about it, and she didn't know what to say.

"Let's take that tour now," Gray said, using the armrest to help him stand. "Dad, did you get the chores done this morning?"

"Most of them," he said.

"I'll make something for dinner," Bev said.

"I want that sausage and orzo soup, Mom," Ames said, following Gray and Elise into the kitchen.

"I got dough rising," their mother said. "I wasn't going to make soup."

"Come on," Ames needled. "You can bake the bread and make garlic toast."

"Hunt," Gray said while they continued to argue about what to make for dinner. "Come help me figure out what Grandpa didn't get done this morning."

He got up without being asked again. Just set his pencil down and stepped toward the back door.

"I'll stay here and make sure they don't say anything bad about you," Ames said.

Gray snorted and shook his head. "Sure, whatever."

Ames chuckled and said, "I'll get the orzo out, Ma. What else do you need?"

Elise went outside with Hunter, and the sun was almost directly overhead now. "It's nice out here," she said, breathing in the pure air and bathing in the sunshine.

Gray followed her and plunked a hat on her head. "You'll need this."

"I will? I was just planning to loiter in the shade while you worked." She grinned at him as they crossed the deck.

"I'm the one who ran twenty-six miles this morning. Why does no one get that?"

She laughed as she went down the steps to the yard, glad Hunter was several paces in front of them. "Your parents are great."

"Oh, you don't need to lie to me," Gray said.

"No, really." She giggled. "Your mom was a little intense in the beginning, but she settled down."

"If you're really firm with her, she backs off." Gray reached for her hand. "They do bring up an interesting point."

"There's that *interesting* word again," Elise said, not really liking that word right now.

"We do live in two different cities."

Elise suddenly wasn't warm enough. "Yes." She once again didn't know what else to say.

"What are we going to do about that?"

"I don't know." She looked up at him, and he'd put a cowboy hat on too. Not his usual one, but he still looked country and cowboy and delicious. "School's almost out. Maybe you and Hunter could come to Coral Canyon for the summer."

"That's an idea," he said, nodding. The way he spoke, Elise knew he had other ideas.

"What are you thinking?" she asked.

"Dad," Hunter called. "He didn't do the goat troughs."

"You get 'em done, then," Gray called. Hunter nodded and got to work. Elise wouldn't even know what to do with a goat trough, but it seemed like the twelve-year-old sure did.

Gray stepped in front of her, blocking her view of his son. "It's fairly obvious that my parents can't run this farm," he said. "There's a granny house here, and I want to move them into that, buy the farm, and move out here with Hunter. We'll work the farm together." He took a deep breath, his eyes so deep and so serious. "That way, the farm stays in the family—we've owned it for four generations. Someone's nearby to look after my folks."

He shrugged and looked away. "I guess I'm asking if you think there's any chance you could leave Coral Canyon." He met her eyes again. "Or are we just kidding ourselves?"

CHAPTER 20

G ray hated the knotted tension in his muscles. He hadn't imagined this day being more than the marathon. Elise being here had changed everything. He'd introduced her to Hunter a week early, and she'd met his parents, and now he was talking about a long-term future with the woman.

She reached up and touched his face, her cool fingers like manna from heaven for him. "You don't mean right now, right, Gray?"

"No," he said. "Just…in general. At some point in the future. Can you leave Coral Canyon and come live on this farm?" He looked around at his future. He'd never aspired to be a farmer, but he could see himself working this land alongside his son.

"I think so," she said, making so many of his dreams come true. "People in Colorado need their lawns mowed, right?"

Gray smiled at her. "I'm sure they do, sweetheart." He leaned down and kissed her, a pain pulling through his lower back as he did. He kept the kiss short, because he was aware his parents were probably watching through the big windows at the back of the house. At least his mother was.

And Hunter wasn't far away, and Gray didn't need to be making out with Elise in front of his son. He pulled away and asked, "I wanted to ask you about children too, Elise."

"What about them?"

"You want kids of your own, right?"

She nodded, those clear green eyes mesmerizing him. "Yeah, Gray. I want kids of my own. Not that Hunter won't be mine. He's a great kid."

Gray put his arm around her and turned around, both of them facing the farm now. "He is. What were you two talking about by the table?"

"His crossword puzzles."

"Looked like more than that."

"Can you not be a lawyer for like five seconds?" she asked, pushing against his chest. "Now come on. You promised me a farm tour."

"My legs hurt," he complained, practically limping after her.

"Fine," she said, dancing around from him. "You go back to the house. I'll get Hunter to give me the tour."

Gray's first impulse was to disagree with her. But his legs really did hurt, and maybe that would give her and Hunter some bonding time. So he said, "Good idea. I'll see you in a bit."

To her credit, she smiled and walked away from him,

headed in the general direction of the goat enclosure. It took him a lot of effort to turn and go back to the farmhouse, where Ames had gotten his way. A pot of sausage and orzo soup bubbled on the stove, and Mom had a loaf of bread on the counter, where she slathered it liberally with homemade garlic butter.

"She's wonderful," his mother said the moment Gray closed the door. "I really like her."

"Me too, Mom."

"How old is she, really?"

Gray rolled his eyes. "She's only thirty, Mom."

His mother's whole face lit up, and Gray knew what she was going to say before the words came out of her mouth. "More grandchildren," she said. "I'm so excited." She finished buttering the bread as if doing so brought her untold joy.

"Where did Dad go?"

"He's in his office."

"I'm gonna go get him," Gray said. "I have something I want to talk to you two about."

"Are you going to ask her to marry you?" Mom dropped the knife on the counter with a clatter.

"No, Mom." Gray went to get his father, his mind rolling the word *marriage* through his mind. He was falling for Elise, he knew that much. But marriage? He could commit again— to the right person. The real question was whether Elise was the right woman or not.

"Dad?" He poked his head into the office. "Can you come out here for a minute? I want to talk to you and Mom for a second."

"Sure." His father kept clicking on his computer for another few seconds, and then he got up. Gray let him go first, and he seemed to move so slow. No wonder he couldn't get all the chores done on the farm. And when summer hit in full force, there'd be yard work to do too.

Once they were all in the kitchen, Gray stuck his hands in his pockets, glad he'd had Ames stop by his house so he could shower and change real quick. Ames had gone to get gas, and by the time he'd returned, Gray had been ready.

"I want to buy the farm," he said, straight-up. "Hunter and I will buy it all. The land, the house, the animals, every-thing. You guys can move into the granny house with Grams. We'll be here if you need anything, and we'll make sure the farm and animals get taken care of the way they should."

"What a great idea," Mom said.

"Now wait a minute," Dad said, looking at her. "We haven't even talked about selling the farm. The granny house is much smaller than this house."

"There's three of us," Mom argued back. "And I barely leave the house. Grams certainly isn't going anywhere."

Gray looked back and forth between them. "Dad," he said, trying to make his voice gentle and kind. "You can't take care of this place."

A fire entered his father's eyes, but he didn't say anything.

"You know I'm right." Gray looked at Ames, nodding to get him to help out.

"It's a good idea," Ames said.

"Maybe someone else will want the farm," Dad said. "We should ask everyone."

"No one else wants it," Ames said. "Colt and Wes are in Coral Canyon, Dad. Cy's building motorcycles for the foreseeable future, and I have a *very* demanding job I love."

"Chris," Mom said, but Gray heard a whole conversation there.

"I suppose I'll have to figure out a fair price," Dad said, and he sounded absolutely miserable about it.

"This is a good thing, Dad," Gray said. "Hunter loves this farm, and he'll probably buy it from me one day."

Dad started to nod, and Gray crossed the distance between them and hugged him. "This is good, Dad."

"I know." He hugged Gray back, and when they separated, Mom sniffled a little.

"Is Elise going to come here?" Dad asked, and the question surprised Gray, mostly because it was such a Mom-thing to ask.

"I don't know, Dad," Gray said. "We're going really slow, okay? We've been dating for a few months, but we definitely need several more before big things like moving and marriage will happen." He looked between his mother and father. "Okay? I don't need you to badger me, and I certainly don't need you making things awkward with Elise. I see her very rarely, and you're lucky I'm sharing her with you today at all."

"Okay, son," his mother said. "We hear you." She stepped away from the finished bread and hugged him. "I love you, Gray. You're a good man, and a good father, and if she's the one, everything will work out."

"Thanks, Ma." He held her tight, because there was nothing quite so good as a hug from his mother.

"Thank you for sharing her with us today." She patted him on the back and stepped away. "I'm just so happy you're seeing someone." She sniffled again, and Gray decided that was his cue to join Grams in the living room, where he could doze until his girlfriend returned with his son.

―――――

"ALL READY?" GRAY ASKED THE FOLLOWING MORNING. HE'D dropped Hunter at school and headed downtown, where Elise had said she'd wait for him before she left to return to Coral Canyon. She'd answered the door of her hotel room and brought her suitcase into the hallway.

Right there, he held her face in his hands and kissed her, wanting more time with her in person.

"I wish you didn't have to go," he whispered, sliding his lips to her ear.

"I know." She exhaled, holding onto his shoulders in such a way that told him she liked being close to him. He hadn't been this close to a woman in so long, and a thrill ran through his whole body. "But I do. I'm already behind schedule."

"Hunter and I talked last night," Gray said, straightening but keeping her in his arms. "We're still going to come this weekend."

"Are you sure?" she said. "It's a long drive."

"We're going to fly and rent a car in Jackson."

"Oh, that'll be faster."

"There's good fishing near Jackson," he said, grinning. "So we'll fly out on Friday afternoon. Try to fish before dark. Stay in Jackson that night. Fish in the morning and get to Coral Canyon in the early afternoon." He watched her to judge her reaction. "I know you wanted Saturday to get as much work done as you could. Does that work?"

"It's perfect," Elise said, pressing into him. "*You're* perfect."

He chuckled and shook his head. "Not true."

"Practically perfect," she teased, stepping away. "I better go."

"Okay." Gray picked up her suitcase and headed down the hall to the elevator. "I talked to my parents about buying the farm yesterday."

A couple of beats of silence passed, and then Elise asked, "And?"

"My father is going to put together an offer, and Ames said he'd help me go through the granny house to make sure it's ready for them to move into."

"And when will you move out there?"

"I don't know," he said. "We'll see how things go. My dad has a ton of stuff in his office he thinks he needs."

"How big is the granny house?"

"Three bedrooms, two baths," he said. "So he could have an office over there."

"Grams will move too?"

"Yes," Gray said. "The granny house was built specifically for the older generation to move into when someone else takes over the farm. It's all one level. Wheelchair accessible showers. A ramp already built-in. That kind of thing."

"Sounds very forward-thinking."

"That's the Hammond way," Gray said with plenty of gusto. "Always planning and looking ahead." As he spoke, he realized why his parents asked what they had. Gray had never done anything like this before. He didn't have long-distance relationships, and he didn't do much of anything without a three-year plan.

Elise giggled, and he waited until they were in the elevator together before kissing her again. "Gray," she said, laughing.

"I miss you already," he murmured, kissing her until the ding sounded and he had to step back. He cleared his throat and straightened his shirt while the door slid open. He took Elise's suitcase out and led her out to the pull-in circle.

The valet left to get her car, and they stood out of the way while they waited.

"I hate saying good-bye," Elise said as her car pulled up.

"I do too."

"Now you know why Wes and Bree just got married." She tossed him a smile and went around to the driver's side. He stared after her. What was she saying? Just because he didn't want to say good-bye didn't mean he wanted to get married. Did it?

Did he love her?

He blinked and ducked his head, trying to figure out how he felt. He'd removed himself from his feelings for so long, he wasn't sure what was happening. He did know how to lift a suitcase into the trunk, and he did that before stepping around to where she stood.

She'd put her purse in the car, and she gave the valet driver a tip while he waited. He put his happy face on as he engulfed her in a hug. "Drive safe, okay?"

"I will."

"Call me if you get bored. I'll talk you all the way home."

She laughed, and Gray did too. Saying good-bye was terrible, but Gray wasn't going to make it worse than it already was. When Elise pulled away, Gray let her go. She got behind the wheel, and he waved as she drove off.

He stood there, watching her car until he couldn't see it anymore. Then he took a deep breath and exhaled, saying, "That was awful."

And in that moment, he knew he didn't want to continue the long-distance dating. What he didn't know was what he should do about it.

CHAPTER 21

C y Hammond entered the back door of the shop, the familiar scent of motor oil and concrete meeting his nose. Ah, he loved that smell. It was what good days were made of, and he couldn't wait to add the California sunshine to the mix.

"I put the mail on your desk," Wade said as Cy went by.

"Thanks." Cy hardly looked at the mail, and he didn't much care about it. He stopped to chat with McCall, his best mechanic, and then he wandered into the conference room, where he was soon joined by the team that chose the veteran who would be getting a custom bike built for them.

"Who have we got today?" he asked, facing the huge, white wall at the end of the room where the presentations were projected.

"Major David Darcy," Tammy said. "He retired a couple of years ago, and he's got a service dog who lives with him full-time. His wife wrote in."

The man's picture flashed up on the wall while Tammy detailed what the Major dealt with on a day-to-day basis. Hearing loss. Migraines. Panic in large crowds.

"They moved to Lubbock, Texas," Winslow said. "It's a slower pace of life. They just have the one son left at home; he's a senior."

"And the dog," Cy said, because he knew that dogs were perpetual toddlers.

"And the dog," Winslow confirmed. "Regina said Dave likes hiking and fishing, getting outside, and Star Wars, so our conceptual is a space-themed bike." A new image brightened the wall, first a sketch while Dom went over the specs for the bike.

Dave was over six feet tall, and that required some adjustments from a standard motorcycle.

"And finally," Dom said. "Regina sent us their family motto. Darcy's are winners."

Cy grinned at that. He needed a personal motto that was better than *get up before noon*. He had terrible insomnia, and if he could push past his first initial wall at about eleven, he could stay up all night.

"We thought we'd put that on the gas tank, so the Major can remember that he won."

"I like that," Cy said. He rarely came into the shop these days, and he liked the energy here. He came for the monthly meetings, and yes, he visited the office on the second floor several times a week. He had to pay for things, after all, and manage inventory, handle payroll, and ensure their customer service couldn't be beat.

He missed the weight of a wrench in his hand, and the

thrill of designing a new bike for someone. He only did a couple of projects a year now, and only for the highest profile clients. The rest of his time was spent on advertising and back-end business dealings. The boring stuff no one wanted to do, but someone had to do in order to keep the doors open.

"Cy?"

He looked over his shoulder to the door, where Marissa stood. "You have a call. She said it's urgent."

"She did?" For a moment—one terrible moment—he thought it was Mikaela, finally calling to tell him she'd made a huge mistake by breaking up with him all those months ago. He couldn't believe he had gone immediately to that, and he frowned as he stood up.

"Yes," Marissa said, her eyes holding some trepidation.

He knocked on the table and said, "This is all great, guys. Let's make it happen." That was his motto. *Make it happen.*

He followed Marissa down the hall to her desk. "Who is it?"

"Candice," she said. "She said it's urgent."

"I don't even know who Candice is," he said.

"She owns this building, sir," Marissa said. "Should I transfer it to your office?" She picked up the phone, her eyebrows also lifted.

"Yes," he said, hurrying back down the hall to the huge office in the corner. Some days, when he was restless, he would jog down the hall, tap his knuckles against the elevator doors, and jog back. Over and over.

His parents had never medicated him growing up, and as an adult, Cy had found ways to deal with his extra energy.

He'd bought rubber bands to wear around his wrists to help himself focus, and he did two thousand piece jigsaw puzzles to force his mind to slow down.

The phone was ringing when he opened the door, and he jogged to the desk in front of the windows. "Cy Hammond," he said after picking up the phone.

"Cy," Candice said, her voice curt. She always sounded like she'd just sucked on a lemon, and Cy turned into Serious Businessman Cy in the blink of an eye.

"Hello, Candice," he said.

"Did you get my letter?"

"Oh, um, I haven't opened the mail yet." He looked down at his desk, where an enormous stack of mail waited for him. The boys downstairs sorted it for him, and Marissa was likely the one who'd put it on his desk, despite what Wade had said. Wade ran the shop downstairs, so he'd likely gone through it first. Marissa usually combed through it as well, with a finer tooth than Wade

"Well," she said. "It was days ago, Mister Hammond."

He looked up, aware of the bite in her tone. The *Mister Hammond* gave away her annoyance too. "I'm sorry," he said. "We've been pretty busy around here." They were always busy. Beyond busy.

"I'm afraid you're going to be busier," she said.

Cy pulled the rubber band on his arm. "Oh?"

"I'm selling the building, Mister Hammond. The dates and details are in the letter I sent you. I'm sure you're aware your lease is up at the end of August, and I hate to say it, but I'll need you out of the property on the last day of that month."

Cy just stood there, trying to process her words. The rubber band thwacked against his wrist. *Thwap, thwap, thwap.*

"The end of August," he said. It was the middle of June. That was only two and a half months, and it generally took them longer than that to build a custom bike. Should they even start on the Major's motorcycle?

Probably not, Cy thought, his mind jumping to another train of thought, then another, while Candice started talking again.

He didn't even know how to pack up the two floors his custom motorcycle shop occupied, and move it...where? Where could he move it?

He couldn't just take any space. He needed a multi-functional space, with big bay doors in the back, a shop in the front, offices, a conference room....

"Cy?"

"Yes," he said. "I'm still here."

"Can you confirm that you understand I need that property cleared on September one?"

He very nearly scoffed, his frustration roaring through him now. September one. Why couldn't she just say September first like a normal person?

"Yes," he said. "I understand."

"Anything left behind at that time will become my property, and I'll get to decide what to do with it."

"I understand," he said, his voice on the cold side. He tried to care, but he'd just learned he had ten weeks to find a new building. He thought of his employees. They lived and worked here in Solana Beach. He couldn't expect them to relocate.

He'd just have to find a new building right here in town. The call ended, and he moved around the desk and collapsed into the chair. He faced the windows and looked out. Just past the rooftops of the houses across the street, he could see the ocean.

No matter where he found his next building, he knew it wasn't going to be as good as this one. Here, he could walk a hundred yards and dip his toes in the surf.

"Is this a joke, Lord?" He tipped his head back and looked up to the ceiling. Through it, to the heavens above. "It's not a funny one."

Cy knew it wasn't a joke at all.

He'd been in this building for eight years, and he didn't even know how to go about finding somewhere to lease.

Maybe you should build your own building. The thought came into his mind, and Cy never was one to discount such things. He believed they came straight from God Himself, and Cy picked up his phone.

"Dad," he said when his father picked up.

"Cy." His father chuckled. "How are you, son? How's California?"

"Great," Cy said, wishing he were out on the beach with his board shorts and not a care in the world. But the Hammond boys had not been raised not to care about things. Even he and Ames, though they were a bit eccentric with their clothes and what they'd chosen to do with their billions, knew how to take something seriously. How to work. How to be a Hammond.

"Listen, Dad," Cy said. "I just found out I'm losing my lease, and I need a new building. What kind of advice have you got for me?"

This last building had sort of landed in his lap by divine providence. Cy couldn't hope for such a thing to happen again. But if there was one thing his father was really good at, it was giving advice.

He talked about finding a commercial real estate agent in the area. Then he said, "And you know, Cy, you could build your own building."

"Yeah, I thought of that, Dad." The thought grew teeth and sunk itself into Cy's mind. "I just don't think I can do it in ten weeks."

"Ah, I see. That is a problem."

"And Solana Beach has strict zoning regulations." Cy knew, because he'd been to court a couple of times over the alleged noise violations from his shop. He'd won every time, because he was located in a commercial zone, and he followed the noise ordinances to the T.

"Maybe you go somewhere else," Dad suggested.

"It's an idea," Cy said, his mind starting to wander. He couldn't ask his staff to go wherever his whims took him. Could he?

There were mechanics all over the country, and he reasoned he could possibly pay to relocate his design team and people like McCall and Wade. "If they want to come," he whispered to himself.

"Listen, while I've got you," Dad said. "I wanted to talk to you about the farm."

"What about it?" His focus sharpened again, and he spun away from the windows.

"Gray wants to buy it. He and Hunter are going to take over."

Cy's eyebrows flew toward his hairline. "Wow."

"I wanted to call all the other boys and make sure that's okay with them before I allow Gray to do it."

"I don't want the farm, Dad," Cy said, though he could use the land to build a great, big custom bike shop.... He shook his head. He wasn't going to do that. His father would never allow it, for one. And if Cy thought the neighbors here complained...he knew they'd be worse in Ivory Peaks.

"Okay," Dad said. "I figured."

"I didn't think Hunter and Gray wanted it either. I'm surprised by that."

"Well, Hunter worked out here all summer," Dad said. "I think some of the farming bug bit him. And Gray's retired now. Life is different for him."

"You mean he has more time now."

"Yes," Dad said. "And the farm is a great way to spend your time."

"That's true," Cy said. "All right, Dad. I have to go."

"Love you, son."

"I love you too, Dad." Cy hung up and faced the windows again. He'd never thought the farm was a great way to spend his time, because he'd never wanted to do farm chores in his spare time. He supposed that now, all of Gray's time was spare time, and Cy did crave a small-town life every now and then.

It was one of the reasons California had appealed to him

so much. The laid-back atmosphere in a small, coastal city like Solana Beach appealed to him.

"Maybe you should relocate," he murmured to himself. No matter what he did, he wasn't going to find another building by staring out the window. He turned, picked up his phone, and flipped open his laptop. It was time to find a commercial real estate agent.

CHAPTER 22

E lise had just buttered her toast when knocking sounded on the cabin door. Hutch barked, his voice so loud. He came skidding into the kitchen, his whole body wagging.

Her heart skipped and stuttered even as the doorbell sang. "Yeah," she said. "Someone's here."

Not just someone. Gray and Hunter were here.

"Come in," she called, heading for the doorway that led into the living room. "Shush, Hutch." The big dog stopped barking, but he was so dang excited to have visitors. Elise knew how he felt.

A moment later, Gray's tall frame walked through the front door, and everything inside Elise rejoiced. He wore a pair of jeans with a red, white, and blue polo, and that cowboy hat she loved so much.

He was perfectly patriotic. She giggled as she ran toward

him, and he received her into his arms with a laugh too. Hutch tried to get in between them, and Gray chuckled.

"Oh, it's so good to see you," he said, his strong arms around her so perfect and so tight. He did not let the dog he'd bought for her nose his way between them, not even a little bit.

"I saw you last night," she said. "On the video chat."

He looked up at her, because he'd literally swept her off her feet. "It's not the same." He set her down and kissed her with enough passion to tell her Hunter was still in the truck and wouldn't be coming in.

This was definitely not anything like the video chat, and Elise hoped she could convey her feelings to Gray through her touch too.

Hutch started barking, and Elise found him such a nuisance sometimes.

"Mm," Gray finally said, pulling away. "We better go, or we'll be late."

"The Whittakers saved a spot big enough for everyone," Elise whispered, not wanting to go. She didn't want to share Gray with anyone today, not even his son. But they had a full day of Independence Day festivities planned down the canyon in town, and Elise knew she wouldn't be getting what she wanted.

She stepped out of his arms and did a little twirl. "Well? How's my patriotic outfit?"

He scanned her from head to toe, his eyes taking on a deep glint of desire. "Amazing."

She wore a blue dress with red and white stripes sewn into it like the flag was waving across her torso. She'd designed it herself and sewn it right at the kitchen table. She smiled at him. "Thank you. How was the fishing?"

"Great," he said. "We both enjoyed it. Caught a few things we made for dinner last night."

"And you're at Colton's? Or Wes's?" He reached down absently as Hutch kept pestering him for a pat.

"Colton's for a couple of nights," he said. "I guess Annie's daughter just got engaged, and they've got a whole thing going on in the formal dining room. Plans and all of that."

"Oh, that's right," Elise said. "I think Eden and Mitchell are aiming for a Christmas wedding." She held back her sigh, though a Christmas wedding sounded like the most perfect thing on the planet.

"Then we'll be at Wes's," Gray said.

"And did you buy the farm?"

He chuckled, his hand sliding along her hip again. "You know what that means, right?"

"Buy the farm?"

"Yeah."

"No." She slipped away from him, adding, "Let me grab my toast, and we can go." She hurried into the kitchen, where she not only grabbed her stack of toast, but her oversized bag too. She'd put sunscreen in it, along with bottled water, a bag of black licorice, several miniature American flags, a blanket, a jacket in case she got cold, and a visor. Oh, and her purse.

"Well, I'm not dead yet," Gray said. "Buy the farm means you've died."

She looked at him, trying to decide if he was kidding or

not. He didn't seem to be. "Huh," she said. "I didn't know that. So, did you purchase your father's farm?"

Gray grinned at her from the doorway of the kitchen, and she handed him a piece of toast. "I can't eat this," he said.

"Oh, that's right. How many miles did you run this morning?"

"It's eight o'clock," he said.

"And that matters how?"

"Fine," he said. "I went six miles."

"Before dawn." She loved teasing him about the running. "Now, you better pat Hutch before he goes ballistic." The dog had run around the side of the couch to find a ball just for Gray. He held the bright orange orb in his mouth, and he was so darn proud of himself for it.

Gray bent down and started scratching behind Hutch's ears. "Look at you, bud. You're huge." He grinned at the dog, who smiled right on back. Elise decided she could keep him, even if he did get jealous while she kissed her boyfriend.

"You're staying here," she told the dog. She'd taken him to lots of things before, but he really was huge, and the parade and festival would be much easier without him. His tail wagged and wagged, and Elise felt a little bad leaving him behind.

But they headed outside, where Hunter had been waiting in the truck Gray had rented. "Yes," he said. "I did purchase the farm."

"Oh, that's great," she said. "And your parents?"

"It was hard on my father for some reason. It's like he doesn't understand that he's almost eighty years old." Gray opened her door and took her bag. "Oof. What is in this thing?"

"Everything we need for a great morning at the parade and a great day at the park." Elise climbed into the truck. "Hey, Hunter."

"Hello, Elise," he said, so proper and so sober.

Gray closed the door and put her bag in the back. "Been working on the farm?"

"Yes." He looked down at his lap again, and Elise realized he had a cell phone there.

"Oh, my heck, Hunter." She grabbed the phone. "Is this yours?" She looked up, her eyes searching his. "Your father got you a phone?" She couldn't believe it. Gray was anti-technology for teens, though Elise had tried to explain to him why Hunter had been asking him for a phone.

"Yeah," he said with a smile. "Dad finally gave in."

"I did what?" Gray asked as he got behind the wheel.

Elise held up the phone, questions streaming through her.

"Yes, yes," Gray said quite huffily. "I got him a phone." He buckled his seat belt, and Elise did the same, a giggle coming out of her mouth. She handed the phone back to Hunter. "It's the only thing he's ever begged me for, and I just figured it would work out."

"The only thing he's ever begged you for?"

"Yeah." Gray backed down the long road and onto the asphalt. He got them moving down the canyon. "Usually, he just asks me, and I say yes or no and that's that."

"How amazing," Elise said.

"But he kept coming back to this."

"Maybe you buy him everything he wants," Elise said. "So he doesn't have to ask twice."

Hunter looked back and forth between Gray and Elise, but she was rather enjoying herself.

"Maybe," Gray conceded, and they laughed together. "How's the lawn care business?"

"Doing great things," she said. They'd talked about her business several times since the last time they'd seen each other in person. Gray had confessed that he didn't like the long-distance relationship, and Elise could admit it wasn't working that great for her either. They'd agreed that she'd go through this one last summer and fall season in Coral Canyon, and then she'd be moving to Colorado.

After all, Gray had two homes now—three, if she counted the granny house—and he'd offered for her to live in his home in the suburbs of Denver. He and Hunter, of course, would live on the farm. That way, they could continue building and deepening their relationship without the complication of the five hundred miles between them.

"All right," Elise said. "Give me your number, Hunter. Then we can text secret things about your father." She gave him a teasing look, and Gray just shook his head.

Hunter rattled off his number, and Elise put it in her phone. She couldn't think of a single thing she'd ever text the boy, but it was important for a teen to give out their phone number to people, she knew.

They arrived in downtown Coral Canyon, and Gray found somewhere to park that was only a couple of blocks from the parade route. Elise led the way toward the spot the

Whittakers staked out every year for the Fourth of July parade, and she found the section filling with people.

Patsy and Sophia were already there, and Elise naturally gravitated toward them. "Hey, guys," she said.

"Morning, Elise," Patsy said with a smile. "Oh, Gray's here." She stood up and gave him a quick hug. One of the triplets started to wander out into the street, and Patsy swooped Collin into her arms. "Can't go out there yet, baby."

He smiled at her and started saying something in his three-year-old voice.

"That's right," Patsy said. "There will be cop cars and floats and horses."

How she'd understood the little boy, Elise didn't know. She stood to the side while Gray set up the camp chairs, and then she sat down, reaching for Collin. "Come here, sweetheart."

The little boy curled right into her lap, and Elise sure did love him. Gray sat next to her, with Hunter on the other side.

Collin only stayed on Elise's lap for a few minutes, and then Rose called him over to get a drink and a cookie. Elise reached for her licorice, because there was nothing better to pass the time before a parade started than black licorice.

"I'd offer you some of this, but I know you won't take it."

Gray looked at the licorice as if it were a poisonous snake. "I wouldn't eat that even if I wasn't training for Boston. I'd eat red licorice. Oh, I forgot to tell you."

"Tell me what?" She bit off a big piece of licorice and chewed it, really enjoying the waxy feel of it in her mouth.

"I got third in my age group at Colfax."

"Out of everyone?"

"Out of males age forty to forty-four, yes," he said. "*Third*, Elise."

"That must be really good," she said.

"There were four hundred of us, so yes," he said. "It's really good. I won a little money."

"Just what you need," she said.

He snorted and then laughed, reaching over to take her hand in his. She slid down in her chair a little and turned to look at him. His eyes met hers, and though they were surrounded by people, and crying toddlers, and laughter— and then the motorcycle cop sirens—in that moment, it was just Gray and Elise.

She felt herself fall all the way in love with him, and she hoped she could survive the next three months here in Coral Canyon without him.

Soon, she told herself as the crowd started to rise. The American flag was coming. *You'll be in Colorado soon.*

HOURS LATER, ELISE HAD EATEN WAY TOO MUCH FRIED FOOD. She'd listened to Gray nag at Hunter about his phone for far too long. And her feet hurt from the sixteen thousand steps she'd taken as they went all over the park, where they had food trucks and a few carnival rides, to the fairgrounds to see the animals, and back to Colton's for a barbecue.

"Hunt, you'll be okay here while I drive Elise back to her cabin?"

"Yep." Hunter looked up from the crossword puzzle he'd

been working on. He smiled at Gray, and Gray leaned down and kissed the top of his son's head.

Then he reached for Elise's hand and said to Colton, "I'm taking Elise home. Hunter's staying here."

"All right." Colton met Elise's eye, not Gray's, and so much was said between them. She'd told him more than she probably should've about her relationship with Gray. She could admit that.

But she was lonely at night, and she often came down from the lodge to either Colton's or Bree's. One of them would have food, and they all seemed to gather every night. She was the fifth wheel, but now that she was dating Gray openly, she didn't feel like it.

Annie had been busy with helping Eden to plan her wedding, and Bree was starting to collect things she needed for when the baby would be born. Furniture and clothes, diapers and ointments and accessories. Elise had gone shopping with her when she'd bought the swing, and all of Elise's maternal instincts had cried out to her that day.

She did want to have children someday. A lot of children.

Now that it was summer, she didn't have a ton of time for shopping trips and hangouts with her friends during the day. A lot of her evenings were dedicated to lawn care as well, and she wouldn't have it any other way.

She worried that Two Green Thumbs would suffer from a move, but she'd already committed to it. Right now, it didn't matter if the landscaping and yard care business didn't turn a profit. She had a job at the lodge that paid her bills. The landscaping was bonus money on top of that.

"When I move to Colorado, what should I do?" she

asked as Gray pointed the truck toward the canyon. She'd stayed past dark, but somehow the summer night sky wasn't nearly as menacing as the winter one. "Just run my business? It'll be winter. I'll need to find a job."

"I suppose that's true," he said as if he'd never thought of it. He probably hadn't. Gray and his brothers didn't worry about money—they never had. He looked at her. "Well, your rent will be free, at least."

"I don't need to live in your house for free," she said. "I can pay rent."

"Okay," he said, but Elise knew she hadn't won anything. He wouldn't make her pay rent, and she'd simply have to revisit the topic when it was at-hand. "I need to tell you something."

"Okay." Nerves doused her, but she refused to assume the worst. He wasn't going to break up with her...she hoped.

He cleared his throat. "I kind of lied to you today."

"You did?"

"I mean, kind of. We are staying at Colton's for a few nights. But we're not going to Wes's after that."

"Oh." She tried to see through the darkness in the truck. The lights from the dashboard illuminated Gray's face a little bit, but not enough to see the emotion in his eyes. "Where are you going? Do you have to go home so soon?"

They'd planned on him being there for a week, and "a few nights" at Colton's didn't feel like enough. Maybe she should just move to Colorado now. She'd have to get a job either way. Her clients could find someone else to mow their lawn.

"No," he said. "Hunter and I are staying here."

Elise turned fully toward him now. "I'm sorry. You're staying here?"

"Yes," Gray said, finally facing her and giving her that cocky smile. "I rented a house here. We're going to stay here until your mother's wedding at the end of August. Then we'll head back to Colorado so Hunter can start school."

A new kind of happiness bloomed in Elise's soul. "You're kidding."

"I'm not." He laughed and took her hand in his, lifting to his lips. "I want to be closer to you."

"What about the farm?" she asked. "You literally just bought it because your dad can't take care of it. Summer is the busiest time."

"I hired a manager," Gray said, putting both hands on the wheel again.

"You just shut down."

"My parents aren't thrilled with my decision. I told them it was mine to make, and it'll be fine." He threw a glance at her. "It's not permanent. I'm going back."

"Of course," she said. "I guess they probably just wanted it to be kept in the family?"

"It is," he said. "I bought it. It's okay if someone else runs it and takes care of the horses for a couple of months."

She agreed with him, but she could also see his parents' side. "I'm so glad you're staying," she said. "And we had an amazing day, and you came in third in your age group, and Hunter got a cell phone."

She smiled, feeling drunk on happiness.

"And we're together," Gray said quietly.

"Yes," Elise said. "We're together." And he wasn't leaving in a weekend, or even a week. He wasn't leaving in a month. She'd be able to see Gray, live and in-person, every day for the next two months, and Elise couldn't wait to show him around to all of the amazing shops and restaurants in Coral Canyon.

She couldn't wait to kiss him every night. She couldn't wait to deepen her friendship and relationship with Hunter. She couldn't wait to show up at Colton's or Bree's with a boyfriend of her own.

What a great surprise, she thought. *Thank you, Lord, for merging our paths, even if it's only for a couple of months.*

CHAPTER 23

G ray ran according to his marathon training schedule, often driving up the canyon to get Hutch from Elise. The dog became a good running partner after only a few days, and he had far less energy to annoy Elise with too.

On mornings where he went less than ten miles, he and Hunter would go fishing on Prospect Lake. Gray loved the area, with homes curving around the lake but not crowding it.

No boats with a motor were allowed on the lake, and he enjoyed a quiet, peaceful experience with his son.

"Hunter?"

"Yeah." He pulled his attention from the still water surrounding their fishing boat. It was still fairly chilly in the morning, especially because the first rays of sun didn't touch this lake until at least ten o'clock, nestled as it was beneath all these pine trees.

"How do you like Elise?" Gray sometimes used his

fishing expeditions to talk about difficult things with Hunter. Neither one of them could get out of the boat, and sometimes hard things needed to be said.

"I really like her, Dad," he said. "She sends me funny memes, and she sent me a link to the New York Times crossword puzzle a few days ago. They put it online for free last year, and she thought I'd like it."

Gray smiled, first at his son's love of crossword puzzles. Secondly, at Elise's kindness to his son. "That's great," he said.

"Dad?"

"Yeah." He looked up from the new fly he wanted to try. The one on his line wasn't doing anything.

"How do you like Elise?"

Gray blinked at Hunter, who simply gazed back at him with those big, brown eyes. He cleared his throat and focused back on the fly. "I like her a lot, son."

"Are you going to marry her?"

"Maybe," Gray said, and that was one giant step further than he'd ever been. "We're going to see how things go now that we don't live five hundred miles apart." He smiled at his son. "Do you text Molly still?"

"Yeah, sometimes," Hunter said, looking out over the water again. "She's babysitting a lot this summer. She's saving for Space Camp."

"Good for her," he said.

"Dad?"

"Yep."

"We have a lot of money, right?"

Once again, Hunter had surprised him with a question.

Gray hated being surprised with questions, because he always knew what the defense was going to present, and he had an answer for everything.

But for this, he didn't. Not really.

"Yes," he said slowly. His father had sat him down when he'd turned thirteen and told him he'd inherit two billion dollars the day he turned twenty-one. The expectations in the Hammond family were intense, but Gray had risen to the challenge. In fact, he *loved* a good challenge.

"Why?"

"Someone said something to me about it," he said. "That's all."

"What did they say?" Gray worked to tamp down the sharp edges in his voice. He didn't want Hunter to think he cared at all, even though he did.

"It was Joey Jacobs. He said it must be nice to be able to leave town for two months."

"Mm." Gray wasn't even looking at the flies anymore.

"It was in a group text, and everyone started saying how rich I was." Hunter didn't sound happy about that, and Gray glanced at him. He wore a dissatisfied look on his face as he watched his line. Gray saw so much of himself in his son's face, it was almost freaky.

"What did you say?"

"I said we were staying with my uncle," Hunter said. "And helping my dad's girlfriend with her lawn care business. It wasn't a vacation."

"It kind of is, though," Gray said. "Right? We get to go fishing, and there's no farm to take care of."

Hunter smiled then. "I guess it's definitely more relaxed than last summer."

"We take Sparky to the park all the time," Gray added.

"Yeah."

They did help Elise finish up her work for the day, almost every day. Any of them could push a lawn mower and edge grass, and that was what they'd been doing. That way, the three of them could spend quality time together. They'd gone to concerts in the park, on hikes around the mountains here, and she'd taken them up to another small town called Dog Valley, where they'd eaten at an amazing barbecue house and visited a rescue shelter for dogs and cats.

"I guess I just didn't realize we were rich," Hunter said.

"When I was about your age," Gray said, looking up and out over the peaceful water too. "My dad sat me down and told me I was going to get two billion dollars when I turned twenty-one."

Hunter looked at Gray, eyes wide. "Wow."

Gray made a noise halfway between a laugh and a scoff. "Yeah, wow. All of us worked, Hunt. All the time. We worked the farm before and after school. We did all of our schoolwork. We had chores around the house. When we turned sixteen, we got jobs." Gray had worked and worked and worked in his lifetime. It actually felt amazing to be in Coral Canyon, floating on a lake he could see clear to the bottom of, and relaxing.

"We were expected to take our money and do something good with it."

"What did you do?"

"I went to law school," Gray said. "At HMC, we hire for

those big positions from the family first, if possible." The lawyer who'd replaced him wasn't a Hammond, but all the other senior-level positions were. "I invested my money in stocks and real estate. Uncle Wes went to business school after he finished his chemistry degree, and he founded a pharmaceutical company."

Hunter just looked at him, and Gray knew the boy didn't understand how much money there was in drug development. Wes did, though, and he'd doubled his money in only four years.

Gray's increase had been a much slower burn, but with plenty of big paydays too. "You know how I check my stuff every morning on the computer?"

"Yeah."

"That's my investment. Over the past twenty-three years, I've made my two billion into seven and a half."

Hunter didn't say anything, and Gray struggled to put into words what that much money meant. It was impossible. No one knew what that much money meant. It wasn't something they could conceptualize.

"Bottom line," Gray said. "We're *really* rich. Beyond rich. Like, we can't even spend that much money even if we tried."

"Is it bad to be rich?" Hunter asked.

Gray smiled at his innocence. "Depends, son," he said. "On what you do with the money. That's what Grandpa would always say. Do something good, boys. Make sure you're always giving glory to God. Be thankful." He spoke in a deeper voice for his father, and Hunter chuckled.

"That sounds like Grandpa."

Gray grinned too. "Yeah." He watched Hunter for a minute. "I've thought about giving you two billion when you turn twenty-one."

"You have?"

"What would you do with it?" Gray asked. "What do you want to be when you grow up?"

"I like computers."

"It's a good field," Gray said, nodding. "Are you upset we bought the farm?"

"No."

"Last year, you didn't want to buy it."

"I like the farm, Dad," Hunter said. "I love animals. Maybe I'll be a vet."

"A tech vet," Gray said, smiling at his son.

Hunter just shook his head. "I'll tell them it's not bad to be rich."

"You don't owe any of them any explanation," Gray said.

"Molly was in the group," Hunter said, ducking his head now. "She didn't say anything, but I don't want her to think I'm some spoiled rich kid."

"Hunt, you're as far from that as a person can be." He reached out and tapped on the brim of his son's cowboy hat. "Okay?"

"Yeah." Hunter looked up. "Okay."

Gray felt like he was in a boat without a rudder, on stormy seas. He had no idea how to navigate this unknown terrain of girls and group texts and their personal finances. He hadn't been planning to have the same talk with his son that his father had given to him.

"Oh, I've got a bite," Hunter said, and Gray turned his

attention to the fish and watching Hunter carefully reel him in.

"That's a good one," Gray said when his son had landed the fish. "Probably eight pounds."

Hunter beamed at him, and said, "Let's get home so I can find a recipe for it."

"Deal," Gray said, reaching for the oars to row them to shore.

———

A FEW DAYS LATER, GRAY REACHED THE TWO-WEEK MARK SINCE he'd been in Coral Canyon. He really liked this town, and he could easily see himself living here. He and Hunter had rented a house, and he could buy one here. He and Elise could split their time between Coral Canyon and Colorado....

Winters in Ivory Peaks were milder than here, and summer in the Tetons was shaping up to be the most amazing thing Gray had experienced.

He'd just finished emptying the dishwasher when his phone rang. Someone knocked on the front door too, and he nodded to it. "Get that, bud. It'll be Elise." He picked up his phone and saw Cy's name on the screen. "Hey," he said, keeping an eye on his son as he answered the door.

Elise stepped inside, her face lighting up when she saw Hunter. She hugged him, and she was shorter than Hunter by a few inches. Gray's heart expanded every time he saw the two of them getting along, and he had to turn away from the front door to focus on his brother's voice.

"...so can I stay at the farm?"

"Wait, what?" Gray asked. "Sorry, I was distracted."

"I closed my shop," Cy said. "I'm back in Ivory Peaks, and Mom said you're in Coral Canyon for a couple of months. Can I stay at the farm?"

"Sure, of course," Gray said. "How long will you be there?"

"Just until I can find a new place for the shop."

"Why'd you leave Solana Beach?"

"The building I was renting got sold, and I had to be out by September first. We finished all our active projects, and I closed it up for now."

"I'm sorry, Cy."

"Thanks." He sighed, the sound so full of longing.

Gray could sense his brother's stress. "You don't want to stay in California?"

"Nothing in Solana Beach that fits my needs," he said. "Dad suggested building something, but that takes time."

"You have time, right?"

"I suppose I do."

"Where are you thinking?"

"I have no idea." A pause came through the line, and Cy added, "No, Grams. Let me get that."

"Oh, you're already at the farm."

"Yes," Cy said. "I didn't know you weren't. Mom had to tell me."

"I didn't know I needed your permission to leave town," Gray said dryly.

"She said you're staying in Coral Canyon so you can ask Elise to marry you."

"What?" Gray spun around, hoping neither his son nor Elise had heard that. Cy had a loud voice, and he'd practically yelled that sentence. "That's not true."

"That's what she said. What did you tell her?"

Elise met his eye, and she was clearly asking if they were going to lunch.

"Give me a second, Cy." He covered the phone. "It's Cy, and I have to talk to him. Why don't you to go ahead, and I'll catch up?"

"Okay, we're going to Sluggers," she said, approaching him. "You can find it?"

"I'll be fifteen minutes behind you," he said. "No soda for me."

"Of course." She tipped up on her toes, and Gray kissed her quickly.

He put the phone back to his ear as she left with Hunter, and he waited until the front door clicked closed before he said, "I told Mom the long distance dating was hard on us," he said. "And I wanted to come up here to have more time with Elise. That's it."

"Well, she's positive you're going to come home with a fiancée," Cy said.

"That's ridiculous," Gray said.

"Is it?" Cy asked. "I don't know, Gray. You—where are you living up there?"

"We rented a house for a couple of months."

"Do you see her every day?"

"Yes."

"You just sent your son to lunch with her, alone."

Gray didn't confirm, because Cy had obviously heard him despite Gray trying to cover the receiver.

"Outsider perspective: you're in deep with this woman," Cy said.

Gray could see him shrugging like what he'd just said was no big deal. "Okay," Gray said. "Maybe I am."

"So Mom's statement might not be as ridiculous as you just said it was."

"I can't confirm or deny that," Gray said. "But you know what, Cy? You should come up here and look for a building. There's a ton of growth and construction here, and I know I saw some huge plots of land for sale."

"Really?"

"Yes, really."

"Coral Canyon."

"Wes and Colton live here," Gray said. "I can drive here in my sleep now, and honestly, I'm thinking about maintaining two residences."

"You already have two residences," Cy said.

"So maybe three," Gray said, lifting his chin though Cy wasn't in the same room with him. "I'll sell the house on the cul-de-sac eventually."

"Why haven't you yet?"

"Honestly?"

"If you can't be honest with me, who can you be honest with?"

"I haven't told anyone this," Gray said.

"Lay it on me, Beans."

Gray chuckled and shook his head. Cy hadn't used that

childhood nickname for years. "Elise is going to live in that house."

"Dude, you should just ask her to marry you. Don't have a long engagement. Ask her today. Get married by September. Sell the house."

Gray burst out laughing. "I am not doing that," he said. "It sounds so ludicrous. Do you even hear yourself?"

"What are you waiting for?"

"I'm waiting to be sure," Gray said.

"Sure of what?"

"Just…sure." Gray didn't have to explain anything to Cy. They'd had a special bond since they were the only two brothers who'd been married, at least before Colton had come to Coral Canyon.

"Do you love her?"

"I'm late for lunch," Gray said, suddenly in a foul mood. "Have fun at the farm."

Cy managed to say, "Good-bye," before Gray hung up. He let out a frustrated sigh, his mind now whirring in a thousand different directions.

"Don't change the plan," he muttered to himself. "You're here until the end of August. She's moving to Colorado in September. You don't need to ask her to marry you today." He shook his head as he grabbed his keys from the drawer next to the fridge and headed into the garage.

What a ridiculous idea.

But is it?

The thought nagged at him, and he finally asked out loud, "Lord, what do You want me to do? Is this another one of those leap of faith things?" He didn't even have a ring, and as he drove toward Sluggers, he thought maybe he should get one.

Or maybe he should just make sure Elise was the right woman to be his wife and Hunter's mother before he did anything else.

CHAPTER 24

"I'm not going to be able to hit it," Elise said, adjusting the batting helmet. She glanced at Hunter, who was testing the weight of the bats in his hand.

"You want a wooden bat," he said, putting the metal one back. He handed it to her. "You'll be able to hit it, Elise. Put your hands together like this." He showed her how to put her hands on the bat. "And you turn sideways, and just look down there. He put it on the slow setting."

"Yeah, and that doesn't make me feel any better."

"Why not?" Hunter asked, looking at her. He was such a sober child, though he had a great laugh too. She saw him every day too, as Gray brought him to help Elise with her yards, and they spent the afternoons in parks, at the lake, or in an air-conditioned house or movie theater.

"If that's your level, that's your level," he said. "Everyone starts at the beginning." He turned sideways, the bat in his hands completely natural. "And you just watch.

Don't look away from the ball. Don't look at the bat. Just look at the ball and swing the bat. You'll hit it."

He handed her the bat and stepped out of the cage. He'd already taken his turn, and he'd been brilliant. She'd taken a video to show Gray, and several pictures where she'd captured Hunter's perfect form.

The machine down at the end of the cage made a thwacking noise, and Elise found the ball easily. She kept her eyes on it, just like Hunter had said. She had no idea how to time the swing, because she wasn't particularly athletic. She'd learned to sew and garden growing up.

She swung, and she connected the bat to the ball. "Oh!" she said, the vibration from the contact moving into her hands and causing her to drop the bat.

"Nice job, Elise," Hunter said, clapping. "But get the bat. There's another ball coming."

"Oh, dear," she said, shaking her hands though they didn't really hurt. She scrambled after the bat, the machine making that noise again. She didn't have time to set up, but she managed to stay out of the way so the ball didn't hit her.

"Hold onto it this time," Hunter said, his fingers curling through the chain link fence. "Just watch the ball. You hit it great last time."

Another ball came, and Elise hit it. She looked at Hunter, who applauded her again, a wide smile on his face. Out of the ten balls, she hit six of them, and she didn't drop the bat again. Her adrenaline streamed through her as she left the cage.

"That was awesome, Elise." Hunter took the bat from her and hung it back on the rack. "You did great."

"Thanks for showing me." She stepped toward him smoothly and drew him into a hug. He was a bit stiff at first, but he quickly relaxed in her arms. Her heart had a spot just for Hunter Hammond in it, and she hadn't known it until then.

She stepped back and nodded to the skeeball. "That next? I'm actually good at that."

"Sure," he said. They started walking toward the arcade games.

"Hunter, do you see your mom ever?"

"Yeah," he said without missing a beat. He took several quarters from her. "Sometimes. I usually go to Florida in the summer, but she didn't call Dad this year." He glanced at her and fed the machine three quarters. "And sometimes she has me come for my birthday, but I didn't go in February either."

"Do you—I mean, do you want to see her more often?"

The balls came down the machine and Hunter picked one up. He held it in both hands and looked at her. "Not really."

Elise nodded, her throat narrowing. "But you go if she invites you."

"Yes," he said. "Dad and I agreed that if she reaches out, I should go."

"Even if you don't like it?"

"It's not that I don't like it," Hunter said. "It's just... whatever. She buys me a bunch of stuff and lets me eat out all the time and we go to the beach. It's not terrible. It's just...." He shrugged and rolled the ball up the ramp to the holes.

"It's what, Hunter?" Elise asked. "You can tell me. I'm just trying to get an idea of what that relationship is like."

He picked up another ball and rolled it too, this one going in the very middle hole for the highest points. With another ball in his hands, he looked at her. "It's just nothing," he said. "Like, I love my mom, because she's my mom, but there's nothing...I don't know. Dad says it better than me."

"What does he say?"

"He says it's okay to go to make her happy, as long as *I'm* not *un*happy. And I'm not, so I go."

"That makes sense."

"He says it's okay to love her because she's my mom, and I do. But he says it's okay if we're not really friends or don't really have that great of a relationship."

Elise nodded, wanting more than that with this beautiful, kind boy. She didn't understand his mother at all. "Do you think we're friends?"

"Yeah," he said, not looking at her as he rolled another ball. "I like doing stuff with you, Elise." He ran out of balls and looked at her. "You're fun, and you're nice."

Fun. Nice. Elise warmed at the adjectives, simple as they were. "Thanks, Hunt. I think you're fun and nice too."

He smiled at her. "Do you want to play?"

"No," she said. "You can go again."

Hunter's face started to turn red, and he didn't move to put more quarters in the game.

"What is it?" she asked.

"Nothing," he said, turning away.

"You can tell me."

He shook his head. "It's embarrassing."

"Why's that?"

"Hey," Gray said, and Elise turned around. "Skeeball. Nice. Hunt is really good at this."

"Yeah," Elise said, taking Gray's hand. "He's good at everything."

"Everything? What else have you guys done?"

"The batting cages," Hunter said, rolling the ball up the ramp. "Elise did great."

"She did?" Gray looked down at her.

"You don't have to sound so surprised." She nudged him with her shoulder, which caused him to chuckle. "I do plenty of physical work, just not with a baseball bat."

"I wish I could've seen that." He grinned at her.

"I got a video," Hunter said, turning from the skeeball ramp. He handed Gray his phone and looked at Elise again. She smiled at him and reached to put her arm around him.

He stepped over to her, a smile on his face too.

"You're a good boy, Hunter," she said, leaning toward him as she heard the video start on his phone.

"Oh, wow," Gray said, his face radiating life and happiness. He handed the phone back to Hunter. "You've got quite the swing, Elise."

"Please, I dropped the bat the first time."

"I mean it," he said. "It looked good."

"Okay," she said. "Let's go get a table. I'm starving."

"I'm gonna finish my game," Hunter said.

"I'll stay with you," Gray said.

Elise left the two of them standing there, but she clearly heard Hunter said, "Dad, she hugged me." Her heart zinged around inside her chest, and she pretended to drop something so she could listen a little longer.

"Oh?"

"She's—I liked it," Hunter said.

"I don't hug you enough," Gray said.

Elise straightened and turned around to see the man hugging his son. Everything aligned for Elise in that moment, and she was so glad she'd hugged Hunter earlier. Gray met her eyes over the top of Hunter's head, and he mouthed the words *Thank you*.

They looked dangerously like *I love you*, but Elise knew he wouldn't tell her that in an arcade, without any sound to his voice. She tucked her hair, a smile moving through her soul, and went to get them a table.

———

A WEEK LATER, ELISE HELD ONE OF GRAY'S HANDS AND ONE OF Hunter's as they steadied her so she could step from dry land into the boat. "Whoa," she said, her body rocking right when it should've stayed still.

"Just step right there," Hunter said. "By the cooler."

She did as he said, and everything evened out. She really didn't like how the ground wasn't solid, but she'd made it into the boat. She flashed a smile at Gray and then his son, the heat of embarrassment filling her face. "I haven't been on a boat in a while."

"It's like a lawn mower," Gray said, his smile so wonderful and warm.

Elise tipped her head back and laughed. "It is nothing

like a lawn mower." She shook her head and gathered her hair into a ponytail. She wore it up so often, she could tell how it looked just by feel, and she secured it with a white elastic before accepting the fishing pole from Hunter.

"I can't say I've been fishing before," she said.

"Ever?" Hunter asked, plenty of incredulity in his voice.

"I suppose I did when I was younger," she said. "I did grow up on an island. I just don't remember it. We'd catch crabs and lobsters, but fishing wasn't something you did from the shore." She held the pole in her hands like she didn't know what to do with it. Because she didn't.

"Help her out, son," Gray said, and Hunter moved from his bench to hers.

"Oh, okay," she said, throwing her arms out to steady herself, but there was nothing to grab onto but the twelve-year-old.

He grinned at her and reached up to adjust his cowboy hat. "It's not that bad, Elise."

"It's *awful*," she said, nudging him with her shoulder. "Now, what do I do?"

"We've got to bait the hook," he said, his voice smooth and even. Elise looked at Gray, who watched his son with a measure of admiration as he rowed them out into the lake. They'd learned that the fish at Prospect Lake liked live bait, and they'd started taking their flies to the rivers and streams in the foothills between Coral Canyon and Dog Valley.

Elise hadn't wanted to get suited up in waders, so they'd brought her to Prospect Lake for her inaugural fishing trip.

Gray's powerful arms stroked, and the boat glided smoothly over the still water. Elise was used to getting up early in the summer, and though it was Sunday—and her one day to sleep in—she didn't mind at all.

In fact, there was nowhere she'd rather be than right here, with these two.

Hunter bent and opened the cooler, and Elise looked away from Gray. "Oh, you have got to be kidding me." She actually jerked away from the worms in the cooler. "I thought you had breakfast in that thing."

She looked at Hunter, her eyes wide. He looked back at her and blinked once before he started laughing.

"Oh, you stop it," she said, though she wasn't upset.

He quieted and shook his head. "When you saw that mess of snakes by that shed this week," he said. "That was a reason to freak out. These are just worms." He reached into the cooler and grabbed one, no hesitation at all. "You thread it right on the hook like this, Elise."

He got the job done in a swift movement. "And you toss it in." He threw the line out, the reel clicking as it went, and handed her the pole. "Done."

She had no idea how to do that, but she figured if she had him to help her, she could just sit here and hold the pole. "So now I just hold it?"

"Yep, you hold onto it," Gray said.

"Or put it in the rings there," Hunter said, nodding to the set of three silver rings mounted to the inside of the boat. "When a fish pulls on it, it goes unless you prevent it."

He moved back to his bench, wobbling the boat around. Elise sucked in a breath, but she managed not to "freak out." She held onto her pole, and Gray stopped rowing. He and

Hunter cast their lines out, and both of them sighed in near unison.

She looked at Gray, then behind her to Hunter. "Now what?"

"Now we relax," Gray said with a smile.

"This is it?"

"This is it, sweetheart," he said with a chuckle. "Sometimes Hunt and I have real good conversations while fishing."

"What should we talk about?" Elise asked, glancing back at Hunter again.

He shrugged, his eyes out over the water. Silence draped over them, and some of Elise's tension ebbed away. She could see what they meant by finding solace and peace out on the water. She closed her eyes and breathed in through her nose, rooting herself right in the center of her soul.

She felt powerfully the love of the Lord, and she sighed too.

"Dad says you're going to move to Denver," Hunter said, startling the silence away.

Elise's eyes flew open, and she met Gray's. He wore an unreadable mask.

"Yes," Elise said, turning to look at Hunter again. She didn't know what to ask him. Was he upset about that? They'd been getting along so great. Did she need to reassure him of anything? And if so, what?

"Go on," Gray said. "Ask her."

Elise nearly got whiplash she looked at him and then immediately back to Hunter. He cleared his throat. "I was wondering if you'd come pick me up from school sometimes." He looked up, right into her eyes, and something amazing and bonding flowed between them. "If you can. I mean, Dad says you don't really know what job you'll have or anything."

"Of course," she said. "Of course I will, Hunter."

"I have friends in that neighborhood," he said. "And Dad says—"

"If you say that one more time," Gray warned. Elise looked at him, and he wore lightning in his eyes. "Tell her what *you* think."

Hunter glared at his father, a bit of teenager attitude in his eyes. They softened quickly, though, and he ducked his head again. "I think it would be nice to do stuff with you."

"Stuff," Elise echoed.

"Yeah," Hunter said. "Like, I don't know. Mother and son stuff." By the time he finished talking, the words came out in a mumble. It took Elise a moment to understand them, and then she handed her fishing pole to Gray.

She stood up, though her heart was pounding very fast. "Oh—whoa." She managed to step over the bench in the middle of the boat, and she sat next to Hunter. He'd put his pole in the rings, and he looked at her.

"I would love that so much," she whispered, linking her arm through his. She moved her arm around his shoulders, and he turned into her, hugging her tight. She closed her eyes so she wouldn't let the burning tears out as she held this beautiful boy.

She loved him so much, and she silently thanked the Lord for opening the doors of her heart to him—and for opening his to her.

CHAPTER 25

Cy rumbled into Coral Canyon, the sun shining overhead. He'd gotten a bit of a late start, but it didn't matter. He'd broken the eight-hour drive from Ivory Peaks into two days, but he was still ready to get off the motorcycle.

They were great for cruising around neighborhoods, or even going up into the mountains on paved paths. But his was not a touring bike, and after a couple of hours, the vibrations wore him right to the bone.

Still, it was mid-July, and that screamed for a drive across two states under the open sky. The wind in his hair, and his forearms taking the brunt of the sun.

At the moment, the sun moved behind a cloud, and Cy looked up into the sky. Gray clouds foamed in the distance, and Cy was struck by the beauty of the mountains. It had been a long time since he'd seen the magnificence of them.

Yes, he'd just come from Ivory Peaks, where he'd been living for the past two weeks. But there was something different about the Grand Tetons. They seemed to rise up much faster and much steeper than the Rockies. He could still see snow on the tops of a few of the highest peaks, and that was unfathomable to Cy.

His soul filled with wonder and awe, and Cy smiled to himself. "So this is it, huh? You want me here, Lord?"

Cy felt a very strong call to Coral Canyon, and a sigh moved through his body. Wyoming wasn't anything like California, and he wondered if he could get McCall and Wade to make the move. Even if he paid for it, they might not. After all, the mountains weren't anything like the beach.

He pulled into a gas station and filled the tank of his motorcycle. He adjusted his bandana, which kept his hair out of his eyes and watched a mother lean into her minivan and say something to her children that had a lot of bite to it.

She reminded him so much of his mother, and how she used to tell him and his brothers the rules for going grocery shopping with her. "You will not ask for everything you see. You get one thing. *One* thing. It has to cost a dollar or less. If you ask for even two things, I will put the one thing back and you get nothing."

Cy chuckled to himself. He'd only made that mistake once, and he'd cried for days over his lost box of Lemonheads.

Today, he went into the convenience store and bought some Lemonheads, a pack of gum, and a Monster energy drink. He'd need the sugar and the caffeine, because he was meeting three people that afternoon for commercial land showings.

He wasn't even sure what that entailed, but he was ready to take the first step toward getting his shop open again.

Taylor Terry was way too over-eager, but Cy shook his hand and let him walk him around a plot of land that sat across the street from an elementary school. Cy could already hear the calls of complaints from teachers and parents alike.

No, he didn't want to be right downtown, and he didn't want his motorcycle shop to be in a residential neighborhood. A strip mall wasn't a good location, and neither was the huge plot of land the city had just released near the hospital.

"I just don't see anything that's going to work for me," Cy said. He shook Taylor's hand, thanked him for trying, and sat on his bike, his phone in his hand.

"Gotta give me a gentle push," he muttered to the Lord. "None of those pieces of land were even close to working for a motorcycle shop."

He found the address for the office of the next agent, and he drove the few blocks to it. Clint Bailey didn't seem like he knew much about the land in Coral Canyon, because he asked Cy three times what they were going to look at. He did manage to take him to a large plot of land on the Eastern outskirts of town with a huge commercial real estate sign just behind the fence.

"Great water rights here," Clint said.

"Water rights?"

"You're the fellow doing the horseback lessons, right?"

"No," Cy said, his mood darkening. The sky did too, and he looked up to find the clouds he'd seen hovering over the mountains in the distance had arrived in the valley.

"What are you looking for again?"

Cy glared at Clint. "I need three acres to build a motor-cycle shop."

"A motorcycle shop?"

Cy didn't know how to say it any other way, so he just nodded.

"Well, you can't do that out here. Mrs. Fletcher lives right over there, and she calls the police when the wind blows too hard and wakes her up in the night."

Cy definitely didn't need to deal with Mrs. Fletcher. "I think we're done here," he said.

"Let me call Duane."

"You do that." Cy leaned against the fence and looked out at the fields. Had he been doing a facility for horseback riding lessons, this would be the perfect land for it.

"Yep," Clint said. "Uh huh. All right." He hung up and said, "We've got something out north."

"Let's see it," Cy said.

Clint drove them to the new piece of land, and Cy gazed around at it. It actually wasn't bad. It was big enough for the two-story building he needed, with plenty of room for a parking lot. "What's out here?" he asked.

"What you see."

"No neighbors who get upset if the wind blows?"

Clint chuckled and shook his head. "Nothing like that."

"What's the catch then?"

"No catch," Clint said, but there was something false in his voice.

If there was something Cy loathed more than green peas, it was a liar. "What is it?" he pressed. He hadn't taken his two billion dollars and opened the country's biggest and best custom motorcycle shop by being a pushover.

"Some say this is a Native American burial ground," Clint finally said.

"So if I buy it and start building and come across graves or bones…." Cy turned away from the land. "It's over."

"Could be," Clint said.

"What else have you got?" He checked his phone for the time. Hopefully, Clint was done, because he was supposed to meet Betty at her family orchards. Apparently, they were selling a lot of the land as her father had gotten quite ill and couldn't keep up with the enormity of the orchards he had.

"Nothing," Clint said.

"Let's go back," Cy said. He'd thanked Clint for his time and looked up Betty's address before the first drops of rain fell.

His mood only worsened as he drove through the rain to the orchards. They sat on the northwest side of town, a mountain rising to his left and a road leading north to his right. He'd pulled over next to a building the size and shape of a single-story barn, but it was boarded up and closed down. It didn't bear a name on it, and he wondered if he was in the right place.

A hundred feet down the road, a sign said *Dog Valley, 12,*

and he stayed put. Betty had said it was on the highway leading toward Dog Valley.

The rain wasn't cold, but the wind sure didn't heat things up. Cy sat on his bike, waiting in the rain for five minutes.

Then ten.

Annoyance filled him, and he looked at his black leather pants. Ruined.

He'd just lifted his phone to call Betty when a giant SUV came skidding into the parking lot.

Cy yelped and jumped from his bike, because he wasn't keen to get smashed between the grill of a Hummer and a fruit stand that had seen better days.

He landed on his hands and knees, and the pain fueled his anger. The mud on his clothes and fingers downright spiraled it.

"What in the devil are you doing?" he demanded. He got to his feet and tried to wipe off as much mud as he could. It seemed to be made of super-sticky dirt, because it just smeared everywhere.

He marched toward the SUV, which had come to a stop less than a foot from his motorcycle. "Hey," he called to the person getting out on the driver's side of the enormous, boxy vehicle.

They must've been fairly short, because he couldn't see them over the hood. He couldn't fit around the front of the SUV, so he went toward the back, saying, "Hey, what kind of driving was that?"

A woman came around the back of the SUV, and she wore sourness on her face like she sucked on lemons for a living. "Stop yelling at me," she barked. "I can hear you."

"Can you?" he tossed right back at her. "You dang near hit me with this thing." He tapped the taillight.

Her gaze flew to it, and her eyes narrowed as she looked back at him. They glared at one another, a silent battle which Cy would not lose. He would not look away from her first.

She had very short, golden blonde hair that had been cut into a stylish pixie cut. It wasn't really his style, but he could appreciate that it fit her face. She wore a pair of jeans with a black pair of boots that had never seen snow or muck, and a pale yellow sweatshirt that seemed to be fitted as it flowed right along the curves of her body.

She deflated after several long moments, and she said, "I'm sorry. It's my brother's truck, and I don't really know how to drive it. And Betty threw this in my lap last-minute, which isn't your fault but doesn't make anything any easier for me." Her bright blue eyes glinted with anger, and Cy kind of liked it.

She was also sort of familiar to him, though he couldn't place where he would've possibly met her.

"So...you're not Betty?"

"No," she said. "Sorry, I'm Patsy Foxhill. Welcome to Foxhill Farms." She stuck out her hand for him to shake, and Cy put his in hers, her name tickling a memory he couldn't quite grasp.

He wasn't prepared for the shockwave of heat to move from her hand into his. She sucked in a breath as if she'd felt it too, and their eyes met.

Cy swore he fell in love that very moment, because he hadn't felt any attraction this powerful since meeting Mikaela, months ago.

"Who *are* you?" Patsy asked, her voice somewhat hushed.

"Cy Hammond, ma'am," he said. "And I swear I know you. Have we met?" He cocked his head and waited for her to answer, but all she did was stare at him with those big, beautiful, blue eyes.

CHAPTER 26

Patsy's ears rang with the words *Cy Hammond.*
Hammond.

Hammond.

Everything around Whiskey Mountain Lodge had changed the day the storm blew in Colton Hammond, eighteen months ago.

Yes, she knew who Cy was. One of the twins who wore weird pants to a wedding. Patsy had sized up this man as he'd done the same to her, and he was wearing those same leather pants right now. They actually fit with the leather jacket and the bandana on his head. They had not fit with the suits and dresses at a wedding.

He has nice shoulders, she thought, immediately horrified at the thought. This was Colton's brother. Wes's brother. Gray's brother.

Patsy was not going to be charmed with a pair of dark, deep, midnight-colored eyes....

She shook herself and looked away from Cy. She'd met him before and felt no sizzle. Her hand was still in his, though, and there was a downright scalding happening where her skin touched his.

"We've met," she finally said. "You're Colton's brother. I was at his wedding."

Cy pulled his hand away, a smile taking over his face. And wow, what a smile....

Stop it, she told herself.

He snapped and said, "That's right." He looked up to her hair and down to her feet again. "Your hair is different."

She automatically reached to touch the ultra-short hair on the back of her neck. "Yeah," she said. "I changed it."

"I like it," he said, but she couldn't tell if he was being serious or not. That was another thing she remember about Cy and...his twin. They didn't seem to take a whole lot seriously.

"So what are you doing here?" she asked.

"I'm looking for land," he said. "I'd like to build my custom motorcycle shop here."

"In Coral Canyon?"

"Yes." He cooled considerably, and Patsy told herself she didn't care. They needed to sell at least half of the orchards. Number one, her father couldn't keep up with them anymore now that he'd been diagnosed with cancer.

Number two, they needed the money to pay off the debts he'd accumulated throughout the years. Since her mother had shocked everyone when she'd filed for divorce one day and left Coral Canyon the next, her father had been doing a lot of therapy shopping, usually from a television station late at night or early in the morning.

He had boxes from the Home Shopping Network he hadn't even opened.

Patsy told herself to get over to her dad's and find everything she could, send it back, and finish her day at the post office. That would put some money back in his pocket too.

But Patsy wouldn't be ending her day at the post office. She had a ton of work to finish at the lodge, and she'd likely be there until the late hours of the night getting everything ready for the payroll the following week.

Not only that, but Sophia would be gone all of next week, and Patsy had a fill-in chef coming to the lodge. That stressed her out, because she didn't know how things would go. Her usual fill-in chef hadn't been available, and Patsy had been on the phone for a couple of hours to find someone else.

The job situation in Coral Canyon meant people could be picky about what they did, and by the time she'd found Tim, she'd been ready to cry. Even now, her chest felt too tight. There simply weren't enough hours in the day to get everything done at the lodge and deal with her family.

"Patsy?" Cy asked, and she blinked her way out of her mental to-do list.

"Yes."

"This looks like an orchard." He gazed out at the apple trees. "I'm not looking to buy an orchard."

Patsy joined him a few feet away at the fence. "It is an orchard. It's my family's orchard." Unhappiness filled her as she looked at the trees. They'd opened up this section of the orchard for anyone to come pick the apples, and the season had just started. Usually, Betty worked in the building to the left, and she assigned people to a couple of trees.

"Keep talking," Cy said. "I feel like I'm losing you every few seconds."

Patsy drew in a deep breath and looked at him. A smile crossed her face, and it shook a little. "I'm sorry." She sighed, trying to find her professionalism. She needed to sell this land, and she knew Cy had enough money to buy it.

"The Foxhill Farm has thirty-three-hundred apple trees across fifty acres," she said, this speech memorized. She'd been giving it for so many years. "We have three varieties for cross-pollination: Snowsweet, Frostbite, and Honey-gold." She paused, the Snowsweet trees in front of her with several apples ready to pick. If someone didn't bring their baskets and bins to get the apples, they'd fall to the ground and rot, just like they'd been doing for the past couple of years.

"They've just come into season," she said. "And my father is getting older, and he's sick, and he can't take care of the orchards anymore. My sister does the best she can, but she has four kids. My brother is going through a divorce, and—" She stopped talking, because Cy didn't need a Foxhill family history lesson. She actually wished she'd given the history instead of airing their dirty laundry.

She was really losing her touch, and she told herself it was because of stress, not because Cy was as handsome as all of his brothers, even with the long hair. Besides, Patsy liked a little longer hair on a man.

No, you don't, she told herself, shaking off the last couple of hours. "It doesn't matter," she said. "Bottom line, we need to sell part of the orchard, because we can't take care of it."

"And you're going to lose all the trees?"

Sadness blipped through her, because she'd worked hard in the orchard growing up. It took years—up to a decade—for a tree to produce fruit, and she couldn't stand the thought of having someone cut them all down to build a warehouse.

"Well," she said. "We're hoping that whoever we sell the land to will keep as many as they can."

"How can they do that, unless they're just going to take over the orchard?"

"How many acres do you need?" she asked.

"Ideally, four. But I can use three."

"Three acres?"

"Four, if possible."

"This half of the orchard is twenty," she said. "The back third are trees that are less than eight years old, and most of them aren't even producing fruit yet." A new hope filled her, and she looked at Cy. "Do you want me to show you?"

He met her eyes too. "Yes," he said. "Yes, I do."

She took her keys out of her pocket and said, "Let's go."

"You're driving?"

She eyed his motorcycle. "Yes, I'm driving." She headed for the Hummer, and to his credit Cy got in the passenger seat. "I was just in a hurry to get here," she explained as she backed up and started down the road to Dog Valley. "And Joe is a huge pig, and there was a water bottle that came forward when I braked, and it was just a moment of wondering if I'd be able to stop."

"Felt like a lifetime," he said, glancing around. "But I can see what you mean about this thing being a mess."

"Sorry," she said, but it wasn't her SUV she needed to apologize for. She made a turn onto an unmarked road and started bumping down the dirt path. "It's about a mile and a half back."

"Easy enough on a paved road," he said. "But it will be quiet back here, I suppose."

"Yes," Patsy said. "Behind our orchards is a stream that runs into Prospect Lake, and those are the nearest neighbors."

"How far?"

"Oh, probably four or five miles." She glanced at him. "And there's nobody going north until the outskirts of Dog Valley."

"Hm," Cy said, but she knew he was thinking something.

"So, are you relocating here because of your brothers?"

"Gray mentioned this place was growing, yes," Cy said. "And I, uh, lost my building in California."

"You lost it?"

"It was sold to someone else," he said. "And they didn't want to extend my lease."

"What do you do?" she asked.

"I build custom motorcycles," he said.

Patsy dang near drove the SUV into an apple tree. She jerked the wheel back, and Cy said, "Whoa. Hey," and reached for the handle above the door.

She straightened the vehicle out, now at war with herself.

"You don't want my shop here," he said.

"It's not that," she said carefully.

"That's *exactly* what it is," Cy said, his voice as cold as a Wyoming winter day, and Patsy had experienced some that had literally frozen the breath in her lungs. Maybe not literally, but it got mighty cold in Wyoming in the winter.

Patsy clenched the wheel in her fingers. Her jaw tightened too.

"There's no point in showing me the land if you're not going to sell it to me," Cy said.

She kept driving, because they really did need to sell the orchard. Who cared what Cy did with the land?

"I'm fine with motorcycles," she said, though she'd never ridden one.

"Is that right?" he asked, plenty of sarcasm in his voice. "Have you even ridden one?"

"I've ridden plenty of horses," she shot back. "How different can it be?"

Cy burst out laughing, but Patsy wasn't sure it only contained happiness. He was definitely mocking her too. "Sweetheart, a horse and a motorcycle are two completely different things."

She bristled at the word *sweetheart*. "How would you know?"

"I grew up on a farm," he said. "In fact, I live on a farm right now. Trust me, they're different. So different, they're not even on the same planet."

"Funny how horses and motorcycles exist on this planet." She threw him a look, but he just shook his head. Thankfully, the trees started to get shorter and shorter, and Patsy slowed down. "Here we are," she said. "These trees haven't produced fruit yet, so they'd be the easiest to take out. There's probably five or six acres back here."

"Can we get out?" he asked.

"Sure." Patsy went a little farther before stopping the Hummer. They got out, and Cy looked around, even going so far as to walk over to an apple tree and knock on the trunk. Patsy stayed by the SUV, and she wasn't sure, but she thought the man was talking to himself.

He came back toward her, and she said, "Well? What do you think?"

"Depends."

"On what?"

Cy looked around again, and she wasn't sure what he saw. She saw trees that hadn't been pruned properly and were thus not growing ideally for apple picking. Troughs that hadn't been hoed right, and mud from the rain. She saw neglect, and she saw what the orchards would become if she didn't do something about it.

The problem was, Patsy was the youngest in her family, and no one had ever listened to her. She'd gone to college for a few years, and she'd returned to Coral Canyon and started working in administrative roles. She was organized, and thoughtful, and she could've been running the orchards with the precision needed to keep them in the family for a long time.

Her father hadn't wanted her to. Joe had resisted. Betty was the oldest, and she'd technically inherited the farm, but her focus was somewhere else entirely.

She's going to lose it all, Patsy thought. While she'd walked away from the orchard a long time ago, it still held a place in her heart. Losing it would leave a blight on her soul she'd never get rid of.

The rain started to fall again, and Patsy moved toward the driver's door. "Let's talk inside," she said.

Cy took a few extra seconds to join her, and when he did, he looked at her with resignation on his face. "Well, I've had a good long argument with the Lord, but He's insisting this is the place for me. So." He blew out his breath as if he were truly unhappy. "How much for the entire thing?"

"The entire thing?"

"Everything on this half," he said. "You said it was half, right?"

"It's twenty acres on this side of the highway," she said, her mind barely able to process what he'd said. "Thirty on the other side, where the house is."

"How much for the twenty acres?"

"You want to buy all twenty acres?" She looked at him, because they weren't moving. She suddenly felt cold on the inside, and it was very unsettling.

"Depends," he said, his dark eyes taking on a glint of impatience. "On how much it is."

Patsy didn't know what to say. In her mind, the land was priceless. "I'd need to talk to my father."

Cy sighed like she was being difficult on purpose, and her irritation with him grew. "Fine," he said. "I'll be in town for a couple of days. Can I give you my number, or should I expect Betty to call me?"

He was a complete answer to her prayers—in more ways than one. Betty would probably be fine taking care of this, but Patsy wanted his number....

"Give it to me," she said. "I'll call you for sure by tomorrow."

Cy smiled at her, and wow, that was downright devastating to her health. "Is this your phone?" He picked up her device from the cup holder, and started tapping. "I'll put my number in."

She swallowed and nodded, telling herself she'd only use it for business. *Just business,* she thought. *Yeah, only business....*

CHAPTER 27

Gray had never had such an enjoyable summer, even if Elise did make him mow lawns and weed flowerbeds almost every day. Even if he'd chased Hutch through the park once to get the labradoodle to come back. He was a good dog, but spirited, and Elise loved him with her whole soul, which meant Gray did too.

He'd just put a white shirt and tie in his suitcase when someone called his name from the front of the house he and Hunter had been living in.

Their time in Coral Canyon was up. They were flying to Las Vegas in the morning, and then back to Denver. School started on Tuesday. Hunter would be in junior high, and Gray would be running and working the farm, and Elise was coming back here for a week to pack everything before she and Hutch made the move as well.

Just thinking about it had Gray's throat stuffed with cotton.

Elise called his name again, much closer this time, and he turned from the suitcase just as she appeared in the doorway, a radiant grin on her face. "Guess what?" She giggled immediately afterward, and Gray thought she was the most amazing and most beautiful person he'd ever had the pleasure of knowing.

He couldn't keep the smile off his face either. "What?" He moved toward her as she danced toward him.

"We won Yard of the Month." She laughed as he took her into his arms, her hands moving right around to the back of his neck.

"Yard of the Month?" he asked, gazing down at her.

She was full of light and life, laughter and love, and Gray wanted her in his life for a long, long time. Hunter loved Elise, he knew that. He'd spent plenty of time with his son in the lakes and rivers around Coral Canyon, and Gray hadn't realized how starved for a mother his son was. He knew he couldn't be both mother and father, and yet he'd thought he was doing a good enough job.

Elise had proven him wrong. They both needed her in their lives, and his heart started pounding. He still hadn't bought a ring, because he hadn't been sure.

Was he sure now?

"Yes," she said, bringing him back to the present. "Colton's yard won Yard of the Month for August. The city gives an award, and some prize money, and he gets to display a banner in his front lawn."

"Oh, wow," Gray chuckled. "That's gonna go straight to his head."

She laughed again and shook her head. "He said he'd

give me the money. And it really helped convince him that he had to take Hutch for the next week."

"Good for him," Gray said. "He should give you that money and take care of your dog. That man doesn't know a hedge from a rose bush."

Elise giggled and stepped out of his arms, backing toward the door. "You're packing?"

"We leave in the morning," he said. "Aren't you packed?"

"Not yet," she said. "I haven't been home yet today."

"Want me to bring dinner up? Hunter would love to visit the horses for a bit." That was code for, *my son will leave us alone so I can kiss you.*

They'd taken dinner up to Elise's cabin several times in the past two months, and Hunter really did like the horses at Whiskey Mountain Lodge. He loved Hutch too, and the dog followed Hunter around like he'd finally found his master.

"Yes," she said. "Bring dinner up to the cabin." She smiled at him and took a step out into the hall. Gray followed her into the kitchen, which felt less intimate than his bedroom. She opened his fridge and took out a bottle of water, and Gray just watched her open it and drink almost the whole thing.

She wore a pair of cutoff shorts and a gray T-shirt that had seen a lot of mud in its time. Tennis shoes and work gloves and her hair in a ponytail often completed her gardening look, and Gray sure did like it.

"Listen, Elise," he said, clearing his throat. "I was just wondering how you feel about...well, I'm wondering what your thoughts are about marriage."

She lowered the bottle slowly, her eyes locked on his.

"Dad," Hunter said, bursting into the house from the backyard. He held up his phone in triumph. "Guess what just happened?"

"What, bud?" Gray tore his gaze from Elise and looked at his son.

"Molly just texted to tell me there's a back-to-school dance the first Friday." He shoved the phone into Gray's hands. "Read it."

Gray was aware of Elise coming to stand next to him, the scent of sweat and earth coming with her. He swiped on Hunter's phone and looked at the text from Molly. She had told him about the dance.

"Oh, my," Elise said, but that wasn't what Gray was thinking.

He looked up from the text—*do you want to go together? Maybe we can dance to a couple of songs*—and into his son's hopeful eyes.

"Can I go?" Hunter asked. "It's three dollars, Dad, but I have tons of money from working on the farm last summer, and tons from all the yard work this summer too." He shot a glance at Elise before focusing on Gray again. "Please?"

Gray handed the phone back to him. "Do you know how to dance with a girl?"

Hunter dropped his phone, his expression turning to horror now. "No."

"Oh, don't look like that," Elise said, stepping between Gray and Hunter. "I'll show you." She took his hands in hers. "So you're twelve, so you don't need to be all handsy, okay? And you're not a monster, so we're not doing the Frankenstein dancing."

She put his left hand on her waist. "This hand goes here."

Hunter turned white and dropped his hand. She giggled, and said, "Hunt, if you can't dance with me, you can't dance with Molly."

He cleared his throat and put his hand back on her waist. Gray leaned against the counter, grinning at both of them. If he didn't keep the smile in place, he'd drop to both knees and propose to Elise right then and there.

She was so good to Hunter, and so amazing with him, and as he watched her teach him how to dance, Gray was pretty sure he fell all the way in love with her.

"Now," Elise said, turning toward him. "It looks like this." She reached for him, and he had no problem putting his hand on her waist and securing the other one in hers. They stepped and moved around the dining room while Hunter watched.

"See how he's not too far away? You were too far away." Elise swayed with Gray as she beamed up into his face. "But he's not too close either. We can look at each other and have a real conversation. It's not weird. It's what people do."

Gray would like to bring her closer, and have her rest her head against his chest, but he didn't want Hunter doing that with Molly. So he kept the respectable distance as she finished the demo. "And that's it," she said, smiling at him. "You can dance with me at my mom's wedding, if you want to practice."

"Okay," Hunter said as his phone chimed again.

"You better answer her," Gray said. "You don't want to leave her on read."

"Yeah." Hunter bustled out of the kitchen, and both Elise and Gray watched him go.

Then Gray growled in the back of his throat and drew Elise to his chest the way he'd wanted to. "I'd rather dance much closer to you," he whispered.

She laid her head against his chest like he'd imagined, and they did sway back and forth slowly together. She never did answer his question about her thoughts on marriage—at least not verbally.

———

"How do I look?" Gray asked Hunter as he adjusted his tie. The boy faced him, and Gray reached for his tie too. "Yours isn't right, bud." He smoothed it under the collar on the right, and said, "There."

"You look great, Dad."

"Good enough for Elise's mother's wedding?" Gray was nervous for some reason. Elise had spent the quick flight telling him and Hunt about her mother, and the words Gray had heard more than any others were "free spirit" and "the nicest person you'll ever meet."

They'd gone to dinner with her and her fiancé, Henry, the night before, and everything Elise had told him about her mother had been true. But he was still nervous for this wedding for some reason.

"I guess?" Hunter said, making it sound like a question. "I don't know, Dad. You look great."

Gray drew him into a hug, because he'd realized that he didn't hug his son enough. Hunter hugged him back, and when they separated, he looked up at Gray. "Dad, are you going to marry Elise?"

Gray pulled in a breath as he searched his son's face. "What do you think about it? Would you like that?"

Hunter took a few seconds, and then he nodded. "I— she's the best, Dad. I really like her."

"She loves you, you know," Gray said.

"She does?" Hunter lifted his eyebrows. "How do you know?"

"I can see it on her face when she looks at you."

"I think she looks at you like that too, Dad."

"Does she?"

Hunter shrugged. "I don't know."

Gray didn't have to ask if Hunter loved her. He knew he did. Hunter talked about Elise often, and he wanted to spend time with her. He wanted her to pick him up from school, and he wanted to show her around the farm, and Ivory Peaks, and the suburb where they lived closer to the city. He couldn't wait for her to meet Molly, and Gray could admit that that one stung a little. After all, he'd been told not to even talk to the girl, because he'd say something embarrassing. But Elise?

Oh, Hunter couldn't *wait* to introduce Molly to Elise.

He smiled at the thought, because while he'd been hurt for five minutes, he was also thrilled that Hunter had another opportunity to have a mother. A real mother this time, one who wouldn't abandon him when things got too hard. One who loved him for who he was, not how it made her look.

Elise knocked as she opened the door. "They're getting lined up." She reached for him, and Gray went toward her, slipping his fingers into hers. "Come on, Hunt," she added. "You're right by me too."

She wasn't walking in the wedding party. In fact, there was very little pomp and circumstance to this wedding. They met Elise's mother at the end of the hall, and she drew her daughter into a hug. "I'm so glad you're here."

"Me too, Mom."

Petra looked at Gray next, and she gave him a hug too. "I'm so glad you came with her."

"So am I," he said. "Congratulations, Petra."

"And you, Hunter," she said, gazing at him too. Hunter really did have some sort of magic about him that everyone loved. Sheila had been the same way, so Gray shouldn't be so surprised.

"All right, Mom," Elise said. "We'll see you in there." She led them into the hall where the wedding would take place, and Gray was just glad it wasn't an outdoor wedding. The heat here in Vegas was strong enough to kill someone if they stayed out in it for too long. At least Gray thought so.

Elise sat on the very front row, and Gray took the seat next to her. Hunter filed in too, and they'd only been sitting for maybe a minute before the soft, classical music that had been playing turned to a drumbeat, which was quickly followed by some keyboard music from the eighties.

"Let's get married," came through the speakers, and the preacher said, "Everyone please stand for the bride and groom."

Gray got to his feet, somewhat surprised to see Petra and Henry dancing down the aisle. Dancing. People laughed and started clapping along with the music as the chorus came on again.

"Let's get married."

Once Petra and Henry reached the front of the crowd, they moved into a clearly choreographed routine, complete with facial expressions and a dip-and-kiss that was impressive for a woman Petra's age.

Gray's back hurt just looking at her.

The song faded to silence, and they raised their joined hands as if the ceremony had already happened.

Everyone clapped, and a few people whistled and whooped. Gray looked at Elise, who watched her mother with that same love he'd seen on her face when she looked at his son.

"Please be seated," the preacher said, and Gray took Elise's hand as they settled back into their chairs.

"I don't want to dance down the aisle when we get married," he whispered.

Elise gasped and jerked her attention to him. "*When* we get married?"

Gray realized what he'd just given away, and he shook his head as the preacher started talking. "Shh," he whispered. "This is your mother's big day."

Beside him, Elise leaned into him and squeezed his hand, and Gray figured he better get a diamond ring and get down on his knees pretty dang soon.

CHAPTER 28

E lise soon learned that Colorado was quite similar to Wyoming. At least the little suburban area where she now lived. People got up and went to work each day. They dropped their kids off at school. They walked their dogs. They worried about their seventh graders going to junior high dances with girls.

The weather was probably a bit milder for this time of year, though the third week of September sure hadn't brought any snowstorms yet. She'd settled into Gray's house, which was about a half-hour drive from the farm in Ivory Peaks where he and Hunter lived.

It was less than five miles from Ames's house, and as she pulled on her running shoes, a sigh of exhaustion stole through her.

She'd been in town for two days before she'd called him to ask a favor. He'd been over to the house in less than ten minutes, dressed and ready to begin her training.

She hadn't even changed out of her pajamas yet. Ames was a cruel taskmaster, that was for sure, but he had started her off easy.

They walked for the first few days. Then he'd given her the task of running a half a mile during their walk. Elise had thought she might die, and she honestly had no idea how anyone could go farther than that.

After a few days, he increased it. And kept her there for a bit.

Today, he'd texted to say she was running a full mile.

"Don't let me die today," she prayed as she went out onto the front porch and started stretching. That was a very important piece, Ames said.

Hutch joined her, and she plucked his leash from the hook on the back of the pillar. "You're going to run a mile today," she told him. "I know you used to run with Gray, and he worked you to death, but it's been a while."

She didn't dream she could ever keep up with Gray—in anything—but she wanted to be able to share something he absolutely loved with him. And that was running.

Ames came huffing and puffing up to her house, calling, "You ready for this?" He had his German shepherd with him too, and Hutch perked right up as he usually did when they got to see Ames and Georgia.

Elise lifted her head and adjusted her visor. "So ready." She tugged on Hutch's leash and started toward Ames in an easy jog, and then slowed to a walk. He always let her walk in the beginning, and he recovered quickly as they went down the street.

After the first few blocks, he said, "Okay, let's go." He

took Hutch's leash from her and picked up the pace. Elise did too, trying to find this elusive rhythm he talked about. "Stride," he called it.

"There it is," he said, and in the next moment, Elise *felt* it. Her arms and legs simply worked together in sync, and with them, she could breathe in and out without having to think so dang hard about it.

"Wow," she said. "I'm running."

"And at a good stride, too." Ames gave her a grin, but smiling was asking way too much of Elise in this moment.

After what felt like a long time, she asked, "How much further?"

He barely seemed winded, but Elise literally felt like she might collapse at any moment. She was a hard worker, but there was a difference between planting a rose bush or pruning a tree and running.

"Just a bit," Ames said. "We're almost there."

"How close is almost?" She wondered if she could use Hutch as an excuse, but the silver dog just trotted along happily.

"We're at point-nine-five miles," he said. "It's literally less than a block."

A block. Less than a block. She could do that. She had to finish the whole mile.

"All right," he said a few seconds later. "That's it."

She slowed instantly, but she kept walking. The first time she'd run, she'd stopped completely and bent over, sucking at the air. Ames hadn't been happy about that—and neither had her calves.

She walked fast too, feeling a power in her legs she

hadn't felt before. Eventually, she felt human again, and she looked at Ames. "That wasn't so bad."

"No?" He grinned at her. "Then, great. You can run back home too." He picked up his pace, but kept going in the direction of his house. "See you tomorrow, Elise."

"Yeah, bye." She lifted her hand in a wave, though he wasn't looking at her. "Thanks, Ames!" she called after him.

He held up one hand in a thumbs-up and kept going.

Elise did not run any of the way back to her house, and she could practically hear Gray's voice in her head telling her how the breakfast casserole she heated up and ate had just undone all of her hard work on the streets.

But she wasn't trying to lose weight, and she wasn't trying to win a marathon. She just wanted to be able to run with Gray on his easy days. Ames had said even those would be three or four miles, and Elise had a long way to go before she could do that.

She showered and dressed, and opened the back door for Hutch. "Be good, buddy," she said, and he lifted his head from the couch.

Lucky thing got to sleep all day on the couch. She smiled at him, and she'd just opened the door to go into the garage when the door started to lift. She paused, her heart pounding as if she'd just run another mile. She hadn't pressed the button to open the door.

She'd been afraid to sleep in her cabin alone at night in Coral Canyon, and that fear came roaring back.

As the door lifted, it revealed a truck she knew well. "Gray?" she asked, going down the steps and toward the vehicle.

He'd just gotten out and he paused as he looked at her. "I got in." A smile overtook his whole face, and he started to laugh. "I just got the email, and I tried to call, but you didn't answer, so I just came over."

"Got in?" Confusion ran through her. "Oh. Oh, my heck. Boston? You got in to Boston?"

He laughed again, rushed toward her, and scooped her up into his arms. "I got in to Boston!"

She squealed as he twirled her around, the joy pounding through her with every beat of her heart unlike any she'd ever experienced before. He set her on her feet, his face radiating that same joy.

"I'm so proud of you," she said, smiling up at him. As she looked at him, Elise felt a very real and a very powerful sense of love.

He bent down and kissed her, and that only solidified everything in Elise's mind. They belonged together. Now she just needed Gray to realize it and do something about it.

––––––––

Wait a second, she typed and sent back to Hunter. *Let's go back for a minute. Your dad's birthday is in three weeks?*

Yeah, Hunter said.

We have to do something.

We do?

Of course. Elise shook her head. She was surprised Gray and Hunter had made it this long without her. *I'll make him a cake. We should have a surprise party or something.*

Dad hates surprises.

She chuckled, because that sounded so much like Gray. He'd taken on some corporate law consulting in the several weeks he'd been back in Ivory Peaks. He ran a lot, and he drove Hunter to school, and he worked around the farm too.

Elise had found a job at a daycare center as a secretary, and she worked until it was time to pick up Hunter from school. They usually spent the afternoon together, and he'd introduced her to several of his friends. Not Molly, though. Not yet.

She'd been teaching him how to cook, and he'd been showing her and Hutch around the city. Some days, she mourned the loss of Two Green Thumbs, which she hadn't wanted to try to start up here so close to winter. Gray had never told her how much the rent for the house would be, and she'd decided to let the topic drop.

So while she didn't have much money, she had enough to pay for her car and her food. And, as it turned out, she needed new running shoes more often too, and Hutch was eating more and more since he went jogging too.

She was up to two miles of running now, though the mornings were starting to get too cold to run. Ames had told her that usually by Halloween, the weather started preventing a lot of outdoor activities.

What do you think we should do? she asked Hunter.

He won't eat the cake either.

"Dang it," she muttered to herself. Hunter was right. Gray and his insane marathon dietary restrictions. *I can make a meatloaf and mashed potato cake and make it look like a birthday cake,* she suggested. *What do you think of that?*

He'd probably like that.

What will you get him? Want to go shopping sometime this week?

Sure, Hunter said. *I usually just get him something stupid like new running socks.*

Elise scoffed right out loud. *That's not happening this year.* She looked up from her phone, the house around her utterly quiet. For how many people lived so close together, that always surprised her. Gray's house did sit in the back of the cul-de-sac, and his backyard took up the entire corner.

Hutch lifted his head too, questions in his expression. She reached over and stroked his side, her mind trying to find the perfect birthday gift for Gray. The dog flopped his big lion head back down to the couch cushion.

She'd made him all the quotes for Valentine's Day, but she'd done that when she had a lot of free time on her hands. She didn't have that luxury now.

I'll be thinking of something, she sent to Hunter. *If you have any ideas for what I can get him, let me know.*

Everything Dad wants costs a lot of money.

"And he probably just buys what he wants." Which was why she'd thought of the running quotes. Maybe she could do something like that again. Even as she thought of it, she dismissed the idea.

I could just ask him for some money, if you want, Hunter said. *See what he says, and maybe he'll give it to you.*

It's worth a shot, she agreed. *Now you better go get your chores done, so your dad doesn't ask what took you so long again tonight.* She added a smiley face to the text and sent it.

Hunter didn't respond, which also reeked of Gray. When

the conversation was over, it was simply over. No need to send a thumbs-up or an *okay* or anything.

Elise stayed on the couch and closed her eyes. What could she get Gray for his birthday? What could she afford?

She got up and went to the drawer in the kitchen where she'd put her sketchbook. If she just let her mind wander, maybe she'd come up with something amazing. The dress she was working on was pretty amazing, she knew that, and she picked up her pencil to continue what she'd started.

CHAPTER 29

Gray swept the last of the dirt and dust from the kitchen out the back door and onto the patio. "That's it, Mom." He looked at her and Dad sitting under the canopy, holding hands. "It's all cleaned up. All finished."

"Thank you, Gray." She smiled up at him. "You're such a good boy."

Gray smiled back, using the last of his energy to do so. Now that he was back on the farm, he was working more than ever. He'd been telling himself for a week that as soon as the remodel on the granny house was finished and his parents were moved in, his load would lighten.

Then he'd think of the marathon in just seven short months, and he'd recheck his training schedule. He drove thirty minutes one way to get Hunter to the junior high he wanted to attend. He worked around the farm, cleaning up things that had long been neglected in addition to the usual animal feeding, building repair, and equipment maintenance.

The guy he'd hired over the summer had started a lot of it, and Gray was glad he was coming in after the work had begun. Matt Whettstein was a good cowboy, and he'd said Gray could call on him again.

Gray had been back on the farm for six weeks now, and his birthday was coming up in two more. He'd been meaning to tell Elise, but something else always came up. Tonight, it was Gray's sheer exhaustion. That, and Hunter still hadn't come in from his evening chores, and Gray was going to have to take the boy's phone again.

He should never have gotten him the blasted thing in the first place. He'd been sitting out in the barn texting when he should've been working.

"I'm gonna head out," he said to his parents. "I'll see you later, okay?"

"Goodnight, Gray," Dad said.

"Love you, son," Mom added, and Gray took the broom to the pantry and propped it against the wall. He left the granny house and began the short walk back to the farmhouse. They were about a hundred yards apart, and because Gray had done his hills that morning, his calves hurt with every step.

"Hunt," he called as he entered the back door.

"Right here, Dad." He looked up from his homework at the dining table, literally a few feet from Gray.

He took in the open math book, Hunter's notes, and his assignment, and his anger faded. He wasn't really angry.

More frustrated. Tired. Fed up with everything, for a reason he couldn't name.

"Did you get the hay moved?"

"Yes, sir."

"Goats fed?"

"Yes, sir."

Gray nodded. "Almost done here?"

"Two more," he said.

"Good boy, Hunter," he said, stepping over to him. He took off his cowboy hat and bent down to kiss the top of his son's head. "I'm going to go shower, and then it'll be time for bed."

"Okay." Hunter went back to his homework, and Gray went down the hall to shower.

He'd been moving furniture, boxes, and belongings for ten straight days. Even on the Sabbath, he hadn't found any rest. If he wasn't clearing out his parents' stuff, he was receiving deliveries of the new things he'd bought for him and Hunter.

He showered, making the water as hot as he could stand. He breathed in the steam, finally finding some relief from the aches and pains in his body.

He dressed in sweats and walked back into the kitchen, expecting to see Hunter's backpack ready for the next day, the table cleared, and Hunter gone. Instead, he found his son exactly where he'd left him.

"Those last two problems must be impossible," Gray said.

Hunter flinched and looked up.

"I'll take it," Gray said, holding out his hand.

Darkness entered Hunter's expression, but he handed over his phone.

"Who are you texting?"

"Phil," Hunter said.

"Finish your math." Gray looked down at the phone, and sure enough Phil's name was at the top. "You aren't erasing texts, right?" He sat down at the table and looked at Hunter.

"No, Dad."

"Good, because if you do, you'll lose this thing permanently."

"I'm not," Hunter said, shooting him a daggered look.

Gray ignored his son's attitude and tapped on Phil's name. He and Hunter had been texting for a solid twenty minutes. First about their history homework. Gray couldn't be too mad about that, especially because Hunter had helped Phil with the project.

The conversation had quickly moved on to a girl named Rachel. "Who's Rachel?" he asked, glancing up.

"A girl in our art class," he said. "Phil likes her."

"And you're going to say something to her tomorrow about him?"

Hunter's face was turning a dark shade of red. "Maybe. If you keep reading, you'll see it's up in the air."

"Oh, I'm going to keep reading."

"Dad, I'm not doing anything bad."

"I get to know who you're talking to," Gray said. "And what you're saying."

"*I'm* not saying anything wrong."

"It's not you I'm worried about," Gray said, his eyebrows drawing down.

"You know Phil. He's not saying anything wrong either."

Gray returned to the conversation, and he finished it. "No, he's not."

"Can I have my phone back?"

"Is your math done?"

Hunter closed his book and said, "It is now."

Gray was just about to hand the phone back when another text came in—from Molly. "Molly texted." Gray watched Hunter tense, and he didn't want to tease his son about the girl. He just wanted to make sure they were being good. He'd gone to the dance the first week of school, and he and Molly had danced three times.

Gray had heard all about it as Hunter told Elise over the phone. Otherwise, he probably wouldn't have gotten a word.

"Should I read it?"

"I don't care," Hunter said, folding his arms. He obviously cared, and Gray's curiosity increased.

He met his son's eyes. He held his gaze for several long seconds. Then he handed the phone back. "I trust you."

"Thank you," Hunter murmured as he took the phone.

"I still want it plugged in out here."

"As always," Hunter said, focusing on the device.

"I'm going to bed in twenty minutes," Gray said. "You should too."

"Okay, Dad." Hunter's thumbs flew across his screen as he responded to Molly.

Twenty minutes later, Hunter got up and plugged his phone into the charger next to the fridge. "'Night, Dad." He leaned over the back of the couch where Gray sat, and Gray patted his shoulder.

"'Night, bud. Love you."

"Love you too." He took a few steps away. "Oh, what are we doing for your birthday?"

Surprise ran through Gray. "What are we doing?"

"Yeah."

"Do we normally do something?" He switched off the TV and stood up to face his son.

"I mean, we should," Hunter said. "I need to get you something too."

"I can talk to Grandma."

"Actually...." Hunter looked at his feet for a moment, then looked at Gray. He was getting so tall and so grown-up. He looked like a mirror image of Gray at that age, and he knew how his son's mind worked.

"You want Elise to take you."

"Yes."

"I haven't told her it's my birthday. She knows it's in October, but she didn't ask what day."

A frown pulled at Hunter's eyebrows. "Why haven't you told her?"

Gray shrugged. "Didn't want to make a big deal out of it. She'll make a cake I won't eat, and I don't want her to feel bad."

"She'll feel bad if she can't celebrate your birthday with you."

"Yeah, probably." Gray nodded toward the hall, and they started down it together. "You told her, then?"

"I mentioned it," Hunter said. "She wanted to know what you wanted."

"I don't want anything," Gray said, actually horrified at the thought of Elise buying him something. "She doesn't need to get me anything."

"Right, Dad," Hunter said, pausing at his door. "Because that's going to happen."

"When did you get so sarcastic?"

Hunter blinked at him. "Sorry, Dad. It's just…I thought you knew more about girls than I did."

It was Gray's turn to blink. "What does that mean?"

"It means, Dad, that you and Elise are like, super serious boyfriend and girlfriend, right?"

Gray swallowed. "Right." *Super serious.* Hunter wasn't far off, and Gray thought of the diamond ring he'd bought a few days ago. He hadn't even taken it out of his truck yet. He'd been busy, for one. And for another, he had no idea where to put it in the farmhouse. Elise hardly ever rode in his truck, as she drove her own car out to the farm when she brought Hunter back in the evenings.

"And you honestly think she doesn't want to get you something? Girls love to give presents. It's like, what they do." He shook his head. "You should tell her, and she'll make a cake out of meat or something. A meat pie. That's like a cake."

"Okay," Gray said.

"Okay." Hunter nodded like that was done, and he went into his room, pushing the door closed behind him. Gray stared at the white-painted wood, wondering when his son had started requiring the privacy of a closed door.

So many things had changed in the past year, and Gray felt like he couldn't keep up.

He also wanted to know what Hunter had said to Molly in the last twenty minutes, so he padded back into the kitchen and picked up the phone. The bulk of their conversation was about Halloween and whether or not they'd dress up.

Hunter had never enjoyed dressing up for Halloween all that much, and Gray wasn't surprised that he'd gently led Molly to the conclusion that they shouldn't wear costumes to school.

Gray backed out of the text string and tapped on the one below that. Elise. He looked at the timestamps, and sure enough, Hunter had been texting when he should've been working.

"With Elise," he murmured. Gray had a hard time being upset when Hunter did anything with Elise, because he wanted them to have a strong, healthy bond. They did talk about his birthday, and then Gray read a text that made his blood run cold.

I could just ask him for some money, if you want. See what he says, and maybe he'll give it to you.

He closed his eyes, but he'd already seen the text. He got transported back in time five or six years, and Hunter's childlike voice asked him for money. When Gray had asked him what it was for, he'd said Maddie. Maddie needed the money.

And now Elise did too.

He dropped the phone as if it had caught fire. His heartbeat throbbed in every muscle and pounded in his ears. He sucked in a breath, trying to find a thought to latch onto. Everything seemed coated in redness, and he grew angrier and angrier with every moment he stood in the kitchen.

He spun away from the counter with the phone with the horrible texts and hurried into his bedroom, where his phone was plugged in. He picked it up and dialed Elise, his breath coming in short bursts.

"Gray, hey," she said as if nothing was wrong. As if she'd done nothing wrong.

"Elise," he said, the name grinding in his throat. He'd never felt so betrayed, and he couldn't say anything else.

"Is everything okay?" she asked.

"No."

"What's wrong?"

"I…I—we can't see each other anymore."

A moment of silence came through the line. "What?"

"It's over," he said, well-aware his voice was icy. "And stay away from my son."

"Gray," she said. "What's going on? Why are you doing this?"

"I saw your texts with him," Gray said, his whole world crashing down around him. His anger changed to despair in the blink of an eye, and he needed to get off this call before his voice choked up. "Good-bye."

"Gray," she said again, but he hung up. He sank onto the bed, his chest so, so tight. He watched the phone darken, and he felt the same thing happen to his soul.

"I loved her," he whispered to the empty bedroom. His breath hitched, and his head grew too hot.

The phone rang, and Elise's name sat there. He couldn't

talk to her again. He didn't know how. He silenced the phone and turned it over.

He just wanted this day to end. He'd never been so tired, so frustrated, and so hurt. He got into bed and turned off the light, wishing sleep to claim him instantly.

It didn't, and Gray lay there with his eyes closed, Elise's betrayal burning through him. After what felt like a very long time, he started praying.

Please shoulder this for me, he thought. *I can't deal with this. I don't even know how. Why did this happen again? Am I really that blind?*

"Please help me sleep," he whispered aloud before he rolled onto his side, where his tears could fall into the pillow.

———

GRAY DIDN'T SLEEP WELL AT ALL, DESPITE HIS PETITIONS TO THE Lord. He didn't get up and run, and when he met Hunter in the kitchen, his son already had that blasted phone in his hand.

"Ready for school?"

"Yeah." Hunter shoved the phone in his back pocket. "You didn't run this morning?"

Gray shook his head. "Rest day." It wasn't a rest day, and Gray hated that he'd just lied to his son. He'd gotten up so late that he didn't even have time to make coffee. "Let's go."

Hunter followed him out to the garage. "You don't look good, Dad."

"Didn't sleep very well," Gray said. And that wasn't a lie. They got going down the road, and Gray mourned the quick eight-minute drive he'd used to have to get Hunter to school.

"Hunt, I'm going to pick you up from school today."

"What? Why? Elise picks me up on Fridays."

"She's not going to pick you up anymore," Gray said.

"Why not?"

"She's just not."

"Is that why she said she can't text me anymore too?" Hunter pulled his phone out. "I texted her this morning about an idea I had for your birthday, and she said she couldn't talk to me anymore."

Gray's fingers clenched around the steering wheel, trying to find a way to tell Hunter the truth. He hated this part of breaking up the most. He should've never involved his son in the relationship with Elise. He was never dating again, period.

The thought of being alone forever made his chest deflate, though he knew he hadn't gotten a proper breath since ending everything with Elise last night.

"Dad, what happened?"

"I broke up with her," he said.

"What? Why would you do that?"

"She asked you to get money." Gray glanced at Hunter, trying to gauge how much his son remembered about the situation with Maddie.

"She did not."

"I saw it on your phone."

"I said I'd ask you for some money so she could take me

shopping for your birthday. That was it. Elise didn't ask me to get money for *her*."

"That's not what the text said."

"Yes." Hunter started swiping, and a sob came out of his mouth. "I said, 'I could just ask him for some money, if you want. See what he says, and maybe he'll give it to you.' It was my idea to ask you. It was for a gift *for you*." He swiped angrily at his eyes. "You can't break up with her."

"I already did."

"Then undo it," Hunter said.

"Hunter." Gray sighed, because now he could only feel doubt and stupidity moving through him. "It's not that easy."

"Yes, it is. You call her and you just tell her you made a mistake."

Gray just shook his head.

"Oh, that's right," Hunter said, his voice hard. "You don't make mistakes."

"Hey."

"What, Dad? You don't. At least you act like you don't. You always know exactly what to do, and you're never wrong. Well, guess what? *You were wrong*." He folded his arms and looked out the window, still sniffling.

Gray didn't know what to say. His son's words stung him, and every time he opened his mouth, his emotions welled in his throat. The closer they got to the junior high, the calmer Hunter became. He wiped his eyes, opening the console to get out a napkin.

Gray pulled up to the school and stopped at the curb.

"Hunter," he said. "Is that really true? She didn't ask for money?"

"Of course she didn't." Hunter threw Gray a death glare. "I think you've just been waiting for her to mess up, because you're afraid."

"I am afraid," Gray admitted. But he wasn't sure he'd been waiting for Elise to mess up. "Maybe we're okay, just the two of us."

"No." Hunter shook his head. "No, Dad. I love her, and I want her to be my mom. I want her to come live with us on the farm." Tears spilled down his face again. "Fix it, Dad. Please." He yanked on the console to open it again. "You bought her a diamond ring. I know you love her too, and you want her to come live with us on the farm too."

Gray looked at his son, his beautiful, emotional son, and he knew he'd done something very, very wrong. He did love Elise, and he'd literally dreamed of having her on the farm with them. "How do I fix it?"

"Let's go to her house right now," Hunter said, pulling in a breath. "I can't go to school like this anyway." He wiped his face, and Gray looked out the windshield.

"Dad."

"All right," Gray said. "Let's go to her house right now."

CHAPTER 30

E lise felt like a satellite floating through space. She was the only one for miles, and she had been for hours. No one knew where she was, and she could take the next exit and quite literally disappear from the Earth.

It was strange how a couple of phone calls could change things so quickly.

First, Gray's had thrown her completely off her axis. She'd called him back—three times—but he hadn't answered. Desperate and heartbroken, she had her keys in her hand when the second phone call had come in.

It had been Wes, of all people. *Bree's having the baby*, he'd said. *She wants you to come if you can.*

Elise had the keys in her hand, and she'd simply walked out of her house with nothing but a jacket and her purse. Oh, and her dog. Hutch had been by her side the whole time, and she'd never been more grateful for his presence as she made the trek from Colorado to Coral Canyon.

She'd been driving all night, and she'd only sent one text to Hunter in all that time. He'd said he'd thought of a great gift for his dad—a Keurig coffee maker—and she'd told him she couldn't talk to him anymore.

She might not understand what Gray had done, but she could respect his wishes. He'd always been so protective of Hunter, and the moment he'd thought she'd taken advantage of him, everything they'd been building for the past nine and a half months had disintegrated.

Hunter had asked her what she meant that she couldn't text him back, and the petty side of her wanted to tell him to ask his father.

A fresh wave of tears threatened to drown her. Her eyes felt so heavy, and she coached herself to keep going. She was only a few minutes from Coral Canyon, and she could rest when she got to the hospital. Wes had also texted to say Bree's labor was progressing very slowly, and she likely wouldn't have the baby for several hours.

Elise hadn't responded. She didn't want either of them to know she'd come immediately. Embarrassment squirreled through her, along with a healthy dose of self-loathing. She reached over and stroked Hutch's neck, something she'd been doing every few minutes when she needed comfort.

She'd had all night to think about her shortcomings, and the worst one by far was the fact that she'd followed yet another man wherever he dictated.

She'd moved to Jackson Hole to be with Brandt, and he'd broken her heart into small shards.

And now she'd moved to Ivory Peaks—kind of—to be with Gray, and he'd done the exact same thing.

"There were no signs," she said to herself. With Brandt there had been signs that things weren't great between them. But with Gray, Elise felt absolutely whole. She loved him with her whole heart, and she couldn't imagine a day without him in her life. And returning to the house he owned so wasn't happening, though she'd left everything she owned behind.

Maybe she could get Colton to come help her pack it up and move it back to the cabin. He'd been talking about coming down to visit Ames and his parents while Annie and Eden worked on the wedding.

If she did that, she'd have to explain everything to Colton.

"That's out," she muttered as she crossed into the city limits of Coral Canyon. She'd thought she'd feel like she was coming home, but oddly enough, she didn't. She truly was simply drifting through space, without an anchor or even a place to belong.

She pulled into the hospital parking lot and checked her appearance in the rear-view mirror. She certainly looked like a woman who'd been crying for the majority of the last eight hours. She hadn't slept, and that wasn't hard to see either.

She had her famous lip gloss in her purse, and she went inside and slipped into the nearest bathroom to freshen up. She ran back out to the car and let Hutch out so he could relieve himself, and she told him, "It'll just be a minute, okay, bud?"

He jumped in the back seat and turned toward her. "Just take a nap. I'll take you up the cabin in a bit. You can chase squirrels all day." She smiled at him and gave him a quick pat before closing the door.

By the time she arrived in the maternity ward, she felt sure she could chalk up the bags under her eyes to her haste to get there to support Bree.

"Elise." Colton rose from a chair and came toward her, a giant smile on his face.

Elise's tears started again, and she stepped into her best friend's arms. "Has she had him yet?"

"No word yet," Colton said, holding her. "What's wrong?"

"Oh, nothing." Elise scoffed and put a smile on her face before she stepped away from him. "I drove all night, and I'm just so excited for Bree." She wiped her eyes. "Have you been here all night?"

"No, I just got here about thirty minutes ago." He returned her smile, and they went back to the chairs where he'd been sitting. He sighed as he sat, and Elise picked up on something there.

"How's the wedding planning coming?"

"I'm dying," he said, meeting her eye. "There was quite a big argument just last night." He leaned back and closed his eyes. "I didn't sleep well, and I'm going to Colorado whenever you are."

"Really?" Her heart skipped a couple of beats. If he came to Colorado, he'd find out about her and Gray. She should tell him anyway. The only reason he didn't already know was because he'd lost sleep last night too.

"Really," he said. "I just need a break."

"Annie's okay with it?"

"Yes," he said. "She's trying to get the girls to be nice to each other, and if she doesn't have to worry about me, she can just focus on them."

Elise's phone rang, and Hunter's name sat there. She quickly angled it away from Colton and silenced it. He didn't even open his eyes, and Elise moved over to a couch and laid down. She'd been awake for over twenty-four hours, and it wasn't hard to fall asleep, despite the less-than-ideal conditions.

Sometime later, Elise didn't know how long, Colton said, "Elise, sweetheart. Wake up. He's here."

Her eyes snapped open, and she tried to remember where she was. Colton and the medical smell in the air reminded her, and she sat up. "She had the baby?"

"Yes," Colton said. "And Wes said we could go back." He helped her stand, and they went through the huge double-doors together. Elise could hardly contain her excitement, despite the heavy weight of Gray in her mind.

"Right here." Colton led the way through the door and into a room, and Elise followed him. Bree sat up in the hospital bed, her baby in her arms, and everything in Elise sighed.

"You came," Bree said, already crying.

Elise rushed to her side and hugged her. "Of course we came."

"We're your best friends," Colton added.

"You drove ten minutes," Bree said, shaking her head as she smiled. "I meant Elise."

"So my sacrifice isn't appreciated because it's less than hers?" Colton grinned at the two of them.

"I appreciate it," Bree said, gazing down at her newborn. "This is Michael Wesley Hammond." She spoke in a reverent voice, and Elise knew why. This baby seemed to have bits of heaven still clinging to him, and she wanted to hold him so badly.

Bree seemed to sense Elise's need, because she lifted the infant toward her. "Michael, this is my best friend, Elise."

"Oh." She settled the little bundle of a person in the crook of her elbow, and the baby squirmed and grunted. "He's beautiful, Bree." She gazed down at the tiny human, her own desire to be a mother doubling and then tripling. And she'd thought she'd been getting close. Now she was all the way back to square one, and she didn't even want to play anymore.

If she couldn't have Gray, she didn't want anyone.

She moved over to Colton. "And this is Colton," she said. "He's your uncle, but he's also Bree's other best friend." She gave the baby to Colton, and she wanted to take a snapshot of this picture of the three of them with Michael.

"Where's Wes?" she asked.

"His mother called," Bree said. "Come tell me about Colorado." She smiled warmly at Elise, but Elise couldn't talk about Colorado without talking about Gray. And she couldn't talk about Gray without crying, and then her best friends would know how terribly wrong everything was right now.

Who else should you rely on? she wondered, and she pulled up the only chair in the room and sat down. "Colorado is okay," she said.

That got Colton to look away from the baby.

"Just okay?" Bree asked.

Elise nodded and looked down at her hands. "Actually, it's pretty terrible." She sniffled. "Gray broke up with me last night."

"You're kidding," Colton practically yelled. "Why?"

"Something about how he saw the texts I'd sent to Hunter." She shook her head. "I don't know why. He called, and he said we couldn't see each other anymore, and he told me to stay away from Hunter. When I asked him what he was talking about, he said he'd seen the texts, and that was it."

"He sabotaged." Colton shook his head, his expression furious.

That didn't make Elise's heart any less shattered, and she couldn't look at Bree or Colton. She knew neither of them had enjoyed a golden path to marital bliss, but she still felt like the loser of the group.

"I tried calling him back, but he wouldn't answer." She looked up, and that made her tears stream down her face. "I love him so much, and I just—I can't go back there."

"Oh, Elise." Colton handed baby Michael back to Bree and returned to Elise. He crouched in front of her, and she embraced him. "I'm so sorry," he whispered.

"I just don't know what I did," she said. "Look at the texts, Colt, and tell me what I did. I'll fix it."

"He loves you too," Colton said. "He's just so scared." He took her phone and looked at the texts, frowning all the while. He handed the phone back. "I don't know what he saw here. You want me to call him?"

"No," Bree and Elise said at the same time. She felt like a

real jerk for ruining what should be a sweet experience for Bree.

She got to her feet and leaned over to hug Bree. "I'm sorry," she said. "No more talk of Gray." She drew in a deep breath. "But I did drive all night, so I need to find somewhere to take a nap. Oh, and Hutch is in the car."

"Go up to the cabin," Bree said. "It'll be quiet, and you can sleep all day."

"I can take your dog," Colton said.

The door opened, and the three of them turned toward it as Wes came in. "Oh, you guys made it." He wore such a happy smile, and Elise took the opportunity to slide behind Colton and wipe her eyes before she said hello to him.

She left only a few minutes later, with Colton right at her side. "Are you going to go up to the cabin?" he asked.

"Yes," she said. "I can get Patsy to unlock it for me." She gave Colton the best smile she could muster. "You need a nap too, Mister."

"I'm worried about you," he said.

"I'm worried about me too," she said, trying to be brave and failing. "But I'm going to eat and sleep, and things will be okay." She had to believe that, or she'd simply go up to the cabin and never leave again.

Colton hugged her in the parking lot and said, "Call me if you need anything. And come down for dinner tonight to my place. I really will take Hutch for as long as you need me too. Sparky loves him."

"Okay," she said. "Thanks, Colt." She made it up the canyon without incident, and Patsy had unlocked the door for her. She went down the hall to her old bedroom, the place as familiar and as comfortable as it had ever been. Hutch ran around, obviously excited to be back where he'd grown up.

She plugged in her phone, ignoring the texts and missed calls she had, and though she was exhausted, she still had a few moments to wonder if any of the texts or calls had come from Gray.

She'd check when she woke up, because if they hadn't, she didn't think she'd be able to sleep.

CHAPTER 31

Colton wanted a nap the moment he walked in his house. The scent of beachy perfume told him Eden was at the house, and her car sat in the driveway too. "Hey," he said, putting a smile on his face as he went into the living area. Annie and Eden sat at the big kitchen table against the back wall, every available inch of it covered with something wedding-related. Announcements. Flowers. Cake.

Or maybe the cake was just for him.

He bent down and kissed his wife, then smiled at her daughter. "How are we this morning?"

"Okay," Eden said, meeting his eye briefly. "Sorry about last night, Colton."

"It's okay," he said. "I get siblings. I've got four brothers, and let me tell you, I don't get along with all of them one-hundred percent of the time." He smiled at her.

"But she only has Emily," Annie said, her voice already

tense. "So she better figure out how to get along, or she won't have anyone."

"I know, Mom." Eden ducked her head. "I already said I'd apologize."

Colton moved into the kitchen. "Can I have some of this cake?"

"Yes," Annie said. "It's dry, just so you know."

Colton didn't care about that. He could soak it in cream, and it would be just great. He cut himself a thick slice and opened the fridge. "Did you tell her about our gift?"

"No," Annie said, clearly still distracted.

Colton returned to the table and took a seat. "Should I tell her?"

"It's your money." Annie met his eye.

Colton looked right back at her. "No, it's *our* money." They'd had this conversation before, and he really wasn't in the mood to have it again. He'd promised Elise he'd stay out of her relationship with Gray, but he really just wanted to call his older brother and ask him what the devil he'd been thinking. Why couldn't he have just stayed calm for once? Found out the truth before he went and did something so rash?

His patience was already thin, and he didn't want to argue with his wife. She softened and reached for his hand. "Okay. I'll tell her." She looked at Eden while Colton took his first bite of cake. It was dry, and to add to that, the chocolate was too bitter. Definitely not his favorite as he preferred a lot more sugar than this.

"Honey, for your wedding, we're going to give you the same thing we gave Emily. See, in Colton's family, when they turn twenty-one, they inherit a sum of money. They're expected to do something amazing with it, work hard, all of that." She glanced at Colton, and while that was a really watered down version of the truth, it would do.

"So we'll be gifting you and Mitchell one million dollars, and—"

"What?" Eden asked, her eyes widening. She looked at Annie and then Colton. "What do you mean?"

"She means that we'll be transferring a million dollars into your bank account," Colton said calmly. Emily had reacted this way too. "And we expect you to do something great with it. Start a business. Follow a dream that can have a positive impact on your life or the lives of others. Be smart. Work hard. Double it or triple it. Trust in the Lord, and be happy."

Annie nodded along with everything Colton said, a smile stuck to her face.

Eden exploded to her feet and ran her hands through her hair. "I can't...a million dollars?" She looked like she might throw up.

"I got two billion when I turned twenty-one," Colton said. "This is significantly less."

Eden just blinked at him as if she didn't understand the English language.

"Sit down, dear," Annie said gently. "It's just money."

"No, Mom." Eden sat down and leaned toward her mother. "It's more than money. It's insane. We can't take it."

So that was different than Emily's reaction. She'd burst into tears and hugged Annie and Colton, as had Kelly, minus the tears.

"Of course you can," Colton said. "It's a lot to take in, I'll give you that. I knew I'd be getting my money for eight years before I got it. The responsibility I felt was enormous."

"So while we want you and Mitch to be responsible and do something great with it," Annie said. "Don't feel so much pressure."

Eden covered her face with her hands for a moment, and when they fell away, she had tears in her eyes too. "I don't know what to say."

"You say thank you," Annie said. She stood up, and Eden did too, and they embraced. Colton enjoyed watching the tender moment, and his heart filled with love for Eden. He understood Eden, and he found himself always siding with her over Emily. He wasn't sure why, only that he knew exactly how it felt to have to live up to a perfect, older sibling.

And he had two of them.

Turned out Gray wasn't as perfect as everyone thought though, and as Colton stood to embrace Eden too, he determined to make a phone call as soon as he could. "Thank you," Eden said to him.

He stepped back and held onto her shoulder. "Your mother and I love you very much," he said, his voice catching. He didn't have biological children of his own, but he did love these girls. "And Mitch too." He smiled, because his emotions seemed to be ricocheting around in the back of his throat.

"Can I go call him?"

"Go ahead," Annie said. "This floral catalog will still be here." She threw it a dirty look and then looked at Colton while Eden rushed from the room. "Thank you for loving them."

"Thank you for sharing them with me." He hugged her too, ending their embrace with a kiss. "Now, I have to go call my brother."

"Which one?" Annie asked. "And what did he do?"

"Gray," he said. "He broke Elise's heart, and I suspect his own too." Colton picked up his bowl and put the rest of the cake in the sink. "That's really not good."

"I tried to warn you," she said with a smile. "I can't wait until this wedding is over."

Colton silently agreed, but he just nodded as he stepped outside to make the call.

Gray picked up after only the first ring, as if he'd been stationed beside the phone. "Colton," he said, plenty of resignation in his voice. "Go ahead. Go ahead and tell me what an idiot I am."

"Why would I do that?" Colton asked, watching as Sparky darted down the steps from the deck to the backyard.

"You've spoken to Elise, I assume?"

Colton didn't want to lie. So he just said, "Tell me why you did it."

"Because I'm a fool? Because I wanted to be sure in a world where you can never be one-hundred percent sure? Because I'm in love with her, and I'm terrified of that, and I don't know how to admit it?" Gray sucked in a breath and blew it out. "Pick one."

Colton felt his brother's agony from five hundred miles away. "I'm so sorry, Gray."

"Do you know where she is?" he asked. "Hunter's plenty

upset with me, and he's tried calling her a few times. Texting too. She won't answer."

"Maybe she just needs a day," Colton said, dodging the question.

"If you talk to her again, could you please let her know it's okay to speak to Hunter?" Gray carried only remorse in his voice. "He's very upset, and I hate that it's my fault."

"He loves her too."

"More than me, I'm afraid," Gray said, his voice changing. A couple of seconds of silence came through the line. "That's another thing, Colt. He loves her more than me, and maybe I don't like that. Maybe it frustrates me, and maybe I thought if I pushed her away, we could go back to how we were, just the two of us."

Colton nodded, though he couldn't even fathom the emotions tied to having a son and trying to build an instant family after what Gray had been through. "Maybe that's something you need to work on with him," he said. "And then with Elise."

"I know."

"I'm coming down to stay with Ames for a bit," Colton said. "I can help with Hunter if you need it."

"Why are you coming?"

"Oh, there's all this wedding planning happening here," Colton said with a sigh as he turned back to the house. "And it's causing a lot of friction in my own family too, and I need a break."

"I'm sorry," Gray said. "I didn't know."

"No one did," Colton said. "It's not a big deal. Annie and I are fine. It's just a stressful situation. She wants the wedding to be perfect, because Em didn't involve her much, and Eden seems to be involving her too much." Colton sighed and shook his head. "It's fine. She's just so busy with that, and there's been some fighting, and we decided I'd just get out of town for a bit until things are less stressful. She doesn't like worrying about me, and she knows if I'm down in Colorado, she won't have to."

"You can stay at the farm," Gray said.

"I'll come visit," Colton hedged. "Drag Ames out to ride horses and bring Sparky to chase the chickens." The dog looked up at the mention of his name, and Colton grinned at him. He wondered what Gray would do if he showed up with Sparky and Hutch.

"Okay," Gray said.

"Okay," Colton agreed. "Now, give Elise a day or two. And then find her, get down on both knees, and beg her to forgive you."

Gray chuckled, the sound quite dark. "Okay, Colt."

"I mean it, Gray. She loves you."

"Did she tell you that?"

"I just know," Colton said. "Just like I knew months ago that you loved her."

"When did you know?"

"I don't know," Colton said, blowing out his breath. "May? Sometime in May. Did you know she asked Ames to teach her how to run?"

"She did? Why would she do that?"

"Because, you dolt. She wants to spend time with you, doing what *you* love to do. And that's running. So she's training to be able to run a few miles with you every day."

"Hunter's coming back," Gray said. "I have to go."

"Give him a hug for me," Colton said. "And tell him not to worry about Elise. She loves him, and even if you screwed up, she's not going to abandon him."

"Okay," Gray said, his voice thick. "Thank you, Colt."

"Love you, Gray. You can do this." Colton knew, because he'd done it. Gray was a different breed of Hammond though. The kind that knew what to do in every situation. Who could divorce feelings from fact and make decisions that would help the most, no matter how he felt.

Men like Gray rarely made mistakes, and when they did, they were very hard to overcome. Hard to admit out loud. Hard to move past.

Colton pocketed his phone and said a prayer for his brother. "Lord, he needs You more than ever right now. Please help him, open his mind to the right road, and please, please protect his son from his father's stupidity." Tears came to Colton's eyes, because he loved Hunter too.

"And bless Elise to text that boy back."

———

A COUPLE OF DAYS LATER, COLTON WAITED ON HIS FRONT PORCH with a suitcase. He'd already kissed his wife goodbye. She'd left for the lodge, and as Elise pulled into the driveway, Colton was ready to leave for Colorado.

"Ready?" she asked through her open window.

"Pop the trunk," he said, not super happy about the giant dog in the passenger seat.

She did, and he put the bag in the back before opening

the passenger-side door. "Get in the back, Hutch," he said. The dog stubbornly stayed where he was.

Elise reached over and grabbed his collar. "Go to the back, Hutch."

The dog finally obeyed, and Colton slid into the passenger seat. "I'm so ready for this. Can we get a breakfast burrito on the way out of town, though? I've only had coffee this morning."

"No cupcakes?" Elise teased. "Seems hard to believe." She backed out of the driveway, and while she seemed normal, Colton knew he was dealing with a whole new Elise. He hadn't asked her about Gray or Hunter in the past couple of days. They'd spent time with Bree and Wes and Michael in the hospital, and then last night at their home, after Bree had been released.

She'd cried and hugged them, wondering what in the world she was going to do the next day—today—with a baby all by herself. "Someone's made a mistake," she'd said, wiping her eyes. "Letting me bring him home like I know what I'm doing."

Both Colton and Elise had reassured her that she did know what she was doing, and that everything would be fine. He looked at Elise now, wondering if she believed that for herself.

"What?" she asked.

"Nothing," he said.

"Good, because it's a long drive, and I'm not going to tolerate any talk about your brother."

"Still haven't spoken to him?"

"No," she said, glancing at him. "I've talked to Hunter a

couple of times." Her fingers tightened on the wheel, and she reached to adjust how hard the air was blowing. "Gray hasn't even called or texted, Colt."

Frustration built inside him too. He hadn't heard from Gray either, so he didn't have an update for her. "Maybe he just wants to talk in person."

"Maybe he meant what he said."

"All he said was not to talk to Hunter," Colton said. "And you're doing that."

"He said it was okay." She glanced at him, fear in those light green eyes. "What if Gray doesn't know he's been calling and texting?"

"Have you met Gray?" Colton asked, smiling as he shook his head. "Elise, the man knows exactly what his son does with every second of his day."

She nodded and looked out her window. "You're right." She pulled into the fast-food restaurant drive-through to get the breakfast burritos, and then they got on the highway headed south.

Elise turned up the music and started belting out the lyrics for the Broadway musicals playlist she'd made. Colton suffered through it, though he did think some of the songs were catchy. He'd never tell her that though.

Once they'd listened to no less than thirty of Broadway's "best hits" according to Elise, he plugged in his phone and said, "Okay, now we get to listen to some real music."

"Oh, jeez," she said. "What playlist did you make?"

"It's a good one," he promised as the first strains of "Take On Me" by A-ha came on.

"Eighties?" She gave him a dry look.

"Just because you weren't born yet doesn't mean anything," he said. "There's some great songs on here. *Girls Just Wanna Have Fun. I Wanna Dance With Somebody. Livin' on a Prayer.*" He watched her for signs of recognition of any of those.

She just shook her head and kept driving. She didn't protest though, and Colton took that as a win.

Several songs later, he happened to look over on the lonely stretch of Wyoming highway and see a truck coming toward them. "Elise," he said, quickly reaching for the radio's volume knob to turn the music down.

"What?"

He peered at the dark brown truck, wishing her sedan were higher, and that they weren't going seventy miles-per-hour. "I think that's Gray's truck."

She looked at it, pulling in a breath. It had Colorado plates, and Colton definitely saw his brother as the truck drew close. Then, just like that, the two vehicles passed one another.

"I have to stop," Elise said, plenty of panic in her voice. "Call him, Colton."

"He's going to Coral Canyon," he said, looking over his shoulder at the truck. It rapidly moved away from them, though Elise had started to slow down.

"Yeah, and we're going to Colorado," Elise said. "Call him."

"Okay." Colton fumbled for his phone and jabbed at the pause button to stop the music. He made the call and put the call on speaker as it connected.

Elise's car bumped over the shoulder, finally coming to a

stop. "Why isn't he answering?"

"Again," Colton said. "Have you met Gray? He's so perfect and so buttoned up, that he doesn't use his phone while he drives."

"Call Hunter," she said. "Was he in the car? Did you see him?"

"I couldn't see that far."

"I'm turning around."

"You'll never catch him."

"Colton." Her voice only possessed desperation.

He looked at her, and he too desperately wanted things to work out for her and Gray. He ended the unanswered call to his brother and said, "Hang on. I'm trying Hunter."

CHAPTER 32

Gray had given Elise two days. He had not bothered her. No texts. No calls. Hunter had burst into tears the first time she'd texted him back, and then he'd bustled down the hall to his bedroom to call her.

"She's okay, Dad," was all he would give to Gray.

He existed in a layer of torture that would not go away. He'd called Ames and confirmed that his brother had been walking and running with Elise every day since she'd moved to Colorado. "She's getting good," Ames had said. "Almost up to two miles now."

Gray had never felt so foolish. He'd asked Hunter a dozen times if he would please forgive him, and every time, Hunter just hugged him and told him he loved him. They'd had a heart-to-heart about Gray's feelings regarding Hunter wanting to share more with Elise than him, and Hunter had admitted that he was a bit worried about what Gray would think of him for liking a girl or texting in the barn.

"It's always about being the best with you, Dad," he'd said. "Because you *are* the best. But sometimes that's hard for me to live up to."

"What's different about Elise?"

"I know she's going to be happy for me, and excited for me, and ask me questions just to know more about me and the situation. No matter what. She doesn't judge me."

"And I do?"

"Feels like it." Hunter had mumbled that last part, and Gray hadn't known how to assure his son that it wasn't judgment coming from Gray. It was worry.

He'd finally said as he'd pitched the last forkful of straw over the fence, "Hunter, I worry about you constantly. I worry that I'm not good enough. I don't know what I'm doing. I just make stuff up on a day-by-day basis."

Hunter had looked at him, and they'd shared another embrace. "So forgive me," Gray said. "There's no manual for this. I'm just doing what I think is right, and I'm sorry if I've been coming across as judgmental or like I don't want to know about your friends and your life. I do. I desperately do."

"I know, Dad," Hunter had said. "Sometimes it's all about how fast I can get the chores done, not that they got done with a little bit of texting, you know?"

Gray had nodded. "Okay," he said. "I can accept that."

He'd left Hunter with Ames for this trip to Coral Canyon, because he'd finally called an old neighbor to find out if Elise had come or gone from the house at all, and he'd said no. No movement or activity at the house.

Which meant Elise had left the house, and Gray knew of only one place she'd go: Coral Canyon.

He'd immediately packed a bag, complete with the diamond ring he'd bought, and called his brother. He'd dropped off Hunter very early that morning, and he'd started the trip north. If he was lucky, and he didn't spy any cops along the way, he'd be there just after lunchtime.

He was trying to decide if he should call her first, just to find out where she was. It would be more romantic if he could somehow just show up where she was with dozens of roses and the ring.

His stomach tightened. Maybe she didn't want him anymore. Maybe roses, and a ring, and Gray himself simply weren't enough.

His phone rang, and it was Colton, and Gray's first impulse was to answer the call. Find out where Elise was and maybe chew out his brother for not telling him two days ago that she'd left town.

In the end, he didn't want to involve her best friend. Gray was a grown man, and Gray could solve his own problems. The call cut off before it went to voicemail, and Gray sighed in relief.

A few minutes later, Hunter called. He should be in school, and Gray's heart skipped a beat. He tapped the phone icon on the screen, and the radio cut off as the call connected. "Hunt? What's going on?"

"You have to pull over," he said, his voice full of excitement.

"What? Why? Aren't you in...." He glanced at the clock. "Art?"

"It's science today," Hunter said, and how he kept track of his alternating classes, Gray didn't know. "And Uncle Colton called, because he saw you in your truck going to Coral Canyon."

Gray looked in his rear-view mirror, but there was no one behind him. "He did? How?"

"He's in the car with Elise, and they're on their way back here," Hunter said. "Dad, pull over."

Gray eased his foot off the gas pedal and started to apply the brake. He wasn't exactly in a spot where he could just pull over, as the highways up here were two lanes, one in each direction, with a shallow shoulder. "I'll call Uncle Colt," he said. "Go back to class, Hunt."

"Dad, you've got the ring, right?"

"Yes." He pulled off the road and brought the truck to a stop. "You think I should ask her right when I see her?"

"Yes," Hunter said. "That's the plan, Dad." He laughed, and Gray wished he had his son's optimism. "Okay, call Uncle Colt. I have to go." The line went dead, and Gray took a moment to look into the rear-view mirror and his own eyes.

"You do love her," he told himself. "You don't know everything, but you know that." He reached into the back seat and retrieved the ring box from his bag. With it sitting on the console, he dialed Colton.

"Did you talk to Hunter?" his brother asked.

"Yes," Gray said. "I pulled over."

"Great," Colton said. "We're on our way to you."

His heart started to pound in a most unnatural way, and Gray reminded himself of the facts. He loved Elise. He wanted her in his life. He needed her to be a mother to Hunter.

It seemed like no time had passed at all, before Elise's sedan pulled off the road behind him, Colton at the wheel. Gray got out of the truck at the same time Elise got out of her car. The wind was blowing up here, as it seemed to perpetually do in Wyoming, and Gray gripped the ring box tightly.

He went around the front of the truck so he could avoid any traffic that might pass by on the highway, and he paused at the hood while Elise stopped at the tailgate.

"I'm sorry," he called to her. "I love you, and I'm an idiot, and if you can find a way to maybe just give me one pass, I'd love to forget about that phone call from a couple nights ago."

A strong gust of wind had him reaching to hold his cowboy hat on his head a moment too late. It went tumbling off into the field alongside the road, and Gray watched it. He stepped forward so the tallest part of the truck would protect him from the wind.

He watched Elise do the same, and before he knew it, she stood right in front of him.

"You're beautiful," he said. "I'm sorry. I love you." He didn't know what else to say. He dropped to both knees and held up the box. "I want you out at the farm. Hunter wants you to be his mother." He took a deep breath. "Will you marry me?"

Elise just kept looking at him. She bypassed the box and reached toward his face, sliding her cold, slender fingers along his jaw. He leaned into her touch, for it was an exquisite form of pleasure and torture.

"You're asking me to marry you in the breath right after you asked me to forgive you?"

"Hunter said I should."

Elise finally cracked a smile. "So we're taking our directions from a twelve-year-old boy now."

"I've disappointed him greatly," Gray said, his throat on fire. "I made a mistake, Elise. A really big one, and it impacted you, and me, and him, and he was so, so mad at me. He explained everything, and as usual I jumped to a conclusion that fit my paradigm." He let the ring box drop, and his knees weren't particularly happy with the gravel digging into them.

"Do you really want me at the farm with you?"

"More than anything in the world."

Elise leaned forward, and because she was so short, he could wrap his arms around her waist as she drew his head to her chest. "I love you, Gray Hammond, but I really don't want to go through another phone call like that one."

"I know," he said. "I'm sorry. It won't happen again."

"Even when you get mad?"

"Even if."

"Even if you're scared?"

"I'm so scared you're going to say no," he whispered.

"Even if you're not sure?"

"I'm sure about us, Elise." He inched away and looked up at her. "Did you say you loved me?"

"I've loved you for months, Gray," she said with a smile. "Maybe from the moment I met you in Colton's kitchen."

Tears splashed her face, but she didn't wipe them away. "And if you really mean this proposal, then my answer is yes."

"Oh, I mean it," he said, his heart singing as it beat in the back of his throat. He took the ring out of the box and slipped it on her finger. He used the truck to steady himself as he stood, and he took his fiancée into his arms, whispered, "I've loved you for months too," and kissed her.

"HE SAYS HE CAN GET HIS OWN LUNCH," ELISE SAID, GLANCING up from Gray's phone.

"Good," he said. Colton had stayed in Elise's car, except for a brief minute to let Hutch out to take care of his business, and Gray had set his truck behind it, with her in the cab with him. They'd been driving back to Colorado for a few hours now, and Gray had suggested stopping for lunch. "If we time it right, we can pick Hunter up together."

Elise pressed her lips together and nodded. She'd been fighting tears for the entire drive, and every time he saw them, Gray felt a little guiltier. He hadn't apologized after she'd told him to stop doing it. She didn't blame him, and she didn't need to keep hearing it. "I'm just emotional," she said. "My best friend had a baby, and he's beautiful, Gray. And Hunter wants me to be his mom...." She'd trailed off then, the tears fresh as she looked away.

"I talked to Hunter," Gray said, bringing her attention back to him. "I've been a little jealous of the relationship you two have."

"What do you mean?"

"I mean, I'm the disciplinarian, and you get all the good stories. You get to know what's going on in his life, and you just tell him how wonderful it is." He cut a look at her out of the corner of his eye. "I'm the one who has to remind him to be smart with girls, and not to dawdle during his homework, and to make sure he pays his lunch money."

"Gray," Elise said. "I didn't realize you were upset."

"Upset isn't the right word," he said, sighing. "I just…I guess I felt left out? And he's *my* son, and yet, he wanted to tell *you* about the dance. And *you* about Molly. And you get to take him shopping and have his friends over to the house. Then, when he gets back to the farm, it's me on his case all the time. Eat dinner. Do your chores. Get your homework done."

He shook his head. "So we talked about it, and he said he does see me as more of a taskmaster, and someone less safe to tell about personal things."

"I'm sorry," she said. "I wasn't trying to do that."

"I know that." Gray reached over and squeezed her hand. "I know that. It was a good talk."

"I'm glad."

"I'm wondering…how do you think we should split the parenting of Hunter? Some couples in situations like this, only the biological parent disciplines."

Elise looked at him with wide eyes. "I have no idea."

"He sees you as his mother," Gray said. "Or at least, he wants that relationship with you. I think I'd like to try co-parenting him. Where you can get after him if he's not getting good grades just as easily as I can. You can make him eat dinner and do his chores before he texts."

"Okay," she said. "I'll do my best."

"Are you scared?"

"Absolutely," she said. "You've known him for twelve *years*, Gray. You got to watch him grow up and learn his personality. I've known him for twelve months, and really didn't even start talking to him until six months ago." She swallowed and tucked her cornsilk hair behind her ear. "I'm terrified. I don't know what I'm doing."

"Heads up, Elise," he said. "Neither do I." He chuckled, and she just gaped at him.

"No, seriously."

"Yeah," he said. "Seriously." He looked at her again and smiled. "We'll figure it out."

She nodded. "Okay, I'll do my best."

"That's all anyone can ask," he said. The miles rolled by under his tires, and as the great city of Denver spread before them, hours later, a sigh moved through Gray. He did love the Rocky Mountains, and his soul rejoiced to be going home.

"I wanted to talk to you about something else," he said.

"Oh, all right."

He grinned at the light tone of her voice. "It's about where we live."

"We're going to live on the farm." She turned fully toward him, but he didn't dare look at her. "Right?"

"I've been toying with the idea of split residences," he said. "Buying a place in Coral Canyon—a mountain home. A cabin in the woods we can run away to in the summers. Or on holidays. Or for the weekend." He finally glanced at her. "What do you think?"

"I think as long as I don't have to stay there by myself, I'm in."

Gray laughed, pleased when Elise joined in with him. "I know your best friends live there," he said. "And I can hire someone to tend to the farm while I'm gone. In fact, I was thinking I'd hire someone anyway. Then Hunt and I can fish more often."

"Who took care of it over the summer?"

"A guy named Matt Whettstein," Gray said. "I think I'll call him again. He can be the manager. Or the foreman. Hunter and I can feed horses and pigs."

"The farm would still be in the family."

"And I think Hunter will take it over eventually," Gray said. "He has hay in his blood, even if he thinks it's too much work."

"That he does," Elise said. "So…when were you thinking of getting married?"

"I have no idea."

"I have a crazy idea," she said.

"I'm not usually crazy about crazy ideas," he said.

"Well, you might have to let your hair down," she teased. "Unbutton that very top button, Gray."

"Okay," he said, rolling his eyes. "What's the idea?"

"Annie's been planning a wedding for her daughter at Whiskey Mountain Lodge for months. I bet if I called her, I could make it a double ceremony…maybe we could just pay for half of what she's already planned."

"You don't want your own wedding?" Surprise moved

through him and came right out with the words.

"The only thing I want at my wedding," she said. "Well, there's three things. You. Hunter. And the dress I designed."

Another dose of shock flowed through his veins. "You design dresses?"

"You're the only person over the age of twelve I've ever told," she said. "Well, and Hutch knows. But yes. And I've been working on my wedding dress for a decade."

Gray looked at her. "Over the age of twelve?"

"I may have told Hunter, but I've never shown him any of the designs." She smiled at him, a bit of anxiety in her eyes. "Remember how you said we were talking about more that one day when I said we were talking about crossword puzzles? I'd mentioned it to him then."

Gray nodded, several emotions zinging through him. "I'm glad you told him," he said. "Can you get it made in time? When is the wedding at the lodge?"

"Christmas," she said.

"*This* Christmas?" Gray's first reaction was to say no. No way. Hammonds had long engagements, with plenty of fanfare. Didn't they?

Wes literally got married on the beach, he reminded himself. *You watched online.*

"This Christmas," Elise said. "It's more than two months away, Gray. What do you need to do?"

"Well, I need a new cowboy hat, for one. A tuxedo. One for Hunter."

"We can do those things this weekend," she said.

"What about your dress?"

"I'll sew it myself," she said. "I can get it done on time."

"You'll sew it yourself." He didn't even know she sewed.

"Gray, every dress you've ever seen me wear, I've sewed myself."

"You have?"

"Designed it too," she said. "It's kind of a little...secret I have. Something I really like doing that soothes me."

He looked at her again, trying to see more about her he didn't know. This was sewing, and he had seen a sewing machine in her cabin before.

"Can you make a special tie for Hunter and I?"

"I'm sure I can. One for Hutch too." She grinned at him, so much hope in her eyes.

"Then I think we can get married at Christmas."

Elise squealed and reached for her phone. "I'm going to call Annie right now."

Gray shook his head and listened to her end of the conversation, marveling at how this day had gone. He'd left this morning heartbroken, with a promise to Hunter that he'd make things right.

Now, he was engaged and going to be married before the end of the year. *Wild*, he thought. *But amazing.*

Forgiveness was *such* an amazing thing, and he sure hoped he could be worthy of it in all aspects of his life.

CHAPTER 33

E lise stood outside the truck and tried to find Hunter through the streams of students coming down the sidewalk toward the pickup circle drive. Colton had Hutch, and he was taking the dog to the farm they both loved.

Her heartbeat thrashed in her chest, and she wasn't even sure why. Only that she wanted Hunter to know she loved him too, and she wanted to be his mother more than anything.

She told herself she would not cry in front of the junior high. She'd lose major points with Hunter if she did that, and she didn't want to be the uncool step-mom from the beginning.

She finally spotted Hunter's full head of dark hair, his bright brown eyes laughing as he walked with a couple of other boys. Molly was with him too, and the kids right in front of Elise moved so that she could see the two of them holding hands.

Her heart warmed, though she had a sudden flash of worry over him. In that moment, she knew exactly how Gray felt about his son. Elise needed to talk to Hunter, stat, and make sure he knew not to do anything stupid with that girl. From texting, to kissing behind the building, to anything—her mind whirred with the possibilities—he needed to know she expected him to be nothing but a gentleman.

He said goodbye to his buddies, and he swept the pickup area, looking for Ames, probably. His eyes landed on Elise, and he instantly dropped Molly's hand. He didn't even say anything to her before he started jogging toward Elise, and a wide smile filled her face.

She opened her arms, and Hunter ran right into them. "Elise," he said, hugging her tight.

She laughed with him, glad that was the reaction over shedding tears. He lifted her right off the ground, but set her down quickly. "You're here."

"Yes," she said, stepping back and running one hand down the side of his face. "I'm back."

"For good?" He looked toward the truck, but the tinted windows wouldn't allow him to see much. "You and Dad are good?"

She held out her left hand, which bore the sparkly diamond. "We're great."

"He did it." Hunter's face split into a grin, and he whooped as he reached for the door handle. He pulled open the door, and said, "You did it, Dad."

Gray said something Elise couldn't catch, because of all

the teens chattering on the sidewalk nearby. Hunter turned back to her, his face glowing.

"You didn't say goodbye to Molly," she said. "She looks a little lost."

Hunter stepped to her side, and they looked at Molly. "Be right back."

"Hunter," she said, her voice firm enough to get him to pause. "You be nice to that girl."

"Yes, ma'am," he said, smiling as he stepped back over to her. He kept his back to the truck, and Elise climbed in, her eyes barely leaving the pair.

"I worry about him," she murmured.

"Join the club," Gray said.

"He's a good-looking boy," she said. "He's going to break a lot of hearts." He hugged Molly, and then came trotting toward the truck. He climbed in the back and slammed the door so hard it made Gray flinch.

He said nothing though, except, "How was school, bud?"

"Good," he said from the back seat. Gray and Elise looked at each other, a silent conversation happening between them. Elise knew exactly what Gray was thinking, because it was the same thing she was.

One word? I show him we're engaged, and we see him hug Molly, and we get one word for how his day was?

She stifled her giggle and shook her head.

"Who wants pizza for dinner?" Gray asked.

"I do," Hunter said.

Elise was still quite full from lunch, but she muttered, "Well, at least we got two words that time," under her breath.

Gray burst out laughing, and Hunter asked, "What's so funny?"

"Nothing," Elise said, though she was giggling too. "I'm just so glad to be back with you two."

"Where's Hutch?" Hunter asked, and Elise assured him the dog would be waiting for him at the farm.

————

"OH, ELISE." BREE SUCKED IN A BREATH, HER EYES WIDE. "IT'S gorgeous." She came forward to run her fingers over Elise's shoulders, her eyes dipping to the bodice and then the waist. "I can't believe it. Where did you *get* this?"

Elise felt like a fairy princess in her wedding dress, and she turned to look into the mirror. With Bree beside her, wonder still shining in her face, Elise felt ready to get married. "I made it," she said.

"You did not." Bree ran her hand along Elise's hip. "No wonder it fits like a glove. It's flawless, Elise." She hugged her. "You've always been flawless."

"That's not true," Elise said with a smile. "Have you forgotten about those caramel swirl brownies?"

Bree laughed, and Elise turned into her to hug her. "Thank you for coming to help me get ready."

Her best friend held her tight and whispered, "You don't need it."

"Oh, but I do," Elise said. "I have no makeup on, and you're a master at that. My mother will be here in a minute to do my hair."

"What's she going to do with it?"

"She swears she has a way to give it a curl that will last longer than ten minutes," Elise said. "But I have my doubts." She looked at herself in the mirror again. Her wedding dress simply was stunning, and she loved the sleeveless design, and how the top half was covered in lace, with carefully placed sequins for shine under the Christmas lights.

She'd thought she'd be nervous on her wedding day, but she wasn't. She was ready to become Mrs. Gray Hammond, and she actually couldn't wait.

"I think you should leave it straight," Bree said. "You don't want to look at your wedding pictures in ten years and not even recognize yourself."

"You're right," Elise said as the door behind her opened again. Her mother entered, carrying a bin full of hairstyling tools.

"Oh, Elise." She dropped the bin and rushed at Elise. "You're so beautiful. It looks so good on." She held Elise's arms, which were bare all the way to the shoulder, and drank in the dress. "It's lovely. I should've had you sew my dress." Her mom met her eye, and Elise had never felt such happiness.

She hugged her mother and said, "Okay, now I need you guys to make me shine." She toed the train of the dress out of the way and stepped over to the closet. She'd change first, and then sit in the salon chair. Annie had arranged for everything at the lodge, and Elise, her mom, and Bree were currently in one of the guest rooms on the second floor.

Eden had planned it so that the magnificent staircase that curled down to the main floor would be the aisle. The

Christmas tree would already be lit, and that would be the only light and provide the scene for the altar.

She was getting married first, and then Elise and Gray would take the stage. Because they were doing their tree-lighting ceremony and stocking exchange first, Elise had given up the superstition of the groom not seeing the bride before the wedding. She wouldn't change into her gown until right before, but she'd just wanted to make sure the final alteration was right. And maybe she'd wanted to show off the dress to her mom and Bree.

She shimmied out of it and into a much more casual, yet still festive, holiday dress, which she'd also made herself. Bree gaped at it. "You made that too."

"Yes, I did." She grinned at her friend. "What gave it away?"

"Well, I think it's this bow around the middle." She fingered the bright green bow, which was supposed to signify the ribbon on a package. The rest of the dress was made of a textured, silver fabric that gave Elise shape in places she didn't have it. "It's like a Christmas present."

"Bingo," she said, grinning at her friend. "Now, come on. We only have forty-five minutes until the tree-lighting ceremony."

Her mother didn't even ask about the curlers. She plugged in a flat-iron and went over every piece of Elise's hair before beginning to braid it back on the sides. She pinned it somehow in the back, saying, "The veil will go here," and stepping away. "Yep. It's perfect."

Bree swept on the last bit of makeup and proclaimed she was done. She turned the salon chair toward the mirror, and

Elise looked at herself. She still looked like herself, thank goodness. Just a better version than the woman who wore gardening gloves and often had smudges of dirt on her neck and face.

"Let's go," she said, and the three of them went downstairs and into the fray of people. Normally, Elise didn't like the noise. She could handle it for a while, and then she needed an escape. But the energy at the lodge today was welcome, and she moved over to where Gray stood with Colton.

He scanned her from head to toe and whistled. "Wow, look at you."

"Merry Christmas," she said, hugging her best friend.

"I put Hutch downstairs, because he looked like he might take a bite of the tree."

Elise nodded, then she turned to his brother. "And to you, Mister Hammond." She grinned as she curtsied.

Gray took her hand and kissed it. He wore a pair of black slacks and a white shirt—nothing terribly Christmasy about his clothes. "You look great."

"Are you ready for this?"

"Absolutely."

"Where's Hunter?"

"He's with Stockton and Bailey," Gray said. "I've got him a seat right here. We'll head back together as soon as Eden's wedding ends."

"We don't want a riot," she said. "We'll have to hurry."

"Sweetheart, I'm five minutes away from being ready."

"It's time to start," Beau said, as he was in charge this year. He stepped over the mic and repeated it. "Everyone take your seats, please. We have a lot to do tonight before dinner." He grinned out at everyone as they settled down. Elise sat in the front row next to Gray and Colton, and Hunter joined them a moment later when he came upstairs with the other teens.

Gray held one of his hands and one of Elise's.

"Welcome to Whiskey Mountain Lodge," Beau said. "We love gathering here each year with our friends and family, and this year, we have two weddings to celebrate." He smiled at Elise and Eden and turned to face the tree.

It stood as tall as it ever did, with ornaments, bows, ribbons, crocheted pieces, and tinsel decorating its boughs. "I love this tree," he said, turning toward the crowd again. "It's a reminder to me of how I'd like to grow straight and tall, reaching for heaven." He paused for a moment, and the feeling in the room could only be described as pure.

Elise felt the pure love of the Lord. She felt pure joy. She felt purely fulfilled.

Beau cleared his throat and said, "As most of you know, we have someone light our tree every Christmas Eve. It's a special job, and one I was proud to do when it was my turn. It's an honor to be chosen, and we try to make sure everyone who comes to Whiskey Mountain feels like family."

He paused again, and Elise thought it was for dramatic effect this time. She'd never had the chance to light the tree, and she didn't expect to be called this year either. Patsy had done it a couple of years ago, though, and Bree last year.

"This year, I'd like to invite Opal Hammond to be our guest of honor."

Gray pulled in a breath, and Elise started looking for his

grandmother, her heart filling and filling with love for the Whittakers. They had plenty of people in their own family who would probably like to light the tree, and yet, they'd welcomed the Hammonds and their staff into their fold as if they too had Whittaker blood.

"She'll be assisted by her grandson, Cy, who's recently purchased some land here in Coral Canyon and will be opening his motorcycle shop by spring."

"This is amazing," Gray said, turning to watch Cy escort Grams over to the light switches.

"On three," Cy said in a loud voice. "All right, Grams?" She nodded, and he said, "One...two...three!"

She flipped the switch, and the tree lit up in holy, white light. Elise gasped and started clapping with many others, and Beau said, "We're going to do the stockings, and our first wedding will be in fifteen minutes."

"Did you pass out our gifts?" Elise asked, suddenly panicked.

"We did," Gray said. "Now, come on. I saw Celia with homemade caramels, and I want to see if I got some in my stocking." He stood, but Elise didn't.

"You want me to get yours?"

"Yes, please," she said. She just wanted to sit there and bask in the awe and merriment of Christmas at Whiskey Mountain Lodge. She wanted to be here every year, and she couldn't wait to start looking at mountain homes next week with Gray.

They'd decided to split their time between Ivory Peaks and Coral Canyon, and Elise couldn't be happier about that decision.

Gray returned with her stocking, and she simply held it while he and Hunter rooted through theirs. "This is so cool, Dad," Hunter said. "Can we come every year?"

"Yes, bud," Gray said, pulling out a handful of caramels. "I think we'll come every year." He smiled as he removed the wax paper from the candy.

Elise opened her stocking and found an assortment of trinkets and treasures. She had plenty of treats too, and she loved going through the stocking in the silence and privacy of her own cabin later, thinking about each person as they'd dropped the gift into the sock.

"All right," Beau said. "Let's start to take our places again, please."

Elise put her stocking on the floor beneath her chair. It was time for the weddings to begin—and one of them was hers.

CHAPTER 34

Gray's anticipation built and built through Eden and Mitchell's wedding. It was a beautiful ceremony, with Colton walking her down the steps and giving her to Mitchell. Gray had realized in that moment that his brother didn't have children of his own, and he wondered how he felt about that.

The moment Eden and Mitchell kissed as man and wife, Gray stood up with Hunter and said, "Let's go, son." They left the massive living room that was doubling as a wedding hall today, while Elise went upstairs with her mother and Bree.

He quickly pulled on his vest and his bow tie, then changed out his cowboy hat for a deeper shade of the one he'd been wearing all day. He helped Hunter with his tie and straightened his hat. "You better get upstairs."

"Yes, sir." Hunter stepped out of the room, and Gray's

nerves doubled. Elise didn't have a father to walk her down the aisle, and she'd asked Hunter to do it. She also wanted him right up front with them, as he was a core part of the family they were officially creating today.

It was everything Gray had always wanted, and he couldn't believe he was about to get it. Ready, he dropped to his knees beside the bed and bowed his head. "Dear Father," he started. "Thank you for all of Thy many blessings. Please help me to be the husband and father I need to be for Elise and Hunter. I love them with my whole soul."

He paused, because he'd loved Sheila like this too, and it hadn't been enough.

"Please bless me to be enough this time." Even as he said it, Gray knew he already was enough. He'd make mistakes in the future. He'd have to ask for forgiveness again. He'd learn and grow. But he was already enough for Hunter, for Elise, and for the Lord.

He stood up and brushed his hands down the front of his vest. He put on his tuxedo jacket as Wes knocked on the door and then entered. "Getting married again," his oldest brother said, and Gray grabbed onto him and held him in a tight embrace. Neither of them said anything for several seconds, and the bond Gray had with Wes was strengthened.

"Time to go?" he finally asked, stepping back.

"I got the signal from Bree," Wes said. "Elise is ready. Colton brought up Hutch."

"Time to go then." Gray went first down the hall and toward the Christmas tree, taking Hutch's leash from his brother. He'd been at the lodge last year, so he'd witnessed the tree lighting before. It was just as magical and just as stunning this year.

The wedding march started again, and he craned his neck back to try to see the second floor above him. Slowly, Hunter and Elise descended on the stairs, and Gray couldn't look away from the woman.

Just like the very first time he'd laid eyes on her, she took his breath away. Her dress was gorgeous, with lace all over the top half, and sequins reflecting the white light from the Christmas tree. She wore a wide belt around her waist, and the bottom of the dress flared to the floor, with a small train behind that.

Hunter looked like a prince with a princess on his arm, and Gray reached for both of them as they arrived where he was. Hunter went around to his left, and Gray linked his right arm with Elise, leaning down to press a kiss to her temple.

Hutch barked, and Elise giggled and shushed him.

The officiator was actually Eli Whittaker, who apparently had the power and authority to perform weddings. Gray didn't know him well, but Elise did, and he gave a pretty perfect speech about what it meant to love and cherish someone.

"Think of them first," he said. "Employ patience. Be forgiving. In all things, put your spouse first, and I promise you'll be happy for your whole lives."

Gray couldn't agree more, and Eli moved onto the vows. Eden and Mitchell had read theirs to each other, but Elise gestured for someone to come out of the crowd.

Colton stood, buttoning his suit coat. He stood next to her while Ames of all people came to stand next to Gray.

He looked from brother to brother and then at Elise. She simply grinned at him and nodded at Colton.

"Gray," he said. "Elise has never been in love before, and she didn't know what love at first sight looked like or felt like. Though the two of you started off with a bad first date, and dealt with a lot of distance between you for months at a time, she knows her life would not be complete without you in it. She loves you. She chooses you. She will stand beside you through snowstorms and marathons and raising a teenager."

A few people twittered, but Gray worked very hard not to let his emotion show too much.

"Elise," Ames said, and Gray wondered what in the world he was going to say. He hadn't given his brother any vows to read for him. "Gray loves you with his whole heart. That heart hurt for a while, and he wasn't sure how to love with it at first, but you healed it. You healed him. He wants you. He loves you. He chooses you. He will stand beside you through tough days on the farm and sewing mishaps and raising a teenager."

They both looked back at Eli, and Gray couldn't have said his vows any better.

"Do you, Gray Hunter Hammond, take Elise Ellen Murphy to be your lawfully wedded wife, to love, to hold, and to cherish, from this day until death shall separate you in mortality?"

"Yes," he said.

Eli turned to Elise. "Do you, Elise Ellen Murphy, give

yourself to Gray Hunter Hammond, and accept him to be your lawfully wedded husband, to love, to hold, and to cherish, from this day until death shall separate you in mortality?"

"Yes," Elise said, her smile so big and her eyes so bright.

"I now pronounce you husband and wife," Eli said. "You may kiss your bride."

Gray grinned at Elise and took her into his arms. He kissed her as her dog barked, as the crowd clapped and cheered, the feel of her fingers along his face like heaven to him, as everything in his life aligned.

He turned toward the audience and raised his and Elise's joined hands, his eyes seeking his mother's. She came forward and hugged them both, and Beau announced that dinner would be served in ten minutes.

All the Hammonds came to offer their congratulations, as did Elise's friends. Once all the hugs and kisses were done, Gray found himself in a semi-quiet corner of the room, nearly smashed between the wall and the Christmas tree with his new wife.

"Who wrote what Ames said?" he asked.

"It was a collaboration between me and Hunter." She beamed up at him. "What did you think? Did we get it right?"

"Hmm," he said, unable to look anywhere but at her. He lowered his head until his forehead touched hers. "I do want you." He dropped a kiss close to her ear, breathing in the scent of her flowery perfume. "I do choose you." He skated his lips across her neck. "And I do love you with my whole heart." He looked into her eyes. "So I think you got it right."

"I love you too, Gray," she said, and she kissed him. Gray took her face in his hands and fully enjoyed kissing his wife.

———

Read on for a sneak peek of **HER COWBOY BILLIONAIRE BEAST** featuring motorcycle shop owner Cy Hammond and Patsy - the manager of the lodge.

SNEAK PEEK! HER COWBOY BILLIONAIRE BEAST CHAPTER ONE

C y Hammond stayed close to his parents and grandmother while people seemed to be moving in every direction. The lodge was a massive building, with plenty of high-end finishes, and it fit in this mountain landscape perfectly.

The Whittakers knew how to put on a good holiday party, that was for sure, because simply keeping track of everyone that would be at the lodge for the Christmas Eve tree lighting and ensuring they'd have a stocking with gifts was a huge feat.

He knew exactly who'd taken care of it, because Cy was low-profile enough here to blend into the background, with the racing thoughts that kept him looking from person to person, watching them.

Observant, he liked to think about himself.

Patsy Foxhill was the one who directed everything here

at the lodge. She talked to several other women, as well as Beau Whittaker, and the whole system ran without a hitch. If she didn't do that, everything would fall apart.

Cy knew, because he had a guy at his motorcycle shop who did the same thing. Wade knew every little thing that happened at Rev for Vets, but he wasn't the public face of the operation. In that situation, Cy *was* the high-profile one, and he always knew everyone was watching him.

Beau had just announced the Cy's shop would be open by spring, and it would be. The building was coming along great, especially now that the walls and roof were done. For a couple of weeks there, he'd thought the weather would prevent him from getting the shop back up and running before next Christmas.

He'd called Wade last week, just to make sure he couldn't relocate. He'd offered him the job the moment he'd spoken to Patsy and gotten confirmation on an asking price for the twenty acres of apple orchards he now owned.

Wade had said no, for the third time, which meant that Cy had no manager for his shop. He knew who he wanted, and the blonde came into the living room, those pretty blue eyes obviously searching for someone.

"Graham," she said, spotting him. "We need you in the kitchen."

The tall cowboy went with her, and Cy wondered if she felt any spark for him at all. His skin and muscles still vibrated with the electricity from her touch, and it had happened months ago. He had her number, but he'd only communicated with her about professional things, and once the contract was signed, there was nothing else for them to talk about.

Cy had rented an old house on the north side of town, and he was planning to build himself a house on some of the twenty acres he now owned. The shop took up four in the back corner of the lot, and Cy had actually considered adding a third floor to the building design and simply living above everything.

In the end, he didn't want his whole life wrapped up in one place, and he'd hired an architect to start designing him a house that would be lavish and comfortable, but wouldn't require the removal of too many apple trees.

Cy didn't even really like apples—he couldn't remember the last time he'd eaten one—but the orchard meant a great deal to Patsy. And for some reason he could not name, he wanted her to be happy with the decisions he made with her orchard.

Your orchard, he reminded himself as a dinging sound filled the air. He glanced toward the front door, but no one else seemed to be. "All right," Patsy said. "We're gathering in the dining room. Dinner will be served in two minutes."

Cy's heartbeat filled the back of his throat at the sound of Patsy's voice. It carried a sense of authority he liked, as well as the kindness that spoke of her femininity. She didn't hide behind her hair, and she accented it with big earrings and the perfect amount of makeup. Tonight, she'd been wearing a skin-tight pair of black jeans with a bright yellow sweater with a white star in the middle of it.

People started moving into the kitchen, and Cy reached for Grams. "Stay with me, Grams," he said. "I'll get you a good seat." He turned toward the doorway, and his eyes finally met Patsy's. They'd been dancing around one another all afternoon and evening, and now he stood face-to-face with her.

"Hello, Cy," she said easily, giving nothing away.

"Hey, Patsy." He gave her what he hoped was a bright smile. It felt good on his face, and her mouth curved upward too, so maybe it had worked. "Merry Christmas."

"Merry Christmas." She looked at Grams. "I have a spot for you, Opal." She reached for her, and Cy passed his ninety-eight-year-old grandmother to Patsy's care.

He felt like he couldn't breathe, and he stepped through the doorway and let his parents go in front of him too. He lost sight of Patsy behind the width of his father's shoulders, and he ducked down a side hall that had a door at the end of it.

He didn't go all the way outside, because without a coat, doing so would be a death wish. He cracked the door and took a slow, deep drag of the fresh air, the temperature difference between inside and outside probably a hundred degrees.

"What am I going to do about a supervisor?" he asked. "You led me here, Lord. I need help." He'd managed to get McCall to agree to come to Coral Canyon in March, as well as two other mechanics. Winslow and Dom from his custom design team had agreed to come, and his secretary, Marissa.

He'd employed a lot more people, but in the past six months, they'd all gotten different jobs. McCall and Winslow had too, but they'd been willing to quit when Cy had called with his job offer, which included a moving package.

"A lot more help," he added to his verbal dialog with the Lord. He reached over and flipped the rubber band on his wrist, the *thwap* comforting him. Outside, the wind blew, rattling the ajar door.

He quickly reached for the knob to make sure it didn't get stolen off its hinges. Lightning flashed, and only two seconds later, thunder grumbled through the sky. Loud thunder.

Cy pulled the door closed and locked it, peering through the glass as hail started to pummel the ground. He flipped the rubber band again. Then again.

"Why do you do that?"

He flinched and turned toward the very woman who'd been in his head in some form since she'd almost run him over in that giant Hummer. Cy looked at Patsy, wishing he could be as verbal with her as he was with the Lord.

His thoughts moved in and out of his head so fast, he couldn't grasp onto them. He'd just prayed for a solution to his supervisor problem, and Patsy had appeared.

Without giving it too much thought, he asked, "Would you come run my motorcycle shop?"

Patsy blinked at him, the surprise laid out in her eyes. He saw doubt as it moved quickly across her expression, and then her rejection. "I have a job," she said.

"Yeah, but you're bored in it." He walked away from her, foolishness streaming through him. He didn't know her. He shouldn't have said that.

"Hey," she said, her voice angry behind him.

He stopped near the corner and turned around to face

her again. "Sorry," he said, holding up one hand. "I'm sorry."

Patsy once again looked like he'd thrown cold water in her face. She marched toward him, her face broadcasting anger. She paused a couple of feet from him. "How—how did you know I'm bored in the job?" she asked. "Not that I'm bored in the job. This place is a zoo most of the time."

"They need two people to do what you do by yourself," he said. "Anyone can see it. Why haven't you told…whoever your boss is?"

"Graham," she supplied. "And I don't know."

"Have Wes do it. I think he's still consulting with them."

Patsy sighed as she looked past him. "He is." She shook her head and reached up to brush her short bangs off her forehead. They weren't long enough to tuck or stay back with her other hair, and they just fell back into place. "I'm not going to ask him to say anything."

"I shouldn't have said anything either," Cy said. "Moment of desperation." He'd had a lot of them lately, and he really needed to school his mouth during those moments.

She dropped her eyes, and she looked soft and beautiful in that moment. She was organized and knowledgeable, and to an untrained eye, she came across as cold. Cy had thought that the first time he'd met her too.

"Apology accepted," she murmured.

The next thing he knew, her fingers touched his, and he sucked in a breath involuntarily. She heard it, and she lifted her eyes to his. That electricity that pulsed through the sky and then called down thunder now coursed between the two of them.

As she looked down again, her fingertip ran along the thick rubber band on his wrist. "It helps you focus, right?"

"Yes," he said, his voice much lower than normal. He told himself in a very stern mental voice not to clear his throat. *Don't do it*, he thought, easily switching it to a prayer. *Please don't let me clear my throat.*

He backed up a step when she met his eye again. His back bumped into the wall behind him, and he stilled.

"My brother used to wear one," she said, finally dropping his hand.

Cy's fingers immediately started rubbing the area of his wrist around the rubber band where she'd been touching. He shifted to the left a little, his shoulder blade running into a box there.

A rousing round of laughter erupted from around the corner, but Cy didn't even look in that direction. He didn't care what was happening in the dining room. He only wanted this moment to continue.

"Would you like to go out with me?" he asked, and he was so deep inside the moment, he heard the words echoing outside his head. It took a moment for him to realize they actually had echoed through the house.

He glanced up at the ceiling as if it held the answer to his confusion. "What's…?" He heard that piping through the speaker system too, and horror filled him.

Colton appeared around the corner, taking in Cy and Patsy standing there, facing off. He knocked on the wall a couple of times as pure glee filled his expression. "You might, uh, wanna turn that off before she answers." His grin was the size of Texas, and he disappeared as quickly as he'd appeared.

Cy pressed his eyes closed and stepped to the other side of the hall. When he turned and opened his eyes, he saw the box on the wall and the speaker embedded into the wall above it, where Patsy had spoken the announcement for dinner.

SNEAK PEEK! HER COWBOY BILLIONAIRE BEAST CHAPTER TWO

Patsy Foxhill traded places with Cy Hammond, her pulse pounding dangerously loud in her ears. She hadn't heard the dinging that always preceded an announcement through the public address system at the lodge. The laughter in the dining room had covered it.

They'd all heard him ask her to go out with him, though, and Patsy honestly had no idea how to answer him. The truth was, she'd very much like to go out with Cy Hammond. He'd worn a regular pair of slacks to the lodge tonight, and with the bright blue dress shirt and paisley bow tie, he was downright handsome.

He ducked his head, his black cowboy hat cutting off their connection. Across the hall, she heard the distinct sound of his rubber band slapping against his skin.

Without obsessing any longer about his question, she twisted back to the wall, leaned forward, and said, "Yes."

The word filled the lodge, and she had enough time to turn and face him before a roar in the dining room filled the air.

Cy's head jerked up, and Patsy reached to brush at her bangs again. She really needed to stop doing that, because it accomplished nothing, and it revealed her nerves.

"Patsy?"

Patsy spun toward the child's voice to find Ronnie and Averie standing there. "Yes?" She took a couple of steps toward them. "I'm coming. Did you guys save me any of those meatballs?" She put her arms around each of them and didn't dare glance over her shoulder to see what Cy was doing.

In the kitchen, she found trays and pans of food, a lot of it taken already. Averie asked for another roll, and Patsy got it for the seven-year-old. Ronnie wanted pie, but Patsy could tell it wasn't time yet. "You'll have to ask Celia," she said. "Or your mother."

"No pie," Laney said from the other side of the counter. "We're still eating, bud. Come sit down."

With the extra table in the dining area, there was hardly room to move around. Patsy kept her eyes down as she put mashed potatoes and meatballs and gravy on her plate. Celia had made her fancy lemon-garlic peas, and Patsy noticed there were plenty of those left.

She felt a lot of eyes on her, and trepidation accompanied her as she picked up a red plastic cup of punch and finally allowed herself to look up.

Sure enough, everyone in the dining room was looking at her. Heat filled her face, and she didn't know what to say.

"There's a seat over here," Elise said. "I saved for you." She glanced out into the hallway and back to Patsy.

Patsy went that way, and thankfully, one of the triplets chose that moment to spill their juice, which caused a commotion and offered the ice-breaker everyone needed to move back to their own conversations and lives.

Patsy put her plate down, as well as her drink, and took the seat beside Sophia on one side and Todd Christopherson on the other. She glanced at him, hoping he didn't care about her love life.

He flashed a grin at her and then turned back to his twins. "Did you hear, Patsy?"

"Hear what?" she asked.

"Vi and I are expecting another baby."

"You are?" Patsy looked past him to Vi. "That's so great. Congratulations." Happiness filled her, and she pushed against the thread of jealousy as it threatened to stitch her lungs too tight.

"Thanks," Vi said, reaching for a napkin and using it to wipe Mary's face. "Hey, let me clean you up. Stop it." She got the job done, and Patsy went back to her dinner.

Sophia leaned toward her. "Did you really just say you'd go out with Cy Hammond?"

Patsy nodded as she cut a meatball in half and scooped up a bite of meat, potatoes, and gravy. Celia's onion brown gravy was the stuff dreams were made of, and Patsy realized how hungry she was. She couldn't remember if she'd eaten lunch, and she knew she'd only had a protein shake for breakfast.

There was always so much to do at the lodge for this

evening, and Patsy worked a lot during the holidays when others didn't. As soon as dinner ended, she'd slip out the front door and head down the canyon to her father's house. She'd invited him up to the lodge over and over, but he'd never wanted to come.

Betty was making dinner tonight at the house where they'd grown up, and Patsy had promised to be there in time for dessert. She loved spending time with her nieces, and Joe had started coming back to the land of the living after his divorce had been finalized just after Halloween. He'd bring his son and daughter tonight, and his ex-wife would have them tomorrow.

"How did this happen?" Sophia asked, her voice still a hiss in Patsy's ear. "What happens if you fall in love with him? You realize these Hammonds are taking over this lodge, right?"

"They are?" Patsy asked. "None of them live here." She turned toward Sophia and searched her best friend's and roommate's eyes. Sophia possessed a bit of a salty streak, and her chocolate-brown eyes held plenty of it right now.

"They've taken three of our friends," Sophia said as if Patsy didn't know.

"He bought half of my dad's orchard," Patsy said. She hadn't told anyone that, even Sophia. The two of them shared a cabin in the corner of the backyard, and they'd grown close in the last three years since they'd been working here at Whiskey Mountain Lodge. "So I met him a few months ago."

She glanced around to see if Cy had come in. He hadn't. A blip of betrayal slid through her veins with every beat of her heart. He'd left her to face the whole crowd—people she knew way better than him—by herself.

Maybe she shouldn't have said yes to his dinner invitation so quickly. Patsy didn't normally let her hormones dictate what she did, and she certainly didn't date men like Cy Hammond.

"Have you been talking to him since he bought the orchard?" Sophia asked.

"Sophia, I'm not going to fall in love with him."

Sophia shrugged one shoulder and said, "You might."

Patsy didn't argue further, because she didn't need to get into her personal insecurities at the Whittaker family dinner on Christmas Eve.

The truth was, Sophia was right. She might very well fall in love with Cy Hammond, but Sophia didn't need to worry about one of the Hammond brothers "taking" her from the lodge.

Even if she fell for him, no one she ever dated had ever fallen in love with her. Her last boyfriend hadn't even noticed when she'd cut off ten inches of her hair.

Cy noticed your hair at the orchards, she thought, and Patsy really hated that she remembered that from months ago.

She finished eating and started cleaning up, picking up dishes children had left behind. About the time the ice cream came out of the freezer and the Everett sisters brought their guitars out of the master bedroom, Patsy slipped into her coat and out the door to go to her father's.

"Oh," she said when she encountered a cowboy on the front steps. "It's cold out here, Cy. What are you doing?"

He looked up at her. "Thinking." He stood up and shuffled a couple of steps back. "Sorry about that in there."

Patsy's annoyance flared. "Which part?"

Cy blinked and cocked his head, the same way her father's dog did when she talked to him in a high-pitched voice. "I...don't know."

"Why didn't you come eat?" she asked. "You threw me to the wolves." She hitched her purse higher on her shoulder, unable to stay for much longer. "I have to go. I'm late."

"Where are you going?"

"My father's," she said as she walked away.

"You didn't have to use the intercom to say yes," he called after her.

Patsy had half a mind to spin around and march back to him to really give him a piece of her mind. Instead, she turned and walked backward as she said, "I take it back, then. I don't want to go out with you."

She waved and continued to her car, surprised Cy didn't say anything else. She got behind the wheel, her heart pounding. She had no idea what had just happened in the last hour. She'd asked him a very personal question, which he'd answered. He'd made an innocent mistake pressing the public address system, but he had asked her out.

She liked that he'd asked her out, but she had zero confidence in her ability to hold a man's attention for longer than a few minutes. And now she'd taken back her acceptance.

A sigh filled the car, and she looked into her own eyes in the rear-view mirror. She hardly recognized herself, and that only added another layer of unrest to her already weary soul.

"Help me get through tonight," she whispered as she fitted the key into the ignition. As she backed out of her parking space and headed for the exit, she added, "And what just happened with Cy Hammond? Can You give me a little more direction there, please? Would that be so hard?"

It obviously was, because Patsy's mind ran around and around the long-haired Hammond brother all the way to her father's house, which sat in the middle of thirty acres of apple trees.

Joe's Hummer sat closest to the garage, which meant he'd been here the longest. His children were eight and five, and he was probably exhausted. He didn't have them very often, because literally the day after his wife had filed for divorce, Joe had lost his job. He'd picked up a new one driving the new bus around town, and since it was a new system, he worked a lot.

He seemed to like it though, and the last Patsy had heard, his boss liked him and had told him he was a smart guy who had management potential.

His ex-wife, Kathy, still lived in town, but she'd moved to a house across the street from her parents, and the kids spent a lot of time over there. Patsy actually missed her. No one had ever talked about what happened to the extended family in a divorce, and Patsy felt like she'd lost a friend she'd known for fifteen years.

Betty's minivan was parked behind Joe's truck, and it looked like it had been driven through a mud field to get to their father's. It probably had been. Betty and Cory lived on a farm on a muddy piece of land off a dirt road about halfway to Dog Valley. They had four teenage girls, and

Patsy sat in her car for a few extra minutes, trying to gear herself up to go inside.

It would be loud, she knew, and she'd just come from somewhere with the same pulsing energy she'd find behind the front door.

When her phone chimed and the curtains on the front window fluttered, Patsy knew she'd been spotted. Betty probably wanted to know why she was sitting in her car when she could be inside with the family.

Patsy sighed as she got out of the car and hurried to the safety of the covered front porch. The hail had stopped, thankfully, but the sky looked like it could easily start to dump more. She opened the door to the wall of noise she'd been expecting, but it actually made her smile.

"I knew that was you," Betty said from her spot next to the window. She stood taller than Patsy, and she'd never had her blonde hair cut above her shoulders. In fact, when Patsy had shown up to their father's for dinner one week and Betty had seen her hair, she'd been downright dumbfounded at what had "possessed" Patsy to cut her hair so short.

Betty had curves Patsy didn't, due to carrying and giving birth to four children, but her eyes were just as bright blue, and her skin freckled in the summer, just like Patsy's.

"Who else would it be?" Patsy worked hard not to roll her eyes. She stepped around the couch while she unzipped her coat. She tossed it on the back of the couch and hugged her sister. Betty was a dozen years older than Patsy, and she'd met and married Cory when she was only twenty-four, and their first child had come along only a year later.

"Aunt Patsy," Laura said, coming around the corner from the dining room, where all of the noise came from. She wore the hugest smile, and she hugged Patsy too. She was seventeen, and trim, with beautiful blonde hair and blue eyes. Apparently, she had a lot of boys interested in her, and Betty had "lost so much sleep" worrying about her eldest daughter. Patsy knew Betty liked the drama of literally everything, and she'd actually been encouraging her girls to have boyfriends since the time they turned thirteen.

"I'll tell Gramps we can have pie now." Laura stepped back, her smile still in place. "And I wanted to show you that new program I coded. Do you think you have time to see it?"

"Sorry I held you up," Patsy said, refusing to look at her sister. "I'm sure I have time to see it. I can't wait."

"You didn't hold us up," Laura said. "Gramps wants to eat pie twenty-four-seven." She laughed as she went back into the kitchen and dining area that was one big room. Her father also had another set of couches back here, with the television and his beloved record player. He spent almost all of his time in this one room that served different purposes, and Patsy tried to tell how he was feeling just by looking.

He sported a lot of color in his face today, and he was grinning at Betty's youngest daughter, Jessica, while she acted out something. Everyone else shouted at her, and Patsy had no idea how Jess would even be able to tell if someone got it right.

She detoured over to her father and bent down to hug him. "Merry Christmas, Daddy." She took in a deep draw of his distinct smell, which was the perpetual scent of apples and leather, a unique blend that he'd accomplished early in his life from his mutual love of two things: horseback riding and growing apple trees.

"Hello, darling," he said, his voice raspy. He should probably be on his oxygen, but Patsy couldn't even see the tank out here. He'd probably left it in the bedroom, as if the grandkids didn't know he had it.

"Yes!" Jess squealed, and she pointed at Wendy. "It was a monkey riding a bike."

The noise lessened after that, and Joe said, "Aunt Patsy's here, so we can have pie." He grinned at her, and his five-year-old daughter slid off his knee and ran to Patsy.

She giggled as she scooped Angie into her arms. "Howdy, partner," she said to the girl. Patsy had been taking Angie to ride ponies since she was old enough to walk, and they had a standing date every September for the western festival in Dog Valley. They wandered around and ate candied apples, threw horseshoes, and once, they'd gotten one of those black and white old west photos taken.

Betty had followed her into the kitchen, and Patsy turned to watch her sister and her oldest daughter slice the pies, get out quarts of ice cream, and lay spoons next to the bowls. "Okay," Betty said, always confident in the leadership role. Patsy had a word for her sister that wasn't all that nice, but Betty really could be bossy sometimes.

She supposed with four girls, she had to be.

"We're ready for dessert," she said. "Dad, what do you want?" She glared Jess back a few steps, and even Joe held his spot in the living room on the couch.

"Pecan," their dad rasped, and Betty handed the bowl to Laura.

"With lots of ice cream," she said to her. "Okay, we're going to go in age order. Oldest to youngest, so that makes my husband next."

Patsy rolled her eyes, because that was just like Patsy. Serve her father and then her husband. After that, Joe got his treat, and Patsy deviated by giving his children what they wanted too. Patsy thought she could just as easily take a piece of pie from a plate as Betty could, but she helped get Angie situated at the large table in front of the back door, and she waited her turn.

She wasn't the youngest, but Betty went ahead and let her girls go next, so Patsy ended up getting her pie last.

There was plenty of apple, the kind she liked best. It would almost be a crime if the Foxhills couldn't make the best apple pie on the planet, so it was a good thing Betty could. Patsy could too. She just didn't have as many opportunities as Betty did to show off her baking skills.

The conversation was easy as they talked about what they hoped to get for Christmas and what they'd be doing for the next week until school started again. Angie told Patsy all about the Christmas around the world stuff she'd done in kindergarten, and Patsy enjoyed the sense of family she felt here.

"I want hairspray," Michelle said, glaring at Laura.

"Hairspray?" Patsy asked, glancing at the girls. "Your mom doesn't get that for you? It's like two dollars a can."

"Hey," Betty said. "Don't judge me. Hairspray is a real commodity around our house." She glared at Michelle and

Laura. "We get enough every month. Some people just need to learn how to conserve it."

"Yeah," Michelle said. "And keep their sticky fingers out of other people's bathrooms if they run out of their own hairspray."

"I told you, I didn't—"

"Girls," Betty said with a sigh. "Do we have to argue about this on Christmas Eve?" She looked like she was poor picked-on Betty, and Patsy hated her oldest sister's act. Since she lived up the canyon, she ordered a lot of her supplies online, and she could easily ship Michelle an extra can of hairspray once a month. Betty would never side with the younger girl, and everyone knew it. Laura, the oldest, was definitely Betty's favorite, and she probably had stolen her younger sister's hairspray and gotten away with it.

She helped clean up and helped her father back to his recliner. "How's the lodge?" he asked, reaching over to pat her hand.

"Good," she said. She came down to visit him alone sometimes, because it was easier to have a real conversation with him when Betty and her entourage wasn't around. "How are you doing, Daddy?"

"Good," he said. "This last round of chemo wasn't bad. I think they might have found the right combination."

"That's great," Patsy said. "I can take you to the doctor this week."

"Oh, Betty's going to do it," Dad said, and Patsy pursed her lips and nodded. She needed to get going back to the lodge, but she decided to stay for just five more minutes.

"Hey," Betty said from the formal living room in the front of the house. "There's a big truck here."

Patsy didn't move, because no one would come here looking for her. No one had called or texted, and she watched Joe's kids set up a checkerboard on the floor in front of her. Alan, the eight-year-old, was definitely the one with all the bossy Foxhill genes, but Angie let him claim the black checkers and put them on the squares just-so.

"Patsy," Betty said, appearing in the doorway, her face flushed. "It's for you."

"What's for me?" She let go of her father's hand and stood up, confusion furrowing her brow.

"The door," Betty said, her eyes wide and astonished.

Patsy hadn't even heard the doorbell ring. Of course, Betty stood at the window like she expected a burglar to be creeping through the front yard. "Who is it?" Patsy started toward the only doorway leading into the front of the house.

Betty turned sideways to let her pass, and Patsy saw Cy standing just inside the front door, a delicious cowboy hat on his head, covering his long hair.

"What in the world are you doing here?" Patsy demanded.

"Can I talk to you for a sec?" He didn't wait for her to answer before he turned and went out the front door. Laura looked at Patsy, and she could feel Betty's eyes on her back too.

So she followed Cy, wondering how in the world he'd even figured out where her father lived.

———

Ohh…things are off to a great start, don't you think? Read **HER COWBOY BILLIONAIRE BEAST** today! **Available now in paperback.**

Keep scrolling to view series starters from three of my other series!

CHRISTMAS IN CORAL CANYON ROMANCE SERIES

Curl up with a cowboy billionaire!

Grab your favorite cup of cocoa or coffee and get comfortable, because you'll get a sweet, clean, and faith-filled romance in every book in the Christmas in Coral Canyon series. Join the Whittaker brothers - cowboy billionaires in Wyoming - as they build strong family bonds, fun holiday traditions, and relationships with the women who make them want to be better men.

Her Cowboy Billionaire Best Friend (Book 1): Graham Whittaker returns to Coral Canyon a few days after Christmas—after the death of his father. He takes over the energy company his dad built from the ground up and buys a high-end lodge to live in—only a mile from the home of his once-best friend, Laney McAllister. They were best friends once, but Laney's always entertained feelings for him, and spending so much time with him while they make Christmas memories puts her heart in danger of getting broken again…

HORSESHOE HOME RANCH ROMANCE SERIES

Fall for a cowboy today in this inspirational western romance series! Journey to Montana for second chance romance, boss-nanny romance, forbidden romance, and friends-to-lovers romance among an awesome ranch setting in four full-length novels from USA Today bestseller and Top 10 Kindle Unlimited All-Star author Liz Isaacson.

The Redesigned Ranch (Book 1): Jace Lovell only has one thing left after his fiancé abandons him at the altar: his job at Horseshoe Home Ranch. Belle Edmunds is back in Gold Valley and she's desperate to build a portfolio that she can use to start her own firm in Montana. Jace isn't anywhere near forgiving his fiancé, and he's not sure he's ready for a new relationship with someone as fiery and beautiful as Belle. Can she employ her patience while he figures out how to forgive so they can find their own brand of happily-ever-after?

GRAPE SEED FALLS ROMANCE SERIES

Journey to the beautiful Texas Hill Country for heartwarming, clean cowboy romance with that hint of faith you'll love. This series includes an Army cowboy, a cowboy billionaire, seasoned romance between older characters, Christmas romance, and three brothers looking for a ranch and a the woman of their dreams!

Choosing the Cowboy (Book 1): With financial trouble and personal issues around every corner, can Maggie Duffin and Chase Carver rely on their faith to find their happily-ever-after?

This is an introductory novelette to the Grape Seed Falls Romance series, with full-length books starting with **CRAVING THE COWBOY**.

A spinoff from the #1 bestselling Three Rivers Ranch Romance novels, also by USA Today bestselling author Liz Isaacson.

ABOUT LIZ

Liz Isaacson writes inspirational romance, usually set in Texas, or Wyoming, or anywhere else horses and cowboys exist. She lives in Utah, where she writes full-time, takes her two dogs to the park everyday, and eats a lot of veggies while writing. Find her on her website, along with all of her pen names, at feelgoodfictionbooks.com

www.ingramcontent.com/pod-product-compliance
Lightning Source LLC
Chambersburg PA
CBHW020015120726
47903CB00004B/1301